Darwin's World

An Epic of Survival
Book One, the Darwin's World Series

Jack L Knapp

Darwin's World Copyright © 2013 by Jack L Knapp
Cover Images from BigStockPhoto. com
Cover Art Copyright 2014 Mia Darien

ISBN:172591249X
ISBN-13:9781725912496

All rights reserved. This book or any portion thereof may not be reproduced or used in any manner whatsoever without the express written permission of the publisher except for the use of brief quotations in a book review.

This book is protected under the copyright laws of the United States of America. Any reproduction or other unauthorized use of the material or artwork herein is prohibited.

This book is licensed for your personal enjoyment only and may not be re-sold or given away. If you're reading this book and did not purchase it, or it was not purchased for your use, then please purchase your own copy. Thank you for respecting the hard work of the author.

Disclaimer: The persons and events depicted in this novel were created by the author's imagination; no resemblance to actual persons or events is intended.

Product names, brands, and other trademarks referred to within this book are the property of the respective trademark holders. Unless otherwise specified, no association between the author and any trademark holder is expressed or implied. Nor does the use of such trademarks indicate an endorsement of the products, trademarks, or trademark holders unless so stated.

Use of a term in this book should not be regarded as affecting the validity of any trademark, registered trademark, or service mark.

Books by the Author

The Wizards Series
Combat Wizard
Wizard at Work
Talent
Boxed Set, The Wizards Series
Veil of Time
Siberian Wizard

The Darwin's World Series
Darwin's World
The Trek
Home
Boxed Set One, the Darwin's World Series
The Return
Defending Eden

The New Frontiers Series
The Ship
NFI: New Frontiers, Inc
NEO: Near Earth Objects
The New Frontiers Series Boxed Set
BEMs: Bug Eyed Monsters
MARS
Pirates (forthcoming 2018)
Short Novel
Hands

For Kevin

Table of Contents

Prologue	9
Chapter 1	20
Chapter 2	27
Chapter 3	33
Chapter 4	36
Chapter 5	44
Chapter 6	51
Chapter 7	59
Chapter 8	67
Chapter 9	75
Chapter 10	82
Chapter 11	93
Chapter 12	100
Chapter 13	105
Chapter 14	113
Chapter 15	118
Chapter 16	126
Chapter 17	133
Chapter 18	140
Chapter 19	148
Chapter 20	155
Chapter 21	162
Chapter 22	169
Chapter 23	176
Chapter 24	182
Chapter 25	189
Chapter 26	197
Chapter 27	204
Chapter 28	211
Chapter 29	218
Chapter 30	226
Chapter 31	233
Chapter 32	240
Chapter 33	248
Chapter 34	254
Epilogue	263
The Trek, an Excerpt	267

Prologue

I waited, as patiently as possible considering the circumstances. I wasn't going anywhere. After all, they'd brought me here to die.

I was ready for whatever waited. Life no longer interested me. Aged muscles and joints, pains, and memory with more holes than a termite-infested stump had seen to that.

My close friends and relatives were dead, most of them long ago.

My thoughts drifted. Was this it, the end? I was wondering when I fell asleep.

But something felt different when I woke up. The pains were gone! This room was different too, not the one the hospital had put me in. The walls were white, not the pale beige I remembered. Why had I been moved? Was it too much to ask, to allow an old man to die in peace?

Where were the machines, the hanging intravenous drip, the wires connecting the machines to my body?

My thoughts wouldn't focus. I drifted, drowsy, half-awake, confused, but my bladder was insistent. There was an open door and I could make out bathroom fixtures in an adjoining room. Could I make it in time? Could I even walk? I felt no pain, so maybe...

Thoughts muzzy, driven by the familiar morning urge, I pulled the coverlet aside and got up. I stumbled briefly, then braced my hands against the wall for a moment. After regaining my balance, I straightened and entered the bathroom.

I used the toilet, cleaned myself, and flushed. My muscles were waking up, becoming useful, but even after washing my hands and face I didn't feel alert.

How could I be walking?

Paramedics had brought me in on a stretcher, terminal, suffering from a variety of age-related diseases. I knew I was dying, and I remembered feeling relieved that the process was finally almost over. I understood, without need for religion, that dead I'd be as I was before I was born, before awareness had come. Living was uncomfortable, the process of dying a bit more so, but being dead, that thought didn't bother me at all. I was ready for life to end.

But I felt none of the symptoms that had plagued my last few years. Walking into the bathroom had been easy, no distress, no pain. Except for that brief stumble, my muscles had worked as they had when I was young. Even the ancient worn cartilage, source of stabbing pains in my back and knees, had felt—resilient.

The bathroom was simple. The walls were also white, but not glaringly so. There was a toilet, a basin with a towel, and a shower enclosure with a larger towel on a rod.

If the lack of pain was due to drugs, I decided to take advantage of the respite while I could. I stepped into the shower and slid the glass doors closed. As soon as I did this, warm water sprayed gently over my skin.

A recessed shelf held soap and shampoo. I washed my hair and bathed, but even this familiar process was different, strange. My hair was short and quite thick, my arms faintly hairy. The hairs were dark, as was the small patch on my upper chest. More strangeness; my hair had been sparse and gray.

Hadn't it? Had that all been a dream? Or was I dreaming now? If I *was* dreaming, it was the best dream I'd had in years.

I saw no controls for the shower, but when I slid the door open, the water flow stopped. I toweled myself dry, hung the towel over the shower enclosure, and returned to the room where I'd awakened.

The bed had been made in my absence. One wall of the room now looked out on a tranquil forest scene. Another change had taken place, one with more significance. A man stood by the wall, watching me. There was now a chair by the bed, so I sat down.

"Your name is Matt," the man said. "Do you remember?"

I did. That much hadn't changed.

"How did I get here? The last thing I remember was paramedics wheeling me in, but this doesn't look like any hospital I've ever seen."

"This is phase one of your rehabilitation," the man said, ignoring my question. "You will be here for some time while we complete your transformation. Don't expect to understand everything immediately, but you will know more next time we wake you."

Rehabilitation? How could a dying old man be rehabilitated?

"How did I get here? Why do I feel different?"

"I will explain as much as I can. You will fall asleep shortly, a natural part of the process, so I have only a few minutes.

"I brought you here from the timeline you were born in. In that time, you would have died. Your body had begun to break down and death would have occurred shortly. We stabilized your condition and brought you here so that more advanced medical treatments could begin. I selected you because you appear suitable for my purpose."

I didn't understand most of what he'd said, but I wasn't worried. Had he given me some sort of tranquilizer?

He continued, "You have been given appropriate medical care. I will now complete your transformation. This will take some time. Some of the procedures are painful, but you will not recall what happens. You will alternate naturally between sleep and wakefulness during the remainder of the transformation process. During wakefulness, you will train your body and mind to accept the changes.

"You will have more questions. I can answer some of them, but despite the changes you've undergone, you lack the capability to understand all that is happening to you."

"How long will I be asleep this time?" For some reason, that seemed important to me.

"As long as necessary," he replied.

I was drowsy, I wanted to ask another question, but he disappeared as I drifted into sleep.

Waking up went faster and this time, there was no residual drowsiness. I now remembered a lot more about my previous life. Growing old, preparing to die, that had been no dream.

I got up and stretched, then bent down and touched my toes. Wonderful! Such a simple thing, so easy now, but I'd lost the ability to do that a long time ago.

The bath worked as I remembered; I showered again, then returned to the bedroom. Clothing lay across the bed now, so I got dressed. The underwear felt silky, yet soft and absorbent. The socks were the sort I remembered, some sort of knitted fabric with a cushioned sole. The boots were soft leather or something resembling it, the shirt and trousers were familiar in cut, although the fabrics were unusual. They were lightweight and had a smooth finish, but the buttons, hook and loop closures, and zippers were familiar. The man appeared as soon as I finished dressing, standing against the wall as he'd done before.

"This is your second waking period and much of the physical work on your body is complete. There will continue to be mental changes, but physical changes will be so small now as to be undetectable. You must integrate your body's muscles and nervous system yourself through exercise. The transformation will add strength and coordination as your body and brain adjust to each other."

"You mentioned that my body was breaking down, that I would die. But I'm not about to die now, am I?

"No. That body was unacceptable for our purposes. We extracted your genetic code and recorded your memories before beginning the transformation. We retained most of those, because they hold the key to your personality. Some that I considered unimportant were excised and others were added. I then regrew your body, using your genetic code but modifying it to delete harmful mutations and correcting defects, before instilling your own memories, augmented by the other memories I implanted. This will prepare you for your new life."

"You did all this yourself?"

"I controlled the process. Most of the changes are carried out by machines. I am one of several engaged in this activity.

"Your memories are important for our purposes. Changes in brain structure and growth of additional neurons would have left you without coherent memories, so I provided what the machines recorded to your new body as soon as the physical restructuring permitted. You're physically equivalent now to what you were at age twenty. Mentally, I estimate that you will be approximately equal in cognitive ability to someone in his late thirties once the integration is complete. Your memories will remain those of a man who lived a long time as your culture measured such things.

"The transformation is nearly finished, needing only final integration. When the process is complete, you will be transplanted to a different timeline.

"You may die after being transplanted, but we cannot estimate when that will happen. It may be that you will live much longer than you expected, or you may die during the first day after transplanting. We cannot predict who will live, but those who do will have the curiosity, determination, and will to survive that we seek.

"For our purposes, it does not matter who survives. Remember that you were terminal when we harvested you, so every day that you survive now is a day of life you would not have had."

"You said about age twenty as far as my physical development is concerned?" I asked.

"Just so," he responded. "The concept has little meaning. It's simply where I stopped development during your rehabilitation, at an age nearing the end of physical adolescence. In your time, such changes began at birth and continued until death. Early development made you larger and stronger as your body morphed from baby through toddler, child, and adolescent, before becoming adult. You are physically adult now, but barely so.

"From that point on, you added experience and learning but most physical changes were harmful. Your cells accumulated damage, and some of the changes altered your genetic code. Your muscles weakened, joints became stiff, cartilage ripped, atrophied, and was resorbed. Over time the changes became so overwhelming that life was no longer sustainable.

"I repaired the damage during regrowth. As a part of preparing your body to make you suitable for transplanting, I also removed the tendency of your cells for programmed death. You should know that the changes cannot prevent future mutations. Radiation and chemical influences will be encountered after you leave here. I cannot predict what will happen to you, except to repeat that your current DNA sequence contains no known weaknesses. Another way to state this is to tell you that you are less susceptible to genetic change, but less susceptible does not mean you are immune.

"It is no longer certain when you will die. Disease is unlikely to kill you in the near term, but we cannot be certain that a disease may not evolve in future which will terminate your life. Still, your own body will no longer kill you until an accumulation of damage cancels the work we've done.

"You can die from a multitude of other causes. Trauma, blood loss, drowning, a broken neck, those things and more can kill you. A knife or spear that pierces your heart, lungs, or brain will cause death. Given time, your body will heal from lesser injuries, but there's no certainty that you will have the necessary time.

"Physical changes within your brain caused your later memories to fade, although your earlier memories remained nearly intact. I supplemented those memories with some that are generic, while others are highly specialized. It would not have been possible for you to acquire all the memories you now possess in a single lifetime."

"Why me?"

"My analysis of your personality, gained initially from records but later by direct examination, persuaded me that you would be a suitable candidate. We have been more selective recently because so many early transplant efforts failed."

I thought that over. "You say that you intend to 'transplant' me? Can you explain why you're doing this?"

"Certainly. I am from your future, in one sense a descendant of yours, but the term is meaningless since so many generations have passed. You are one of hundreds among my direct ancestors. Do you understand the mathematics of this concept? You had two parents, four grandparents, eight great-grandparents. Generations became longer as people waited to produce children, but even so, more than eighty thousand persons who lived during your time are ancestors of mine. Should I go back a few generations more, I am related to everyone in your world. I gained a suite of genes from the genetic pool, just as all humans do, so in that sense we are all related. Some are more closely related than others, such that recent mutations are more likely to be shared, but since harmful mutations have been excised from the human genetic suite, differences between individuals are less pronounced.

"Our science is more advanced, but despite all we've done, humanity is dying. It may be that science has done too much. We have conquered death from what your time called 'natural causes', yet people continue to die. We don't die from age or disease, but we also no longer reproduce. Earth's human population is perhaps a tenth of the peak numbers reached in the 21st Century. Numbers declined naturally thereafter and this continues, as it has done for more than three centuries.

"The human population of your time numbered around seven billion, but there are less than one hundred million people alive today and the decline continues. We estimate that humanity will become extinct within a century or two, possibly less.

"We explored the solar system in the 22nd Century, but found nothing of more than transient interest. There is nothing on other planets that we need. We transform ordinary matter as needed and we conserve and recycle what we cannot transform. We might have established viable colonies throughout the system, but we lost interest in doing so.

"We never went beyond the boundaries of the home system. Einstein's limit prevented that at first, and by the time we gained the ability to evade that limit and colonize planets beyond the home system, it no longer seemed important to do so.

"The Earth provides all that we need, but our society has no future other than continuing decline. A few of us refuse to accept that inevitability, extinction. Simply put, we are attempting to change the future for our species. A discovery, made late in the 23rd Century, may prevent it from happening.

"We have the ability to harvest a human specimen such as yourself from our past. Perhaps a thousand of us are engaged in this effort. Each of us accepts the responsibility for harvesting and preparing a subject for transplant. There are similarities in what we do, but also differences. The differences in method may be beneficial, but we cannot yet say.

"We place our transplants into a parallel timeline on an Earth where humans did not survive. We chose this because the Earth of that dimension is physically similar to our present world.

"Life there is hard, and there is danger. Survival will not be easy and the unfit will not survive. I have prepared you to face the dangers and overcome hardships, but whether you do so is up to you. We believe that some of the transplants will succeed, but we accept that some, even among those we are transplanting now, will not. We cannot say which transplant has the qualities necessary for success.

"I have sent more than a thousand specimens to that dimension. Others have sent as many, and some may have sent more. I have not yet begun harvesting the offspring of my transplants but I will do so when I deem them ready. I will then prepare the selected individuals for transplanting here to my own world and time.

"We do not know what the eventual results of our experiment will be. The harvested and transplanted specimens may adapt to life here and become as the rest, content to live out their lives without ambition. We cannot say. We hope they retain the drive and curiosity that we have lost. If we are fortunate, the transplants will instill those qualities in our own highly-evolved population.

"We will continue the transplanting process and hope that it succeeds. It is worth noting that none of us who are engaged in harvesting or transplanting specimens have terminated our own lives. In the meantime, humans are now on a dimension where they did not naturally occur. They are humans of our type and they may survive, even if all humans on Earth Prime do not.

"Some of the dimensions we've explored have humans that are different from what you are and what I am. We leave them to work out their destiny in their own way and hope they feel the same once they develop the ability to cross dimensions. This, too, was a part of our reasoning when we decided to begin the transplant program. An aggressive population may resist attempts from cross-timeline invaders, where a passive population would not.

"We hope that *your* descendants will possess an enhanced sense of survival. There will also be other qualities that become emphasized by the environment you will find on the alternate version of Earth, and some of those qualities may not be advantageous. We will be as careful as possible regarding which specimens we harvest for transplanting to Earth Prime."

"You've said that I could die from any number of violent processes. Will you help me avoid that?"

"No. We give you a healthy body, a mind that is well developed for your time and culture, and then we release you. We select a location where survival is possible, avoiding transplanting into extremes of weather or climate and places we suspect of being geologically unstable. You may choose to seek such places on your own, but that is a choice for you to make.

"You will be alone when I transplant you, but there are other humans within a reasonable distance. You may seek them out, or not. The choice is yours. Some will be male, some female. Some will have been there a considerable length of time, others will have been transplanted after you. I cannot say, because I do not know what the others engaged in this activity have done or what they will do in future.

"The time period on that alternate dimension is between glaciations. According to your reckoning, the conditions are similar to the late Pleistocene period on Earth Prime, the time you refer to as the 'Ice Age'. However, some geological processes took place there in a fashion that is different from what happened on Earth Prime. Your knowledge of the past will be useful, but you should expect differences.

"Humans have been and will continue to be transplanted to each of the major continents. They are released between 40º north and 40º south of the Equator. There are still glaciers beyond those latitudes."

I was beginning to feel drowsy again. Then, with no further speech, he simply disappeared. I wondered if he was some sort of hologram or if his appearances were 'in the flesh', so to speak. I fell asleep while wondering.

☾

I soon fell into a routine, much as I had when getting ready for summer drills with the Army Reserve. I would wake, use the bathroom, have breakfast, then use the well-equipped gym that opened off the bedroom through a door I hadn't noticed before. I worked as much as I could during each session, took a break, had lunch, and worked again. Break for supper, shower and sleep, wake up, and do it again.

There was no way to tell how long this went on, but it probably lasted weeks. I was soon stronger and more agile than I'd ever been. After a while I stopped gaining strength, but coordination and agility continued to increase.

While I was wiping sweat off at the end of one of my workouts, the man appeared and looked at me. After a moment, he disappeared again.

☾

The next awakening found me in possession of more memories. Some I thought might have been my own, but some I was certain were of things I'd never done. Still, they were there; I wondered how long it would take to integrate them into my own memories, the ones I'd acquired at the cost of joy, sorrow, and pain before the Futurist had found me.

The 'bedroom' now contained a table, and a knife and an axe lay on it. The knife had a blade that was a bit more than three-eighths of an inch at its thickest and was about ten inches long, two inches wide at the guard and tapering to a wickedly sharp point. It had riveted wooden grips for a hilt, and a small cross-guard separated this from the blade. A heavy pommel balanced the knife. I picked it up and examined it. The blade had a clouded, mottled appearance. I concluded that the knife had been made by repeated forging and folding to produce a strong blade that would take and hold an edge, while still retaining flexibility. It was both tool and weapon. I liked the feel of it in my hand, and the edge was razor sharp. I tried shaving my arm and it easily removed the hairs.

The axe was larger than a hatchet but smaller than a standard woodsman's axe. I estimated the head would weigh about a pound and a half compared with four or five pounds for a full-sized felling axe. The haft was wood, about two and a half feet in length. The back of the blade was flat, so it would be useful as a hammer. Call it a camp-axe, more useful than a hatchet, but not heavy enough to be unwieldy.

I had nothing better to do, so I examined the knife and axe carefully. Some of my memories had to do with knives and axes, and some of them clearly were of places I'd never been and people I'd never met. For whatever reason, the memories left me pleased with the appearance and apparent usefulness of the tools.

How would I use that axe and knife after being 'transplanted'? Pioneers in North America had considered themselves adequately equipped if they had an axe, a knife, and a shovel. I had no shovel and the axe was small, but the knife was superb.

Still, some primitive societies had lacked metal shovels. They'd made do with sticks or carved branches and those had worked well enough, so perhaps I could do the same.

I hoped that the knife and axe would go with me when I was transplanted. I couldn't think of any other reason the Futurist had left them on the table.

The two were fine weapons, but too valuable to risk unless there was no other choice. I would need weapons that *could* be risked, even used up in an encounter. Those weapons would necessarily be things I'd made and could make again if they broke. A club, a spear, and eventually a bow and arrows would be needed.

Meat or fish would provide protein. Vegetable protein would help, but I couldn't count on finding it where the Futurist placed me. I would have to hunt or trap, and I would also need to defend myself.

The Futurist appeared as soon as I laid the knife and camp axe on the table.

"Our work with you is done. It is now up to you to make your way as best you can when you are transplanted. This will happen after your next awakening, and the tools you see will go with you. I will also provide a sturdy costume of undergarments, shirt, trousers, a belt, socks, and boots. The items are similar to what you are familiar with, and both the shirt and trousers have pockets. There is a leather scabbard for each of your tools. You may choose to carry them in your hands or wear them when you are transplanted."

"How long before I'll be released?"

"You will sleep first, and when you wake you will be provided food before you depart. Transplanting is painless and does not cause disorientation. You should consider what you will need to do immediately on arrival. While there will be no immediate danger, I caution you that it may not be far away, so you should plan accordingly."

I was getting drowsy again as he disappeared. I wondered how he did that; I supposed that it was not important, but it would sure be a handy ability to have.

I woke up energetic and hungry. There was a meal ready, the same type I'd had before, and the clothes I'd been told about lay on the table. I ate the meal, whatever it was. I had never been able to identify the ingredients; the meals had been tasty and that's all you could say for them. If one of the dishes was meat, I hadn't recognized it as such. There were no obvious muscle striations or the connective tissue that separates individual muscles. Just... something.

I got dressed, hatchet on my left side, blade facing to the rear. The knife hung at my right hip. The tools felt comfortable hanging from my belt. Regardless of what the Futurist had said, I did not intend to take unnecessary chances. He had mentioned the Pleistocene epoch, and I knew from memory that the time featured apex predators such as dire wolves and saber-toothed cats. Even the huge bison, ground sloths, and mammoths were dangerous.

As soon as I'd finished dressing, the man appeared.

"It is time," he said. "Come with me."

He walked toward a different part of the wall and another door opened. Beyond the door was a small chamber with no discernible features. It was simply blank; a floor, a ceiling, three walls, and a door that closed behind me as I walked through.

Another door immediately appeared where the opposite wall had been. Beyond it was grass, and three hundred yards away there were large trees. I stepped through the door, then glanced back. There was nothing there.

I was alone. I had near-perfect freedom, I could live or die, I could prosper or fail.

I was a very small entity surrounded by a very large and dangerous world and there was no way back, even if I had wanted to go.

Chapter 1

I had never felt so alone.

I was on Earth, but that didn't mean much; a planet is huge to a man on foot.

Based on the vegetation I was seeing, I could be anywhere in the temperate-to-subtropical zones. The Futurist said he transplanted his 'specimens' to North America; that helped a little, but even so, that put me somewhere in a region measuring thousands of square miles.

I was not well equipped for survival, wherever I was.

No shelter. No food. I was wearing what the Futurist had provided, clothing, a knife, an oversized hatchet. Other than that, I had a brain with real memories and some that had been implanted. I was young, healthy, and fit.

It was enough; it would have to be.

The time appeared to be late morning, judging by the sun. The sky was partly cloudy and a faint breeze stirred the leaves. The temperature was comfortably warm and the air was humid.

The small clearing around me was surrounded by trees, mixed hardwoods mostly. Low bushes and berry vines grew near the edge of the clearing. Sinking down until my head was just above the bushes, I examined my surroundings.

Any feeling of safety gained from hiding in the bushes was an illusion. Crouching to remain concealed, I moved upwind. Only faint forest sounds were detectable, the rustling of leaves and occasional chirps from insects or birds. Something, far off, made a chattering noise. I paused for a moment by a tree at the edge of the clearing, gathering information, then moved farther into the forest.

None of the animals of this time had reason to be wary of humans. I was prey, not predator. I had a better brain, but at the moment that didn't fill me with confidence; rabbits were better equipped to survive. They had better hearing, greater speed, more agility.

Darwin's principal, survival of the fittest, controlled my life now.

My immediate needs were water, food, and shelter. As soon as those were satisfied, I would need fire and better weapons. Tools, another necessity, could wait.

But providing for those needs required that I be cautious. I was no match for the bears, cats, or wolves that preyed on the giant animals of the late ice age. Carnivores included the huge short-faced bear, as well as the grizzly of my timeline; plus saber-toothed cats, lions and wolves, all larger than the predators of my timeline.

Water would be found downhill, so I moved down the slight slope, remaining watchful of the breeze's direction. Moving air would carry my scent; if a predator was downwind I could expect him to follow his nose. Streams would be my water source here; springs, which probably provided better water with fewer parasites, were not commonly found in this type of southern lowland forest.

For my food needs, I would be a scavenger when possible and a grazer on berries, nuts, and vegetation until I could make traps and better weapons.

This truly was a world where only the fittest survived, Darwin's World. I grinned; the Futurist had called his planet Earth Prime, now my Earth had a name too.

My first weapons would be a club, a spear, and strings. The club could be as simple as a piece of thick, heavy wood. The spear would be crude because I needed something *now* and couldn't take the time to make a better one. The strings would be used for traps and snares. They could also be woven into bags for carrying things.

With traps and a spear to kill what I caught, I would become hunter as well as hunted. The knife and axe were close-in weapons, nothing I wanted to face a cat or bear with; until I got better armament, my only options for avoiding danger were hiding, climbing, or running.

The idea of hunting, of killing even a deer, was laughable; sneak up on him and chop him with my axe? Stick him with my knife? More likely, the critter would stomp me into a bloody paste!

Some bears could climb trees, but I could climb higher and farther out onto limbs that wouldn't support the animal's weight. So trees were my immediate refuge if I encountered a predator.

I soon spotted a sapling, tall, straight, and a little thinner than my wrist. The axe made short work of cutting through the trunk and trimming the top to length. A few additional chops left a sharp point at the thicker end; I had my first spear. Unlike the knife or axe, I could use the spear while remaining out of the animal's reach, yet still be able to inflict lethal wounds.

There was a small stream ahead, but I looked warily around before approaching it. Water sources are dangerous; predators drink from them and often ambush prey nearby. Nervous, I drank quickly by scooping water in a cupped hand. Even while drinking, I was aware of trees I could climb quickly.

A large tree stood thirty yards ahead of me, smooth of bark and with low, spreading branches. Fruit hung high in the canopy, though there was none on the lower limbs. Had something eaten the low-hanging fruit? The lack meant that the upper ones were probably edible.

Climbing the tree was awkward, but I wasn't going to leave my spear. It would hopefully discourage any possible pursuit.

The fruits were some kind of fig, smaller than the ones I'd eaten during my previous life but they tasted better. Color told me which fruits were ripe; not-ripe also meant not tasty. My first attempt to eat an unripe fig left my lips puckered.

The tree divided into two main branches midway up the trunk. One of the two, about eighteen inches in diameter, had a smaller but substantial limb extending to the right and another a few inches farther on that projected to the left. I chopped thinner limbs of the necessary length and wove them through the branches, making a platform where I could sit while working. It would also serve for sleeping. The platform was not particularly comfortable, but at least nothing was going to approach unseen.

I sat down and began working on my spear.

Trimming the shaft, I shaved away bark and some of the wood underneath. Half an hour later it was done; the finished spear was slightly longer than six feet, tapered, but less so than it had been when I cut the sapling.

It was crude; there was no other word for that first spear, but it was still better than nothing.

The forest around me wasn't true jungle, but the leaves of the plants beneath the main canopy were large. I could use them in a number of ways, including toilet wipes. Such would be necessary soon because the figs had left me with an urgent need. I added the lesson to my memories, beware of eating too much fruit and especially unripe fruit!

I climbed down, did what was necessary, and used some of the leaves to clean myself. I gathered handfuls of others before climbing back to my platform 'home'.

Pounding on the leaves, using a chopped off branch for a hammer and another limb for a work surface, loosened the long fibers from the matrix. I extracted as many as possible, then dumped the remaining material on my platform, making it smoother and more comfortable for sleeping.

With enough fibers on hand, I began making string. The result was almost as thick as my little finger, fuzzy where I had spliced in fibers, yet strong.

The next morning found me hungry, but wary of eating more figs. They had not given me diarrhea, but I was certainly very loose! Still, the green figs had a kind of milky, sticky sap that could be used for sticking things together, so the experience wasn't a total failure. I had a number of projects in mind and glue would be helpful.

Back at the tiny stream, I drank and examined the bottom carefully.

A large rock near the edge looked promising, so I turned it over and grabbed a crayfish before he could scuttle backwards to deeper water. He managed to snap a pincer closed on my finger but I repaid his impertinence by eating him raw. There were also insect nymphs in the leaf litter on the bottom and I ate those too. I was hungry, not fussy.

Moving upstream, I crept around a small bend in the stream and found a small turtle sunning itself on a half-sunken tree trunk. The animal would provide a crude pot as well as a meal if I could catch it.

I swung my spear shaft, knocking him onto the land, and grabbed him as he scrabbled to turn himself upright.

Raw, or cooked? I decided to cook the turtle, which meant I needed a fire.

I knew the theory but had never practiced it. Finely-crushed dry material scraped from inside a piece of fallen bark made tinder and two dry branches were my tools. I shaved the straightest of the dried branches for an upright piece, then carved a starter hollow and a channel in the larger one that led to my tinder. I was ready to begin, the turtle was waiting, and I was hungry.

There are easier ways to make a fire, but they require things like flint and steel. I didn't have those, so I used what I had.

Hold the stick upright with the point in the carved hollow, feet on the large stick to keep it stable. Palms on the sides of the upright near the top, then press downward *hard*, spin the upright piece back-and-forth while my hands slipped down the stick.

Eventually, I got a tiny spark in the tinder from the friction of branch point rubbing inside the socket I'd carved. The tinder smoldered and I blew carefully on the spark. When the first tiny flame appeared, I carefully added small twigs. When they caught fire, I fed in larger pieces.

Humans love fire, other animals don't. For the first time since I arrived here, I felt safe. My eyes smarted from the smoke as I prepared to cook my turtle.

I lopped off the animal's head (turn him over, wait until he sticks his head out, a fast swipe with the knife) and let the carcass bleed out. I wasn't yet prepared to drink the blood as a source of salt and additional nutrition; for now, I simply cleaned out the entrails.

Turtles stink when the shell is opened, but I didn't complain. I made a quick trip to the stream, washed the turtle thoroughly, then made a hasty retreat back to my fire.

The turtle was soon cooked, more or less, and I ate him. The bones were small, but I saved them; they would be useful at some point. I hardened the tip of my spear in the coals, then tied a sling on for easier carrying. Finally I scraped the live coals together and covered them with ashes, I hoped they would still be hot enough tomorrow morning to restart the fire.

I collected more birch-bark before climbing a tree to spend the night; the bark had long fibers. I extracted the fibers and made more string, smaller but equally strong. Now I had enough for a safety loop to make sure I didn't roll off the platform in my sleep. The powdered bark remnants I scattered over the woven branches of my second platform home, added a layer of green leaves for comfort, and was soon asleep.

The trees offered concealment and a place to sleep in relative safety, plus a refuge from predators, but I needed a better location where I could trap small animals and catch fish.

My first spear shaft had begun to dry and overnight it warped. I could still use it, but the second one would be better.

A thin layer of mud inside the turtle shell had dried overnight, making a basin for carrying fire. I hoped to avoid making another fire from scratch; still, I could if I needed to, and next time I could use my string to make a fire drill rather than depend on my still-tender palms.

Blackberries were in season and the ripe fruit proved tasty. This also told me that the season was sometime in early summer. It meant I could count on having at least four, maybe even six months before cold weather arrived.

The oaks I'd seen included southern live oaks, easily identified by their wide spreading branches, and I'd seen magnolia trees too. The forest seemed familiar, the kind of country found in western Louisiana where I'd grown up.

If so, the Gulf of Mexico should be to the south and I might have a better chance of surviving winter near the coast. The fruits and berries wouldn't last, but there would be clams, crabs, and fish along the shore, easily caught. Salt, another need, could be evaporated from seawater.

I could head southwest, avoid the worst of the swamps, and maybe reach the Gulf within a few days; if that didn't work, I could go northwest. To the east lay hundreds of miles of thick forest, most of it like the area where I was and offering no advantages. There were also huge rivers to the east, dangerous for a lone man to cross.

Heavy forest, the kind where I now stood, was not my preferred habitat. Vision wasn't particularly useful because I could only see a few yards in any direction, meaning a predator might be lurking just out of sight. Animals use scent and hearing more than sight in heavy forest, giving them an advantage. Many forest carnivores could climb as well as I could.

The only real advantage the thick forest offered was temporary summer foods like figs, berries, and nuts. There was timber available for building shelter and making improved weaponry, but at the same time large game would be scarce. The forest didn't provide enough grass for grazing, and as for browsing animals like deer, there was too much cover to make hunting easy.

I would also need to find other humans at some point, not easily done in heavy forest.

Routine took over; travel, look for food, find a safe place to sleep, work on improving my equipment in the afternoon.

My strings made a net bag, crude, but it would serve. Lining it with leaves helped, and I learned to put my turtle shell with its live coals into the bag, tighten a drawstring around the top, then secure it to my belt before heading southwest.

I had a better weapon now, the replacement for my early effort, and a lot more confidence than I'd had when I first arrived.

The predators were out there, so I was still wary.

Depending on weather, I was also prepared to sleep on the ground now and rely on my fire for protection.

My food was frequently the sort of thing I'd have rejected in my earlier life, but it was keeping me alive and well fed. I wasn't losing weight; the clothing I'd been given by the Futurist still fit me and was holding up well.

I had adapted. Darwin's World was home.

Chapter 2

A month had passed since my arrival on Darwin's World.

The trail of a deer led me to a muddy salt lick. A lot of tracks were around the site, some from animals I didn't want to encounter. The salt was also poor quality, as much dirt as salt.

Soaking the mix, pouring off the liquid, then evaporating the water would give me usable salt; for now, it was too much work for too little result. Still, it meant I could find salt without going all the way to the ocean.

I had worked my way southwest without much difficulty, but then I encountered a large river.

Creeks hadn't been a problem, but this river was much more dangerous. The water ran sluggish, murky, and wide, at least a hundred yards. It was too deep to wade and I had no idea what might lie under the surface. Might there be alligators, even crocodiles? For that matter, were there predators I didn't know about? Was the bottom quicksand? There was no way to tell without wading in, and if I blundered into trouble it might be too late to turn back.

Swimming would be equally dangerous, and if I suddenly had to swim my boots would be a hindrance. Pushing my weapons and boots across on a small raft might work, but if I lost the raft I would then be barefoot and unarmed. I had a momentary vision of scrambling back to the bank, a crocodile in pursuit, my equipment floating away downstream.

Carry my spear, or dump it in favor of making a better one after I crossed? I rejected that idea. I might have immediate need for the spear on the other bank, so it would have to go with me. A wrong decision could kill me.

Building a raft and cutting a push-pole would take at least a day, maybe two, and then I would simply abandon the raft after it had served its purpose. A dugout canoe would be better in that I would have directional control, but would require a lot more labor and time to construct. That would only be worthwhile if I intended to use the craft afterward. I could travel farther by canoe, even go upstream, but even so I could go only where the river flowed.

I would also have to take time away to hunt and gather edible fruits or nuts. By contrast, traveling on foot allowed me to forage along the way as well as choose the path I would follow. That latter thought made the decision for me. I would go upstream and look for a safer crossing.

A low-growing palm-like plant had leaves arranged in a fan shape, each with sharp edges and a wicked point. I cut the stems and chopped off the sharp tips for ease in carrying.

After stopping for the night, I removed the long, strong fibers from the palmetto leaves. Much superior to what I'd harvested from other sources, palmetto would be the fiber of choice whenever I could find the plants. My strings and ropes were weapon, tool, and building material combined. Leather or rawhide would be better than plant-fiber cords, but I needed string in order to make the traps that would catch the animals.

I hung my newly-woven cords from a heavy limb, then added another limb to stretch them while they dried overnight. Coils of finished cords were easy to carry in my woven bag.

It was time to add more meat to my diet.

Hunting only works if you're there when the animal is present; trapping or snaring is much more efficient. Rabbits, squirrels, and large birds were common, if I could only catch them. They'd found it easy to avoid me so far, but now I had the means to build efficient traps. I might even catch a raccoon. I had seen tracks near the streams.

My deadfall traps, tree trunks suspended over a trigger, hadn't caught anything. I had enough cords now to put out a dozen snares each afternoon when I found a good place to stop, so hopefully my trapping success would improve. More traps and better traps should result in more catches.

My life settled into routine. Get up each morning, take care of personal necessities, then drink water from a gourd I'd cleaned by swishing dry sand around the inside. Breakfast was whatever I'd caught during the night, augmented by edible roots, greens, and fruit. Check the wind direction, look around for danger, then move out. Direction of travel was determined by the wind direction and the river. It originated somewhere to the northwest, so that was the course I followed whenever possible.

Weather was more annoyance than problem. I sometimes huddled under a spreading canopy to wait the rain out, but given enough warning, I built a tree shelter.

Adding a cover over my arboreal sleeping platform kept me dry as well as safe. Branches, arched, tied, and overlapped shingle-style with leaves made a fast and easy roof.

If birds and small animals ate fruits, that was recommendation enough to at least try them. Some I liked, some I tasted only once. The only things I refused to eat were mushrooms. Knowledge of which varieties were safe had accumulated as people got sick or died. I wasn't hungry enough to experiment.

The blackberries were gone now, most eaten by birds or small animals. A bush huckleberry had ripened since and the fruit provided a pleasant snack. The huckleberries weren't as large or as tasty as the blackberries had been, but I picked a few whenever I found them. My diet varied with location and changing of the season, but I was eating well, the result of not being picky.

Among the signs of rabbit, squirrel, and raccoon, I saw a large cat's track. It might be a puma, and if so I wasn't particularly worried. Pumas, sometimes called panthers, aren't likely to attack a full-grown man. But it might be a jaguar or some kind of cat I didn't know about, and some of the big cats could climb. Even so, they would find it difficult to creep out onto the limbs where I slept without waking me.

Giant lions and saber-tooth cats lived in North America at the end of the Pleistocene, but supposedly they couldn't climb. Face a saber-tooth on a tree limb with a wooden spear? No, thank you!

A fist-sized rock, found near the stream, gave me an idea. A thick branch from an ash tree, carefully split at one end, made a haft. I worked the rock into the split, then strengthened the joint by wrapping it with cord. As a final step, I coated the joint with milkweed-sap glue to make it stronger. Similar easy-to-make clubs had been used by early humans.

The point of my spear was relatively fragile. It was useful, but the club was almost equally so and it was certainly not fragile. Best of all, if either weapon broke, I could make another.

Armed with spear and club, I was ready to try living full-time on the ground. Trapping, cooking, and other activities necessarily took place on the ground, so living where I worked made sense. Fire would be my primary protection, backed by my club and spear, but if I lost the fire I would be forced back into the trees until I could kindle a new one.

My new traps were easy to construct. Straight sticks, laid crosswise in a hollow pyramid, were held together by tension. Strings, attached to the bottom sticks and stretched to the ends of a bow-stick across the top, provided the tension. Figure-four triggers, easily carved from three branches, supported one side of the trap, and tossing bits of bait around the trigger stick finished the job.

With practice, building and setting the traps took only a few minutes work. Most days, the traps caught birds. Cord snares took even less time, so I usually set out twenty or more each night. Rabbits soon became the core of my diet.

Fish, crustaceans, rabbits, raw shoots and roots, these things had kept me alive and would continue to do so. But I hungered for different foods. If you've ever eaten a cattail root, you'll understand. It's survival food, but no gourmet treat. Dandelion leaves and thin green shoots from milkweed plants are edible too, but both are an acquired taste that I intended to un-acquire as soon as possible.

My daily routine changed. Instead of a tree platform, I constructed a lean-to shelter each afternoon, then kindled a fire from the coals in my clay-lined turtle shell. The lean-to would protect me, but more importantly, it would protect my fire in case of rain. After building the fire, collecting fuel and building a shelter, it was time to set up a fish weir if the stream was suitable. I built the weirs with a wide, enclosed end upstream and a smaller mouth opening facing downstream. Fish entering the weir would swim forward because there was no room to turn around. After reaching the larger enclosed end, they would be unable to find their way out, because they tended to swim upstream. I tied easy-to-catch crayfish inside my weirs for bait.

I also fished, using gorge-hooks made of small, sharp-ended bones with carved grooves around the center. Thin cords tied around the grooves completed the assemblies. I made the hook-and-line sets in advance, then coiled the strings around the bone hooks before placing them in my woven bag.

Each afternoon, it was a simple matter to tie the remaining string end to a tree or pole, then toss the baited hook toward the center of the stream. Catfish, my usual catch, alternated with rabbit for my suppers. Even a small amount of variety in my diet made a difference.

I used a long, thin branch with a tied crosspiece to rake crayfish from the bottom. I added braces between the branch and each end of the crosspiece, thus stabilizing my makeshift 'rake'. An added piece, tied parallel under the crossbar, made the device even more effective. The tool wasn't pretty, but it was easy to construct and use. The crossed end went into the stream as far out as my arm would reach, and I held the crosspiece against the bottom as I raked it to shore.

I usually caught several large—and angry—crayfish, some of which I'd boil in one of the turtle shells I'd acquired. The others got used for bait.

Bamboo-like canes, if present, made superior fishing poles. The long, lightweight canes allowed me to toss the baited hooks farther. Angled cuts on the ends of the poles made them easy to stick into the dirt. So anchored, they resisted the pulls of even large fish.

Traps set, shelter built, bed of green leaves waiting under the rear of the lean-to, a fire burning for cooking and protection; so ended my days.

After placing my weapons where I could reach them, even in the dark, I ate a little cooked rabbit or smoked fish, fresh or from the previous day's catch. Water, from the stream or collected during a rainstorm, was my drink. As the light faded to dimness I lay down, sometimes damp, but not too uncomfortable and definitely not hungry, to sleep as much as possible during the night.

The chunky animal looked to be a kind of cross between a bull moose and an Irish elk, but was neither. Its body was a light brown with a whitish belly, while the upper back showed a faint dappling of lighter spots. A darker-brown growth of longer hair covered the withers and extended down over the shoulders. It grazed on the long bunchgrass near the stand of trees, raising its head occasionally to look around and test the breeze before resuming feeding. The antlers were palmate, but with long tines extending out from the flattened sections. The main beams extended rearwards, while two lesser beams with wider flats pointed forward and diagonally to the side, a kind of counterbalance for the main antler mass. In addition, two straight prongs projected forward from the bases, inside the secondary beams, one half as long as its fellow and with a broken end. The rear antlers protected the animal's back from predators, while the forward palmations gave it an offensive weapon to dominate other bulls. Perhaps fighting accounted for the broken tine.

A figure slipped silently through the trees, moving easily to avoid the underbrush. A slight movement of the hand cautioned two others, following ten yards behind the leader. They paused, obediently, managing to stop without alerting the bull, though neither moved as smoothly as the leader.

The animal fed on, unaware, as the leader brought up a crossbow and took careful aim. The buzz of the string was followed immediately by a solid thump as the bolt punched into the rib-cage behind the beast's shoulder. It bolted but soon stopped, head hanging. Finally, with a loud, rattling sigh, the animal collapsed.

The two followers moved forward, only to be interrupted by a hissed command. "Stay back until I get this thing reloaded!"

Moments later, crossbow ready, the leader signaled the others forward. "Stay behind me," she whispered. "Those things take a lot of killing."

But the animal was dead, and the three stood looking down at the carcass. "I'll keep watch while you dress it out. Keep your eyes peeled and your ears open. I may not have much time to warn you if I see something."

The other two, also women, nodded and set to work. Their butchering skills were on a par with their woodcraft, unpracticed. The leader looked at them with a kind of amused contempt. Well, she'd once been green herself, but at least she'd been raised on a farm. These two? You'd think they'd never seen an animal, much less had to prepare one for supper!

Chapter 3

One of my pyramid traps had caught something large and aggressive. It had destroyed the trap, which was just as well; I probably wouldn't have wanted to eat it anyway. I wasn't going hungry. Raccoon? Maybe, or a bobcat or coyote, but not a wolf; this wasn't their preferred habitat.

My kit now included a net bag. It was easy to make; I knotted the strings together fishnet-style, with the vertical and horizontal strands about an inch apart. Making the first bag took time and small objects tended to fall through, but carrying things in the bag was more comfortable than stuffing them in my pockets.

I had a bundle of fibers ready each afternoon. I generally stopped early, so I would have time to set up camp and put out traps and hooks. After my other chores were done, I wove the fibers into string. When I had enough strings, I plaited them into rope.

Weaving additional fibers and long leaves between the knotted strands improved the bag's ability to carry small objects. The resultant hybrid was stiffer, as much basket as bag. Needing both, I made another fishnet bag and this time wove extra strings through the mesh, producing a kind of coarse 'cloth'. A drawstring closed the top and attached the bag to my belt.

Travelers need to carry stuff, but when you find something useful you have the problem of how to transport it. My hands had to be free for carrying my spear and only a few items would fit into my pockets. Bulging pockets might hamper my movements, and that could be fatal.

Everything had to pass a needs test. Can I carry this with me, perhaps for long distances, and not be exhausted at the end of the day? Will it be helpful in the future, or more of a hindrance now? Most things got left behind.

Even so, a flexible basket-like container now hung over my left shoulder, along with the net bag I'd tied to my belt. I held a wooden spear with a fire-hardened point ready in my hand and the club hung at my belt as did my knife and axe. The system wasn't comfortable, but it worked. I got used to the annoyance because my situation improved with every tool or weapon I made.

I'd been working and traveling each day since arriving on Darwin's World. My current location was pleasant, my traps and hooks were set, so I decided this was a good place to rest and think.

Somewhere out there were other humans. Some had come from my time period, according to what the Futurist had said, some might be slightly more primitive or more advanced. Did they get the same equipment as me? It wouldn't make sense to limit one person and give another more; survival turns on such small differences.

What would the harvesters have sought among potential transplants?

The primitives of Pleistocene Earth had required thousands of years to develop civilization and science; the harvesters had probably selected people from my timeline because we already had an evolved approach to thinking but might still have the capability to exist here. It would be easier for us to survive without civilization than it would be to educate ice-age humans to fit into a modern civilization. And people from my time still had the kind of curiosity and ambition that the Futurist's sought.

As for me, in addition to what I'd had on arrival, I'd gained a lot more confidence. I had not only survived, I was now thriving. I had advanced from 'rabbit' to at least the level of 'coyote', a predator of small game and scavenger.

I felt good about how much I'd accomplished. The war club felt comfortable in my hand, the haft balancing the stone head well. The spear was less useful, but I would make a better one later with a stone point.

The spear, club, and net bag made a lot of difference, the cords and traps being at least as valuable as anything else I'd made. They kept me fed without having to always depend on hunting and gathering.

What solution had the Futurists found for transplanting women? They historically lacked the strength or speed of men. They might have stamina and certainly had other qualities, but if they'd been dropped alone and almost weaponless they'd have had little chance of surviving.

Would women have been transplanted as male-female pairs, or had the Futurists found a different arrangement?

A light rain began falling, but it didn't concern me; I had shelter to keep the rain off and a comfortable bed of leaves. The fire provided comfort as well as protection and it was located beneath the lean-to's overhang, hence protected.

Meantime, a fish splashed in the stream as it struggled to escape one of my lines.

I hurried to the stream and grabbed the cane pole. A heavy fish, if determined enough, might pull the pole out of the bank. If it did, my supper would be gone.

I leaned over the stream and reached as far up the pole as I could to get a better grip, then pulled. The fish tugged back and I felt a sudden twinge in my lower back as something popped loose, but I was able to land the fish. I began cleaning it there on the bank, where I could toss the offal into the water. Left on the land, it would almost certainly attract scavengers. And I would wash the fish's body cavity in the stream before heading for my shelter.

The muscles of my lower back were cramping by the time I finished cleaning it. I gimped my way back to camp, then gathered as much wood as I could.

The pain soon came in waves, leaving me gasping and sweating after each spasm. I didn't dare lie down, I might not be able to get back up.

I cooked the buffalo-fish, a quick task and not well done, but good enough considering. I sat down under the oak tree and ate some of the fish. Leaning back very carefully, I tried to give my lower back as much support as I could. The pain subsided for a time, but every time I moved to put more wood on the fire a spasm wrenched my back.

I was in serious trouble.

Between recurring attacks, I dragged up more wood. The spear was my crutch; it was fortunate that I didn't have to use it as a spear, because I doubt I could have.

The cramps soon became almost continuous. Waves of pain were followed by panting relief, then pain again. I held onto the tree during the attacks and waited them out.

Reaching for that buffalo-fish might well have killed me. I would have laughed if I hadn't been hurting so bad.

Chapter 4

Time was not on my side.

The pain would pass, eventually; but until then, the fire was my protection and I had to keep it burning.

Fuel was plentiful, but gathering it wouldn't be easy. I had already picked up everything nearby. I couldn't bend, lift any substantial weight, or even drag the bigger pieces back to camp. Even more pressing, I had only a little food on hand and I couldn't get more until my back recovered. Without food, I would soon begin to weaken.

Living a primitive, subsistence life is only fun when someone else is doing it.

During that night and the next day, I ate sparingly and drank rainwater that I captured in my turtle shells. I pissed near the lean-to. It might repel predators, and lack of sanitation was the least of my worries.

Grasping a branch, I hung by my hands for a time to see if whatever had popped loose in my back would pop back in. Maybe it helped.

That second day was pure agony, there's no other word for it. The spasms left my back muscles sore, and still they continued. The pain would begin, muscles would begin to cramp, then seize up for long moments before finally relaxing.

Each episode left me sweating and gasping. There would then be a short pause, perhaps a minute, sometimes ten minutes, before the cramps would start again. The soreness got worse, making the spasms even more painful.

I held onto my tree when I had to, hung from the branch when I could, and toughed it out the rest of the time. Between spasms, ignoring the pain as best I could, I put a little wood on the fire. To give in to the pain was to die.

During the brief, chill showers, I let the cold rain drip onto my back. I was desperate enough to try anything.

I learned what misery and pain were.

I endured.

The spasms lessened during the third day, intervals between cramps lasting longer. I had slept for brief periods, but now got more sleep as the pain lessened. I had been on my feet for the entire time, even while I drifted in and out of sleep, and I was exhausted. But I had survived.

Even while I was nearly helpless from the pain, *still* I had somehow kept the fire going, creeping out to drag in more fuel whenever the fire burned low.

It had been three days since the injury, three days I never want to relive. I survived not by cunning, stealth, and knowledge but by pure dumb luck and determination. The luck part was because the worst of the storm held off for two days, and by the time it finally arrived, I'd begun to recover.

On the fourth day, driven by thirst, I was able to use the spear as a crutch and stumble to the stream. The sky was still overcast and thunder grumbled in the distance.

Hanging onto the spear, I slowly crouched, bending my knees, favoring my sore back. Dipping up water with my turtle shell, I drank. I did it again, then once more. After drinking, I made my slow way back to camp.

Rain was falling in earnest by the time I got there. I huddled under my lean-to, trying to stay warm while listening to water drops hiss on my fire. I salvaged some of the burning sticks and brought them under the shelter. A turtle shell, placed upside down over the flames and supported by sticks, added more protection. My fire endured, just as I had.

Damp wood steamed near the fire; by the time I added it to the flames, it was dry enough to burn.

The spasms stopped and the worst of the soreness left my back while I sheltered from the storm. I was hungry, cold, damp, there was still residual soreness, but those things would go away as soon as I could begin foraging.

That Futurist may not have done me a favor by putting me here.

There was no letup in the rain that day. Lightning flashed, thunder rumbled, drops pattered around me where they dripped through the trees.

I was cozy under my shelter despite the lingering pain. I was damp, but the fire warmed me. My shelter didn't provide much of an advantage, but sometimes it doesn't take much.

The rain stopped during the night. As soon as it was light enough, I sloshed and slipped down to the stream.

The river now extended past its banks. The poles and gorge-hooks I'd set out before my injury were gone, washed away.

I drank some of the river water, despite the muddy color, before looking for my traps. But they were washed away too.

How far would the river rise? If the storm was the remnant of a hurricane, flooding would extend for miles inland. The dying storm might also spawn tornadoes, and I didn't want to be anywhere near one of those. It was time to look for a better location, a small rise that would not flood.

The clouds hid the sun so that I no longer had a good idea of directions, but by heading upstream I would be moving northward, more or less. Going downstream, south, would put me where all that water was going and maybe into more storms; upstream it would be.

My fire had finally gone out, drowned by the rain. But

I had the Futurist-provided weapons, plus the club, spear, and bags I'd made. In one of the bags I had some small bones and several hanks of string. There were three turtle shells under the lean-to for cup and cooking-pot. I would take them with me.

These were all that remained of the tool kit I'd assembled. Not much, but more than I'd had when I arrived here.

I looked around, making sure I'd forgotten nothing, and headed upriver.

Despite the flooding, there were still berries and edible plants around. I ate while I walked north. My back muscles loosened up and the pain subsided. Muddy ground slowed me from time to time, but I kept moving; there was no other choice.

Until now, I hadn't been seeking people, but now I would keep going until I found them. Having companions to turn to in time of need was clearly a survival measure.

Two days later, still following the river, my course bent to the west. The skies cleared, the ground dried, the flood subsided. Three days later I located a shallow ford and crossed the river.

I wove strings to replace what I'd lost, then assembled them into thin ropes to replace my lost snares. Traps I assembled from materials I gathered each night.

Ground-level vegetation soon changed and the forest became more open. I decided I was now in what would have been Texas on Earth Prime, west of where Arkansas and Louisiana bordered that state and possibly as far north as the border with Oklahoma.

Memory, real or implanted, told me there were likely remnant glaciers farther to the north. They would likely be bordered by wide permafrost expanses. Ranges of steep mountains bordered the permafrost belt. The Ouachita Mountains, lightly weathered in this time, would be a major barrier to any northward movement.

There was nothing north of them that I wanted to get to anyway; people would likely be south of the mountains and west of the great North American forest belt, extending all the way down into what would, on Earth Prime, be Mexico. Perforce, I would head west.

Ten days had passed since the storm. I was now at least a hundred miles north of where I'd been transplanted, probably more. The river was behind me as I headed due west.

Traveling got easier as the forest thinned more, but I still had to be cautious. Snakes were around. I'd eaten some, including poisonous varieties. But I avoided thick brush and snakes don't hunt in the open.

Something had screamed off in the distance one night, a cat most likely. Panthers, what farther west would be called a cougar, were known to be in this area, and wasn't there an American cheetah too? My memory, likely implanted, mentioned it. The animal wasn't really a cheetah, more of a cougar, but built along the cheetah's body plan.

Coyotes yipped nightly, but no wolves howled. I wondered; had the Futurist dropped me into relatively-benign territory, so I could have a short time to adjust to my new life?

My large net bag became a small backpack after I added shoulder straps. I was now making rope from tall grasses as well as fibers extracted from leaves.

There were more varieties of berry in the open areas too. I ate them regularly and only the occasional bout of light diarrhea kept me from eating more.

My strength had fully recovered and I had gained back the weight I'd lost during my period of enforced fasting. I was eating two meals a day now as well as snacking while I walked.

I stopped every afternoon, usually about two hours before dark. Because of the openness, I built a fire first using the coals I carried, then put up a lean-to and set out traps, mostly snares. I also set hooks and fish weirs whenever possible. I ate what I caught or went hungry, but that rarely happened.

Even so, my dreams were often about what I'd lost. A thick, rare steak; I could almost taste it. Lobster, dripping with butter. Eggs, potatoes, and bacon, bread from a French or Italian loaf. German brotchens or Italian rolls, layered with cheese and cold cuts or spread with a thick layer of butter and jam...

I was more than ready when I spotted the deer a short distance ahead.

He, for the head had small nubbins of antler covered with velvet, had come to the stream to drink. His front hooves were in the fresh mud, the rear hooves on the dry area just off the stream's bank. That small circumstance cost him his life.

Bad luck for him, good luck for me.

His head came up at some tiny sound, or possibly he spotted my movement. But his front hooves slipped as he tried to turn and my hard-thrown spear took him just behind the ribs.

The buck humped his back, floundered for a moment, then finally lunged for the bank. Too late; I was close enough by then and the stone club was in my hand. I swung as hard as I could for the area between the antler buds above his eyes.

My movement, the deer's movement, it made no difference; my aim was slightly off. But even so the stone club-head crushed the deer's skull. He dropped in his tracks, quivered slightly and kicked his hind legs twice.

Riches! In my situation, that's what the deer represented.

The spear was undamaged when I removed it from the carcass. It was my first thought, because it might be needed again.

The time was barely past noon as I set up camp a few yards from the deer's carcass, building the fire somewhat larger than I usually did. The lean-to could wait, and today I wouldn't need to set out traps.

Even with the fire for protection, the spear remained within my reach while I field-dressed the deer.

Cutting carefully to avoid nicking the bladder or intestines, I opened the body cavity and soon had the entrails out. I saved the heart and liver, then dumped the rest in the stream. The lower legs went into the stream too; there was little meat on them anyway, and the scent glands above the joint of the rear legs give venison an unpleasant taste. I split the breastbone and pelvis, then spread the carcass open to cool. I wasn't slavering, not quite, but there was a suspicious amount of saliva in my mouth!

I left the butchering task long enough to put up my shelter and gather firewood, then returned to the deer. I made a rough job of skinning the animal, rolling the carcass in order to cut through the skin over the backbone. He was smaller than I might have expected, about the size of a domestic goat, so handling the weight wasn't a problem.

There are two long muscles along an animal's backbone, the backstraps. They're called filets or loin if the animal is a cow, but whatever they're called, they're tasty, and I craved the fresh meat. I soon had two skewered chunks of backstrap sizzling as the fat dripped over the coals at the fire's edge.

I left the rest of the meat piled on the skin and dragged it closer to my fire. A scavenger would now have to face the fire as well as a desperate human with a spear before he could steal my meat!

While the meat cooked, I built a simple drying rack of poles to preserve the rest before it spoiled. It was finished by the time my steaks were ready.

I stuffed myself; there's just no other word for the appreciation I gave that slightly-charred-on-one-side venison. My stomach felt uncomfortably full, a sensation I'd not felt since the Futurist dropped me here.

The flames died down and a nice bed of coals formed while I butchered the carcass. The heart and liver, cut into manageable pieces, replaced the chunks of backstrap on my skewers. I let them cook while I sliced the remaining venison into thin strips, then laid them on a rack of poles I'd made while the meat cooked.

The fire's coals I raked apart to spread the heat evenly. Small hardwood twigs, plus green chips hacked from an oak tree, provided extra fuel and smoke. I saved the liver and heart, well cooked and wrapped in large oak leaves, for breakfast.

It would take a day for the deer meat to dry into jerky, a welcome addition to my load when I resumed traveling.

The landscape became hilly, with thin forest and occasional large clumps of oak, beech, and hickory. I was able to see farther, so I felt safer and moved faster.

Watercourses became smaller and less numerous as I continued on, but small streams were found at the bottoms of most hills. Springs became common, a feature not found in the deep forest. I could also see numerous animal trails; these marked preferred travel routes, and in those well-traveled trails I would set snares.

The deer convinced me that I could find larger game and dine well in this new terrain, but there was another reason I had been happy to see it. They require salt, so somewhere around would be a salt lick.

I was sitting on a fallen tree, resting while eating some of my venison jerky, when I spotted a thin tendril of smoke rising from beyond a distant hilltop.

A dozen men lounged in the shade of a huge oak tree. They wore breechclouts and moccasins of soft leather. One, somewhat better dressed than the others, wore a scarlet-dyed headband made of deerskin. This one, the leader or commander of the band, sat apart from the others.

They'd rested about half an hour when another man trotted up to the leader and took a moment to catch his breath. When he was ready, he reported.

"No sign of alarm, Boss. They're working in the fields, except for two men building walls. I can't tell how long this has been going on, but the walls aren't very high. They won't do more than slow us down."

"How are they armed?"

"Simple spears, not tipped with anything far as I could tell. I'd guess the spears are to keep animals away. No sign that they're expecting a raid."

"Too bad. Not that they'll get a chance to learn, the ones we don't kill. How far ahead is the village?"

"Two hours if we push it, three hours if we take our time."

"We'll camp here, then. You'll stay with us tonight and guide me tomorrow morning."

The leader called softly to get the attention of another man, who stirred himself and ambled over to join them.

"Rennie says about three hours, so we might as well camp here. The moon's down, so it's too dangerous to travel after dark.

"You know the drill, set up a framework and thatch it with blackberry vines. That should be enough to discourage critters from slipping into camp, but double the guard tonight. We'll have breakfast, move out an hour after that and plan to hit the village at noon.

"With luck, they'll all have come in from the fields for lunch, but we'll play it by ear. If necessary, we'll take the village first, then sweep the fields for anyone we missed."

"Think this bunch will fight back, Boss?"

"Does it matter? They're farmers, we're warriors."

"I guess so. Maybe they'll have women! Did Rennie say anything about women?"

"Don't worry about it. There are women back at our camp."

"Yeah, but we could use some new ones. Those are pretty used up, you know."

"We'll get new ones. If not this time, next time. Who's going to stop us?"

Chapter 5

My course led northwest toward the smoke, but I was ever watchful for what the wind was doing. If it shifted, I looked for a path across the wind rather than going downwind. Prey that goes downwind doesn't survive long enough to breed, and despite my weapons I was still more prey than predator.

The smoke vanished after an hour, but I knew which direction to go.

I was wary of encountering big predators, but they can't afford to wander aimlessly; the hunter's behavior is based on what his quarry does. There was only one of me and I wasn't following a pattern. Most probably hunted by night and they would instinctively avoid my fire. So long as I remained wary and alert, I was safe enough. Still, I always knew where the nearest tree was. I didn't want to run into a stupid saber-tooth, one who didn't know he wasn't supposed to hunt at random!

The streams became smaller, more infrequent; I usually drank from springs now. The tiny streams I crossed were too small for weirs and pyramid traps also stopped working. Snares were more efficient and easier to set, so I stopped early and put out more of them each afternoon. I judged that I was averaging at least ten miles a day, more when the wind and animal trails led where I wanted to go.

A snare is among the simplest of killing devices. Tie a small loop into the end of a cord, run the other end through the loop making a larger loop and a slip-knot, then hang it in an animal trail. Improve the location by cutting and laying brush to guide the animal into the snare.

Animals are suspicious, but they're also creatures of habit; they follow established trails and might step around a snare if they notice it, but they're unlikely to back up or detour around an obstacle. This is particularly true if they find themselves between two small trees whose branches have been hacked off, leaving points that guide them funnel-like into the snare. I set out at least two dozen every afternoon and improved the sites when I could. Large snares were for deer trails, smaller ones in places better suited for rabbits. An animal would catch the loop around its neck, struggle, and choke to death.

The simple design could be improved by attaching the snare to a springy tree, which was held under tension by a rope. The rope led to a trigger across a forked twig planted solidly in the trail. This cross-twig held the tree under tension until an animal pulled on the snare's loop, releasing the trigger. The tree then snapped upright, yanked the animal off the ground, and killed it. I hoped.

Two rabbits and a porcupine waited in my snares when I ran my trap-line just before dark. I collected the rabbits first, then made sure porky was dead before freeing the carcass.

The loop was buried in the quills around his neck, so I cut the cord. I skinned it, hung the carcass from my belt, and moved on to check my other snares.

The spring-snare had almost worked.

The animal's front legs had been lifted off the ground by my spring-pole. The trigger had released satisfactorily, the bent tree had snapped upright, but the unhappy creature was not dead. No indeed; the spring-pole had not been strong enough.

The beast had a pig-like head, short tusks, and jaws that snapped angrily as I approached. Wheezing, it tried to keep me in view by swinging its body around.

My crude spear would work better from the side, so I took three fast strides around the pig—a peccary?-- and slammed the spear in behind its shoulder. The animal squealed and sagged, still supported by the loop; a sudden smell of dung told me it had died. I was still shaking from adrenaline when I saw a tan shape crouching across the cleared area.

Cougar? No; the nostrils were too large, the legs too long. Whatever the cat was, it had a long tail with a dark tuft at the end. The pig had seen the cat and faced it, attempting to defend itself. By moving around to where I could spear the pig, I had put the pig between me and the cat. A twitch of that tail-tuft had caused me to notice it.

My spear was still stuck in the snared pig; I yanked my axe out with my right hand and with my knife in my left, I slowly backed toward the nearest tree. But the cat made no move to attack. It remained crouched, watching me warily.

Had it seen humans before? Or did the sudden death of the pig cause it to hesitate?

The cat finally backed away, spun, and disappeared into the undergrowth, and as it did I jumped for my spear. The spear allowed me to keep my distance from teeth and claws if the cat came back, but I needed both hands to use it effectively. Pulling it out, I replaced the knife and axe in their sheaths and immediately felt better.

I backed to the tree behind me and just relaxed against the bark, shaking a little from fear and letdown. My face was sweaty, my shirt was soaked through. I hadn't felt afraid, but apparently the body reacts to stress whether you're consciously aware of it or not.

I'd left a fire burning back at my camp. I quickly field-dressed the pig, leaving the entrails, and dragged it to the fire.

After a short rest, I built a drying rack for the pork. I added fuel, and while the fire burned down to coals I prepared the skinned porcupine and one of the rabbits for dinner. I had decided not to keep the quills. They have tiny barbs, so if one stuck into my finger I'd have to cut it out.

While the carcasses broiled, I sliced up the pig. The strips of pork went on the rack to dry while I ate my supper. The other rabbit I cooked for breakfast.

I went looking for a stream after eating. I could hear the water a few yards away, or so I thought. It turned out to be more like five hundred yards, but animal trails eventually led me there.

The stream was in a small ravine, shoulder-deep, twenty-five yards wide. The walls sloped gently to a small beach of sand and another beach lined the far bank. I saw numerous tracks, some on my side but even more across the stream.

The tracks led to a seam of salt, which turned out to be mixed with something when I tasted it. I had no idea what the gritty substance was, but animals had been using the salt lick so I could too. After drinking and filling my water gourd, I headed back to camp with some of the salt.

I made a second trip and gathered more salt, using a turtle shell as scoop and container. I added water from my gourd and ended up with salty water and a white substance that wouldn't dissolve.

I dredged some of the pork through the salt water and wondered what to do with the gritty stuff. It was fine in texture, almost flour-like; diatomaceous earth, perhaps? DE had a number of uses, so I poured the material onto a leaf and laid it aside to dry. I salted the rest of the pork strips and put them back on the rack to finish curing.

Waking up periodically during the night, I added fuel and raked fresh coals under the drying rack.

After breakfast, I added more fuel to the fire and returned to the stream for more salt. While I was there, I took a closer look at the rocks on the stream's bottom. A rounded rock looked like a flint nodule, a white crystalline rock was probably quartz, and a dark rock might be obsidian, all washed down from who-knows-where by flooding.

I got more salt and brought the rocks back to camp so I could work on them while my meat dried. The flint nodule, cracked open, yielded two cores; the obsidian lump cracked into two fist-sized pieces with moderately sharp edges at the top and bottom.

That gave me an idea. I collected the white gritty stuff and tried placing it between the pieces of obsidian. Rubbing the two halves against each other, I rotated them periodically to even out the effect. When I examined the two pieces there was evidence of scratching, but I realized that the very-fine grit would take forever to make much headway. It was more polish than grinding material.

Still, it might be useful someday for polishing spear or arrow points, so I tied the powdery stuff into a packet made of leaves.

The fire smoldered, the pork cured, and I chipped at a rock core. Striking carefully, using the quartz for a hammer-stone, I got half-circle conchoidal fractures and a number of thin, sharp, chips. The stone chips could be used as scrapers for converting skins to rawhide or leather. The piece of quartz, held in my hand, allowed more precise strikes than I could get using the heavy club.

Wrapping the cured pork slices in leaves, I added them to my pack next morning. The pack was heavy but the extra weight was welcome. I picked up my weapons, shouldered the pack, and followed the creek upstream.

There were still scattered copses of trees, but now shrubs, briars, and ferns grew under the trees. I picked a few tender shoots and ate them along the way. Mid-afternoon found me at the edge of the forest.

A grassy plain spread away to the west. I could see more forest, but it was at least a mile away. This area was a savanna rather than true plain, not forest or grassland but a mix of both. Scattered groups of trees interrupted the grass, a dozen or more trees in each clump. The grass extended across the direction I wanted to go, so I left the trees and walked out into the grass.

Mistake! Fighting the thick, chest-high bunchgrass was exhausting and the clumps grew so close together that I couldn't walk around them. If I encountered a problem, I couldn't run away; lacking trees, I couldn't even climb to safety. I might also end up with a sprained ankle from the shifting grass stems.

There was a small grove of trees to my right and I decided to go there. Stepping on the grass, I attempted to form a surface for my feet to push ahead, but the resulting surface was unstable. Even so, I reached the copse of trees without incident and stopped to rest and catch my breath.

I was in excellent physical condition, better than I'd ever have dared hope to be, but fitness wasn't enough to fight my way through the grass.

I explored the trees and found a few more of the grasses, but now they were widely scattered and easy to avoid. The long stems would be useful for rope and the grass would make a resilient bed, but I resolved to avoid the grasslands in future. They were just too dangerous. I would also not build a fire tonight; there was too much loose, dry vegetation on the ground. I couldn't even set out snares, but at least I had jerky for my supper. I'd seen no large animals and hoped the lack of grazers also meant no predators, but to be safe, I slept in a tree anyway.

I ate a slice of pork the next morning, still sitting in my tree, and looked for a path back to the forest. I'd had enough of fighting the dense grasses. I spotted a game trail, probably dangerous considering the environment, but it would have to do.

I waited until mid-morning before starting to give any grazers time to bed down. Hopefully the predators would also be sleeping. I was wary and kept my spear ready as I hurried down the trail, but nothing threatened.

Reaching the edge of the woods, I resumed my course to the northwest and soon spotted a dark object off to the northeast. It was a little aside from where I wanted to go, but I changed course to investigate. Finding the source of the smoke could wait.

The dark object was something totally unexpected, a long-abandoned dwelling. Grass grew in front of the doorway and around the sides of the dwelling; no one had walked here for years.

Could the people have become transplants, taken from Darwin's World to the world of the future? The Futurist hadn't told me of a timetable, only that eventually some of the survivors would be brought into that future time. Had that happened here? I prowled around, looking for whatever evidence might remain, and examined the dwelling's construction.

A dirt mound rose to a low roof which was itself covered with dirt. Log ends stuck out like the spokes of a giant wheel. The black thing I'd seen was the door opening, so I poked the end of my spear through the doorway before stepping inside. Critters, including large, dangerous varieties, like caves and cave-like openings. They make excellent dens.

The walls were crafted of logs, palisade-like, ends buried in the ground and supporting the roof. The highest part was in the center, the roof supports sloping away toward the walls. The floor had been dug out inside to a depth of two feet below ground level. A dirt ledge extended around the inside of the walls, probably for sitting or sleeping.

There had once been a skin covering for the door but most of it was now gone. Animals might have gnawed it away or it might simply have rotted; I couldn't tell.

Fires had been built in a pit beneath a smoke hole in the roof's center; charred wood and ash still lined the fire-pit. I found small points fashioned of chert on a ledge near the back of the dwelling, looking as if the worker had simply laid them aside. There were several small, dart-like objects tipped with similar points, but no evidence of flight-control feathers.

The matter was soon resolved; another object lay near the darts, likely an atlatl, and there was a spear shaft of better workmanship that mine. The shaft had no point, but one end had a deep conical socket designed to accept a dart. The other end had a shallow cup, and the atlatl had a knob designed to fit the hollow at the end of the shaft. Pleistocene North Americans had used such a system, replaceable darts and an atlatl to throw their spears.

A hollowed grinding stone lay near the fire pit, two hand-sized stones nearby that had been used for grinding grain. I couldn't carry the heavy stones, they would have to remain behind in the ancient dwelling, but the other objects I would take with me.

This hut had been home to a family and there might be more dwellings about, but I wouldn't take the time to search for them. I had all I could carry comfortably, so more discoveries wouldn't do me much good.

The spear-shaft and the darts were dry, but usable; the atlatl was rotted. Perhaps it had picked up oil from the user's hands. I fixed the shape in mind and left it behind. I took the flaked points; for now I could use them to make replacement darts and I would copy them later. A dart went into the spear's socket, the others went into my pack, points up and ready for use.

The dart was a bit loose. It might have been a snug fit when new, but it had dried out and shrunk over the years. I kept the point of my new spear up so that the dart wouldn't drop out. It was more lethal than the wooden one I'd abandoned in the old dwelling and tomorrow, I might find the source of that smoke.

Chapter 6

After setting up camp that afternoon, I soaked the ends of the darts and put more water into the spear's socket. The darts expanded overnight, enough to resume their snug fit by next morning. It was a simple, yet effective, weapon; friction held the darts in place until they were embedded in an animal, then the shaft dropped away. It could be picked up, a new dart inserted, and immediately used again.

Leaving the stream, I followed the edge of the forest toward where I'd seen the smoke. During a short pause, I chopped a piece of wood suitable for carving into an atlatl, which in simplest form is no more than a lever to add force to spear casts. I improved my version by adding a cord loop, which allowed me to store more energy by pre-tensioning the cord before launching the spear.

Eventually there would be a leather loop; the cord was strong, but rough, and it might blister my hand. I would make a new spear too, one with a longer, heavier shaft. The salvaged one could then be used for practice. The makers of the spear I'd found might have been smaller; considering what I might use the new spear on, bigger was better.

I remained close to the edge of the trees, with the grassy plain off to my left or south. I could make out dark objects far across the grass that slowly moved. They were probably grazing. But whatever they were, they wouldn't be friendly. And even with an atlatl and a reloadable, socketed shaft, the creatures were too large to attack.

The atlatl got more attention during my midday break; I might need it at any time.

The wood I'd cut was a two-foot-long branch with a fork extending from near the end. Carving the smaller forked limb improved the fit where it fitted into the spear's hollow base, and trimming the larger part to size finished the task. I adjusted the hand-loop until it felt right, then tucked the device into my belt. Smooth stones or river sand would do for final shaping, but the atlatl-spear-dart system was usable.

I topped a small rise later that afternoon and saw more smoke. Slipping closer, taking advantage of small bits of cover, I finally had a clear view. The smoke was rising from an earth-colored, beehive-shaped object standing next to a large, shingle-roofed log cabin.

I watched for a moment, trying to make sense of the scene. The rectangular cabin's logs had been squared and notched to fit tightly with the cross-logs at the narrower ends. It looked well built, solid; I suspected I couldn't improve on it if I had a workshop and helpers. At one end was a chimney. A thin wisp of pale gray-brown smoke rose from it, different from the darker smoke I'd seen from a distance. A door opened while I watched and a dark-haired young woman came out.

She added dried branches to a hole in the beehive-shaped object, then carefully selected and added a green branch as well. In a moment, there was a renewed plume of dark smoke. Satisfied, she turned around and went back in the cabin.

Had the cabin been put here by the Futurists? Or was there some other group involved, perhaps the people from the dwelling I'd found? At any rate, I wanted to make contact, so I stepped out of the edge of the wood. I was visible to anyone in the house, but close enough to dodge behind cover should that prove necessary. My spear shaft, dart still inserted, I leaned against a nearby tree.

"Hello, the house!" I called out as loudly as I could.

After a moment I saw movement at a window, closed until now by an internal shutter. I made sure my hands were visible and turned them palm-forward where they hung at my side.

I got a reply. "Hello." She spoke English; there had been no assurance that she would.

"I'm friendly. Can I come up to the cabin?"

"OK," she replied. "Keep your hands in sight, please."

I realized that she had some sort of weapon, probably one that cast a projectile. The dark smoke had most likely been a deliberate attempt to attract others, but even so, she was cautious.

Hands extended slightly from my side, palms still facing forward, I walked about halfway to the cabin and stopped. I was cautious too.

The door opened and a different woman stepped out. Like the other, this one wore a skirt, but her hair was so light brown as to be nearly blonde. So; there were at least two women in the cabin. It looked large enough to house half a dozen people if they were really good friends.

"I saw your smoke," I told her. "I've been alone since I arrived, so I thought I'd check on the smoke."

"We caused the fire to smoke. If anyone was near we thought they'd see it. You're the second to come here."

"I saw a different woman earlier," I said. "As I said, there's only one of me. I mean you no harm."

"You can come on up," she said. "But be careful. There's a crossbow aimed at you."

Suspicions confirmed; the crossbow was a surprise, but I could get killed by an animal as well as by a bolt, so I walked toward her. I still had my slung knife, axe, and club, but I kept my hands away from them. I noticed her move aside so that she would not be between the window and me. If the other woman was watching from inside the house, as I supposed, she was concealed in the shadows.

"I didn't expect to see anything like this cabin," I said. "This is all I was given." I gestured at the slung axe and scabbarded knife at my hip.

"Are you from the future too?" she asked.

"Sort of, but not from the same time as the man who transplanted me here. He led me to believe that all of us would begin with just a knife and an axe."

"Maybe they realized women needed more. They gave us knives, the crossbow, and the cabin, but we need to start growing plants soon or we'll have to leave it."

"How many are you?" I asked her.

"There were three of us originally." A bleak look flitted across her face. "But some kind of wild cow killed Amanda three weeks ago. She insisted on taking chances, more than Sandra or I thought was smart, but she wouldn't listen. I'm Millie, by the way."

"I'm Matt."

"Come on in. Are those your only weapons?" She gestured at my axe and knife.

I hesitated a moment before responding. "No, I've also got a spear. I left it in the woods."

"Bring it with you, then. If you meant to attack, you could have remained hidden and ambushed one of us when we came outside. I'll trust you, at least for now."

I went back, recovered the spear, and removed the dart. The dart and atlatl went into my pack and I carried the spear-shaft in my hand, now no more than a heavy staff of wood. The door stood open, so I went in.

Sandra and Millie, as I now knew their names to be, stood near the fireplace. And yes, there was a cocked crossbow, but it was standing bow-end-down. I saw no quarrel or bolt, but there was probably one nearby. Loading the crossbow, aiming, and firing it would take bare seconds.

Glancing around, I saw that the cabin contained a fireplace, three wooden chairs, and a platform bed. The bed was high enough to store small items underneath and easily large enough to accommodate three. The fireplace, centered in the wall to the left of the door, had a swing-out metal crane for holding a cook-pot. A metal grid with an extended handle leaned against it.

The fireplace was for cooking and heating the cabin, then; the outdoor item was probably an oven. Not much, but a lot more than I'd started with. Or had, for that matter. I looked at the nearest chair and raised my eyebrows in question.

"Sure, sit down. But. . ." she hesitated. "We can't feed you."

"That's OK. I've got food."

"Do you have enough to share? We'll let you stay in the cabin tonight if you share your food."

I had enough cured food to last three people for possibly two days, one day for sure, but after that, I'd have to set traps or go hunting. Still, finding food hadn't been a problem before, so probably it wouldn't be now. I decided to share my dried meat. "I've got pork, smoke cured."

A look of relief crossed her face. "Great! We haven't had pork since we got here. We had beef, but after Amanda got killed we were afraid to go after any more of the wild cows. We've got bread that we make from grass-seed flour, and we grind nuts and seeds from a gourd to add a little flavor."

I nodded and set the pack down, then removed my cured meat. Millie brought out a loaf of bread and cut it into thirds. She gave me the middle third and I sliced off chunks of my pork. "It's a bit salty and if there's any grit on the meat, just brush it off. It won't hurt you." I paused while I estimated how much meat to give each of them. They looked hungry, so I added more than I'd originally intended.

Sandra had been quiet until now and she'd not left the vicinity of the crossbow. Now she released the bowstring, using a cocking lever that was part of the bow. It was clearly a chore; this was a heavy weapon, suitable for killing large animals such as the wild cow she'd mentioned. I might have thought it too heavy for light muscles, but Sandra managed.

No question, the two were hungry. They grabbed onto the smoked pork and took large bites. After a moment, they slowed down and ate some of the bread. I'd been eating too, but slower.

I cut off two more pieces of the pork and offered them. There might be enough remaining for breakfast, but there would be no more after that.

"Couldn't you trap animals, even small ones?" I asked. This time it was Sandra who answered. "We tried, but I think we were doing it wrong because we didn't catch anything. We've had bread, but that gets old pretty quick. There were no other flavorings except for salt and some wild onions we found. We haven't been starving, not quite," she admitted.

"Why don't I set out a few snares before it gets dark?" I suggested. The two were happy to have me do that, so spear in hand, I set off to circle the cabin. There was a spring behind the cabin, only a few feet from the back door, and with a tiny rivulet leading off to the west. I decided this was the cabin's water supply, but I decided to investigate where that rivulet went when I had time.

I put a snare near the spring's drain and set others wherever I found a likely spot. Pyramid traps could wait until tomorrow, when there was enough light to see by.

It was dark enough that I was glad of the half-moon in the sky by the time I got back to the cabin. I knocked gently at the door before going in.

There was a small fire burning in the fireplace. Millie was drinking from a gourd. There were several of these hanging from a peg and near them stood several crude pots. From the shiny appearance, I thought they'd managed to fire the pottery.

Sandra picked up a thick bar and secured the door after I came inside. The shutters were already closed and barred in a similar fashion. "We always do this," she explained. "Animals sometimes come in from the plains off to the southwest. We've seen sloths and huge things we think are bison, or maybe they're buffalo. They're like what we saw in zoos before we were brought here, but bigger and with straight horns. They've never come close to the cabin.

"Sometimes there are lions and we saw huge wolves once. They're after the bison and maybe the sloths too. We also saw tracks that we thought might be a bear, but if a bear made the tracks, it's huge. The only thing we've seen that was funny and not dangerous was a giant tortoise. It saw us watching and slowly crawled away, so we left it alone."

"I noticed you have gourds and that you're making pottery," I said. "How are you making the pottery?"

"We tried coiling long clay rolls and wrapping them into a round shape, then smoothing it before the rolls dried. The rolls are easy to make, but that first effort was a disappointment. Now we coil the clay rolls around a small gourd first. The gourds aren't good for anything else, they're too bitter, but we can coil the clay around one, remove the gourd, then smooth the clay with water.

"We also have a larger round gourd we found growing down in the creek bed. We're trying to use it too, but we've only found a few of them.

"We have plenty of clay. We dried the pots near the fireplace and when they were dry enough, we moved them out to the oven. We have to fire the bowls slowly. That's when we use the smoke, to see if anyone wants to come in; we just add green branches on top of the dry firewood while we're baking the pots. There was a man who arrived before you, but we ran him off. We'd have killed him if he hadn't gone."

I looked at her in surprise.

She answered, somewhat defensively. "He thought we were going to be his harem. He expected we would feed him and warm his bed every night, *our* bed at that. He would be the king rooster and our cabin would be his hen house.

"But he didn't like the looks of that crossbow and Amanda was just itching to shoot him, so he left. I really miss Amanda. She could do a lot of stuff we can't do, either of us."

"Well, I knew how to do some things when I arrived and I've learned more since. I've kept myself fed, first by trapping, but then later on I got a deer. The pork came from a pig, or maybe it was a peccary, that I caught in a snare. I couldn't decide which one it was, but it tasted good after I washed the meat in salty water.

"I cured it over a smoky fire for a day and a half. So far it hasn't lasted long enough to go bad. Anyway, I don't mind teaching you what I've learned."

"Matt, you're welcome to stay as long as you contribute. Just don't expect to be the boss; there are two of us and one of you, and if we can't work together you'll have to leave. We don't intend to be servants or any man's harem."

I couldn't help but become a little cautious after that statement, but not enough to leave. "I have no problem with what you said. I don't plan on being anyone's boss, but there really is safety in numbers." Both nodded in agreement.

"Where will I sleep? Considering what you just told me, I don't want to make a mistake."

"You can sleep on the bed. With us, I mean, but we need to talk first before anything happens. One of us could end up pregnant, maybe both of us. You understand, don't you? We can't take a chance if you decide to move on in a day or two."

"I can stick around for a while," I said. "But eventually, I'll want to look around farther west. Right now, I'm wondering if the Futurist lied to me. Did the one you saw tell you this world was empty, that humans had not developed here?" The women glanced at each other, nodded.

"Well, I found a hut, not like this cabin at all. It was well built and still strong, even though it looked really old. Somebody had lived there for a long time. They also knew how to make tools and craft weapons; the spear and the darts are the ones I found in the hut.

"That's where I got the idea for the atlatl. The one they left wouldn't work, but I made another one using their pattern. The spear had shrunk, part of the reason why I thought no one had been there for a long time, so I soaked the ends of the darts to make them fit tight in the socket. I also re-wrapped the socket end of the spear with cord and glued it in place. It seems strong now, but I plan on making a new shaft and keeping the old one for practicing. I didn't want to chance breaking my only spear. If it's going to happen, I want it to be while I'm killing an animal."

I went to the pack and brought back the darts to show them the finely-flaked stone tips. I also demonstrated how the darts fitted into the socket and showed how the atlatl added force when throwing the spear. They quickly understood how everything worked; this system was obviously superior to carrying a bundle of spears. As I finished the explanation, I noticed yawns coming from the women. Both had fed well, probably better than usual. They had reason to be tired.

"Why don't we wait until tomorrow for the rest of it?" I asked. They agreed, so we went to bed. I lay down and simply listened for a moment. So strange, hearing the breathing of others after being alone so long! We were soon asleep.

Chapter 7

I slept for four hours straight, the first time since arriving on Darwin's World; the feeling of security from being inside four sturdy walls, of having a real roof overhead, allowed me to sleep without waking long enough to add wood to the fire.

My clothes needed washing; I had planned to do so but that hadn't happened. Still, it had seemed like removing my stinky clothes was the thing to do, the first time since being transplanted that I'd had that luxury. I could still reach the clothes quickly if necessary, and I avoided at least some of the smell. I had planned on wearing my underpants, but they virtually fell apart as I tried to adjust them. I sighed; at least the cabin was dark, and I habitually woke up before dawn. I could be dressed before the women got up and there would probably be someplace down at the stream where I could wash. The clothes, and also me!

The faint glow of coals barely showed where the fireplace was located; all else was dark when I woke up. I got out of bed, picked up my spear, and glanced through the peephole before opening the door. After a careful look around, I stepped outside.

Crickets burred softly; likely, there was no threat around, so I took a few steps away to water a bush. Waking up and a full bladder go together. It was pleasant outside, more pleasant than in the cabin, truth be told; I wasn't the only one that needed a bath and clean clothes. After a final shaking, I glanced at the sky and admired the stars. The moon was no longer visible.

I went back in after a moment and secured the door. From there, I made my way back to the bed and tried to find 'my spot' by feel. It was a very interesting process. A hand grabbed mine and led me to the open space in the bed, and then led my hand farther.

One of the women, I had no idea which, had not been nearly so sleepy. So much for assuring me that they wanted to be careful. Someone had undergone a change of heart.

I don't know if the other woke up when we started, but I heard a mumbled "Slut," before I dropped off to sleep again. It's so hard to keep secrets when you're sleeping three in a bed, even in the dark!

I woke up later than usual next morning. My new companions slept late too. Had the late-night activities kept them awake? Finally my insistent morning need got me up and out to find someplace to take care of matters. I decided that yes, I would definitely find someplace to wash up before the day was over!

The two women were up when I returned. I said, "Good morning!" and waited to see if there was any reaction. If there was, I missed it. I was greeted with essentially the same tone we'd used when we wished each other a good night.

We worked together fixing breakfast; I set out the last of my cured pork, they provided more bread. There was water to wash it down and we took turns drinking from the gourd. Little things are important; having your own personal drinking vessel and dishes constitutes wealth.

I mentioned I was going to look around and check the traps, and they'd be welcome if they wanted to come along. The snares would need to be moved anyway, and if one or both came along I could explain trapping and how to improve a trap site.

There was also a stream not far from the cabin and I wanted to see how useful it might be. There might even be a pool where I could catch fish, which would certainly improve to our diet. I could wash my clothing, even manage a bath for myself!

The women decided that Millie would go with me while Sandra worked around the cabin, opening the windows and letting the air blow through. An excellent idea I thought; perhaps the bed would be aired out too. Sandra would also bake a few loaves of bread and grind more flour while we were out. The raw materials, already collected, were in pots against the back wall.

I rapidly fashioned a pack for Millie; Sandra would get one later. I carried my spear even though we weren't going far, and Millie had her knife. We probably wouldn't need the crossbow; even hunting for three, I had no intention of confronting a big animal today.

Millie and I made the rounds of my traps and collected four dead rabbits. Most of the snares were undisturbed, but I picked them up anyway, putting them into my pack to be reset elsewhere. We quickly gutted the rabbits and lopped off the heads; skinning could wait until we got back. Millie put the carcasses in her pack, since I carried my atlatl and spear. If there were predators around I didn't want to find one the hard way, and if we surprised a deer I intended to be ready.

I reset the snares in several of the many animal paths, showing Millie how I placed the trap and improved the location. We finished the task after about two hours and returned to the cabin. The rabbits would be our supper, along with whatever greens or fruit we might come across later. Thanks to Sandra, there would also be fresh bread; we'd eat well tonight. We left the rabbits with her and headed out again, this time toward the stream.

The women hadn't been attacked, but they'd worked outside only for brief periods. We couldn't assume the area was safe. Amanda had been killed somewhere nearby, and where the grazers went, carnivores followed. The women had survived as much by luck as skill, I decided; we had that much in common.

Maybe I could convince them to be more alert, more cautious. Tackling a big bovine was something to do only when you had a handy tree to climb. That had been a dumb move on Amanda's part, shooting when you couldn't be certain of killing immediately. Overconfidence kills.

I would be sure to explain this to them, several times if necessary. Amanda's lack of wariness might be what Darwin's World was expected to weed out of the gene pool.

The spring behind the cabin was a reliable water source, and close; take a few steps outside, fill a gourd, step back in the cabin. The water would also be pure, something I hadn't been certain of regarding the places I drank. I had never known if some animal had been pissing just out of sight or had died and was rotting upstream. I'd depended on the 'immunity' that the Futurist told me I had. I'd been lucky too, or perhaps this region wasn't as wild as I'd assumed when I was first transplanted.

The stream was less than half a mile from the cabin, running roughly north-to-south. It flowed in a narrow gully that was slightly more than six feet deep and would probably flood if we got a heavy rain such as I'd experienced.

We followed an animal trail down the gully's fairly-steep side. The vegetation near the stream was thick and varied, with willows the dominant species near the banks. There were no gourds, though they might be growing upstream.

I couldn't see over the gully walls, but then, no sight-hunting predator was going to spot us either; terrain can provide advantages as well as disadvantages. I looked for tracks along the banks, but found nothing new. Old tracks indicated that large deer frequently came to the stream. If not deer, they might have been left by something I had no knowledge of. What else might exist on Darwin's World?

I had good knowledge of fossil discoveries from before the twentieth century, but that didn't mean everything had been found. Fossil creation depends on where the organism dies and what happens afterwards. Luck plays a large part in fossilization, so there might be entire families of organisms that never left evidence of their passing.

Should I set traps by the stream? There were tracks of birds, and the cross-stacked pyramid would serve nicely as a bird trap. A large, heavy snare might catch the deer that had left the tracks, but at the same time I didn't want to discourage animals from visiting. They might decide to move away. It was something to think about, our current requirement for food balanced against future needs.

We moved upstream. Millie had mentioned they needed to find a new clay deposit. Looking down, I noticed that the stream-bed was well supplied with rocks which might be useful later. But for now, we were more concerned with finding edible vegetation or berries and clay for making more pots.

Cress grew in the water near the bank, the cattails had edible roots and green shoots. Millie gathered foods while I kept watch, then we moved on.

We soon found a spreading pool, shallow, but deep enough to bathe in and wash my filthy clothes; two new blood spots, gained while butchering the rabbits, had joined earlier stains. I brought up the subject.

"I really need a bath. If you like, you might move up to the top of the bank and keep a lookout?"

Millie gave me a funny look. "I suspect I need a bath as much as you, maybe even more. And I need to wash my clothes too. You're not turning shy, are you?"

"No, but I don't know enough about you; it should always be the lady's choice."

"This lady will choose to be clean. Do you think we're safe enough?"

"Wait; I'll look around."

I crossed the stream but found nothing threatening on that side. Climbing to the top of the small gully, I looked around the countryside. Nothing moved. I slid to the bottom and crossed to where Millie waited.

"I couldn't see anything dangerous, just woods and grass. I think we're safe for a while."

"Good!" she said, then immediately began removing her boots and the shirt and pants she wore today. She had no underwear, but did have socks. The Futurists had been nicer to the women than me, giving them the dresses they'd been wearing when I first saw them as well as shirts and trousers.

Watching her undress was exciting, but I'd been alone since being transplanted. A cloud or a bush had occasionally been exciting. I waited until she was in the water, then put my backpack down and laid the spear across it, shaft toward the stream.

Following Millie's example, I shucked my own clothing. My underwear had rotted, but I still had socks, serviceable, if dirty. I laid the socks across my outer clothing. Everything was placed so that I could quickly get to the weapons; I might not have time to get dressed, but at least I would be armed.

Millie took her other clothes in with her. As relaxed and carefree as an otter, she slid into the water and sighed with pleasure. "This sure beats washing up by using a gourd for a bucket!"

"I got used to washing in streams," I said. "It works, not as well as soap, but if you do it every day or so it's not bad. I didn't cross any streams during the last week before I found your cabin."

Millie made a production of sloshing her clothes in the water, wringing them out, then repeating the process several times. I was content to soak and watch her. Sitting was best, I thought. She was female, and part of me was taking due notice.

She waded to the side, spread her clothes on the grass to dry, then slipped back into the water. This time, she was quite close to me.

"How long do you think we'll be safe here?" Her voice was a soft murmur.

"I didn't see anything up top. Predators hunt when the prey is active and a lot of animals don't move around during the day, so I think we're safe for a while."

"Oh, good. I was hoping you'd say that." And she slid the few inches closer until she was in contact with my hip. Her hand was underwater. I knew exactly where it was. And what it had found to hold on to.

"I got tired of waiting for you to make a move, Matt."

"Millie, I'm not sure this is a good idea. I don't know if I can watch out for danger if we—do this."

"The Futurists gave me this new, young body. It works really well, but then they put me here with two women! I'm tired of waiting!"

Well, shucks. I didn't want to get killed, but I was beginning to forget about saber-toothed cats. I was wavering. I knew what I wanted to do, and what I should do. Wanted was winning.

Even so, I was insistent. "Look here, if we're going to do this, it's got to be quick, and we've still got to watch for danger."

"*You* watch for trouble. Some other time I might need to be persuaded, but not now." I understood exactly what she meant. Sandra had probably been my partner last night; Millie was too eager.

"So you're here and I'm here and Sandra is back at the cabin, and I don't want to wait until tonight!" How do you say no to that? I had no idea, so I didn't.

She was naked, I was naked. I looked around, and then put my hands on her hips. I leaned forward and kissed her. Well, I was always polite. Everyone said so.

We explored each other's tonsils for a minute and I explored lower. Very nice, even perky. Yes indeed, perky was the word. I was happy and eager to see this go further, even after last night, so the kissing was less protracted than it might have been. I tried to concentrate on her, but I couldn't get that hypothetical saber-tooth completely out of my mind. The critter was possibly out there somewhere, deciding that inter-species voyeurism wasn't fun and could we please hold still while he used those long fangs on us?

But we finished, satisfactorily for me at least, and Millie wasn't complaining; job well done, more or less. And no saber-tooth showed up to interrupt our fun.

Finally, I just sat down in the water. She saw what I was doing and decided to do the same. Perhaps she washed a bit longer than was necessary for cleanliness. Well, people say women need time to get there and time to come back down. At least I was now watching for danger instead of watching Millie!

I could cheerfully have lain down in the stream and gone to sleep. I wonder if women know just how much sex takes out of a man? But I didn't. She was still washing—or maybe trying for seconds—but I needed to rinse out my clothes.

The weapons stayed on the bank, the clothes got a good sloshing around in the water. As soon as they were as clean as I could get them, I wrung them out and got dressed. They would dry on the way back.

I picked up my knife and axe, installed them in their respective carriers, and picked up my spear. Millie gathered up her mostly-dry clothes and dressed. I put my boots on and looked at her questioningly. She nodded, showing a lot more energy than I had. I was tired, if not quite exhausted. She was still—perky. Women are different. Mostly I like the difference, if I'm not too tired.

We headed back the way we'd come, moving downstream now. I had the urge to look behind me to see if there were furrows in the grass. But no, my butt wasn't really dragging the ground. I'm almost sure of it.

Maybe the saying isn't meant to be taken literally.

We had almost reached the path when I saw a fresh track, a human one.

The footprint was large. It probably belonged to a man. There was still a bit more adrenaline in my system; I felt a sudden jolt as the flight or fight reflex overcame the exhaustion.

I held out a hand to check Millie and looked around carefully, but saw nothing threatening. Looking again at the track, I saw it was still damp; he'd just crossed the stream. Millie was opening her mouth to say something when I looked at her and shook my head, lips pressed firmly together. I looked at everything in view. I took my time, examined every place the maker of that track could be hiding, finally decided he'd kept moving.

Still, he'd been here. It had to be a he, large foot, enough weight to make a deep impression on the soft ground near the stream. Maybe he was a stranger. Or maybe he was the one that the women had chased away.

And maybe he was heading for the cabin where Sandra was alone, maybe alert to danger, but maybe not. I glanced back at Millie and headed for the cabin, running.

Chapter 8

Millie ran behind me, trying to keep up. I had the spear in my right hand and I fumbled to shrug the backpack's straps from my shoulders. I eventually got them free while I kept running. Finally, I saw the cabin through the trees. There was no one outside, but the door was slightly ajar. Sandra wouldn't have left it that way if she'd had a choice. I slowed down and concentrated on moving quietly. The noise Millie made was far enough back not to be detectable.

My spear was ready when I reached the door, left hand just behind the socket, right hand far enough down the shaft to provide strength to a thrust. This grip would ordinarily leave the spear slanted across my body, but by extending my left arm forward and pulling the right elbow in tight, the lethal stone tip was at eye level, pointing forward when I pushed gently against the door.

As it swung slowly open, it revealed a stocky man, facing away from me. He wore leathers, deerskin I thought, and held a small buckler in his left hand. I couldn't see his right hand, but Sandra was facing the man, knife in her right hand held by her hip, left extended forward in guard position.

There was a bloodstain on her right side, just above the hip. It was enough.

I lowered the spear tip slightly and lunged forward, my weight behind that chipped-stone point. It entered his back just below the ribs and to the left of the spine. He straightened in shock, and as he did I saw the short sword in his other hand. The blade was long, leaf shaped, and made of metal. It wasn't like my Futurist knife; this weapon was made for stabbing.

My dart sank in until the end of the spear-shaft dimpled his skin. He grunted and stumbled forward. As he did, I pulled back and the shaft came free just as it was supposed to, leaving the dart in his body. I held the shaft up as a guard against surprise—the spear was a weapon in its own right—as he collapsed, never knowing what had killed him.

Let that be a lesson to you, close the door when you come in! But then I got a surprise of my own. I saw movement to the side of the door, revealed as the door swung further open. I had brushed it with my hip while spearing the first man, and as it opened it revealed a second man looking at me. Like the other, he held a buckler in his left hand and short sword in his right.

Also like his partner, he had an astonished expression on his face.

My dart tip was gone and the others were in the pack I'd dropped back along the trail. But as he brought up the small round shield, I thrust forward with my empty spear shaft. The socket-tip punched him in the face just below his left eye and skidded up beside his nose, finally ending up in the eye socket.

Well, there went the old binocular vision; I'd probably ruined his whole day too. Still, he was tough and determined. That small shield was coming up and the stabbing point of the long, heavy blade now pointed toward me. He should have been in agony from the eye injury, but maybe he hadn't felt it yet.

While I was wondering what to do next, Sandra saw her opportunity. As the man faced toward me, his attention focused on the point of my spear, she sprang forward and used both hands to plant her knife into the back of his neck where it joined his body.

He collapsed and she stumbled forward as he fell. I grabbed her, yanked her upright, and pushed her behind me. I switched my spear shaft to my left hand and fumbled for my axe, trying to watch everything in the cabin at the same time.

There was a movement to my rear; I spun around and almost gutted Millie, but she squawked and jumped back in time to avoid the strike.

I took a deep breath and began to recover from the adrenaline-fueled fear and combat madness. I was panting and trying to get my breath, I was spattered with blood, there was blood all over the floor of the cabin. One man was dying from a knife that still stuck up from the back of his neck, the other one was dead or nearly so; I'd had to step over him as I turned toward Millie.

To make sure, I drew my axe and turned it hammer-side down. I swung hard at his head and brained him. If he wasn't dead before, he was now. His companion got the same treatment.

I glanced outside, then pulled Millie into the cabin and slammed the door behind her, holding it in place while she dropped the bar into the locking hooks.

So much for airing out the cabin; it stank of blood, shit, piss, and whatever smelly things are in the human abdomen. Butchered humans smell a lot like fresh-killed animals, only worse.

My spear was done. The socket at the end had split when it hit the bones of the second man's face. A triangular piece had broken off the old wood, despite the reinforcement I'd wrapped around it. The cord and glue had also come loose, but the old spear had done its job one final time.

The second man, the one Sandra and I had killed together, was the reason for the blood on her dress. He'd used his long blade to try to convince her to drop her knife and had ended up putting a two-inch gash above her hip. Well, she'd returned the favor, her cut not so long but better placed and much more lethal. I spread my arms near the door and the three of us huddled against the wall, shaking with reaction. I listened to see if there might be more of them outside that my cursory examination hadn't discovered, but heard nothing.

Recovered, I was finally able to leave the two women holding each other while they wept from the shock and fear. My first move was to free the short swords from of the hands of the dead men; it took less than a minute and we might need them. Their fingers still gripped the hilts, even after death, but I managed.

The weapons were reasonably well balanced, likely copied from ancient Roman or Greek versions; swords intended for thrusting had been the weapon of choice for foot soldiers back then. I had my axe and knife, so I was better armed than the women. I handed each a sword, then looked out through the peephole in the door. Nothing moved, but I would have to scout the outside to be sure; there might still be more of them.

One surprise, finding a second attacker in the cabin, was enough.

I had to speak sharply to get through to them, but finally Millie was able to function. Sandra had acted when she needed to, so if she was a little hysterical now I could forgive her that.

I told Millie to bar the door after I went out. That might provide them a little short-term protection, but I realized that the cabin wasn't a safe refuge. An attacker likely couldn't get through the walls, but we'd be forced to come out sooner or later and face whatever waited. Meantime, I needed to be sure.

I crouched low as I ran, then scuttled into the trees some thirty yards away. I carried my knife and axe in readiness and tried to control my breathing, even while listening for any disturbance. But I heard nothing. Even the usual forest sounds were missing.

Waiting, just inside the trees, gave me time for my breathing to slow. I remained there for a long five minutes, then continued around the edge of the clearing while stopping every few paces to listen and observe. The whole process probably took at least an hour, but I found nothing, not even the tracks of the two men who'd died in the cabin.

By the time I finished the sounds of the forest had returned to normal. Insects, birds, a squirrel chattering in the distance; if they'd been disturbed before, they weren't now. Reassuring, I thought.

I thought about something that hadn't occurred to me at the time, the war club I'd made; I realized that it might be preferable to my knife or axe. Clubs kill by crushing, unlike stabbing tools such as the attackers' shortswords. And they don't get stuck, as had happened to Sandra's knife.

Perhaps I would make new clubs, better than my first effort. It shouldn't be too difficult to chip an edge, making it more useful, and Millie and Sandra could use lighter versions.

Finally I went back to the door and tapped on it. A voice whispered "Who?" and I barely kept myself from giggling. Reaction is a funny thing, and all that came to my mind was the thought that we'd been invaded by owls. But I whispered "Matt" and the door swung open.

We began putting the cabin to rights. Millie and I grabbed an arm apiece, dragged the nearest dead man out, and left him just inside the edge of the forest. We went back, got the second one, and gave him the same treatment. I have no idea why dead men feel so much heavier than live ones, but they do. Still, we managed. After a short break to catch our breaths, we dragged the bodies farther into the woods.

I collected the belts and scabbards that each was wearing. The covering they'd worn over their private parts was a loincloth made of thin leather. They could keep the loincloth and the sleeveless vest that covered their upper bodies, the leggings too. Those things weren't worth salvaging, nor were the crude shields. I couldn't think of any possible use for those, other than combat between humans.

There wasn't much we could do about the bloodstains. I began carrying in double handfuls of dirt before finally remembering my turtle shells. I used them to scoop up dirt which I spread over the stains to soak up as much of the blood as possible.

While the women prepared food, I went out and fashioned a broom from branches. Cord tied the leaves and stems into a bundle around a long handle; I used this to sweep the bloody dirt into a pile. I scooped it up and took it outside, then repeated the process with fresh dirt. After dumping this, I tossed the soiled broom toward the forest. The floor was better, not perfect, but it would have to do. By the time I finished, the women had cooked the rabbits.

It was not the most appetizing food I'd eaten, and certainly the surroundings weren't the best. But the rabbits and bread vanished and I felt better. The cabin still stank, but we would just have to live with it tonight.

There was nothing I could do to keep scavengers away. I couldn't carry the bodies far, and we had no tools to dig graves. So the big animals would certainly come. There was just too much easy meat in the woods.

Predator, scavenger, those were human words; the animals wouldn't care. Lions, bears, wolves, even saber-tooth cats lived in part by robbing other animals.

Kill, feed fast, hope you get a belly-full before some bigger, meaner animal moved in to claim your dinner, that was the rule among predators. When that bigger animal showed up, abandon what was left and head off in search of more prey.

I'd salvaged Sandra's knife from the dead man's neck and returned it to her, but I had forgotten the dart in the other man's back. Perhaps I could find it, or at least the worked-stone head, after the animals had fed. I'd also recovered my pack from where I'd dropped it, not that the darts inside would help. The socket in the end of the spear shaft was unusable.

I asked Sandra, "The guy you ran off before, was he one of the two we killed?"

"I think so. It all happened fast, but I think that was him, the one I put my knife into." She looked to Millie for confirmation, and Millie nodded.

"That was him, but that other one was a stranger. I've no idea where he came from. And those knives, they were like nothing we'd seen before. The man that was here before didn't have a knife like that, or that thing on his arm. I would have noticed."

It was something more to think about. Where had they gotten the knives?

Did our activities in the pool have anything to do with the events at the cabin? It was almost certainly coincidence. The episode at the stream had lasted only a few minutes, not long enough to affect what those two had been planning. A number of thoughts had gone through my head after we left the pool. Not just about Millie's invitation, but whether I could develop a relationship with the only two people I'd seen up to that time. They'd already run one man off, and if I had offended Millie by rejecting her, they might decide they preferred me gone.

It might also cause problems between them if one wanted me to stay and the other wanted me to leave.

I'd decided at the time to take the risk. There was a slight risk from animals discovering us in the act, but possibly a greater risk if I denied Millie. The inconvenient fact remained that if I were alone, something so minor as a sprained ankle could result in death. So it had been my own logical thinking, not just the urge for sex that had convinced me.

I was almost certain of it.

The quickie had been only a brief distraction, and if anyone was at fault for permitting the surprise attack to occur, the fault fell mostly on Sandra. It couldn't have happened had she been more cautious, kept the door barred while Millie and I were out.

"Millie and Sandra, you need to keep that door secured. Not just occasionally, all the time, even if you're inside. Sandra, you'd have likely been raped or enslaved, maybe killed if I hadn't got here in time. There are no laws on this world and no one to enforce them if there were. You take care of yourself or you take the consequences." My voice and expression were grim. I didn't know if they understood what they'd barely escaped, but I did. Rape, slavery, even cannibalism; human history has a lot of dark chapters.

"Something else; this cabin isn't a fort, it's a trap. The cabin is fairly roomy for three, but there's not enough room to store food or water, even if we do make more of those pots. We don't have excess food, and no place to store much if we *can* gather a surplus. Even that spring out back isn't walled in, so going out for water exposes you to attack. An attacker can starve us out or burn the cabin around us. How bad do you want to try to keep this place?"

"Matt, I hear what you're saying. But what if I'm pregnant?" Sandra asked. "If we don't keep this cabin, then I'd be left to carry a child through the woods or grasslands. There would be no shelter unless we built something, or protection other than from our own weapons. And we can't depend on those to stop an animal. Amanda found that out the hard way. There might even be packs of wolves or lions or something."

OK, that confirmed what I suspected down at the stream; Sandra had been the one last night. Now Millie might be pregnant too, but she could tell Sandra herself if she wanted her to know. It was her decision as to when she'd do that.

"Sandra, we could probably do something to improve this cabin. For example, we could build a wall around it. Dig a shallow trench, then put up a palisade like a coyote fence.

"I could cut poles four or five inches thick and a couple of yards long, then tie them together with cord. We could bury the bases in the trench and add pole braces to make it stronger. We could also sharpen the tips and set the palisade poles so they slanted out. We'd also have to become farmers. Permanent shelter is only worthwhile if we can feed ourselves.

"But all this depends on whether you want me to stay. If you're not sure, then I'll need to move on."

"Matt, I think we need you." Millie nodded emphatically. She looked at Sandra, and Sandra nodded back.

I had been lonely, more than I realized, before I found this pair. Working together, we could divide up the jobs as well as be safer. I nodded agreement.

"Sandra...well, you're not the only one, you know," Millie said. "I had Matt while we were down at the stream."

When Sandra looked at her in surprise, Millie said, "You had him last night. I decided I wanted him too. I heard what you said, that stuff about not getting pregnant, but that didn't last long. Did it?" Sandra flushed and looked down.

"Anyway, it's done. I may be pregnant too. We need Matt, and that makes him need us too. Especially if we're pregnant with his children."

I looked back and forth between them as they tried to stare each other down. Could I provide for two more people? Gathering plants was easy if there were edible ones about, and the women knew as much about that as I did. But how much did any of us know about farming?

Hunting and gathering can work for a small group, but only if they're nomads. People soon exhaust resources near a camp and moving on becomes necessary.

Of equal importance, could I protect them? At first, I had depended on my ability to run away from danger rather than fight, but that option would go away as soon as I accepted responsibility for the safety of two women. But it didn't appear that I had a choice. I was committed now, just as I'd been committed when the Futurist dropped me here. There was no going back.

It was getting dark outside, and some of my snares were still set. They might catch something during the night. I could hope, and if not, maybe there would be bread or vegetables. Millie had gathered some before we'd come back to the cabin. But it was too dark to set more traps now, especially considering we'd hauled out and left two large pieces of bait that were sure to attract a predator.

We secured the cabin, bar across the door and shutters over the windows, and turned in. I was in the middle this time. We all smelled a bit ripe but they wanted to cuddle so that's what we did. I dropped off to sleep after a minute.

My last thought was that I hoped tomorrow wouldn't be as dramatic as today had been.

Chapter 9

Despite the smell, I got a full night's sleep.

Our cleanup efforts and the attempt to air out the cabin helped, but enough of the stink remained to remind us that yesterday two men had died here. The fact that we'd been defending ourselves made no real difference. They were dead, and the cabin smelled.

Killing animals had become almost routine, but not humans; it was surprising that I slept at all. But yesterday had been physically exhausting as well as stressful, so maybe that's why I slept so well.

After taking care of morning necessities, I found a young tree to serve as a temporary spear. I hacked a point at the end, cut the trunk so that it was equal to my own height, then smoothed the places where branches had been. The spear ended up slightly more than six feet in length and two inches in diameter. It would deliver a lethal wound when backed by strong muscles. While it was not of the same quality as the one I'd broken yesterday, at least I had a spear again.

Scavengers might still be feeding on the bodies we'd dumped, and if so, they were welcome to those two. I hoped to get my dart back, or at least the chipped point, but salvage could wait. In any case, the dart wouldn't be useful until I made a replacement shaft.

I collected a large and healthy rabbit from one snare and there was evidence that another had been caught, but something else had a taste for rabbit. There were no recognizable tracks, just bits of fur, and even the snare cord was beyond salvaging.

Maybe one of the scavengers had abandoned feeding on the human bodies in response to the rabbit's squeals. Simple rule, wait too long before checking your snares and *you* won't get the rabbit.

I cleaned my catch and headed back. One rabbit, shared three ways, wouldn't provide much of a meal. If I intended to provide meat for the three of us, I would have to do better.

Events provided some excuse for the failure; defending the women had taken precedence, and after dragging the bodies into the woods I was tired. But excuses can't be eaten.

Leaving the rabbit at the cabin, I headed for the stream.

I considered whether it might be possible to dam up the gully. It would be a lot of work, but possibly worthwhile. There are advantages in having a plentiful supply of water for irrigation, and wastes could still be dumped downstream.

Farming could make holding the cabin worthwhile. Add a palisade for security, perhaps an outbuilding for storing supplies... such improvements would eliminate two of the cabin's worst failings.

Musing on the possibilities occupied my thoughts. The last few snares I placed in the gully; the final snare was rope, all I had left, but maybe it would work. Heading back, I collected fibrous leaves and long-stemmed grasses for use in making more cord. As I was stuffing them into my pack, I noticed the bees.

They had been visiting a shrub with small whitish flowers. Whatever kind of blooms they were, the bees liked them. There were a lot of them and when they left the flowers, they flew away downstream. I followed their flight path and found the hive.

It was in an old tree, now hollowed out by rot. Possibly it had fallen victim to a lightning strike; the bottom showed a long split extending almost all the way to where the bees were entering the tree. A rotten branch had fallen away, leaving a foot-wide hole. The bees I'd been following entered, even as others exited and flew away.

I moved in a little closer to make sure they were bees and not hornets. But bees they were, and I decided to raid the tree for honey. I suddenly had a taste for something sweet, and I knew the women would like it too.

There's a trick to gathering honey. If you're careful, you can do it without getting stung. I hoped. But I would need a helper, plus gourds or a tightly woven container for carrying the honeycomb. I wanted the beeswax as well as the honey; I had a use for it.

On the way back to the cabin, I cautiously approached the place where we'd dumped the two bodies. There might be tracks there, and knowledge could be a life-saver.

The bodies were gone; only a slight smell lingered to indicate they'd been there. There were numerous tracks, most of them looking like a cross between a cat and a dog. I'd have called it cat, but cats retract their claws and this one showed claw marks ahead of the oval pads. The animal was heavy, too; the tracks were deeply indented into the soil. Had the cat-dog carried a body away?

Might it be some kind of terrestrial cat, as opposed to an arboreal one? A lion, perhaps even a saber-tooth? My spear wouldn't be adequate for either. Whether atlatl-spear-dart or bow and arrows, I knew that I needed a projectile weapon. The crossbow was really too heavy for field use, and it needed to be reserved for defending the cabin.

Meantime, the big cats were best avoided; they were better armed than I was.

I gave up on recovering the dart; I would have to make my own. It would take time, but I had more time since I wasn't traveling. I also had plenty of raw materials, the rocks I'd spotted along the stream.

I considered the types of projectile weapons I thought I could make. The crossbow would be powerful enough, but it was slow to reload. A longbow would take a lot of practice before I became skilled, but it could be reloaded and a second arrow launched while a crossbowman was still cocking his weapon. A sling would be easier to make but would take even more practice, plus it lacked the killing power of a bow.

My new spear might be useful as a replacement shaft if it didn't warp while drying. Meanwhile, I would work on a bow.

Carving a stave wouldn't be a problem, but fashioning a thin, strong bowstring would. Numerous primitive peoples had solved the problem, I could too.

Drying the spear shaft near the fireplace might prevent warping. In the meantime, I would split a straight trunk into quarters, providing blanks for a new spear and three bows. The blanks would also be less prone to warping. I hoped.

Ash or hickory was best, but if necessary, beech or cedar would do. American natives had used a tree called Osage orange, but I hadn't seen anything matching what I thought such a tree looked like. Yew didn't grow here either. Maybe there would be some closer to the mountains where the climate was cooler. But my choice would have to be made from what was available.

What was the rest of this country like? There would be mountains, the spring near the cabin told me that. Surface runoff produces streams, but springs need elevation so that water falling higher sinks in and flows downhill, still underground. Where it emerges is a spring.

This region had not been mountainous in my timeline. The Ozarks and Ouachitas were north of here, but the Futurist had warned me that the geological history here might be different. And I couldn't be sure of my location.

I was probably still in Texas, well north of the big-tree region above the coastal swamps. I was also near grasslands. The mix of plain and forest might indicate the area west of downtime Dallas. There were probably rivers somewhere nearby, though hopefully not equal to the downtime Mississippi.

Central-western Texas had canyons such as the Palo Duro, some caused by erosion of the Edwards Plateau. But the nearest thing I'd seen to a canyon so far was the gully where the stream ran; there might not even *be* an Edwards Plateau in this timeline.

I had been walking as I mulled the possibilities over, and now I was back at the cabin. The women could cook the rabbit while I rested, then I'd head out again after a meal. I wanted to run my snares before dark and also keep my eyes open for the kind of tree I wanted, straight and without knots for six or seven feet. It also had to be small enough that I could split it into quarters. The salvaged short-swords would do for that; my own knife was too precious to risk.

"How would you two like some honey?" I asked.

Both answered at once. Yes indeed, they would like some honey!

"We'll need containers. I've found a bee tree, and the trick to not getting stung is smoke. It tranquilizes the bees, I think. Anyway, that's what beekeepers do, the ones who don't use those net outfits that we don't have anyway.

"We'll build a smudge fire and let the bees settle down, then I'll approach the tree. I might try a coating of mud to protect exposed skin and I'll tie off my trouser legs. Anyway, I think it's worth the effort, and I need the beeswax. I could chop down the bee tree, but I'd rather not. If we can rob the bees without killing the queen, we can do it again later.

"Honey will keep indefinitely but we don't have enough containers. I think we should weave tight baskets to bring the honeycomb to the cabin, then transfer the honey to your fired clay pots. If you can make the baskets tonight, I'll raid the bees tomorrow."

"Are you going to keep using smoke to attract people?"

Sandra answered after glancing at Millie. "No," she said. "We had one bad experience and one good experience, and the bad experience led to a raid. If you hadn't gotten here in time, I don't want to think about what might have happened. We'll use nothing but dry wood from now on."

I nodded. "That was my thinking. We don't know if those two were alone. It's strange; they had manufactured swords, but their bucklers were more joke than shield. The two just don't fit together. And the design of those swords; they're fighting implements. A whole world, plenty of resources, very few people, so why fight a war? It doesn't make sense.

"But we need to store more food and water, just in case. If one person is inside, the door stays barred unless you recognize the person knocking."

I mentioned that the two bodies had been carried away. Whatever had done that was nothing we wanted to treat lightly.

As we talked, the rabbit cooked. The women had baked bread, so we had rabbit and bread and water. They had roots that could be roasted for later, and maybe by then I'd have another rabbit or two.

I had been catching a lot of rabbits. They were probably near the bottom of the food chain here, flourishing by producing lots of offspring. Bigger carnivores likely ignored them. We might get tired of rabbit eventually, but I was glad to have the abundance. Hunger makes an appetizing sauce.

After eating, I worked on weaving new cords.

The heavy grindstone helped with separating fibers from the matrix, so I moved it near the fireplace and turned it upside down. I didn't want to contaminate their grinding surface with the plants I got my fibers from.

Tap with a hand-held stone, heavy enough to break up the stems and leaves, but not to damage the fibers. After picking them from the broken-apart stems, I spread them near the fireplace.

While they dried, I hardened the tip of my spear. It was a substantial club even without a point, but it would work much better if I used the coals to bake out the moisture. I slowly rotated the shaft, heating the sharpened end evenly. The point cooled while I turned the fibers so they would dry evenly. The women worked around the oven while I stayed busy in the cabin.

Not wanting to risk my axe, I left it in the cabin when I went to check my snares. The stone-headed club replaced it, hung from my belt by a loop of cord. The knife was at my hip and I carried my spear. If I had caught anything, I didn't want to be robbed this time. I got a smile from the two women as I headed out.

My clothing was frayed and my boots showed wear. I would have to make replacements soon, maybe moccasins like those raiders had worn. The memory implants didn't mention footwear, but the women might have ideas. I considered options while I walked my trap line.

My snares had been set in a rough spiral, beginning only a few yards from the cabin, then extending outward with each circuit. I found nothing in the first two snares, but something had knocked down the third loop. I reset it and kept going.

Even with the numbers of animals available, trapping has an element of luck. You only catch the animal that triggers your snare.

I'd caught nothing until I got to the stream, but there was noise coming from where I'd set the rope snare.

I slipped closer and sure enough, the snare had worked. Not quite what I'd had in mind, though, because the animal wasn't dead. Far from it; the snare had caught it by the left front leg and it was struggling to escape.

It was not a particularly appealing critter. The head was long and ungainly, the lips dripped with slobber, and the legs were long and knobby. It was light brown in color, shaggy over the shoulders and forelegs. The extra hair was a darker brown. It also had a humped appearance.

Some sort of wild camel? Camels of my timeline had one or two pronounced humps. This one was more like the llamas of South America, but larger and with more hump.

I held my spear two-handed as I approached. The camel laid its ears back and bared its teeth, edging away, but it came up against a large bush that held it in place until I got close enough to spear it. The sharp tip punched into the rib cage and the camel tried desperately to escape, but I kept my left hand on the jerking spear and drew my war-club.

It took me two swings to kill it. The first strike stunned the animal and the next one, delivered two-handed after dropping my grip on the spear, crushed the skull. The camel fell down, kicked, leaked urine, and died. The mouth sagged open as it fell, so I gave it another whack for insurance.

The head had been ugly, and I hadn't improved its looks.

I was breathing hard, but I had a large supply of meat and skin if I could get it back to the cabin without a scavenger getting to it first. I could also boil down the hair and hooves to make glue, and the tendons could be used for making bowstrings. I contemplated the many uses for our new-found wealth while field-dressing the animal. I didn't want to waste time, so I sliced open the body and removed the organs, then used a green stick to prop the cavity open.

Leaving the carcass to cool, I headed off to fetch the women.

Chapter 10

We secured the cabin door with the latch-string before leaving. It was made from a heavy downtime cord, wooden handled on the outside end, that went through a hole and connected to a pivoting lever inside. The lever was mounted on the door and would engage one of the wall hooks when it dropped. Pulling on the handle lifted the lever's bar, allowing the door to be pushed open.

I had exchanged the club for my axe, a better tool for butchering. I knew I would have to chop through the breastbone and pelvis before I could open the carcass fully, and a knife is not the best tool for those essential cuts. The knife would have its uses too, because I wanted to keep the skin in one piece and the animal's tendons intact. The sinew fibers within the tendons are very strong, useful for making bowstrings.

When we arrived at the camel's carcass, I left the women to skin it and cut it into portions we could carry.

Millie decided to save the organs too. Camels, being ruminants, have a stomach and a paunch, useful for waterproof bags. The intestines could be used for sausage casings, and the resulting product could be smoked for storage.

The meat would be heavy and awkward to deal with, even after being cut up for transporting. Getting a heavy green hide up the side of the gully was also going to be a chore. We would just have to manage.

I cautioned them to watch out for scavengers—the crossbow was cocked, loaded, and propped against a nearby bush ready for immediate use—and went off to make a travois.

Two saplings, straight, bare of limbs and about ten feet long made the side beams. Two branches, tied across the main poles, finished the frame and kept the ends splayed apart. The long poles supported the weight, the crosspieces added stability as well as a place to tie the load. Because the load was well back, only about eighteen inches from the end, leverage kept most of the weight on the poles. Dragging them over the short grasses kept friction to a minimum.

I needed one more thing to make the travois complete, and I would get that from the camel's skin.

I left the travois propped against a tree near the edge of the gully. This would allow me to take up the load without having to pick it up from the ground. This made it less-likely that I'd reinjure my back.

I removed a few stones from the side of the gully and cut away dirt on the way down. The steps would make climbing up the path easier. The diagonally-sloped path was longer but required less effort, hence less energy expended carrying the load.

The women had the hide off when I got back to the kill site. I washed my axe-head, then quartered the animal. We left the head behind, but kept the neck; there's a lot of meat on an animal's neck.

I chopped off the hooves and put them aside; I already had enough to carry this trip. The heavier loads devolved on me anyway, while the women carried lighter packs of meat and the organs. The rest, including the hooves, would have to wait.

Hooves and hair, boiled down, make hide glue. It has excellent adhesion and is easily reheated, but it's not waterproof. It's also smelly while being prepared, but I could live with that.

Cutting a two-inch strip of thick belly skin from the hide and punching small holes in each end took only a short time. I measured the length I needed, allowing for stretching of the green hide, then laced the strap to my pack. This left me a loop for the top of my head, just behind my forehead. This tump-strap would help by taking some of the weight off my shoulders.

For transporting the skin, we stretched it out square and rolled it up, hair side out, into a long irregular bundle. I secured this by tying the roll at one end and taking half-hitches the rest of the way along. The flexible package went across my shoulders and neck, a heavy, awkward load, but I could carry it. My spear would help me balance as I climbed.

We tied the unrolled skin between the poles and the crosspieces, hair side down. Excess length got folded over the quarters of meat after they were secured in place. The tump-strap would help support the travois later, after I transferred it from my pack. I tied the ends to the two side poles, leaving just enough length to pass across the top of my head. Sandra put the strap into place and I allowed some of the weight to transfer from my arms to the strap.

The women shouldered their packs and Sandra picked up the crossbow. I would need the protection; both hands were occupied in dragging the travois. My spear lay across the poles, but I wouldn't have time to grab it.

Getting everything to the cabin took more than an hour. The women immediately began butchering the meat, putting three large sections of back-strap aside for cooking. Only a few words were necessary. We'd worked silently at the stream, now the habit continued back at the cabin.

It's really strange how that works. Noise brings danger here, and anyway most conversation downtime deals with things that aren't very important.

I broke the silence long enough to mention, "We'll need salt." The women nodded and kept on with their tasks.

I put empty gourds into my backpack, shouldered it, and headed for the salt lick. I left my axe behind for the women's use and took the club in its place. The bar thumped behind me as one of the women secured the door.

I made the two-mile trip to the salt lick without incident. It was hard work and it took time, but I soon had a pack heavy with salt. I got back to the cabin shortly before dark, offloaded the containers, and made a quick trip to collapse my snares. One held a rabbit, so I sighed and took him along after field-dressing the carcass. We didn't need the meat now, but there was no reason to waste it. The rabbit was dead and I could always use the skin. The tump-strap was uncomfortable and a lining of rabbit-fur would improve it.

I followed my trap-line, this time spiraling in from the distant snares toward the ones closer to the cabin.

A boy, a teenager I thought, stepped out a few yards in front of me. He held a bow, arrow nocked to the string but not drawn.

"Matt?"

I overcame my surprise long enough to answer. "I'm Matt. Who are you?"

"I am Lee. I have been waiting for you."

"You have?" Dumb question, and I knew it as soon as I spoke, but his appearance had surprised me.

"My mother and I have come here," he continued. "She is at the dwelling place. We can talk there." His speech sounded stilted, but it was easy to understand.

"All right. Can you walk guard? I'll move faster if I don't have to watch for danger."

"Yes."

Boy, or man, of few words. I led off, he followed a few steps behind.

I had time to form a quick impression as we finished collapsing the snares; leather breechclout, open leather vest, and moccasins or turn-shoes. I couldn't tell. Everything appeared well made. He had deeply tanned skin, not ethnically white but not black either. Something in between, maybe some sort of Mediterranean mix? Black hair hacked off short and no beard, at least not yet.

I couldn't get a good look at the bow, but the arrow had a chipped stone point and flight-control feathers.

He moved easily, quietly, not truly upright but not quite crouched. He'd be hard to surprise, and if danger threatened he could move in any direction. I approved.

His breechclout had a belt and a scabbarded knife that hung over his right hip. The bow was in his left hand, nocked arrow held in his right. A leather arm-guard protected his forearm and a slung quiver held arrows, feathered ends up.

I took off my pack when we got to the cabin, stretched upright to get the kinks out, then tapped on the door.

"Who?" The owls were back, but I avoided laughing.

"Matt and Lee."

I heard the locking-bar scrape, then the door opened. A woman, perhaps a bit older than the rest of us, looked at me.

More than that, she looked me over, head to foot; I wondered if I passed inspection, but I had work to do. I picked up the pack, carried it inside, and propped my spear next to the door. Lee came in, and I heard the bar thump, locking the door behind me.

"You have salt?" the woman said. So much for civilized introductions.

"I'm Matt, and yes, I brought salt. It's in my pack. Who are you?"

"I am Lilia," she said. Her voice had a lilt to it; English, but probably not my kind of English. "We have seen smoke. It has been two days. We crossed a stream and there were two straight tracks in the dirt. We have followed them. We found this dwelling and I have talked to Sandra and Millie."

I glanced at the two women and got nods in return. "Matt, she's been a huge help. Lee worked a lot too. We wouldn't have managed to get nearly this much done without their help."

"Well, you've certainly done a lot more than I expected. So are Lilia and Lee going to be staying with you? With us, I mean?" I felt a bit anxious; perhaps I would suddenly find myself unwanted.

"They'll stay, at least for now. We were talking about that. Her husband was killed over west of here and she's been alone ever since. They had a shelter, but it was burned and they lost everything."

Well, not everything. Lilia had the knife she'd been using to cut meat into thin strips, and Lee had his weapons too.

I was tired and it was nearing dark outside, but I didn't see how four adults and a near-adult were going to fit comfortably in the cabin. So I asked.

"Lilia will stay inside with us, but you and Lee will need to sleep outside tonight. Will you be OK?"

I nodded. I'd slept out for months, and clearly Lee and his mother had been doing so since their home burned.

"I'll need something to eat first, but after that I'll take a torch and we can build a fire near the edge of the woods."

I got my steak, quite tasty and tender, and a piece of bread that tasted better than what Sandra and Millie had been baking. There were also boiled roots and a kind of fruit I wasn't familiar with. Lilia was showing her worth.

Lee got a similar meal and we ate in silence. Conversation could wait; I was simply too tired. I took time to drink water from the gourd, then fastened smaller branches together to make a torch. I lit it and we moved out, bar thunking into place behind us.

So much for my domestic arrangements.

We found a tree at the edge of the forest with branches that could be easily climbed. I tended the torch while Lee brought up dry branches, then we built a small fire near the tree. He added wood while I went off with the torch to gather more.

He wasn't there when I got back, but he soon returned. He'd been cutting material for beds; now he set them up a few feet apart. Our heads would be near the tree, there was a hollow for our hips, and springy branch tips formed the rest of the simple beds. His quiver and bow, still strung, lay near the head of his bed.

I stacked the remaining fuel close to the fire. It would keep us safe, and sleeping on the ground was more comfortable than up in a tree.

Lee sat down and looked out into the darkness, rather than at the fire. "I will watch," he said, so I stretched out on the bed. Careful, and knowledgeable; I would do the same when it was my turn on guard.

Lee woke me shortly after midnight. I had slept long enough. I stoked the fire, put more fuel where I could reach it easily, and sat looking into the darkness as Lee fell asleep behind me.

He woke up at first light. We each took time to find a handy bush, then gathered the bedding and tossed it on the fire. The leftover fuel wood could be retrieved later. We watched while the fire burned down, then scraped up dirt to smother the final embers. When the fire was out, we picked up our gear and headed to the cabin.

I mentioned building a drying-frame for the meat, but Lee quickly dismissed that idea. "My mother knows how. She will do this." Huh. I might not be necessary at all now. Lilia apparently knew more about living on this world than me, her kid Lee had better armament than I did except for my knife and axe, and he would soon be physically mature.

If he wasn't already.

Maybe I had good reason to feel insecure. Sandra and Millie might decide they liked younger men. Lilia might not even like men, although she'd been married or at least had a partner.

Millie and Sandra hadn't picked me for looks or because I was the best man they knew. I was the *only* one, except for two others who'd attempted to rape Sandra. Anyway, they were now dead. Well; matters would play out as they would. Worst case, I had been looking for people when I found the two of them, I had invested only a bit of time, and had at least learned more about how the Futurists thought.

For now, there was nothing to be gained by borrowing trouble. Relationships would adjust, and if it wasn't something to my liking, I could always move on. No question, getting summarily booted out of the cabin last night had left me feeling nervous.

"Lee, after we eat, I plan on raiding a bee tree. We could use the honey."

"You have found a bee tree? Can you do this?"

"I think so. I plan to try, anyway. You can help if you want."

"I will speak to my mother." With that, we arrived at the cabin and knocked on the door.

We had steak and bread again. I looked at the fireplace and there were coals there and liver and heart chunks roasting on the metal rack. I wasn't sure about the heart or liver, but I wasn't a picky eater after months on this survival-of-the-fittest world; I would eat whatever they prepared.

"I'm going to rob that bee tree this morning. I'd like to take Lee with me, if that's all right."

I got three nods in return. Lilia's habit of not talking much reinforced the habit we'd already developed. I realized that even my thinking pattern had changed; it's funny how isolation can do that to you.

●

We left for the bee tree after breakfast. I had my pack with a basket and gourds for holding the honeycomb, and a shallow bowl with live coals inside that I had covered with ashes.

A fire near the tree, with a few green branches added, would generate smoke. Some of the smoldering wood, placed near the tree on the upwind side, would do the trick. I hoped.

My task, which I would carry out alone, was to chop into the tree after the bees stopped flying; Lee would keep lookout and tend the fire. If the swarm attacked me, I would run to the nearby stream and hope I could get underwater. It wasn't a big stream, but maybe it was deep enough.

Detouring past the stream, I got enough mud to wipe a thin layer over my face and arms; cords already secured the openings in my clothing. Would this be enough?

As backup to my fire-making, I had a greenish-colored rock from the stream, found while I was setting out snares. Attempting to crack it using the hammer side of my axe had produced sparks. If necessary, I thought I could make a fire by using sparks from the stone. As it turned out, I didn't need it. But I would keep it; sooner or later, I knew it would come in handy.

Scraping material from inside a piece of dry bark, I levered out the coals from the shallow bowl. I soon had a wisp of smoke and I blew gently to encourage it. I got more smoke, then small flames.

We built the fire up carefully before feeding the green wood in. Smoke drifted around the tree, and soon the bees stopped flying. They were still there, crawling slowly around their knothole, but hopefully they would ignore me.

I knelt down and peered up the crack at the bottom of the tree, but there was nothing to see. The cavity was dark. There was nothing for it but to remove one of the thin walls to expose the honeycomb.

Tapping gently on the tree above the crack resulted in a dull thump. I decided this was caused by the honeycomb; there was a lot of honey in that tree! So I took a full swing, pulled back my axe, and waited to see what the bees would do.

They crawled faster, but were still not flying. Safe enough, then, so long as I didn't dawdle. Eyes smarting from the smoke, I marked out a hand-wide rectangle beside the knothole and chopped it free. When it cracked, I carefully pried out the wood to reveal the honeycomb inside.

The axe went on my belt, the pack went in front of the opening; I cut out large sections of honeycomb with my knife and scraped them into the basket. It wasn't quite full, so I collected smaller pieces and stuffed those in the empty spaces. I also stowed some of the smaller pieces in the gourds.

As soon as I had all I could carry, I stuck the wooden rectangle back on the tree, using honey as glue. A few stunned bees had come out with the comb, so I carefully scraped them off. Finished, I shouldered my pack as Lee smothered the remnants of the fire. The bee colony should survive; I hadn't taken all the honey, and I hadn't seen the queen. Hopefully she was still alive. If so, I might come back, take out my glued-in plug, and harvest more honeycomb.

Lee led the way back to the cabin. I licked my fingers clean as I went. *He* would just have to wait until we got home, but the honey tasted wonderful.

The women had been busy while we were gone. The scraped camel skin was now stretched across a frame outside the cabin. Two slender trees formed the main supports. The trees had been bent toward each other, then tied so that the upper crossbar held them in position. The crossbar served another function; the skin had been tied to it, then allowed to hang down. Cord loops attached the edges to the trees on each side. The skin would shrink as it dried, but the loops were loose enough that it shouldn't tear. A piece of heavier wood hung from the bottom of the skin, keeping tension on the skin while it dried. Elegant and simple; I knew it had to be more of Lilia's work.

I could smell fresh bread baking and the thought of bread and honey had me salivating. I took my pack inside, removed the basket and pots, and soon we were all eating honey with our still-warm bread.

The squeezed-out honeycomb would be melted to purify it. I wanted the wax for my longbow and spear-shaft, but there might even be enough for candles. It could also be used to waterproof baskets for storage.

※

Arrangements changed again that night. We finished off our meal with cooked rabbit and roasted tubers, then Lee and Lilia got up and left. The arrangement had been decided before we returned.

Sandra barred the door and I washed my sticky fingers. Maybe the women wanted to reassure me, maybe they wanted to reassure each other that I would stick around. At any rate, I didn't get to sleep immediately. The two were quite active, taking turns according to some schedule that only they understood.

Sex is a drive, like hunger or thirst, but in the end, survival is paramount; between bouts, I concluded that sex is part of the urge to survive.

I also came to a decision during the night; we would need to abandon the cabin. It was barely suitable for three, let alone five. No way could we store enough food or supplies inside for that many people.

Another consideration: remaining here without information was to wait for the axe to fall. Predators, some of them human, knew where we were. They could attack whenever they decided, giving them the element of surprise. It was a tactical advantage I didn't want to concede.

※

Over breakfast I told the others of my decision.

"I'm going to take a couple of days to work on a new spear-shaft. One of the shafts I've been drying will do for the spear, the others will be made into longbows. I'll try chipping my stone cores to make a spearpoint and arrowheads. We've got meat for now and I can show Lee how to run my trap-lines while I'm working on improving my weapons.

"In a week or so, as soon as I'm ready, I'm going on a scout. I'm not sure how long it will take, but I've got to know what's out there.

"Two raiders showed up here with weapons that I doubt they made themselves. Lilia's husband is dead, killed during a raid. There's also an abandoned house about half a day's travel from here and no indication what happened to the people.

"We don't know where the raiders came from or who made those short swords. I'm wondering now if the Futurist told me the truth. That hut had been there a very long time, people had lived there for years, then they disappeared. And Lilia and her husband had lived where *they* were for a long time too. Conclusion, we can't be safe as long as we stay here. I don't see that we have a choice; if we intend to survive, we have to look for a better location, one that will be easy to defend."

Lilia, still not wasting of words, spoke. "Lee was born on this world. It was fifteen years now. My man, husband, was here when I came and he had been here two years by that time. He helped me when I came. We lived for long time before raiders killed him."

"That settles it, then. I have to go; other raiders will probably find us and we can't defend the cabin."

"Lee will go with you. He can help."

Surprise! I hadn't thought of that. I suppose I still had the loner mindset I'd developed before finding Millie and Sandra.

"What about the three of you?"

Lilia shook her head. "I have bow and arrows, I can make more. Sandra and Millie have crossbow and swords. We will be safe."

I still wondered, but if Lee was fifteen he was a little older than I'd thought, adult enough to take the trip I had in mind. He also wasn't inexperienced, because he'd been living in the wild with his mother. I'd seen for myself how confident he was, how easily and silently he moved.

"We'll get everything together," I agreed, "and as soon as that's done, we'll go. We will be back when we know what's out there. But we'll need to move in a hurry, so I'll be looking for a route while I'm scouting.

"I'm thinking that if I can find a cliff, something like what the Anasazi used, we can build a place we can defend. They built cliff dwellings, lived in them for centuries, and we can too. We could take up farming below the cliff and do some hunting, trapping, and fishing to supplement what we raise, just as they did.

"But we don't advertise for more people. If you think we need more, we should find them before they find us. We decide we want them to join us, then we can make them an offer.

"Something else; if the Futurist lied to me, maybe to all of us, then I think we need to go somewhere they don't know about. They may be able to follow, but maybe not. I just don't trust them; they have their aims and we have ours, and since they aren't helping us, we don't need to stay here where they put us." We left it at that. Lee and I had work to do, and so did the three women.

Lee was fifteen, man grown. I decided I liked the idea of taking him with me. I wasn't certain of what the women might think of him, but I didn't want to leave a young rooster in the hen-house. I intended to work on developing a permanent relationship with Sandra and Millie later. There was safety in numbers too, and with two of us to forage for food we could travel longer before making camp. Yes indeed, it would be best if he went with me.

Chapter 11

We breakfasted on fresh camel meat the next morning.

After eating, I went back to the kill site and recovered the hooves. Hair, scraps of rawhide, and chopped-up bits of hoof, boiled down, would make the glue.

Lilia had collected camel hair for my experiment; it was useless for any anything other than making rope, and there wasn't enough for that. We had plenty of rabbit fur, but it was better saved for padding and making into felt boots for winter.

A clay pot, crafted specifically for the purpose, held the ingredients. Thinner than other pieces and with a separate lid, it had been slow-fired in the oven to convert the earthenware into true pottery. The lid would help keep the mess hot while it cooked down to glue.

I heated water in the pot, added the hoof bits, hair, and rawhide, then let them boil. I stirred the mess from time to time, trying not to breathe in the smell. Water and more scraps went in as the mix boiled down to a brown, semi-liquid mass.

Coals covered the pot sides and kept the mix hot. I added more water and raked in fresh coals when needed, remaining upwind as I did so. Even so, it was an unpleasant job.

Between tending the cooking glue, I shaped blanks for a spear and three bows. The staves came from a hickory tree, selected for its desirable size and knot-free trunk. I carefully split the tree into halves, then split the halves into quarters. I dried the quarters near the fire, being careful to keep the wood from drying too rapidly; warping or cracks would ruin my work.

One of the captured swords worked well as a makeshift froe. I laid the edge on top of the trunk and tapped the exposed end with a billet of firewood, forcing the blade lengthwise down the bole's center.

The blades would need sharpening periodically; river stones would do the trick if carefully selected. Coarse stones work fast, fine-grained stones are slow but better for smoothing cutting edges.

The swords had been intended as stabbing weapons, but that wasn't the best use I could make of them. One would make a froe for splitting wood, or, after sharpening and reshaping, a drawknife. The other would make an excellent spear blade. The metal was superior to anything I could craft from stone.

Each hickory quarter formed a right angle with the sides joined by an arc where the bark had been. The semicircle would be the bow's back, shaving down the sharp angle formed the belly. The three best staves would be bows, the fourth would be my new metal-bladed spear. Shaving the quarter round to make the shaft wouldn't be difficult and the tree I'd chosen left me plenty of wood to work with.

Chipping and slicing with my axe, I rough-shaped the staves. People had used axes for a long time to make boards before saws became commonplace; I could do the same. Drawknives are precise, but the added precision brings loss of speed. That's what I did, chip gently with the axe, then shave the blank smooth with the knife.

Smoothing the spear-shaft allowed me to practice draw-cutting before I worked on the more-demanding task of shaping bow staves.

I used a thick fold of rabbit skin to cover the pointed end of the sword's blade, providing a safe place to grip. One hand on the knife's hilt, one on the rabbit skin, I shaved off thin slices of wood by drawing the blade toward me. I worked from the center toward the ends. Any exposed fiber ends would be in compression, not tension, which might cause them to splinter.

Tend the fire, add water to the disgusting glue mix, shave the spear-staff to shape. I rotated the blank periodically and continued. My imitation drawknife was crude, but it worked well and was easy to control.

Axe and drawknife, chip, chip, slice, tend the fire. The work went slowly, but I had time. By the end of the day I had three bow staves roughed in, ready for tillering and sanding. I also had a spear-shaft that only needed a socket or steel blade to be better than the one I'd found.

A stick with a chip of flint glued to the end would do for drilling the socket hole. It would be slow work, but when finished, I would have a weapon I could throw as well as a spear for thrusting. It had the advantage of reusability, but once I had a working bow and arrows, I wouldn't need that. For now, it was the best option I had; there would be things to learn while making the bows and I needed a weapon *now*.

My hide glue had boiled into an evil-smelling brown mass that wasn't quite solid. It would require reheating before every use, and the surfaces I used it on had to be clean and dry, but in many ways hide glue was superior to more-modern adhesives. I stirred the hot mess to make sure it was thoroughly mixed.

It was not the same formula as the hide glue used downtime, but it would work far better than the milky sap I'd used. Even if it wasn't as strong as I hoped, it might kill an animal by smell alone! Best of all, I could make more by using animal scraps that otherwise would be thrown away.

The camel's tendons, after separation, yielded sinews. Lilia twisted them into long, thin cords that I could make into a bowstring by twisting two or three of the cords in a direction opposite to the one Lilia had used. The counter-twisting would prevent the bowstring from unwinding.

The final string was long, but could be shortened by more twisting. In this way I could adjust the string's length if it stretched during use. The finished string would have a spliced loop at each end and a coating of beeswax.

Arrow shafts came from small sapling trees. As the shafts dried, they tended to warp, so I steamed and straightened them. Lee and Lilia helped. Her husband had made their bows and arrows, but both knew the basic techniques.

I had a bow and a dozen shafts by the third day. Not yet arrows, they had no flight feathers or points and only notches for nocks; even so, I could kill a bird or rabbit with one. For that matter, *any* small game could be killed if I could hit it.

Stringing the bow, I adjusted the limbs to curve equally by careful scraping and smoothing with stones, a process called tillering. This was likely a memory implanted by the Futurist. The only part of bow-making I didn't 'remember' was how to make the string, and fortunately Lilia knew how that was done.

I wrapped the middle of the stave with a long strip of wetted rawhide, double-wrapping one end for an arrow rest. This was the grip. The rawhide shrank as it dried, and as a final step, I rubbed beeswax over everything.

The bow wasn't as powerful as I'd hoped, but it would do. Lee advised me to begin with a lighter bow; it would be easier to use while learning and if I liked the feel of this particular bow, I could always add draw weight by gluing sinew to the back.

While I'd been working on weapons, Lilia had shown the others how to stitch smoked and greased skin into a quiver. It had a strap for my shoulder and a loop to hold it to my belt.

The quiver had a sewn-in divider so that I could carry different types of arrows. Arrows for large game aren't suitable for small animals or birds, so having different types made sense. A brace of turkeys, a few ducks or geese…I could almost taste one!

Along with the quiver, the women had made a forearm guard for my arm. Bowstrings, especially when used by novices, leave bruises from the elbow to the wrist. I would appreciate the forearm guard when I began practicing.

And practice I did. I strung the bow, working to gain speed without losing precision. String in the right hand, held just below the loop, lower arm of the bow braced on the instep of my right foot; put my left leg between the bow and the string. Then bend the bow, using the muscles of my trunk. Stringing the bow using arm muscle alone wasn't possible.

After stringing the bow, I practiced pulling the string to full draw. Draw, anchor the hand along my jaw, slowly let off on the string. Draw, imagine aiming, let off, relax. Releasing the string would only be done when I had a shaft in place.

Unfamiliar muscle use left my back and arms sore for the first few days. Fortunately, this time there was none of the cramping I'd experienced before.

During pauses, I made more arrow blanks. The task was now routine; straighten the shaft, carefully notch the end, adjust the notch's fit on the string.

I reinforced each shaft by wrapping thin string from the bottom of the notch down the shaft, extending the wrapping for an inch. More wrapping would be used later to support the flight feathers as soon as I had them. Once the feathers were glued in place and wrapped, the missiles would need only points to be complete.

Finally, I had twenty shafts that I considered acceptable and a dozen I'd rejected. The rejects could still be used; they wouldn't be as accurate, but I could draw, aim, and release the string to propel them until they broke. Present the bow, remove an arrow and lay it above the rawhide 'grip', nock it on the string, draw, aim and release. Then do it again. And again.

I taught myself flint knapping in the afternoons.

Percussion...striking with a hammerstone...was how I split blanks away from the stone core. Pressure-flaking the blanks followed, no easy task; it was accomplished by pressing a tool against the blank, *hard*, until a chip popped free. Final flaking of tiny chips from the edge took less force.

Estimating the 'grain' of the blank, learning to vary the pressure to make the flakes larger or smaller, took longer. My points got better. By the end of the week I was flaking points and short knife blades that were functional, if not aesthetic. Knapping was a craft I could improve over the course of a lifetime.

I picked up techniques from Lee, who had learned them from his father. Perhaps his father had arrived with the knowledge implanted. I had only a vague idea that one should begin with a larger stone and crack off medium-sized chunks which could be slowly worked down to shape. Longer pieces could be knives or spear-points, shorter ones arrowheads or scrapers.

My metal knife wouldn't last forever, and the ability to smelt iron would be necessary before making steel. It wouldn't happen anytime soon. In the meantime, the ability to knap a flint knife would be very useful.

Small flakes could also be used. A single large stone might yield several large blanks for blades plus smaller pieces for arrowheads, dart points, awls, or drill tips.

The chips were sharp! Where two flaked surfaces met, a razor-like cutting edge resulted.

My routine was simple; leave the chips where they fell, continue flaking the blank, then salvage what was usable the next time I paused to rest. Mistakes I fixed by making an intended knife into a spear-point. The final core, too small to flake smaller, would become a scraper. I picked up the remaining pieces, selected the ones that could be used, while the rest went into a small leather bag Lilia made. Very little waste remained after I finished.

My darts were thicker and longer than those I'd salvaged from the hut, so I used larger points. This wasn't a redesign so much as it was the result of my limited technique. I couldn't drill a small enough hole in the end of the spear, nor could I yet produce finely-flaked points such as the ones I'd found. As a result, my spear, while it outwardly resembled that earlier one, was crude and heavy by contrast. On the plus side, it was a lot stronger than the original.

The new spear was more usable for thrusting than casting with the atlatl, but I intended to use the bow for longer-range killing anyway. The socket would accept the salvaged darts, although they were a loose fit; I wrapped a layer of string around the end of each and glued it into place. The salvaged darts were my reserve; I would use my own darts as long as they lasted.

A flint-tipped stick was my bit, a bow-drill spun it in the hole, and I used a dart as the template, enlarging and deepening the socket until half the dart was inserted. It had to bottom-out in the hole or it would split the shaft during use. For insurance, I reinforced the outside of the socket end. The wrapping material this time was rawhide, soaked, stretched, and wrapped so that the loose ends could be pulled underneath. I trimmed what remained and let the rawhide dry and shrink. A final thin coat of hide glue finished the job and I sealed it with beeswax to make it water-resistant.

I added a sling, but the spear was not a serious burden. But it retained enough heft to be lethal.

I found it best to work on a project, then lay it aside while I worked on something else. This allowed the wood to dry; if it was going to curve while shrinking, I wanted it to happen before I put too much work in.

My flaked points were soon fitted to spear-darts and the twenty arrow shafts I'd made. Notch the ends, insert an arrowhead coated with glue where it joined the shaft, then wrap the joint with string. Coat the assembly with more glue, then put it aside to dry. This took only minutes, but I allowed a half hour just to be sure.

I had no feathers yet, but there were turkeys and there might be other large birds too; I'd heard them, but hadn't yet seen any. Still, the noise and the tracks we'd seen were promising.

Lee hunted and ran our trap-line while I worked. He usually brought back something small, but near the end of the week he killed a deer.

I envied him the opportunity to hunt, but I couldn't spare the time. I had to have weapons; two men on a scout worked better, but only if both contributed equally.

Lilia had organized Sandra and Millie so that the three now functioned as a team. They foraged, ground the seeds and nuts into coarse flour, baked bread and cooked. When not otherwise occupied, they made earthenware containers, tanned hides, and stitched leather. A flaked stone awl simplified their leatherworking.

My weapons were good enough; refinements would continue and there would be improvements to make the spear and bow function better. It had all taken time, but now that the biggest tasks were finished I could fit lesser ones in as time permitted.

I used the atlatl when I practiced with the spear. My first throws were under-thrown; I hadn't realized how much force would be needed to cast the spear effectively. After adjusting, I found I was throwing too high, but if an animal was reasonably close, I could put killing force into the cast.

By the end of the week I was hunting small game with the bow. I still depended on traps and snares, but in time I'd get better at the quick snap-shots that hunting requires. I understood the principles of archery and tried to keep all factors nearly the same from one shot to the next. Time and practice would refine my skills, but my motions were already smooth and fast.

Best of all, what I had made I could repair or replace.

Lee and I both had leather backpacks now; Lilia was a marvel.

We talked in the evenings about her history. They had lived in a hut her husband built, several days travel to the west. The raiders killed her husband in the first few moments, but she had hidden Lee and herself. The raiders ransacked the hut, then set fire to it before leaving. After they'd gone, the two had left their hiding place and fled east. Some details of the things she'd seen before finding us were sketchy, but she remembered crossing a shallow river.

The attack on their home had taken place to our west; the two men who had attacked Sandra might have come from the same bunch, but equally there might be other groups of raiders.

We finished packing by filling our packs with jerky.

I had a gourd for water, Lee had a skin bag made from the stomach of the deer he'd killed. Water sources might be widely separated, so it was best to be prepared.

Finally, I decided that we were ready.

Next morning, we said our farewells and headed southwest.

Chapter 12

I intended to travel southwest for several days, then turn right and head northwest. We used the sun as a guide, so our route remained generally straight except for the occasional forced detour around an obstacle.

We entered unfamiliar territory on the second day. I hadn't expected problems before that point, because I'd explored the area while hunting, but tomorrow would be different. We might find almost anything ahead of us short of mountains.

I expected to find large animals where we were going. Some of them we might hunt, but not if there were too many predators.

The trip should take about a month to complete. Go southwest for a week, turn northwest, then northeast a week later. A final east-southeast leg would take us slightly north of the cabin, offsetting to allow for errors. I hoped to find the stream that was near the cabin and follow it until we recognized a familiar landmark; if everything worked as planned, we'd be home in a month. By then, we'd have a general idea of the terrain west of the cabin.

I already knew what lay to the southeast; I had come through there after being transplanted. There might still be things of interest north or east of the cabin, but that would require another trip and I saw no need; I wanted to keep going west or southwest. This trip would tell me which route was safer.

●

We soon worked out a routine. Scout for six or seven hours each day, depending on terrain, then camp. Streams and hills slowed us and we detoured around tall-grass plains. In mid-afternoon we'd begin looking for a campsite.

We'd look for animal paths, set out snares, and wait. We were usually successful; the animals weren't particularly wary. I concluded there were probably no people nearby.

On the fifth day we came to a river, wide, shallow and muddy. There was little current, so I didn't anticipate a problem.

The new layer of soft mud on the bottom of that river saved our lives.

We had gone onto the riverbank to look for a good crossing. Even shallow rivers are dangerous; there might be quicksand or heavy currents, and while you're crossing, you're in the open. You're exposed to predators and if there are any, the water slows your movements. Even when you reach the bank, there's no way of telling what might be waiting. You can't retreat, you can only go forward or to the side, so options are limited.

Lee was making his own estimate of hazards we might discover during the crossing. I don't know which of us spotted the animal first, but it had already seen us.

The cat crouched in thin brush across the river, some five yards back from the water. Yellow eyes watched intently. The cat was motionless except for a nervous twitch of the short tail.

It was considerably larger than a bobcat, built along the same chunky body plan, but smaller than a lion. Not a cougar, the short tail ruled that out, plus the color was wrong. This animal had faint dapples of dark brown among the tan shades of the fur.

The stream was twenty yards wide, maybe more. The cat couldn't cross the river in a single jump. We might have time to get back into the treeline. I glanced at Lee, and without speaking we began backing away, slowly.

The cat saw us as prey, and we weren't cooperating. As soon as we started to back toward the forest it slunk forward, toward the river. We continued backing toward the trees, arrows nocked, bowstrings almost fully drawn. Perhaps the cat's approach was a bluff, but whatever its intention, we had to be prepared.

It was well that we were. The cat sprang into the river, landing almost halfway across. Our arrows struck it before it could recover and leap again, Lee's striking behind the foreleg, mine punching into its throat where it meets the chest.

The cat tensed for another spring; in the brief pause before it gained traction, we had drawn replacement arrows, nocked them, and were drawing back for follow-up shots. The cat hesitated slightly, trying to find firm footing, and two more arrows thumped in.

My arrow was slightly off this time, but still struck the front of the cat's chest, low and inside the shoulder. Lee had centered his second arrow between the front legs. Blood stained the dappled fur.

I registered long canine teeth—saber-tooth!-- as I grabbed my spear. The heavy dart was one I'd made. Was the weapon lethal enough? I was about to find out.

I was closest, so the cat came for me. Lee, standing slightly to my rear, sank his third arrow to the fletching behind the animal's shoulder.

I took a half-step forward and surprised the cat. Prey was supposed to run, not counterattack! He, for it was a male, hesitated briefly. I lunged with the spear and stuck the dart in the center front of the chest, the end of the spear-shaft thumping hard against the animal. The dart was fully planted, the point eight inches into the organs and cutting lung and heart tissue. I pulled another dart from my quiver's second pouch and slid it into the socket.

Breath rasped, bloody slobber dripped from the open jaws as I thrust with the spear. The animal yowled. I took a half-step back and yanked my axe from the belt sheath. Dropping the empty spear shaft, leaving the second dart lodged in the animal's breast, I swung the axe two-handed. The blade sank into the crouching cat's muzzle, just below the eyes.

And stuck.

The animal pawed at the axe handle and yowled again, but the sound was more wheeze than battle cry.

I fumbled out another dart with shaking fingers, picked up the spear, and loaded the dart. My thrust went into the throat, near where my first arrow had struck.

The thing was close! I smelled it, felt the hot spatter of drool and blood, looked into the eyes—and realized there would be no more time to reload the spear.

But the animal remained crouched, rasping breaths sawing in and out. I waited for it to bound forward and rip out my throat, but it didn't happen.

Slicing arrowheads and dart points had left the lungs full of blood, the heart no longer able to beat. I hadn't noticed, but Lee's quiver was half empty and the missing arrows were somewhere in the critter's body. He was standing half-turned away from the cat, knife in his left hand pointing toward the cat, club cocked over his right shoulder. But the weapons wouldn't be needed.

We waited, he with knife and club, me with my empty-socket spear. The cat's eyes never blinked as it died, not that I was prepared to accept that without proof! Finally, I pulled the last dart from my quiver. I still had arrows, but I would have to drop the spear to use them, not something I wanted to do. My dart went into the spear's socket, but the cat didn't blink. The head sank a few inches lower when the animal died, still in its crouch.

The cat had possessed amazing vitality. Had its approach not been slowed by the river, we'd never have killed it before it got one or both of us. Despite the arrows and darts that surely would have killed it eventually, it had been full of fight until the end. It had been a very near thing.

Spears with fixed points, as long and heavy as we could wield, were necessary for close-in work. Bows were useful, but they couldn't hold off an enraged animal the way a heavy spear could. I filed the information away for later.

We salvaged the arrows and darts; where the shafts had broken, we cut out the points. One of Lee's had chipped against a rib, but the others could be reused. Lee cut steaks from the hindquarters and we roasted them. The skin was ruined, but we chopped the long teeth from the skull and removed the claws. There was thick mud between the toes of the front paws. What if there had been a sandy bottom, a better purchase for the animal's claws? I preferred not to think about that.

Lee took half the trophies, I got the other half. Wariness, skill, determination, and teamwork had saved us. There had also been luck involved, luck in seeing the animal and where it landed after that first spring. Neither of us had hesitated; we now possessed something we hadn't had before, confidence in the skill and courage of the other. We had faced death without flinching and come away alive. There had been no need to talk, no giving of orders, no calls for help. We had reacted quickly and correctly; as a result, we survived.

Lee was unscathed, except for a few blood spots from the animal's nostrils. I had a long scratch from something, not from the cat because he'd been almost three feet away when he died, but something. I never felt the scratch when it happened; probably I had mishandled an arrow in the confusion.

Lee and I were closer now, in the way that brothers sometimes are and combat veterans often are. Neither of us mentioned it.

Bloody arrows went back into our quivers, broken material and trophies went into the packs.

Saber-tooth? The canine teeth, while large, weren't as long as I expected. But there might be others, so we decided not to cross the stream until morning. We spent that night in a tree, downstream from where we'd killed the cat. Lee might have slept, but I drowsed most of the night. Adrenaline kept me half-awake. I finally dropped off just before dawn. Birdcalls woke me as the sky turned light.

We would watch that far bank for a while before crossing, to make sure another cat wasn't waiting. Next time, we might not be so lucky.

Chapter 13

Lee watched from the bank, arrow nocked and ready, while I crossed the stream the next morning. The cat had shown that they take a lot of killing. Lee was fast, accurate, and dependable, but I wouldn't be able to contribute much while I was in the water. The stream's bottom was muddy, too slippery for me to use my bow effectively. I slung it and carried the spear, hoping I wouldn't need it; you also need good footing to use a spear.

After crossing I took over guard duty, spear now slung and bow ready, arrow on the string. Lee also crossed without incident.

Still dripping, we left the river behind us, happy to see the last of that place. We had left tracks but it couldn't be helped. Human enemies might see the tracks, so we would have to remain alert. Nothing new in that; survive or perish was the rule, and vigilance the difference between them.

We traveled without incident during the following two days. All was routine; camp in mid to late afternoon, set traps to supplement our jerky, munch on berries and fruit we encountered along the way.

We detoured around the grasslands, remaining far enough back in the shadows cast by the trees to avoid brush. This grew thick along the treeline and wherever sunlight penetrated the upper canopy.

We'd been watchful for cats, but what we spotted was at least as dangerous. I slowly crouched, holding out my hand to signal Lee; he followed my lead.

We were on the southeast side of a small clearing, forty yards across at most. Much of it was grassy, although there were scattered, brushy plants. This type of grass was short, and the open vista allowed me to see two men approaching. I estimated the distance at a hundred yards, and it was shrinking rapidly.

I held up two fingers and glanced at Lee. He nodded understanding. I waved him forward, a slight movement of my hand, and he eased up until we were crouched side-by-side. I pointed to the men, then glanced at Lee to be sure he'd seen them. He had. His eyes were slitted, jaw muscles clenched in anger.

There was slight risk of being heard, so I murmured as quietly as possible, trying to avoid the sibilance that whispering makes. "You've seen someone like that before?"

"I have seen others. They have no bows, but they have the long knives."

Lee had sharp eyes. I looked again at the two men. They had paused to look around before entering the clearing, and I saw the hilts at each man's hip. They had small buckler-like shields strapped to their arms, and each wore a breechclout and leather vest; their shoes were likely similar to what the cabin raiders had worn. Maybe they got their clothing from the same tailor.

The man in front had a decorated headband for his hair; maybe he was the leader.

I nodded "Likely from the same bunch as those we killed at the cabin. They'll cross our tracks if they keep coming. They'll know we're here, they might backtrack us and find the cabin. We can't allow that." Lee nodded and held his bow a little tighter.

We needed to kill them fast; if one got away, he would bring others. They would then backtrack us and eventually find the cabin, if indeed they didn't already know where it was.

The two men walked into the clearing and kept coming, wary at being in the open; their heads turned frequently, eyes looking around for threats. They were thirty yards away now, well within bowshot. I made a slow pointing gesture to Lee and he understood; he was to take the man on the right.

Mine, the one on the left, was slightly in the lead. I intended to trigger the ambush by standing. I would get into firing position, shoot, then charge the leader if my arrow didn't kill him outright. Lee would be ready to shoot as soon as I did.

It was a simple plan, but it began to go wrong almost immediately.

The man spotted me while I was still coming to my feet. The small shield slipped down his forearm into his left hand even as he drew his short sword. Both movements were smooth, practiced. He took up a ready stance, knees flexed, shield toward me. In so doing he turned slightly; this threw my aim off.

Instead of punching into his chest, my arrow passed through his side. I had probably not hit the gut, perhaps causing no more than a flesh wound. He might eventually die of blood loss, but that wouldn't help if he killed me first!

The injury didn't slow him much, nor did it temper his aggressiveness. He bounded across the clearing, shield up, sword ready; I wouldn't get a second shot. He stopped as I reacted, resuming the ready stance he'd showed when he first saw me.

There was no time to unsling my spear. Discarding the bow, I drew my knife right-handed and yanked the axe with my left. The axe would have to be my guard, the knife held back as primary offensive threat. I took up a ready stance of my own, left foot leading, axe slightly forward and held upright.

A short sword and buckler is a good individual-combat system for a man who knows how to use it.

This one did.

He held the sword ready, hilt back and point up to stab for my gut as soon as I left an opening. He was balanced, left foot forward, the shield at arm's length to keep me from closing. He took a half-step toward me, left foot still leading, right coming up to regain his original stance and balance.

Maybe the small bucklers weren't as useless as I'd thought!

I avoided focusing on the sharp point of that sword. It wasn't easy, but you *must* watch the enemy's body and footwork. Blades move around, even his eyes can cause you to misjudge your opponent's thinking, but foot placement and body position tell you what's *possible* for him to do. And Lee couldn't help, not yet.

I hesitated, but *he* couldn't afford to wait; if Lee had killed his partner, then he'd be free to circle the two of us and watch for an opening. My enemy's only choice against men armed with bows was to get in close, attack immediately, and put us down. I was his immediate target, Lee second.

Had Lee killed his man?

I did the only thing I could, step to my right, right foot ahead, but weapons still pointing toward him. By circling, I forced him to change his stance. The move also changed *my* stance from right-handed to left-handed, axe back slightly, knife extended.

The man took another half-step, buckler still held forward but shifted slightly in an effort to cover his torso from my knife, which was now closer to his body as our stances changed. This left an opening; to see was to act.

I hooked the buckler with my axe, pulling it toward me, using his change in balance against him. He stumbled slightly, unable to resist the axe's pull, and I switched my stance again, still tugging on his shield. This move forced his guard to open wider.

I stuck my knife in his gut, wrenching up as hard as I could to withdraw the blade, but it stuck. I also tried to free my axe from his shield—pulling it toward me had done what I intended, pulling him off-balance—but he'd managed to regain his balance. He pushed forward with the buckler and thrust at me with his sword. He'd dropped the point when I stepped forward so the sword went into my thigh instead of my gut. I felt a push, but no pain; that would come later, if I survived.

I let go of the knife and used both hands to yank desperately at my axe. If I lost the axe too...

I pulled as hard as I could and hopped back, briefly dragging him with me. He stumbled again, but this time he dropped the sword and used his free hand to clutch at my knife hilt where it stuck out from his body. I freed my axe and skipped backward again, ready. But the knife had done its work; the man was dying.

I held the axe ready but it wasn't needed. He was holding his hand over his gut, tugging at the knife, but his fingers slipped off the blood-slick hilt. He stopped moving and I was finally able to step back and look around.

Lee had another arrow on his bowstring and was watching wide-eyed. He looked at my leg and I glanced down. Blood slicked the front of my trousers and it had run down into my boot.

My knife was still in the man's gut, so I worked it back and forth to loosen it. It required much effort, but finally it came free. I wiped the knife on his vest and sheathed it, then loosened the belt that held up his breechclout.

I needed the belt and breechclout. The belt I wrapped tightly around my injured thigh, just above the wound. The blood flow slowed, so I wrapped the deerskin clout around the wound, a temporary bandage.

Two more of the enemy warriors stopped at the edge of the clearing, looking wide eyed at us. Even as I watched, I saw one turn and begin running back the way they'd come.

"Lee! Can you catch him?"

Lee nodded and took off, avoiding the other who still stood, frozen by shock, trying to decide whether to attack or run away. He saw Lee sprint past and that decided him; I was the only enemy left to his front, and I was clearly wounded.

He was armed in the same way as the man I'd killed, but not so skilled judging by his movements. He rushed toward me.

I still had my axe. My spear had fallen at some point during the fight—I didn't remember it happening, but the spear lay on the ground, dart missing—but another dart was in my quiver. If I could insert it in the spear socket, I would have a longer reach. I wasn't very mobile, the hole in my leg was throbbing, but the spear would give me an advantage in reach and that might be enough. It would have to be.

I hopped forward, switched the axe to my right hand, and picked up the spear. Holding the shaft under my right arm, I fumbled a dart out and managed to get it into the socket, but the man was almost on me by the time I finished. But finish I did, and he hesitated when he saw the spear in my left hand.

The axe was a threat, but first he had to try to keep the buckler between us to deflect the spear. It gave me more reach than the short sword gave him.

I waited. Lee was somewhere behind him, chasing his partner, but he would come back. This swordsman also couldn't afford to wait.

He attacked. Perhaps he'd only hesitated to see if I was bleeding out or had weakened, but he ran out of patience and then he ran out of luck.

My left hand was weaving the spear around, holding his attention. A small feint forward using my uninjured leg and he reacted. The buckler brushed at my spear, deflecting it downward to protect his chest and gut, but his thigh was open. I lanced forward, a relatively light thrust, but the dart went into his thigh near the femoral artery. I pulled back and blood jetted; the dart remained in the wound.

Holding the shaft, empty end toward him, I backed away. The spear-shaft was the equivalent of a peasant's quarterstaff, usable if needed. I limped forward and circled to his right, the side his sword was on. By circling I forced him to keep facing me, and while he was doing that the buckler was trapped on the disengaged side of his body. Meantime, he was bleeding badly and the dart moved as his muscles flexed, doing more damage.

While he worked out his tactical problem, I poked the end of the spear sharply toward his face. I thrust twice rapidly; there was only a little force behind the thrusts but they made him protect his face, and when he did I chopped at his sword arm. The axe chunked in just below the elbow, coming free when I pulled at the handle. He dropped the sword, unable to hold his grip, and I stepped forward and rammed the spear end into his face. I drew it back and thrust again, much harder. Dead or unconscious, he dropped. I stepped in, reversed the axe and crushed his skull with the hammer face.

Lee had not returned.

I was concerned, but there was nothing I could do; I couldn't run on my wounded leg. I busied myself by collecting the dropped spear darts and the short swords.

I drank from my water gourd, emptying it, and tried not to pass out. I ended up sitting against a tree at the edge of the clearing.

It took more than half an hour before Lee returned. He was panting from his long run.

"That one was fast! Fortunately, he did not have endurance, so I caught him when he slowed and arrowed him through the back of the skull. I cut my arrow free and came as soon as I could, but I saw something where I killed that man and I think you should see it too."

I looked at him questioningly. "What did you see?"

"There is a thing, a building. It is very tall. I do not know what it is, but there are more enemies there. I saw others, too, not armed with weapons. Perhaps some are women. It is possible, but I could not go closer until I returned to see if you lived."

I sighed. I would have to accompany him. It would not be fun, not on my bad leg. Well, I could fashion a crutch later from a forked branch.

We dragged the bodies away from the clearing. With luck, scavengers would take care of them. We cut branches and smoothed the disturbed earth as best we could, though a skilled tracker would know there'd been a fight. There was little we could do about the blood. It had soaked into the ground.

Lee led, I followed. We were vigilant, despite the noise I made limping along. Finally, we came out on a small rise and I saw the body of the fleeing man Lee had killed. A few yards farther ahead the trees opened out, and I saw the building Lee had found.

I studied it for a moment.

"Lee, I think that's the head of a mine shaft. If I'm right, there's a wheel and rope or chain lift in that building. The mechanism operates an elevator when it's time to bring up ore. See that loose material over to the side? That's waste from the mine, a tailings dump."

"Matt, what is an elevator?" I had forgotten that Lee was born on this world.

"It's a device that can be lowered with ropes. There's a shaft that goes down into the earth. The elevator is like a small room with a rope attached to the top. It's much faster than climbing a ladder. Carrying the material up by hand is slow and it's hard work. The mine operators would need a lot of men to do what the elevator does."

Lee nodded. He was untutored but not slow.

"Lee, from what the Futurist told me, this should not exist here."

Lee shrugged. "Matt, perhaps that man lied to you."

"Maybe he did. Anyway, there's nothing we can do here now. We need to start back for the cabin. It will take as long, possibly longer, than it took for us to get here. We won't follow the same trail, and that may slow down pursuit if the other men you saw come after us. I won't be moving very fast, and if there are predators around, they'll find those bodies. They might follow us too.

"We should try going straight back to the cabin instead of following the dogleg course we followed before, offset slightly to the north." I sketched an angle in the dirt, a long leg that led from the cabin to the stream, then a short leg to where we had ambushed the swordsmen, and a connecting line that led back to where we'd begun. "This is how we'll return. It's shorter, so that may help make up for my slowness. I couldn't fight more of those warriors, not now. We'll have to avoid them."

I looked at the sun, now southwest of us, and we started east, Lee leading, seeking a way that would be easier on my wounded leg. My leg was rapidly stiffening and I was feeling the weakness of blood loss. The wound was quite painful. But there was nothing to do but go on, so I did.

Lee was our eyes and ears and he would be our first line of defense, perhaps our only defense. And if he was killed or badly injured, the women wouldn't be warned.

"Lee, if they catch up to us, don't try to stay with me. Run ahead, find the cabin and warn the women. You'll likely have to abandon the cabin and look for cover in the woods. I won't be able to fight, and if you stay you'll only be killed with me. It's more important to save the women."

He nodded. It was only common sense. Even if we didn't see more enemies, I might have to hole up somewhere and wait until my wound was healthy enough to travel. Infection, if it set in, would be a near-certain sentence of death.

We rested early in the afternoon after crossing the shallow river. There were no cats around, a good thing; I was feeling weak and feverish. I dropped off after chewing on a piece of jerky, my sleep troubled. Still, I managed to sleep through the night.

We were left with no choice when I woke up the next morning. The leg was stiff, sore, and when I loosened the bandage my thigh was hugely swollen. The sword-point might have been dirty, or it might have pushed fabric from my trousers into the wound. It didn't matter; the leg was clearly infected.

Lee helped me move until I found a place near the river, then left, headed for the cabin. I would stay here, where I could have access to water and where I could climb a tree if necessary. I would subsist on jerky as long as it lasted, then I would try to set traps as I'd done before.

Could I survive? Infection was an enemy I couldn't face. My body would fight this battle without my direction.

Lee would warn the women, and when I recovered I would make my way to the cabin. Teamwork had brought us this far, but now we'd had to split up.

Neither of us might make it home.

Chapter 14

The fever was worse. The wound was a deep puncture, and it wasn't draining. It had swelled more and turned dark, almost black.

My original garments were ragged and tattered; the sword puncture was a last straw. Astonishingly durable, the fabric had done its job. The shirt and trousers linked me to a different world, but it was time to let go.

I hacked off the trouser legs and the shirtsleeves, leaving me with a pair of shorts and a shirt that ended at the shoulder. My legs were bare, making the wound easier to care for.

My spear-shaft served as a makeshift crutch. I hobbled down to the stream and waded out to the center. Sitting in the water, I let the coolness relieve the pain and pressure. The relief was indescribable.

After washing the strips of cloth and the leather breechclout I'd used for a bandage, I prepared to do what was necessary.

I washed the wound gently. Gritting my teeth, I pressed into the swelling on each side of the puncture, trying to force any pus or foreign material out. Almost weeping from the pain, I pulled at the skin with my thumbs and opened the wound as much as possible to let the water wash around it. I finally twisted the strip of leather around my thigh above the wound. The tourniquet would control bleeding and reduce the pain.

I drank as much water as I felt comfortable doing, sitting there in the middle of that slow-moving river. I filled the water gourd too, both done upstream from where the water flowed over my leg.

I couldn't wait any longer; the chance of losing my leg to infection or gangrene increased as long as the wound remained sealed. Could I amputate my leg, even to save my life? Others had, but there was something I could do short of that final choice.

I carefully washed my knife, trying not to think about what I was doing, then just got on with it. I stuck the knife in deep, just below the wound, and sliced up through the puncture. Fresh blood and more pus flow out. If there had been foreign material in the wound, it probably came out too. I couldn't tell; the water carried everything away.

I washed the knife again, waiting while the water bathed the open wound. Agony threatened my consciousness, washed through my brain; my vision began to gray out, a fuzzy colorlessness that surrounded the clear center.

I couldn't wait; passing out in the river meant I would likely drown. Dragging my leg behind me, I made for the riverbank and crawled part-way out. I sat on the bank with only the injured leg in the water and squeezed the wound again. More blood washed away downstream. At least now I would fall on the land if I passed out.

Finally, after the faintness passed, I dragged myself the rest of the way out and let the wound air-dry.

I tied a rope to my pack and got to my feet. Looping the rope over my shoulder, I let the pack drag as I limped and hopped my way, aided by the spear, to the tree I'd selected.

In that tree's branches I would live or die.

My arms had become uncommonly strong from the work I'd done since arriving on Darwin's World. I was weak, but there was enough strength remaining to pull myself up into the tree.

That journey was the stuff of nightmares, constant struggle, slow progress, pain, seemingly no end to it all. I concentrated on the pain as I climbed, squeezing it into a ball then trying to push the ball away.

It might have helped, a little.

Laboriously climbing, one branch at a time, I finally neared the upper reaches. Animals like the saber-tooth we'd killed might climb, but they wouldn't be able to climb this high. I frequently stopped during the climb, resting, pulling up the pack that contained my dried food and supplies. My quiver I left at the base of the tree. I would recover it later, or I wouldn't need it.

A tree crotch became my resting place. I pulled the pack up and secured it to a nearby branch with twine, then used the rope to tie my body loosely to the tree bole.

The climb left me soaked with sweat. I drank more water and ate a piece of jerky, careful to make sure that the pack was tied in place and the flap was closed.

At some point, after eating and drinking, I passed out.

During the night I woke up for a short time. I drank more water and pissed as far away from the tree as possible. I ate a little more of the jerky and propped my swollen leg atop the branch I was sitting on. The dull throbbing, interrupted by brief stabbing pains, ruled my thoughts. I soon passed out again.

It was afternoon when I woke up. I had a raging thirst and my water gourd was empty. Stiff, sore, but no longer feverish, I made the trip back down the tree. I had to drink or I would weaken more. I took the pack of supplies with me; I might not be able to climb back up.

My shorts were fouled; I had pissed myself during the night and shit myself too. The feces were mostly solid and stayed within the shorts while I climbed down.

Back in the shallow river, the water bathed my wound while I carefully removed my shorts. I washed out the feces as best I could, repeatedly rinsing the shorts, then wringing out most of the water. It wasn't the best job ever but it would suffice. I limped back to shore, supporting myself with the spear, and spread the shorts out to dry.

I examined the leather breechclout that the original owner no longer needed. The long strip of deerskin had two half-ovals cut on each side near the middle. The narrow part, adjusted between the legs, would prevent bunching of the leather around my genitals. I pulled the strip into position, adjusted it for comfort, and secured it in place with my belt. When I struggled to my feet, the belt kept the breechclout in place while allowing the two loose ends to swing free.

Modesty had gone long before; I had no issue now with most of my body being exposed. Things would only get worse as my remaining garments wore out.

I ate jerky, drank more water, then went back to the tree to recover my quiver. I spared a thought for Lee; he might have survived, but it was also possible he hadn't. One man, making the trip alone, would need a substantial amount of luck to succeed.

I would need luck, too; my food was running out. I would have to try to make it back to the cabin on my own.

Taking my bearings from the sun, I headed northeast. Walking was painful and my limping pace was exhausting.

Lee and I had kept watch, traveled, then set up camp when we found a good spot. Alone, I made less distance and stopped earlier. I doubt I covered more than three, four miles at most before I was forced to stop.

Water was my priority; I stopped each afternoon as soon as I found a water source. I remained close enough to the water that I could fill my gourd before limping on the following morning. Snares supplemented my remaining food. I caught a large rat and a rabbit; the fresh meat was welcome. Two days after I caught the rat, I got a rattlesnake. He fell victim to my spear and I ate the flesh raw. That afternoon I ate the last of my jerky.

The leg was useful now instead of being a burden, something I dragged along. Not yet fully recovered, it would support my weight in an emergency. I slung the spear by its sling and strung my bow. The process was painful and stressed the wounded leg, but soon I had an arrow ready on the string and felt better.

The bow would have to remain strung for the rest of the trip, and would likely take a 'set' from being kept so long under tension. The induced curvature reduced the available power, but I wasn't strong enough to pull the bow all the way back anyway. If the bow remained usable long enough for me to reach the cabin, that was all I could hope for. I had left two other unfinished blanks back at the cabin, and I could make them into bows just as I had this one. And I could always cut more blanks.

I camped on the ground most of the time, using a fire to keep predators away, but I slept in the trees on two occasions. I heard noises that made me think large animals might be nearby.

I ate a root from a cattail and considered whether to eat the fuzzy 'tail' part. I finally tried it, but ended up spitting the seeds out; maybe they could be cooked and eaten, but I got no benefit from them. I choked down the root and it temporarily suppressed my hunger. Snails, a pair of insects that looked like grasshoppers, things that hopped, crawled, or swam, I ate them all. I was surviving, but barely so. I punched new holes in my belt as I lost weight. I had begun the trip with little fat on my body, and I had virtually none now.

It was a mixed blessing, I suppose. I had less weight to carry on the injured leg, but I was weaker from malnutrition now as well as the infection and loss of blood.

That was my situation when I caught a raccoon in one of the riverside snares. He was still alive, so I speared him, then skinned the carcass and roasted the flesh. The half-cooked meat was delicious and I ate too much.

I vomited up that first meal and regretted the loss.

I cooked more raccoon and ate again, slower this time, tasting and thoroughly chewing the meat. This time it stayed down. I stopped before I reached satiation.

No steak ever tasted as good as that raccoon!

After scraping the skin, I rolled it up to carry in my pack. I was doing that when I heard a tiny rustle. I whipped around, reaching for my knife and axe, and saw Lee and Lilia watching me from the forest.

"Easy, Matt. We didn't want to surprise you. We were backtracking my trail when we spotted your cooking fire."

"I didn't expect you. How are the others?"

"Stocked up with food and water and forted up inside the cabin. We've been worried, so I'm glad we found you."

For the first time in more than a week, I relaxed.

I would no longer be alone during the trip home.

Chapter 15

Lilia wasn't happy with my sloppy bandage. Nothing would do but that she remove it and examine the wound.

She sniffed around the open cut, then held the back of her hand against my forehead. Another sniff, but this one was a sniff of dissatisfaction. I thought the fever was gone, but she had other ideas.

"Leave it open to the air. I'll be right back." With that, she headed off into the forest.

She returned with an armful of vegetation. I recognized bay leaves and there was a root of some kind, but I had no clue what the rest of the things were. I gave them the scientific name of Weedus curiosa. I wasn't going to tell her that and earn another sniff, though.

She started a small fire and half-filled a small clay pot with water from the stream. When the water boiled, she fed the green material in. It turned the water a dark brown color. The steam smelled good to me, although maybe not to whatever germs were living inside the hole in my leg.

She let the water cool, then gently poured the warm tea over the wound. It stung a little, but that soon faded. She packed the boiled residue over the wound. Finally satisfied, she rewrapped it in a clean bandage. I was pleased; I had been afraid she would want me to drink that stuff or eat the mush that remained!

"We will rest here until tomorrow. I will build up the fires and Lee will set traps and hunt. You need meat, and rest. The trip back will be slow, but that cannot be helped. Lee will conceal our tracks. With luck, we shall be home in no more than four days and enemies won't be able to track us."

Her plan sounded good. Finally I could turn some of the responsibility over to someone else!

If there had been fever, it was gone now. Other than minor pain and stiffness, I felt good when I woke in the mornings, and if I was tired in the afternoon that was only to be expected. I had lost a considerable amount of blood and the weakness had only increased while I was unconscious, kept from falling by the rope. I had barely been able to eat and drink during the brief periods I was awake. It had not been enough to regain or even keep my strength.

The cut scabbed over and two days later Lilia decided I could remove the bandage.

We barely spoke while on the trail, remaining alert instead. Beasts lived in the wilderness. Some of them had four legs.

Lilia led, I limped along behind. We left little sign of our passage and Lee brushed out what there was. I kept moving at the best speed I could manage.

When I tired, Lilia found a sheltered spot to camp and Lee set out snares. We paused while she gathered things along the way that would be included in our evening meal.

I ate a lot of meat; Lee was a skilled trapper and hunter. I regained some of my strength, and our little group moved faster. Even so, it took a full five days to cover a distance that, healthy, I could have traveled in just a little more than a day. At least Lilia had been wrong about *something*!

Late in the afternoon of the fourth day after they'd found me, we came to a stream. We agreed this was likely the stream that flowed near the cabin, that we were probably a few miles too far south. We would make our way up the stream until we found a place we recognized.

We were more than usually careful to leave no sign of our passing from that time on. If those other warriors managed to follow us this far, it wouldn't take much to lead them the rest of the way. The smell of cooking bread, the slight noise I made while chipping points for arrows, spotting evidence where we'd trapped animals or gathered plants, the sight of a set snare; any of these might be the clue that led enemies to us.

We woke early the next morning and, after a hasty breakfast, were soon following the stream north.

I spotted the salt lick just after noon, then we passed the bee tree that Lee and I had robbed. Lee went on ahead at that point, leaving Lilia with me. He was able to move faster, which gave him time to circle the cabin and look for danger before we approached. He rejoined us as we entered the clearing and we reached the door together.

I slept in the cabin that night; I hadn't fully recovered and the leg was still painful. Lilia and Lee camped in the forest.

The following night, Lilia remained in the cabin while Sandra stayed in the forest with Lee. The women made the decision in each case. Was this no more than rotating space on the more-comfortable bed in the cabin, or was something else going on?

Lee, after all, was an adult, even if society downtime might not consider him so. He was a proven warrior, he'd killed enemies, and the occasional scruffy whiskers I saw before he shaved them off indicated he was past puberty. I had no claim on Sandra, but still, I felt a bit of jealousy. Still, if anything happened between them it would be her decision.

In a sense, this too was survival at work. There were three women in our little tribe but only two men. Relationships would have to adjust if we weren't to be forced apart by jealousy. Lilia and Lee would probably not have a physical relationship, but any other shuffling of our personal cards was possible. Even for the two of them, old taboos based on genetics and reinforcing of recessive traits might not control their relationship.

The new arrangements might also not be permanent. Each of us might live a long time on this world if we could avoid accidents, dangerous animals, or dangerous people. Assuming, of course, that what I'd been told downtime was true and the women had undergone the kind of physical and genetic restructuring that I had.

Would pairings be permanent? As people age, they change; those who are compatible might find themselves much less so ten, twenty, even a hundred years later. Could this be the reason so few marriages lasted during my original lifetime, because people changed as they grew older?

What would be the effect of living well past the century mark, assuming the Futurist had told me the truth? How long could we live here on Darwin's World? He'd mentioned that his culture had conquered death from 'natural causes', that he'd reworked my own DNA to the same standards.

Not that living forever on this world was guaranteed; fire, flood, famine, dangerous beasts, and dangerous people would prevent that from happening. Even lethal diseases might evolve at some point; the Futurist had mentioned that too. Meantime, there weren't enough of us to survive a war, just one more life-ending threat among the rest. Finding a better place to live was critical.

I brought up the subject that night.

"Lee and I went southwest first, about thirty miles or so. We found no human sign. We turned northwest after that.

"I came here from the southeast, and the only thing I saw was a long-abandoned hut. There were still things there that the owners wouldn't have left, so probably they died or were picked up by the Futurists. They might have left the grinding stones, but they'd have at least taken the spear and darts if they'd moved on willingly. So figure that whole quadrant from the southeast to southwest is probably safe.

"We had turned northwest when we ran into that patrol, and shortly after that we found an operating mine to the west. We were probably somewhere between twenty-five and thirty miles west of the cabin by then. We also might have been somewhere near your home by that time, Lilia, though maybe we were still a little south of there.

"There were different kinds of people working at the mine, warriors like the ones we killed, some that were probably miners. We don't know who any of them are, where they came from, or what they're doing. We only know they're there and they're probably involved in some way with the Futurists. Those swords were made using advanced technology, so I think the warriors probably got them from the people operating the mine."

I was drawing on the floor to illustrate my thoughts. Even though my fingers left no marks, the movements were short and obvious enough that the others understood.

"We know we want to avoid those people. Two got here to the cabin, but I doubt anyone sent them; if they had, someone would have come looking after they turned up missing. They'd have been here by now if they knew where the other two had gone."

I paused for a moment to give the others a chance to ask questions, but they nodded understanding so I went on.

"We're too close to that mine. It's maybe thirty miles away, a long day's travel due west, but doable. We found it, sooner or later more of them will find us. Next time it might be the people in charge, not just two renegades.

"Another issue, the game will soon be hunted out around here or the animals will move on. The snares aren't working as well and Lee told me he's had to go farther to find game.

"I don't expect an easy trip, but I think we have to go, and go as soon as we can get ready. If we head west or southwest, we'll likely encounter more of the mine people, and they may be the same ones who destroyed Lilia's home. Those raiders could have come from the people working the mine, but that's unlikely. Mining and raiding are different; if you need people to work a mine, you can't afford to have them off raiding. Some of the ones we saw were armed, but others weren't. I think there are probably two groups there and in any case, we need to stay as far away from them as we can.

"As for going southeast, the direction I came from, I can tell you there's not much down that way but deep woods, big rivers, and swamps. It's the same to the northeast, except with fewer swamps. Those rivers are major obstacles by their nature, but the biggest danger comes from not knowing what might be hiding on the far side. It's too easy to be ambushed.

"That leaves northwest. I think that's also our best chance to avoid running into the raiders who hit Lilia's home. We can travel for a week, then head due west until we find a better place to live.

"The country to the north looks to be hilly; I got a pretty good look from the top of a hill. It's probably mountainous if we go far enough, but I don't think we should do that. By staying in the foothills or just outside them, we'll have better visibility, fewer grassy plains, and maybe fewer dangerous animals.

"I know there are huge animals out in the grasslands, I saw them. They were a long way off, but I don't think we should hunt there. They might have been sloths or mammoths. Even if they're smaller, maybe wisent or some other kind of wild cow, that's still probably the kind of critter that killed Amanda.

"They're sort of like the downtime Cape buffalo, the kind hunters consider more dangerous than lions. They may not wait to be hunted, they might decide to hunt us. The animals here have been surviving worse things, bigger lions, saber-toothed cats, huge bears, and dire wolves, so they won't be easy prey. We might hunt them eventually but not until we're better armed.

"The plains animals might be the Pleistocene version of bison, bigger than the ones downtime but probably herd animals just like their descendants. The people who hunted them in that other timeline didn't just get close and spear them, they trapped them first in a bog or pit. And sometimes they drove them over a cliff. They used the same technique to kill mammoths.

"They used fire to drive the animals, but fires can turn on you if the wind shifts and anyway, too much meat would be wasted. We don't want to waste anything; we saw downtime what happens if you do that.

"But in the hills to the north, there will probably be only a cougar and maybe a few timber wolves. There are deer and elk there too. There might even be moose, goats, and mountain sheep.

"It'll be easier to avoid wolves and an occasional cougar in the hills than lions or saber-toothed cats down on the plains. I think they'll stay close to the big herds."

I paused to take a swallow of water.

"Something else about those men. Lee, would you hand me that short sword?" Lee picked up one of the weapons and handed it to me. The edge on this one showed damage, so I concluded it was the 'froe' I'd used to make staves for my weapons.

"Look at this. It's clearly advanced, but the men using them were wearing leather, not fabric. No weaving, in other words. And the shields are flimsy things, probably made locally because they're not equal in quality to the knives.

"If you look at this one and turn it so the light shines along the blade, you'll see faint dimples in the steel. I think those are forging marks. You can forge steel by heating it with coal or charcoal, so I can't tell which fuel was used.

"The forge marks though, those are evidence of advanced craftsmanship. At the same time the people using them are wearing primitive garments and carrying small, locally made shields. The only thing I can think of is that the swords were made by a sophisticated culture, but the rest were produced by someone that's not nearly so advanced."

Lee nodded. "I think you're right. They would carry the swords, because they were better than what they could build themselves, but they might not have wanted to carry a heavy shield. They especially wouldn't want to carry it unless they expected to fight someone, perhaps someone using flint knives."

"Right. So did they make the blades, or steal them? We just don't know.

"We know they're aggressive, even though they're not great warriors according to what we've seen. They might have raided to get the swords, they might also have taken the mine from someone more advanced. We don't know that either. But it really doesn't matter, because we're too few to do anything but avoid them." I paused to let them think it over.

Lilia had filled a pottery jug with berry-leaf tea. I poured some of the drink into my gourd and added honey, stirring the concoction with a twig. The berry tartness meshed well with the honey's sweetness. One day we might use berries to make wine, or ferment the honey into mead.

Someday.

"We could go due north for a few days longer, then decide whether to keep going north or turn west," Lilia suggested.

"Right. I favor the idea of going west, but we'd need to avoid the mine. Still, if we traveled slow and didn't build big fires, we shouldn't attract attention from anyone. We'd need to be careful, but we already do that.

"When we find a place with game, we might stop for a while. But if we see people, we'll watch long enough to get some idea of what they're like before we approach them. If they look peaceful, then we contact one of them. We'll get him away from the others, just to be safe. If they aren't friendly, then we move on. What do you think?"

Sandra answered, "I think it'll work, at least for now. We need more game and vegetables, no question about that. We're not finding much of either around here now, so I agree, we'll have to move. Lilia knows a lot about living off the land, you and Lee are good hunters and trappers, we should be all right."

"Sandra, I don't know all of the plants. I know of the ones near where we lived and I know some of what grows here," objected Lilia.

"You're still better at it than we are. You can teach, and we can learn," Millie said.

Our conference was suddenly interrupted.

There was a scratching sound at the side of the cabin, then something hit the closed window a heavy thump. Fortunately the shutters held. I heard a snuffle, and moments later claws scratched at the door. I was the first to have a weapon in hand, but just barely.

Millie had the crossbow, Sandra held two short swords, Lee was rapidly stringing his bow and Lilia was reaching for hers.

The axe went into the carrier on my left side, the knife went on my right. My club hung from a peg by the door, but I doubted I would need it. My spear leaned against the peg; I grabbed it and hung the quiver of darts around my body, letting it hang near my hip.

My bow hung nearby, but I left it too. Lee and Lilia already had bows, and one more wouldn't make much difference. The danger was close by, the spear was a good close-in weapon, and my bow wasn't in very good shape anyway.

Taking charge was instinctive. "Lee, back by the wall. You can shoot better from there if that thing gets through the door. Lilia, you're with Lee. Sandra, back them up with the swords. Millie, you've got the crossbow so you're up front with me. Shoot as soon as you see whatever that is out there, then get back by Sandra to reload."

The animal snuffled again, then I heard it moving around back of the cabin. The animal might be drinking from the spring. Safer for us, I thought; there was a barred door back there, but no windows.

It was nearly dusk. It would be foolish for us to venture out from behind the sturdy cabin walls, especially if we ended up facing whatever that was in the gloom of evening.

"Nobody goes outside. If that thing is still around tomorrow we'll deal with it, but not now. We'll wait. If it goes away during the night, I'll be happy.

"Two people keep watch. Everyone else try to sleep, but keep your weapons close.

"I'll take the first watch with Millie. Sandra, you'll take over the crossbow from Millie and be second watch with Lee. Lilia, sleep if you can, but you're first on call if anyone gets sleepy."

"Matt, I think that thing's coming back. Maybe it's a different one. There might be two of them!"

Chapter 16

I began removing the wooden grips from a short sword we'd taken after the fighting in the cabin. A second sword, salvaged from the men we'd killed on the scouting expedition, served as a chisel to cut the rivets holding the wooden pieces in place.

The sword would be a spear point after I got the hilt off.

The socket-ended spear I'd made earlier *could* be used as a stabbing weapon, but it wasn't designed for that. Nor could it be; the flaked-stone points became too fragile if they were longer than a finger, the relatively-thin darts also became too flexible if they projected more than hand-length beyond the front of the socket. The two combined to limit how deeply the darts could be inserted and how much damage they could do after they'd penetrated.

There might be no opportunity to pull the weapon back, reload the socket, and create a second wound. For that matter, the lightweight spear and atlatl system was useful as a projectile weapon, but a bow and arrows had much greater range and potential accuracy. The bow could launch more arrows with more penetrating force in a shorter amount of time, and do it from a safer distance. Still, archery depended on distance for safety; shooting arrows into a bear at point-blank range would certainly be hazardous to the bowman's health!

The spear I was making, unlike the replaceable-tip atlatl-driven projectile, was intended for close-in use. Even during my original time, a form of spear survived as the rifle bayonet. Though rarely employed, it remained useful as a close combat weapon.

It was not the best time to begin building a weapon, the night before using it to face an unknown animal in a fight to the death! But needs must; I could always fall back on the socketed spear and hope that with assistance from the crossbow and longbows in the hands of Lee and Lilia, it would be enough.

I was left with a full-tang blade after I removed the wooden grips. The holes in the tang couldn't be used, because I had no rivets to replace the ones I'd chiseled away, but the long tang would provide leverage.

For the shaft, I chose to start fresh using one of the blanks I'd roughed into shape. I'd intended to make it into a bow, but I needed a spear *now* more than I needed a new bow in the future.

My current spear shaft could have been used, but I might end up destroying the still somewhat-usable spear, and if I couldn't complete the other one in time, I would be left with no spear at all. Time was the enemy; I might not have time to finish the project.

I set the hide-glue pot on the fireplace's apron, raked coals around the pot, and left it in place while I began working on other tasks. A long strip of rawhide went into water to soak; it would stretch while being worked, then shrink as it dried, tightening the junction between the shaft and the metal blade. The rawhide would also become rock-hard in the process, and with a coating of more hide glue and beeswax, it should be water-resistant even if not waterproof.

I would have to split the end of the blank to accept the blade's tang. Softening the end fibers with boiling water allowed me to control the speed. Reinforcing the shaft above the split by wrapping it with cord also helped prevent the split from running up the shaft, weakening it.

The split end would be drying while I wrapped the lower part of the spear with the stretched rawhide strip, starting some ten inches above the point where the split ended. The reinforcement was necessary; a sixteen-inch blade, the amount that would project from the end of the shaft, exerts a lot of leverage in use.

As soon as the wood was dry enough, I coated the tang of the former short sword with glue and carefully worked it into the split. Adding more glue over the outside, I wrapped a damp rawhide strip down the shaft until the joint and two inches of the blade were covered, then allowed the whole thing to dry and shrink.

It's best to use hide glue over close-fitting dry surfaces, but adding the extra glue might provide additional support. Anyway, I was depending on the shrunken rawhide to do most of the job of reinforcing the blade-to-shaft joint.

I worked fast, but at the same time as carefully as possible. The spear had to work perfectly the first time. There wouldn't be a second chance for me if it failed. The others might retreat into the cabin, but I would be hand-to-claw with the animal, too close to escape.

I hadn't heard anything from outside in some time, but the ordinary night sounds hadn't returned. That worried me. Whatever that animal was, it was probably still waiting. We couldn't stay inside forever; we would have to drive the animal away or kill it.

Based on the sounds, I suspected the animal was a bear. If we were lucky, it would be a black bear, the smallest and least aggressive of the species; but it might be a grizzly, a much more dangerous beast. There was a third possibility that I didn't want to think about.

Whatever it was, we would find out in the morning. I kept working.

It was sometime after midnight before I could begin the slow process of drying the completed joint. We had only a little fuel remaining in the cabin by that time. I carefully added it, using small bits first. There was a longer and heavier stick that might be useful tomorrow; I kept it aside.

I held the spear-shaft and slowly rotated it in the radiated heat in front of the fireplace. I wanted the assembly to be fully dry, with the glue set, before the morning. At the same time, I didn't want to dry the joint so fast that it might be weakened, perhaps by cracks in the wood.

I finally passed the job to Lee when he took over the watch around two in the morning.

Facing a grizzly with no sleep? Not a good idea; I would need my wits about me and my reactions fast. As it happened, Lee let me sleep later than usual, so I'd had about four hours when he finally called me.

I ate a light breakfast and drank water. I used the corner to piss after that, which is what all of us had done since I made the decision for us to remain inside during the night.

Again, needs must.

The corner smelled. The cabin also smelled from the hide glue I'd been working with, so the urine was just an added stink.

The blade was secure as far as I could tell. I shook the spear vigorously, but there was no sign of wobbling where the blade joined the shaft.

The balance of the completed weapon wasn't great; the blade was slightly too heavy for the shaft. The resultant weapon was as much naginata as it was spear; it could be thrust bayonet-style or used axe-like for chopping. I tried each move in slow motion and decided it would work best as a spear.

I was as prepared as I was going to get.

"Lee, that thing may have gone, but get ready just in case. You and I will be the first ones outside.

"Lilia, you back up Lee. Sandra, you use the crossbow. Millie, I'd like you to help her reload. That torch might be useful, too."

I had put the end of the long, heavy stick into the fire. A nice flame now extended almost halfway up the stick. "Just be careful with the torch. We don't need you to burn the cabin before we're ready to leave!"

Finally, it was time. I took a deep breath, held the heavy spear ready, and nodded to Sandra to open the door.

I saw nothing. I released that held-in breath and breathed a sigh of relief.

But then, a huge furry mass broke from the tree line and came for me. Even limping, favoring a front paw, that thing was fast!

It was a bear, but not a grizzly; it was less chunky than a grizzly and the legs were longer. Still, it was powerful; it brushed aside the vegetation at the edge of the woods as if the plants were no more than cobwebs.

I registered all this and rapped out, "Lee! Back inside!"

The women would need him if I didn't survive. I might have gone in too, but there wasn't time for both of us to get inside and bar the door. At least, I now had a heavy spear that extended more than eight feet from tip to butt. The long blade added length to the shaft, and the extra distance would hopefully keep the bear from mauling me.

Lee ignored me. Worse, Lilia slipped out and moved off to my left as Lee ran several paces to the right. I registered their smooth progress as Lee launched his ready arrow and reached for another.

I heard a twang from Lilia's side and a deeper thunng sound from inside the cabin. The bolt sprouted near the bear's left eye, but didn't kill the animal or even blind it. I didn't know where the other arrows had struck. The bear was so close by this time that the shafts almost certainly had hit.

I could never stop that charging mass on my own; instead, I would let the bear force the spear home and hope those long front claws couldn't reach me. But meanwhile, I would have to stand and take the bear's charge.

Holding the spear with my right hand near the butt, left extended along the shaft, I took a step to the side of the door.

Blade pointed at the bear, butt end braced against the cabin wall, I waited. If the shaft held and I didn't lose my nerve, the long blade would do lethal damage.

If.

I never saw the blade go in. It was there, then it had disappeared into the fur at the base of the animal's neck. The shaft bent and bucked savagely, but it held.

The bear roared his fury, I yelled, the others were yelling too.

The animal hesitated, then spun incredibly fast. I hung onto the spear and let the blade carve its way through the organs inside the rib cage. I was thrown viciously around before finally losing my grip and slamming against the wall of the cabin. I shook off the stars I was seeing and spotted Lee as the bear went for him.

The bear, now standing awkwardly upright with my spear shaft sticking past its head, swiped at Lee with its right paw.

Somehow Lee had gotten my old spear. The flint-tipped dart faced the bear, but Lee was much closer than I'd been while using my longer spear. He poked rapidly at the bear as that first swipe missed, then planted the dart deep into the bear's throat, this time pointing upward so that the wound carved through the blood vessels in the beast's neck.

The second blow of a front paw didn't miss. Blood showered from Lee's arm and it bent impossibly; even so, he kept his grip on the spear with the other hand, pulled back on the shaft, and thrust the empty socket end at the bear's eye before finally collapsing.

The bear roared again, then I saw something I had difficulty crediting. The door opened, Sandra came out and shot the bear *behind the shoulder*, using the crossbow. The two women had managed a fast reload!

Lilia appeared to dance as she moved in on the bloody, roaring bear. She had two of the short swords, both held overhead; as soon as she was in range, her body bent back slightly, then whipped forward. Both swords went in almost half their length before she sprang back.

Note to self. Do *not* get into a knife fight with that woman!

It's funny the thoughts that run through your mind when you're stunned. I finally staggered to my feet and grabbed my axe. I adopted a two-handed stance for more power and got ready.

But I didn't need to attack. The bear collapsed, the great head sinking forward first, then the body slumping, allowing the animal to roll on its side. It was still gasping for breath, but blood flowed in a steady stream from the open mouth and the nostrils.

It seemed to take a long time for the bear to die, but on reflection I decided it had only been a few seconds. While I leaned wheezing against the cabin wall, the great beast stopped breathing. The blood kept flowing for a few seconds more, then stopped. Maybe the heart had quit, or maybe it had simply run out of blood.

Lee lay crumpled where he'd fallen against the cabin door. He looked dead. Lilia got to him and crouched, looking at his face. As she watched, I saw a small movement of his leg. Was he still alive, or was this a dying reflexive kick?

She reached for the mangled arm and Lee gasped. He was alive then, but I had no idea for how long. I limped over to where Lilia was examining his arm.

By the time I got there, Lee appeared to have passed out. He had a claw mark that started near the elbow and extended to just above the wrist. The skin had been flayed back as if by a knife, simply ripped free of the muscle. The wound wept droplets of blood.

"We must get him inside," Lilia said. "Matt, help me, please. If you can carry his shoulders, I will carry his feet. I will fold the injured arm over his chest. I must set the bone before he wakes up."

That was almost the way it happened, except that Sandra and Millie helped with the shoulders. Lee was heavier than I expected, but we moved him inside as carefully as possible. Lilia set his arm while I held his shoulder, then she bandaged his wound with cloth ripped from Sandra's dress.

I surrendered the rest of my clothing, as did Sandra and Millie. The three of us were naked when we went out to work on the bear's carcass.

I gutted it; it had indeed been skinny. It might even have been close to starvation, due to the mangled front paw. Hunger forced it to hang around, because it smelled us inside and had no other source for food.

I dragged the heavy guts as far away from the cabin as possible, then dropped them. Something would take care of the offal, hopefully not something that would then decide to come after us; but there was nothing else I could do.

Millie and Sandra had done a hasty job of skinning back the bear's hide. Almost half the animal's flesh now stood revealed, and the skin had been pulled flat along the ground.

I began dismembering the animal with my axe. The head and neck would be left complete, except for removing arrows or bolts.

We didn't need the meat on the neck; as it was, some of the meat would likely spoil before we could preserve it.

I hacked off great chunks and we carried those inside the cabin. We would get as much as we could, in case some other animal decided to challenge us for the kill. We were in no shape to fight off anything larger than a rabbit; if something bigger wanted that skinny bear, it could have it!

We got most of the shoulder, chopping off the lower parts of the forelegs and throwing them into the forest. I might salvage the claws later, but not now. We then chopped through the ribs and discarded them too, leaving the upper ribs attached to the spine. We would eat the heavily-muscled part that lay along the spine. There was also a slight hump over the shoulder, so I got as much of that as possible; it was mostly fat, the only fat I'd seen on the bear as I chopped the carcass apart. I took the exposed hindquarter too, although it took two of us to lug it into the cabin.

Lilia stopped us at the door on the way back out.

"I would like to have the skin, but it may not be possible to finish skinning the bear. We will cut off the skin that has been stripped back. It's less weight to drag, anyway."

So that's what we did.

The meat was tough and a little gamy, but I ate some later, a supper that was mostly roasted bear with a little bread, then stretched out and fell asleep. I think Lilia may have slept too. I saw Sandra and Millie watching out the open window and one of them closed and barred it as I dropped off. I hadn't gotten a full night's sleep the night before, and it had been a stressful day.

Lee hadn't stirred after his mother set his broken arm. He had lost a considerable amount of blood before she set the arm, bandaged the wound, and protected the arm with splints. Now she simply waited. Lee would wake up naturally, given time.

Or not.

Chapter 17

Our plans to trek northwest were on hold. For the moment, Lee had lost a lot of blood, so we'd have to care for him as best we could and wait to see what happened.

The women had shown courage and more fighting ability than I expected, but physical strength would also be a factor on the trek. Lee and I had it; we could carry more of a load and do it longer before we needed to rest. We'd also have a better chance of surviving encounters with the huge animals I expected to find or attacks by hostile warriors. If we blundered into either, we wouldn't have a cabin to fort up in, maybe not even a tree to climb. We might be forced to fight on the ground, outnumbered, if the enemies were human.

Only the winners get the prize on Darwin's World, a chance to survive for a little while longer.

As for animals, the bear had been injured before the fight started. Despite our combined efforts, Lee had been badly wounded before it finally succumbed. Killing the scimitar-toothed cat had also required luck as well as teamwork and skill. Had the animal not landed in the river, the outcome might have been different. And we hadn't yet faced a large, healthy predator on its own turf.

Could I keep us fed by hunting and trapping? If I couldn't, we would starve. Gathering edible vegetation would help, but as the season progressed such opportunities would diminish.

Dire wolves might be there too, where we intended to go; they were larger than gray wolves and probably hunted in packs. If they caught us in the open...

I had named this world after Darwin for a reason. By almost any measure other than intelligence, those wolves were better suited to survive than we humans were. The same was true of all the other top predators. This was *their* world, not ours.

Technology had made us the top predator downtime. Here, we had no technology other than the most primitive kind. We were prey. The facts spoke for themselves. This world would eliminate the unfit, the unready...

And the unlucky.

Meantime, I had more important things to do than muse about the future. Regardless of whether we left the cabin or remained through the winter, I needed a stronger bow and arrows matched to its draw weight. I also needed better arrow points, and I had not yet mastered the art of flint knapping. My stone points were usable, but they would become much better with practice.

We also needed spears for everyone. The new ones would have longer and thicker shafts, better for use against the huge animals we could expect to face. I could also salvage blades from the short swords, enough for a steel-bladed spear each.

Eventually, when the steel blades broke or were lost, I would need stone points, and they would have to be better than what I'd made so far.

I explained this to the women.

"We can't travel until Lee recovers. I know you're better able to defend yourselves now, but even so, Lee or I would have to help. One of us would need to stay close, maybe do some trapping, while the other hunted.

"I expect we'll be using a travois to haul heavier items. We'll carry everything else in backpacks. We won't be moving very fast and we won't go very far in a day.

"We can pick up the travois' trails during the last hour before we stop and carry them, so that we don't leave drag marks.

"We'll also change course while we're carrying the travois, so if anyone's following, they can't find us by going ahead in a straight line. We can probably evade an ordinary enemy, but a skilled tracker will still be able to find us, which means we'll have to take turns on watch, even though it will leave us tired." I left it at that. They could think about the things I'd said and we could talk later.

We had meat for the time being, but the half-carcass we'd made into bear jerky wouldn't last long. I would have to resume hunting, and this time I would have to travel farther from the cabin. Animals already avoided this area.

Lilia, Sandra and Millie would have to share the task of caring for Lee.

The women would also have to range further afield. Simply put, we had gathered all that were growing nearby. The plants would come back, given time, but only if we stopped harvesting them, and before that could happen I hoped to be gone.

It would be safer for both of us if Lilia accompanied me, she seeking edible plants and herbs, while I concentrated on hunting.

The traps would catch small animals, so that could be a backup in case the hunting was poor; but we also needed fats, and large hides for leather. I would have to kill deer or elk for those things.

Larger animals would be even better, but I had no idea how I would kill something as large as a bison or ground sloth, and certainly not a mammoth!

And I wouldn't be the only one hunting the huge grazers. Big game attracts big predators. Out on the grassy plains, I wouldn't have a handy tree for refuge either, which made hunting them extremely dangerous.

But there was probably no choice; I would have to do the best I could. The heavier bow I planned to make would help, and maybe I could choose my hunting grounds with safety in mind.

Maybe. And maybe the bison, what people downtime often called buffalo, would graze in bowshot of the tree-line. I could only hope.

What kind of bow? The Welsh longbow was excellent for warfare, but less suited for hunting in thick cover. English archers *had* used them in the forests, judging by the legend of Robin Hood; but by comparison, the horse nomads of the Asian steppe had used short, stout bows and American natives had short but lighter bows.

Another consideration; the longbows were so powerful that a bowman needed regular practice just to draw the bow, and they were unsuited to fast snap-shooting.

Something shorter than the longbow, then, but more powerful than the American Indian bows. My old, weakened, bow would suffice in the meantime.

I discussed my thoughts with the women, but Lilia wasn't yet ready to hand over caring for Lee. She insisted on instructing Millie and Sandra before doing that and would help around the cabin until she was satisfied that the others were competent.

Felling trees for spear blanks would need to be done before I could hunt. The blanks could dry while I was away and they'd be ready when I had time to work on them.

As soon as I'd eaten, I took my spear and bow along and went looking for a tree or two that I could split for spear-shaft blanks. There was a bit of residual muscle soreness, some of it from my wound, some from the fight with the bear. I soon worked through it and felt physically good. Mentally, I was still very concerned for Lee.

I soon crossed the stream near where I'd killed the camel. There was now little sign that anything had happened there; the scraps of skin and flesh had been eaten and the scuffs left from the fight had been eradicated by a short-lived but heavy rain. Sic transit camel.

I would likely leave no more sign than the camel when I passed. Pleistocene-age humans, those who lived in the Americas at the end of the last ice age, rarely lived to be thirty years old. My downtime knowledge might help, but it might also not be enough. Those ancient humans had also acquired knowledge, and theirs had been the specialized knowledge of how to survive in a world like this one.

Darwin's World was primitive, violent, and untamed. I decided I liked it just as it was. It might kill me, probably would, but I would enjoy life until it happened.

I found and cut two suitable trees and carried the trimmed trunks back to the cabin.

I went hunting the next morning, circling the cabin while staying between a mile and a half and two and a half miles away. I soon found where larger, cloven-hoofed animals had left tracks and droppings; some of the pellets were the size of my thumb joint, and some were considerably larger. I found other droppings I thought might be coyote or wolf. There was also a larger pile, older, hopefully left by the bear we'd killed.

If not, there were trees I could climb. That bear, likely a short-faced bear, had been built for running, not climbing. The crippling injury to the foreleg would barely have slowed a more-robust grizzly.

If I was wrong about the scat, I had the bow and my heavy spear. Even so, I had no desire to find myself close to a healthy bear; for that matter, I didn't want to be near a big bear with any weapon short of a cannon. I had the same healthy desire to avoid the great cats and dire wolves, or for that matter even the smaller gray wolves. I was strongly in favor of live-and-let-live, especially where the great bears were concerned.

Caution wasn't at all the same as cowardice.

Like the others, I had proven my courage. We had facing the bear, a scimitar-toothed cat, and armed men, all at close quarters. We lived, our enemies did not. Proof enough.

Hunting is best begun immediately before first light, when the herbivores are still feeding. But there were other things that hunted during this time, things that might hunt me. No, not the preferred time for a lone human to be hunting!

I hunted after first light the following morning but found nothing. I would try for success again in the afternoon, when most predators were bedded down. The grazers might be stirring by then, looking for water and a fast meal.

Despite the tracks and droppings, I had nothing to take home for dinner. Even so, the morning wasn't a waste. I found a tree that had been used as a roost by some sort of large bird.

It might have been the favored overnight home of a flock of turkeys; the ground under the tree was covered with droppings and cast-off feathers, showing this was a place the birds used frequently. I collected the best of the feathers and stashed them in my pack before moving on.

I finally arrived back at the cabin, tired, unsuccessful, but at least still safe. After a short rest, I would work on chipping points. The rough points I would pressure-flake to sharpness.

I broke as many points as I produced. Perhaps the early flint-smiths had done the same. More likely, I still had much to learn. I had begun with implanted knowledge, but skill would be needed to make the knowledge truly useful.

Lee had not awakened. The women had cleaned him when necessary, but he remained in a deep sleep or coma. I couldn't tell the difference, and probably it didn't matter.

Lilia decided to remain in the cabin for another day. The women had fashioned a number of clay pots during the time I was out. Someone had even taken the time to decorate the pots, although the etched attempts were not very elaborate. The clay would need to dry for at least another day before the pots could be fired to convert them into pottery.

Tonight, they would bake several loaves of bread from flour they'd made. We didn't want to build a fire during daylight because someone might spot the smoke.

I felt much better physically, no longer sore even if I was tired from the day's travels and an evening's work after that. I considered approaching either Sandra or Millie later, but decided it wasn't a good idea with Lee and his mother in the cabin with us.

Well, I had been celibate for months before I encountered Millie and Sandra. I would just have to forego a physical relationship for now, even though I had certainly earned it!

I had my own bed at least. Someone had stitched rabbit furs together into a pad that covered the camel-skin, and the two provided a cushion for the wooden floor. I needed no cover to keep warm, for now. More skins and furs would eventually be needed when winter arrived, whether we spent it here, on the trail, or in a new, defensible home. It was just something else we would need to plan for. For now, the bed was comfortable.

I had no trouble falling asleep.

Rising before daybreak, I spent a few minutes watching out the window. I saw no movement even though my eyes were well adjusted to the darkness, but I heard normal insect and bird sounds and that was even more reassuring. I went out, spear in hand, and took care of my morning business before passing by the spring to wash up.

Someone had begun the process of enclosing the spring while I was away. It would eventually be a lightweight fence that wouldn't stop a bear, nor be tall enough to keep out the cats or wolves; instead, the fence would be more discouragement than barrier but better than nothing.

I thought we might improve the fence by slanting the points slightly outward, making it even more of a deterrent. The slender wooden uprights had already been cut with sharp points at the top.

There was an implanted memory of something called a 'coyote fence', made by lacing thin trunks together. Continue looping the rope around the trunks, tie every tenth loop into a knot, then continue the figure-8 pattern; implant the bottoms into a shallow trench to anchor the bases, then finally stand the fencing up at something a little less than a right angle. It would also be necessary to support the outward-leaning fence with vertical supports, but it could be done.

Such a fence would work better than a split-rail fence and be quicker to construct too. A wall of sharp points at eye level would cause an animal to back away.

I went back into the cabin. Someone had heard me go out and the women were up and preparing food.

Best of all, Lee was awake.

He was still groggy and unable to move about without help, but he was awake. In a short time we had him up and occupying one of the three chairs in the cabin.

So Lee would live, but wouldn't be able to help me if we left now. It would take at least a month, probably longer, before he was fit. That made the decision easy; we would remain in the cabin during the winter and head northwest in the spring.

Lee was young and healthy except for his injuries. Despite his serious wounds, he should recover, given time. I had been worried about the loss of blood, but that would have killed him already if it was going to. The broken bones would knit, and the cuts on his arm were already scabbed over.

Lee would need to regain his strength before he could even go outside the cabin. The broken arm would cause him to lose endurance as well as strength while it healed. I estimated at least a month before he could go outside. Even then, he would need someone with him.

"Glad you're awake, Lee. How's the arm? "

"Painful. My mother has added more bruises to what the bear gave me."

Lee would need meat in order to make a full recovery. Dangerous or not, I would leave before daylight tomorrow so that I might have the best chance possible of bagging a deer or an elk.

Lilia decided she'd go with me, leaving Sandra and Millie to watch over Lee.

He probably didn't mind.

Chapter 18

We breakfasted before daybreak and slipped out the door, Millie dropping the bar into place behind us. I knew which way to go, based on the direction the cabin faced, and we set off at a slow, cautious pace. We were the equivalent of rabbits in this wilderness, and there were but five of us that could be considered 'friendly'. When you're a rabbit, speed kills.

We still made good time despite the slow pace and frequent pauses to listen. Walk a few paces, pause; listen, and once we were satisfied there was no danger around, resume walking.

There was no need to speak. Lilia was close behind me and whenever I paused, she maintained position by lightly touching my arm. We had traveled at least a mile by the time the sky lightened enough for us to make out objects.

A small clearing lay just ahead, and a few hundred yards away from the clearing was the roost tree I'd found. I hoped there would be deer still browsing in the clearing.

Dawn is prime time for hunting deer. They feed in early morning, then head for a water source. By mid to late morning, they're bedded down.

Bedding areas offer protection; they're often in thick brush that will slow a predator's approach or force him to make noise, or atop a hill where the deer can see anything that moves. And there are always escape routes, regardless of where the deer beds down.

Lilia had her bow and my light socketed spear was slung across her back. I carried my new heavy spear and the weakened bow I'd kept strung too long while recovering from my wound. I also had my axe and knife, indispensable tools for butchering. The axe would also be the tool of choice for fashioning a travois to haul our kill home afterward.

We eased slowly ahead, making no noise, but nothing moved in the clearing.

I had marked the location of a tree during my previous visit, ten yards back from the clearing. It had strong, sloping branches, easy to climb without making excessive noise.

I intended to wait in the tree; deer had been here, as evidenced by dung piles in the clearing, and there was no reason they shouldn't return. Lilia was a complication; she could take this tree, I would find another one. It would be a more difficult ascent, but I was accustomed to climbing.

She went up the tree as easily as I could have. She arranged her quiver so that a second arrow would be immediately available and made herself comfortable.

I used more strength to compensate for less flexibility while climbing my second-choice tree, but soon I was settled in, watching. My bow was ready, my quiver was conveniently placed. I laid the spear across a branch; I might need it eventually, but for now it was awkward and hampered my use of the bow.

Waiting, only my eyes moving, I scanned around the clearing. A glance at Lilia showed me that she was also perfectly still, clearly no novice at hunting. She glanced back at me, and then resumed watching.

The time passed slowly. The clearing remained deserted. A few insects buzzed, but none reached up to where we waited.

I had been sitting unmoving in the tree for two hours or so. It might have been a little more, but probably wasn't much less. I was stiff and I suspected Lilia was too. Was this site a bust? Then I spotted a slight flick on the far side of the clearing.

A dark object, a tiny movement that covered only inches; I couldn't tell what it was at first but it was moving and there was no detectable breeze. Finally I realized I was watching a tail.

The tail belonged to a long, tawny shape crouched in the brush at the clearing's edge. The animal was perfectly still except for the excited twitching of that tail. If the critter wasn't a lion, it would do until a real one came along.

This one was female, and she hadn't discovered us. Sheer good luck, that tiny twitch; had we climbed down, the lion would surely have seen us.

And attacked.

I glanced at Lilia. I hadn't seen her move, but she was watching me. I eased my hand out and wagged it from left to right. To make sure she got the message, I slowly shook my head, no. We didn't want anything to do with a lioness.

She was big and heavy-bodied. She also might not be hunting alone. Lions hunt in prides, don't they? At least, they do in the world where the Futurist had found me.

We would have to roost in our respective trees until the lioness departed. Still, that excited twitch was a sign; she'd seen something, even if I hadn't. I glanced at Lilia to make sure she had gotten my message. To reinforce it, I silently mouthed "Lion", exaggerating my movements.

Her eyes opened a bit and she mouthed back, "Lion?"

I nodded.

I turned my attention back to the lioness. I had a moment's fright, thinking I had lost her, but she was still there even though the tail had stopped moving.

The lioness sank lower as she crept from cover, belly barely touching the ground, great muscles bulging. But she wasn't heading our way. She was clearly intent on something else, stalking instead of moving to a better position.

What had attracted her attention? Finally, I saw it.

The animal was huge, even larger than an elk. It had pale dappled spots on its side, a dark line along the back from neck to tail, a blocky body that was buff-colored but fading to cream along the belly. It had antlers like nothing I'd ever seen; they were huge, long spikes extending from a palmate structure similar to what a moose might have.

Larger even than a downtime moose, this beast represented a species I'd never heard of.

The stag had spotted the lioness when she left cover. The head sank until the nose almost touched the ground, that formidable rack of spikes facing the lioness. The stag slowly stepped back.

The lioness roared and charged. She crossed the clearing in three huge bounds before reaching her full stride. Three more yards and a final bound would land her on the back of the stag.

That turned out to be a mistake. The stag wasn't intimidated. Was it instinct, or had it faced lions before?

Lions normally sneaked in close before trying to spring onto an animal's back. Anchored by claws, the lion could then bite through the spine or hook the nose with a powerful clawed forepaw and break the grazer's neck. If the prey attempted to run, the lion could race alongside and sink its teeth into the throat, suffocating the animal. Almost always, there would be several lions working together. Whether from breaking their prey's neck or suffocating it, a pride of lions usually killed.

Neither approach was suitable for a single lion attacking an alert animal, one with a head protected by spikes.

The stag's head was low, antlers forward and spikes slightly raised. As the lioness sprang, the head swept strongly up and rammed several of the long spikes into her body. She squalled in pain as she spun away. Landing on her side, the lioness scrambled to regain her footing.

The stag-moose now revealed his alternate weapons. He reared up and came down on the lioness, both front legs stiff, his considerable weight behind them. Ribs broke with a crunch and the lioness squalled again.

The stag had been clawed during the attack, although I hadn't seen it happen. Still, he was bleeding. Infuriated, he reared up and landed on her again, then a third time. This time the lioness made no sound. There was little left from shoulders to haunches that didn't show evidence of those killing hooves and antlers.

I glanced at Lilia. She was switching her attention between watching me and the end of the drama below. I made a sudden decision. We were in a tree, no other lion had joined the fight, and the stag couldn't climb.

I didn't have time to explain. I simply glanced at Lilia in her tree, and then pulled back my bow. I released the nocked arrow and reached for another.

I fitted it over the bowstring as Lilia's arrow thumped into the animal's side, behind the shoulder. I could see my own arrow, a bit higher than Lilia's. I planted my second arrow slightly behind that first one. Only a few inches of shaft projected to show where my arrows had struck. The bow had lost some power, but clearly enough remained; it was still an effective weapon.

Lilia might have hit the heart and my two arrows were into the lungs. The stag stood now, front legs wide-spread, head hanging, back slightly humped. Lilia put another arrow into the neck, just forward of the shoulder. The dying animal folded and the front legs collapsed. It looked for a moment as if it might be lying down to sleep. The hind leg kicked twice, the anus and bladder relaxed.

Lilia made the first mistake I'd seen from her; she gathered her equipment, preparing to climb down. I hissed to get her attention and called low-voiced, "Not yet. Give it a moment to see what happens."

We sat in our trees and waited. The quiet of the forest gradually gave way to the buzz of insects and the distant chatter of a small animal. Finally, deciding it was safe, I eased cautiously down. I was waiting, weapons ready, when Lilia reached the ground.

"Thank you for the warning, Matt. It was safer to wait. I should have remembered that, but I thought of all that meat and I got impatient."

"That stag was too eager, Lilia. He forgot to keep watching for danger. I didn't want us to make the same mistake."

"You watch for now, Matt. I do this."

Lilia glanced at where the bright arterial blood from the stag's nostrils had clotted. She tugged at the antlers, rolling the big animal over on its side. I helped her before resuming my post, on guard.

She rapidly opened the body cavity to let the blood drain. A few deft cuts freed the internal organs, and she paused after removing them to let the carcass begin cooling.

"Take a break, Lilia. You get your weapons and watch, I'll get a travois ready."

I cut and trimmed the pieces I needed, assembled the travois, and dragged it back to the animal. I attached the tump-line as before, now improved by a stitched sleeve of rabbit fur where the strap crossed the crown of my head.

I took over watching; dead animals attract scavengers like bare skin attracts mosquitos. Lilia went back to work, skinning the carcass but leaving two flaps of skin attached along the spine. We quartered the carcass, then freed the hide from the final attachments. Tying it in place on the travois, we loaded as much meat as I could carry, then folded the remaining hide over to protect the meat.

The rest would be left to the forest to take care of. Scavengers would appreciate the bounty; we couldn't get the rest of the meat back and preserve it before it spoiled.

Drying and smoking was our only way of preserving the excess; even so, the meat wouldn't last more than a few weeks. It would keep longer after the weather turned cool, but by then there might be fewer animals to hunt.

Before the development of refrigeration, people named winter the hungry time with good reason.

I'd have given a lot for an uptime freezer and someplace to plug it in! For that matter, I'd love to have a big-bore rifle, and a gun-bearer, and enough porters to haul everything around. Someone to set up the camp and pour me a drink of real, smoky tasting scotch while I sat and watched the sun go down.

Yeah.

Those things were fading memories; I would never taste scotch again. I had a momentary glimpse of my future, a constant struggle without respite to provide food, shelter, and protection. There would be few luxuries in that future.

I still had a strong will to survive, but how long would that last? Would events slowly erode my determination? Would I lose my concentration at a critical time? How long would it be before I met the same fate as this stag?

I killed that I might eat. It gave me a feeling of exultation, winning the contest of life and death, but regret always followed. We killed to live, but necessity didn't take away the realization that we'd taken a life to preserve our own.

Well. I was tired already and I would be more tired when I got back. I shook off the morbid philosophy and got on with the task.

We'd killed the stag, but he'd been no Bambi; he'd killed the lion before we killed him.

Lions will attack a Cape buffalo, but only if the entire pride is available. One lion stood little chance of bringing down such a huge animal and it might well die in the attempt. Even a cow moose can drive a grizzly from her calf.

No; this had been no tame grazer. Downtime memories were better not dwelt on; I didn't live in that time, not now. The land was different here, the animals were decidedly different, and many of them were dangerous. To forget was to suddenly become dead.

We had the best quarters of meat lashed down protected by the hide. As a final act, I used my axe to break off a section of antler. The hard bone would be useful.

I picked up the travois and Lilia adjusted the tump-strap. Leaning into the weight, I headed for home.

I took frequent breaks to drink, but even so I got thirsty. Both of us were still bloodstained when we came to the stream. We took turns, one in the water, one watching for danger and guarding the meat. I soon had the worst of the dried blood off. I also drank and refilled my gourd.

Lilia without her clothes was…interesting.

She could decide when, if, she was ready to move on after the loss of her man. I appreciated the view, but still kept most of my attention on our surroundings.

Perhaps she enjoyed the view while I bathed.

I washed as quickly as possible, brushing the water off as I left the stream. Clothes back on, I resumed dragging the travois.

We didn't talk about the bathing. It was a natural thing to do, we did it, and anyway we didn't talk more than necessary while away from the cabin.

Even in the cabin there wasn't very much to talk about. Immediate plans, occasionally thoughts of what we might do in future, those things we discussed. Our usual conversation was about what we'd done during the day, sometimes a report of an unusual or interesting thing that had happened, and we talked while we worked. The women might be grinding grain, I might be knapping a new point or crafting an arrow; there was never a shortage of tasks.

The theatre, doings of celebrities, new developments in music or entertainment, books, the topics common downtime... yeah, right. We weren't going back to those things. And the constant need to work didn't permit the kind of idleness that needs conversation to pass the time anyway.

Medieval peasants had lived much as we did now. Wake, breakfast, work, perhaps a short break at noon, but often enough, simply continue working. Break for supper, then do small chores until it was too dark to see, sleep, get up tomorrow and do it all over again. At least, peasants had an occasional holiday and an enforced day of idleness on weekends. We didn't have that luxury.

Maybe we could take a day's holiday, if we could build up a reserve of food and firewood and arrows...

We reached the cabin late that afternoon.

Chapter 19

The bear attack means we can't leave, at least not before spring. We'd have had to travel light, move fast, and even after we found a good location, we'd have had to build a shelter and collect supplies before winter. It would have been tough, even with all of us healthy. Now, Lee will have to regain his strength after his arm heals. We've got to spend the winter here.

"It's going to get cold. Winters are probably harsh; the Futurist told me he was transplanting me to an Earth at the end of the ice age, the Pleistocene.

"We've got a problem. We're going to need massive amounts of wood and we're also going to have to store a lot of food, enough to last for at least four months. That means harvest everything we can gather. We'll eat what we need and dry the excess. We've also got to preserve meat, which means we'll need more salt.

"Animals are scarce. The last trip was successful, but only because we hunted a long way from here. The hunt was successful, then we had to leave almost half the carcass behind.

"Someone has to stay with Lee. After he's able to take better care of himself we can all hunt, but not yet. So three of us will go on the next hunt.

"After that, I've got to cut firewood. It's going to be nearly impossible. The small axe isn't suited for that, the handle's too short, the blade's too light. It's better than nothing but it's meant for gathering limbs, not cutting trees. There's already a nick in the blade too, from chopping through bone. The Futurists got too creative; the best axe would have been a heavy single-bitted axe with a long handle, something twice the weight of the one they gave me. It should also have been soft steel with a harder edge, not the pattern-welded steel they used. I'm guessing that no one there has used an axe for centuries. They knew that the best knives and swords are made of pattern-welded steel, wootz or Damascus as some call it, and thought the axe should be made from that too.

"Maybe the Futurist made a trade-off; the camp axe he gave me is handy for carrying and doing light tasks but not for chopping trees. A saw would have been better."

"Matt, what is a saw?"

"It's a blade for cutting things. It's like the swords we captured, but it has sharp projections called teeth along the edge. It cuts by sliding back and forth through wood. Even a small one would be helpful. . ."

Lee interrupted, "Would you be interested in a large saw? I saw things such as you've described and an axe that is larger than the one you have. They are hanging in an open shed at the mine. Maybe the miners use them."

I muttered something under my breath.

"I'll have to steal those, but not right now; I need to finish my bow first. But that should only take another day or two; the shaping is done, all I have to do now is glue sinew along the back to give it additional draw weight.

"There's always more to do," commented Lilia. Sandra and Millie nodded agreement.

Neither had said much while we discussed our situation. I wondered if they were unhappy about changing from owners of the cabin, totally in charge, to being two among five. And for that matter, two who appeared to have less ability and less knowledge to contribute than the rest of us. Hopefully, it would work itself out; there was no going back to the way things had been, not now.

"For every need it seems like there's a solution, but the solution then opens up five more needs that have to be met," Sandra said. "How would you steal the tools without the guards noticing? Even if you aren't killed during the raid, how could you escape without leading them back here?"

"You're right, Sandra, I would have to be careful. We can't outfight them, there's not enough of us for that, and you're also right about not letting them follow us. If I can get a head start, I can discourage pursuit."

"How would you do that?" This came from Millie. She looked worried. I had been their only support until Lee and Lilia arrived. There had also been those other activities; no, they wouldn't want to lose me.

I hoped.

"Mantraps. If they're competent trackers, they'll know there were at most one or two people on the raid so they won't be worried. I'll put traps along the escape route, things like snares, spiked deadfalls, shallow pits with sharpened stakes. The traps will slow them down.

"I'll leave a trail away from the cabin, just enough to lead the pursuers into the traps, then change direction. We can circle back to the cabin after making certain no one is following me.

"The traps won't stop them, but they'll have to slow down. Even if they keep coming, they'll be following a false trail. I'm hoping that will discourage them. Anyway, we don't have a choice; I've got to have the tools.

"The raid will take at least a week. I'll have to find a place to put the traps, then mark the locations. A full moon will help. We'll be able to see the markers and it will also encourage the guards to run into the traps.

"I'll need a place to break my trail. I'll set a few traps past that point so they'll keep thinking that's where I've gone. That will give me time to hide my tracks.

"After I get the tools, we cut all the wood we can. We've used it for cooking but when winter sets in, we'll need to keep the fireplace going all the time to keep the cabin warm.

"We'll need to hunt, but that can be done after the first cold spell. Trapping will provide meat for daily use but we need more and bigger skins. We'll need fat too.

"We've got to have warm clothing. Deerskins won't be enough, but maybe with parkas they'll work. We'll also need thick furs for bedding. We might even take a few bears."

"Matt, you're not seriously proposing to hunt one of those short-faced bears!"

"Lilia, the bears will have thick fur and a lot of fat. Short-faced bear, black bear, grizzly, if we can trap one, we stay out of its reach and kill it with arrows. I'm thinking of a pit trap; it would be work, but it could be done. The reward is worth the chance.

"For now, we can make stag-moose skins into leather boots. The skin's thick enough, it should last through the winter. We can line the boots with rabbit-fur or fur-felt for added warmth.

"After the first snow, we'll haul meat on sleds. We can transport more meat and move faster, plus the meat will keep. Tracking through snow is easier too.

"Cold weather and snow are helpful in another way. Bears hibernate, even the big short-faced ones. I don't know about the big cats, but they probably will migrate south. Our main danger will be from wolves, because they're well adapted to the cold.

"The bison won't move as long as they can find graze, even under the snow, the deer might stay around too. They browse on branch tips, so they can find food for some time. The wolves will prey on the bison herds, picking off stragglers and weak animals. We'll have to be careful; I wouldn't want to fight a pack of wolves for a kill!"

As it happened, the plan worked, but not perfectly. Three of us went on the raid, Sandra remained to care for Lee.

Lilia had her bow, Millie had my old one, both had quivers of arrows. The weakened bow was better suited to Millie's strength now. I had my new heavy bow and stiffer arrows.

Lee had put me on the right track; he had more experience using a bow than I had. My accuracy improved after I began using the stiffer arrows as he suggested. Even with his injuries, he helped.

The two women established a rudimentary camp, away from the trail, and began planting simple pit traps. Some were in the trail, others alongside it; if they decided to avoid the path, the side traps would discourage them.

This was our basic system and we repeated it every few yards.

I would leave fairly obvious tracks until just before the traps, then walk westward along a downed log to break my trail. After circling, I would join the other two and we would head east for home.

Our modified plan left Millie waiting where I planned to leave the trail. Lilia would go straight for the temporary camp, I would lay the final trail while brushing out any sign she made. Millie and I would watch for followers until we were sure they weren't coming. If necessary, we could launch an arrow or two and force pursuers to take cover while we escaped.

Lilia would go with me, then wait at the edge of the forest while I sneaked in to do my grab-and-go.

There was a sentry.

He was sitting by a small fire, not very alert. I watched for an hour, but saw no one else. I finally decided to go ahead; it was that or abandon the raid. That wasn't an option; we had to have that axe, hopefully a saw as well, so too bad for the dozy watchman. I would sneak in as close as possible, Lilia would shoot the guard, then I would finish him before he could sound an alarm.

I closed to within five yards, then faced Lilia and nodded. She punched an arrow into the sentry's chest. As he straightened in shock, I grabbed him, my hand across his mouth. My knife, still sharp, sliced through his throat. Carotid arteries squirted and he gasped for air; I held him upright while he died, lowered him to the ground, then took his short sword before rejoining Lilia.

We waited, but nothing moved. There was no alarm, no sound. The dead sentry lay on his side; the others might think him asleep.

I left the captured sword with Lilia. She already had my bow and arrows; I hadn't needed them to finish the sentry and I wouldn't need them to get into the tool shed.

The shed was a treasure trove! I took an axe, a saw, a file, and a shovel. There were other tools, and I hated to leave them, but we might find ourselves running for our lives.

We took our time leaving, Lilia going on ahead, me establishing a trail that would be discovered but not quickly. I *wanted* the guards to follow and run into the traps.

They might find the cabin, even though it wasn't close, but let them take injuries first.

I carried the saw and shovel, Lilia carried the axe and file. There had been no alarm when we reached Millie. We walked along the downed tree, changed course to the north, then headed east.

The file was in my pack, I carried the saw in one hand, my bow in the other; Lilia carried her bow, an arrow on the string, the axe slung by a cord. Millie carried her bow and the shovel, also slung. We moved silently, Lilia leading, me bringing up the rear and erasing evidence of our passing, concentrating on stealth. There was no sound behind us.

Sooner or later, someone would discover the dead sentry. Would they even be aware of the missing tools? Were they careful in how they accounted for things? Perhaps axes and saws were periodically taken out for sharpening, so no one might immediately realize anything was missing.

They'd only know that a sentry had been killed. Had another guard done it, someone with a grudge?

We kept a low profile during the next two weeks.

I avoided using the axe near the cabin; the sound of chopping carries a long way. I still used it, but only when I was cutting farther east. For most cutting, I used the saw, staying on the north, east, or south of the cabin, away from the side closest to the mine. We couldn't conceal *all* the signs of living in the vicinity, but we did what we could.

Lee asked a question one evening when we were working by the fireplace.

"Matt, how did you know about doing all the things you did on that raid? I couldn't have planned it, nor could my father. He was a good man, knowledgeable about weapons, but no warrior. He might still be alive had he been more skilled in fighting," he mused. "But from what you have told us, it was almost like you knew what the guards would do."

I shrugged. "I didn't know. I just considered what I would do in their place.

"The guards are not well trained, we know that from the man we killed by the fire and the others we've killed. I saw no supervision. The guard was sleepy and looking into the fire destroyed his night vision. Maybe they don't expect trouble from humans. Maybe he believed that animals wouldn't approach the fire.

"Anyway, I got a lot of information from books and correspondence courses. I was a weekend warrior, a reservist in the American Army. I trained weekends and during the summer, but I never got called up for duty. I had a commission and I'd been promoted several times, but the active services decided they didn't need an over-aged reservist to take one of the few command slots better given to an officer already on active duty.

"I finally retired. I never heard a shot fired in anger, but I took a lot of courses, waiting for the call that never came.

"I worked on a number of disaster-recovery assignments though, whenever the government needed trained people fast. We deployed to the west during the great California earthquake of 2015 and we fought forest fires during the extended drought years of the early 21st Century. I learned a lot about living and working outdoors during training and while fighting fires. Things got pretty dicey after the earthquake too, so I suppose the government got their money's worth.

"I got old and sick, later on after I retired, but the Futurist grabbed me before I died.

"Some of my experience is useless, of course. I know a lot about modern weapons and how to employ them, about parachuting, commanding large formations of infantrymen, logistics, stuff like using a road net to move troops around, a lot more. But basic woodcraft skills and constructing hasty traps and barriers, how to survive if I was separated from friendly forces and then evade and escape, I learned about those things early from the courses and deployments, and I never forgot them. A couple of the courses I went through were designed to be something you never forgot!

"As to your original question, we had a saying. 'Prior planning prevents piss-poor performance'. The rule of six P's was a joke, but at the same time it wasn't. I was careless when I planned this raid; if I had been planning an operation for a *real* infantry patrol, we would have rehearsed everything.

"After the plans are made, you walk through what you intend to do and refine the plan. Then you rehearse it again, with all the changes. For a night raid, you practice executing the plan at night.

"You plan for things like the sentry, even if you're not sure there'll be one. Contingency plans, supplies, people to execute them, all of those become a part of the final operation plan.

"I didn't do those things because we didn't have more people or extra supplies anyway. So I just made careful plans. They were good enough, this time."

Chapter 20

I examined the tools; the shovel needed sharpening. I used the file sparingly; I didn't want to wear it out. I followed the filing by smoothing the edge with a rock I'd found.

The axe got the same treatment, then I started on the saw.

This one was designed more for crosscutting than cutting with the grain. Saws designed to cut parallel to the wood's grain have a more aggressive tooth shape and a wider offset. This cuts a wider channel and lessens the chance the saw blade will become stuck, a condition called binding. I tried to keep the set angle and the saw's teeth the same shape while I lightly filed the dull edges.

This saw had a wide, heavy blade and an oversized handle that resembled the one on a carpenter's handsaw. The teeth stopped before the blade's end, leaving a gap for the final two inches; for two-person use, a second handle could be added at that point. The rivet holes had already been punched through the blade.

Could I reuse the rivets I'd salvaged from the sword? For now, there was no second person so the second handle could wait.

"Tomorrow I'll start cutting a road to haul wood back. I'll remove underbrush and small trees down to ground level."

"Why a road, Matt?" Lee asked. He got a nod from Sandra. I had noticed that she usually agreed with what he said.

"I can drag a lot more weight than I can carry. I'll build a stone boat…"

That got an interruption from Millie. "Why in the world would you worry about a boat now, and one made of stone certainly won't float!"

I chuckled along with the rest. "A stone boat is a sled to move heavy weights. You select two trees, say about eight inches in diameter, then cut them about six feet long. Cut the front edge at an angle and if you do the same to the back you can drag it in either direction.

"The two trees are the only thing in contact with the ground, so that reduces friction. Fasten smaller limbs crosswise between the runners, that's what the main logs are called, and they hold the runners parallel to each other. You can attach as many cross-pieces as you want or weave ropes between the crosspieces."

I got nods as they visualized what I was talking about.

"You use the axe or camp-axe to chip and rough-shape the runners so they're easier to drag. Chop a narrow notch beneath them so you can tie the crosspieces on. That will protect the ropes. People used the sleds originally to haul heavy stones out of fields and that's how they got the name. Most of the time, they hitched horses or oxen to the stone boat, but we don't seem to have those. We'll attach two ropes instead, and that will allow two people to pull together. Wood isn't as heavy as stone, so it should work.

"We'll make our version about three feet in width. I can only carry about a hundred pounds, maybe a little more if I'm walking along an animal trail, less if I'm carrying stuff cross-country. The stone boat should be able to move ten times that weight if I make a road for it. The road only has to be wide enough so the sled won't hang up on obstacles."

We settled in for the night. Morning would come early and we had no trouble falling asleep. Lee and Sandra were a few feet apart from the rest of us.

Sandra had been providing the primary care for Lee as his wounds healed, so maybe that was why they'd separated from us. Whatever their reason, it was the way it was and there was no need for me to worry about it.

Worry came with the dawn. We were finishing our simple breakfasts when I heard a shout from outside, "Hello, in the cabin. Can you understand me?"

We scrambled for weapons and I moved to the window. There was a man across the clearing, twenty feet from the cabin door. He was armed and dressed much as the men we'd fought. I couldn't see anyone with him, but that meant nothing; they could easily be hidden in the woods.

"I can hear you. What do you want?"

"I mean you no harm. Can we talk without fighting?"

With that, he took the short sword from its scabbard and stuck it point-down in the ground by his foot. He made a production of it to make sure I saw what he'd done. He had the same sort of small shield, although his appeared to be better made, and he dropped that by the sword.

"All right. You can come up to the cabin. For now, let's just talk through the window. I won't take action unless you show you're an enemy."

How had this man found us? Had he followed our trail after the raid?

The stranger walked up to the window, stopped four feet away, and waited. I opened the window and looked at him. He spread his hands wide, then slowly turned around to show he had no weapons, then sat down on the ground.

Keeping my voice low, I passed my intentions to the others.

"Lilia watches through the window. The rest of you, bar the door after I'm out and stay alert. I'll leave my weapons inside. Maybe he's not here to attack us."

Sandra unbarred the door, Millie opened it and I stepped outside. I slowly held my arms out, turned as he'd done, then folded my legs under me and sat down.

Lilia was my hidden ace, armed with her bow and with an arrow on the string. Sandra would also have the crossbow ready by now if it should be needed. He probably also had someone in hiding.

"You the one that raided us?"

After a brief hesitation, I nodded.

"I'm one of the mine foremen. The people I work for sent me to see if I could talk to you."

I simply nodded. Mine foremen? The mine looked like something that might be in use downtime, and he'd now told me he headed a crew, so there were probably other crews.

"I'm guessing you're local."

"I am. I was here before they hired me and they also hired a few others from my tribe. The mine owners pay with metal tools and weapons, but they won't give us anything advanced.

"As for weapons, they give us what you see. We needed the metal; we'd been working on better spears, but we didn't bring them to the mine. They told us we'd get what we needed.

"I brought seven men and a woman with me to the mine. We get fed, clothed, and housed, plus they gave us a few metal tools that we sent back to the tribe. We kept the knives for our own use.

"Cindy's a cook, the rest of us work as miners. We use picks and shovels, plus sledges and drills for breaking up the rock. We also install timber shoring in the shaft. There are handcarts on tracks, but the carts never leave the mine. I don't think they want wheels here unless we make them ourselves."

"None of your people are guards?"

"No. The ones who won't work or that need a lot of supervision are the guards. They're just thugs.

"I'm not at all sorry that some of them have been removed. We've also had deserters. Have you seen them?"

I nodded. "I didn't invite them to stay around."

He nodded in return. He could figure it out. I was here, they weren't.

"So how did you find me?" Me, not us. There was no reason to let him know how many others were inside the cabin. Maybe he knew, maybe he didn't.

"I wasn't looking for you specifically. My supervisor told me to find whoever had taken the tools and try to reason with them. If it looked like talking wouldn't work, then I was to make sure they didn't raid us again."

"What if I hadn't wanted to be reasonable?"

"I didn't come alone. There are others in the woods, but so long as we can talk instead of fight, there's no reason for this to be unpleasant."

I was all for pleasant. Especially since we were otherwise trapped.

"My employers are from the future but I don't think they're the same as the ones who transplanted us here. We can't be sure, though; they don't tell us much about themselves. You weren't born here, right? You were transplanted by the people from the future?"

I nodded, and he continued. "Anyway, they aren't interested in killing unless it's necessary. That's why they've kept the malcontents and thugs employed, better to watch them at the mine than have to fight them.

"They want the ore, not a war. The guards are there to watch for animals, not people. There are big, really bad animals around. Have they bothered you?"

I just nodded.

He continued, "Anyway, I don't think the mine operators are the same as the down-timers who sent us here. They don't seem to be as advanced, even if they *can* cross dimensions. They just seem different. I don't think the ones who brought us here have any need to mine anything."

I silently agreed. Maybe there were two groups from the future involved? Could there be more than two?

"OK. I only raided you because I needed tools. We've got a wounded man, hurt in a fight with a bear, and we can't travel until he's well. We intend to leave, but now we'll have to wait until spring. I needed the tools to cut firewood."

"So if we offer to trade you what you need, hire you to do things for us, you won't keep raiding?"

"Sure. I'd rather trade than fight anyway. We've had a hard time as it is. That bear was really dangerous and there was also a cat. Maybe not a saber-tooth, but big and nasty just the same."

He looked at me with new respect. "You took on a bear and a big cat and survived? I'm impressed. There are two kinds of those, a saber-tooth and a slightly smaller one that we call a dagger-tooth. There's one guy who insists it's a scimitar-tooth, some kind of scientist before he was transplanted. But you fought two of the big animals?"

I nodded. "It got pretty iffy. I prefer they leave us alone and I'm happy to leave them alone if they do. There was a lion, too, a lioness like the ones that lived in Africa."

"Only one lion? They usually hunt in packs or prides. There are sometimes solitary males, but it's rare to see a lone female. Sometimes a young one gets chased out of the pride."

"That's probably it. This one wasn't too smart; she tried to jump a huge deer head on and the buck killed her. We call it a stag-moose. It might be related to the Irish elk."

"Big antlers, palmated and spiked?" I nodded. "We know about those. We don't tackle them unless we've got half a dozen hunters at least; they're bad news. And we don't dare hunt the big animals. There are mammoths or mastodons, maybe both because I don't know the difference, and a kind of hairy ox, antelopes and wild cattle too. These aren't your milk-cows, they're not even the longhorns that lived in Texas. The critters around here would simply kill anything from my home timeline. Tough? The word doesn't do them justice. Black bear, the one you took on?"

I shook my head. "Not even a grizzly. This one was bigger and built for running. The legs were longer and thinner than a grizzly's, I think."

He nodded. "Short-faced bear. Big, fast, and tough, but they don't usually hunt people."

"This one was injured. Even so, he was a hard fight. I wouldn't want to have to try killing one that was healthy. By the way, my name's Matt."

"I'm Robert." He pronounced it Ro-bear, which made me think he was possibly from France down-time. But maybe he came from somewhere else; European naming conventions ignore borders.

"You can keep the things you stole, and we can probably trade you some other stuff. We could use meat and there might be other things you could do. We don't have good, reliable hunters, so our food comes from downtime. The mine owners would prefer it be obtained here and so would we. There's plenty of game around, so if you can kill and butcher it we can provide labor to haul it to the mine."

"I think we can do that. I'll need to talk this over with my people. Can I approach your mine?"

"Better not. Just build a fire and make it smoke, somewhere that's not too far from the mine. I'll come out or send one of the other foremen to meet you. You've killed a fair number of the guards, and even the thugs and failures we use for keeping watch might decide they're not interested in being friendly. The best thing for everyone would be if you didn't have anything to do with them, and if you have women here, don't send them."

I nodded in understanding.

"I'll head back now. Let me know what you decide. So long as you don't raid us again, we'll consider this issue closed. I'll talk to the mine operators and they won't send any of the guards out this way. That will help avoid any future trouble." With that, he got to his feet and I did too.

Robert raised a hand in farewell and glanced at the window above us. No dummy, he knew he was being watched. He simply turned and walked back to the sword and shield he'd left near the forest. As he picked up the weapons, a second man, then a third moved out of the shadows to meet him.

They disappeared into the forest as I went back inside.

I would explain to my four companions what we'd talked about and get their opinions, but I thought it was much better for us if we could work with the mine people rather than try to fight them.

Chapter 21

Three days later I cleared a shallow fire pit near the top of a bald hill.

I soon had a fire going, then added a couple of branches with green leaves. Smoke began rising as soon as the flames reached the leaves. Lilia and I moved back into the trees to wait.

Robert showed up two hours later.

"I was down in the mine, but one of the men spotted the smoke. I came as soon as he told me. How's your injured friend?"

"He's much improved. The arm will be usable within another six weeks, maybe less. Anyway, I talked to the rest of my group. We can do your hunting if you provide people to transport the meat. We would prefer to keep the hides."

"I can send you two people. I trust them; they won't cause you problems."

"Excellent, Robert. I need to gather wood first, but I should be ready to hunt in a week."

"Sounds good, Matt. I just came off shift and I'm tired, so I'll head back now. Ten hours on, fourteen hours off, do it again tomorrow. It's a good thing I'll only be working here another two months."

"You're going back to your group? What happens to our arrangement after you leave?"

"There will someone here to replace me. I'll talk to him before I leave so he'll know to expect your signal."

"That should work, Robert. I'll need to hunt the grasslands, but I'll explore around the edges first. Later, after I know more about what to expect, I may hunt farther into the grass, away from the tree-line, but until I know what I'm facing I want trees close at hand. Do your people use bows?"

"We use spears, but not bows. We haven't figured out how to make strings that are strong enough for the kind of bows needed here. I wouldn't want to try to kill a saber-tooth or a bear with a lightweight bow. For that matter, our spears aren't as good as what you're carrying."

"Can you get more swords, or maybe even forged spear points? I can trade finished spears for labor. I can chip obsidian or flint points, all you want of those, but steel is better. I could also use men to cut and haul wood. I have an axe and a saw, but more tools would also be helpful."

"I can get swords, probably not spear points. The only weapons the mine operators will give us are the short swords. They probably wouldn't expect us to salvage the blades for spears, so I'll keep that a secret. I'll get whatever I can, maybe some broken tools; you might be able to use the metal. Whatever I can get, I'll send it with some people to help you, at least two men to haul stuff and maybe a kitchen helper to assist with skinning and butchering.

"I'll relieve you of as much work as I can if it will allow you to hunt earlier. I'll ask the mine supervisor to transfer replacements to my crew.

"I'll send you people I trust, but I can't say that about some of the others. Most of the miners are okay, but the others are guards because they're useless for anything else." With that, and a final handshake, he headed back to the mine and Lilia and I started for home.

Until Robert's people showed up, I would do as much cutting as possible. I carried the axe and crosscut saw, Lilia and Millie came along to help. Millie gave me a wistful look when I decided to take Lilia, but I needed a guard while I was working and Lilia was second only to Lee for that. Millie was learning, but I wasn't yet ready to trust my safety to her ability. Or her safety, for that matter.

She wasn't up to Lilia's standards, but she *had* made great strides. I'd made her a bow and she carried it now, but the arrows she'd made herself.

Sandra remained behind. Lee was more independent every day, but it might take another month for the arm to finish healing. Until it had, I didn't want to risk him outside without someone to keep watch. The bear had caught us by surprise; even though we hadn't seen other predators, it could happen again. For now, he did as much as he could and chafed at the restrictions.

I selected two trees suitable for blanks, a hickory and an ash. Both had straight trunks about eight inches in diameter and were knot-free as far as I could tell. The ash would need to be cut six inches shorter than the hickory because of a knot, but the rest looked good. I made short work of chopping the trunks to length, then laid them aside to dry.

There were other young trees along the path I intended to use. I cut them at an angle, extending down into the dirt. The stumps came out easily after that. Brush was removed in similar fashion.

By the end of the day, my road was finished so far as vegetation removal was concerned. I still had a couple of rocks to move, but I didn't anticipate a problem; I would change the road to detour around anything I couldn't move.

I rarely saw Lilia, but I knew she was there; I trusted her as I trusted no one else except Lee.

With Millie's help, I cut two larger trees and sawed them to length. These would be runners for the stone boat; I would build it here, chopping away as much excess wood as possible before putting the pieces together. The wood would season during use.

We picked up the trunks for the spear blanks and carried them back, washing the sweat off when we crossed the stream. It was an interesting experience; Lilia and Millie gave each other a serious looking-over. Both then watched for danger while I washed off.

If they also watched me in the water, well, that was only fair.

☾

Next morning, I sawed pairs of shallow crosscuts two inches apart in the underside of the runners. Chipping away the wood between left gaps for rawhide to tie crosspieces to the runners. I squared everything by eye, then tied the crosspieces in place. Added branches stiffened the structure and the simple sled was finished, except for a means to pull it.

The front of each runner got a towrope and Millie and I tried dragging the stone boat. It was fairly heavy, but would become lighter as the wood seasoned and the bottoms of the runners wore away. They would also become smoother with wear.

Placing a light load of firewood on the stone boat, we dragged it back to the cabin. The time used in making the stone boat was well spent; we could now spend our time cutting wood without needing to carry it back in our arms.

We turned the stone boat on end and leaned it against the cabin wall overnight. This became habit over the next few days.

Sandra fired pots and bowls that had dried in the cabin, converting them to pottery. She'd done this in the oven while we worked in the woods. She showed us the results when we came in, the larger pots already filled with drying grain. A smaller one was half-full of coarse meal she'd ground earlier. As soon as the grain was dry enough to stop it from developing mold, the pot would be covered with rawhide. Tiny air holes, punched in by an awl, kept insects out while preventing buildup of moisture.

Food supplies were low. We still had dried meat and the fresh-ground meal, but the more preserved foods we could save, the better. We would eat fresh foods as long as they were available; extras would be preserved and stored.

I found a different clearing for us to watch this time, one with more tracks and droppings than where we'd killed the stag-moose.

Lilia left to check the roost tree, hoping to bag a turkey. Millie and I took up positions in trees near the clearing's edge. We killed a camel an hour later, this one a virtual twin of the one I'd snared. We were skinning the carcass, preparing to quarter it for transport, when Lilia came up.

She had a brace of turkey hens, roughly half the size of downtime turkeys. The feathers would be as useful as the meat. Lilia explained that she'd killed one, recovered it, then heard a second chirp. She shot that one too and cleaned both body cavities, saving the livers and gizzards. She had tied the necks together to make them easy to carry.

We finished quartering the camel, tied everything on a travois, and set off for the cabin.

The women worked at preparing the meat when we got back, while I split the tree boles into quarters for spear blanks. The splits went into the corner to season as I finished.

My next task was building a support behind the cabin for cutting firewood. I used an untrimmed green tree, cutting the legs to length, then lifting the trunk into position on four of the limbs, legs for the cutting 'table'. Shorter stubs stuck out above to hold a log in place during sawing. I would need help lifting the larger logs, but I could then crosscut the log without further help.

If threatened, I could duck into the cabin, but the noise and activity would probably keep animals away. In any case, my weapons were close at hand if needed. I never went outside the cabin without them; I knew just how dangerous the predators on Darwin's World were.

I started in the morning and cut firewood all day, taking short breaks from sawing to split the lengths. There was soon a stack of firewood which would help insulate the cabin during the coming winter.

I expected it to be long and cold. This was the late Pleistocene, after all, the time when much of the land was covered by glaciers.

Three people showed up the following morning, two men and a young woman. All wore leather packs, the men carried short swords and one had a spear. The woman had no sword; instead, she had a knife that resembled mine.

"Robert has sent us to find you. We are to work until you release us. Robert says that you can make us spears and bows. Is this true?"

"Yes. I've got blanks seasoning that I'll use to make them, but I'd like to wait a few days before I start chipping the blanks to shape. Did Robert send metal for spear points?"

"He sent enough to make spears for us and arrow points after we have bows. Cindy is to get the first bow, please; she will go with us on the hunt and help with skinning and butchering. She is also good at preparing food."

They introduced themselves as René and Laszlo "Call me Laz. . . everyone does." They appeared to be my age or a bit younger. Cindy went in to meet the other women, René and Laz joined me cutting wood. It went much faster with three of us. They took over the sawing while I made a wedge for splitting the sections.

I stood the sections on end first. A swing of the axe left a gap if it didn't split the trunk outright. Placing the wedge in the gap, I used the reverse face of the axe to drive in the wedge.

Split the section into halves, split the halves into quarters, and stack the wood for drying. By noon, we had processed all the wood I'd brought in.

We ate a hasty meal, then started the next project.

The cabin wasn't large enough for eight people; we also needed space for storage. Building a second cabin was beyond my skills. For that matter, hauling the logs was likely impossible, given our time constraints.

I had made lean-tos before, this one would just be larger. I hoped to finish within two days.

We cut a dozen trees twenty feet long, then leaned them against the cabin. The three best ones would be the main beams for the shelter, the others would fill in between.

René and I cut the poles while Laz dug a trench paralleling the back wall. We set the main beams in place, the first centered over the cabin's back door, the other two at what would become the left and right ends of the lean-to. The rest of the poles we leaned rafter-like between the mains, butt ends in the trench, tips resting against the cabin's wall. The poles rested against the wall about a foot below the cabin's roof. We sawed the smaller ends off to keep the poles level with each other. The space above would give us room to put branches and leaves under the cabin's eaves; the material would compact over time so that water draining off the roof would run down the lean-to until it reached the ground. Snow would hopefully not build up either, but if it did we'd have to rake it off. The structure was strong, the smaller ends of the poles at least four inches thick.

We laid thinner poles across the slanting ones, squaring them by eye, then tying them into position. We alternated so that a heavier butt end lay between two tips. Branches with the leaves still attached were then tied on in courses, beginning close to the ground, the second course tied paralleling the first and overlapping it. This layer extended until the final course lay just beneath the cabin's eave. The lean-to's roof extended from the ground to the cabin wall, each course designed to shed rain or snow onto the one beneath.

The ends got frameworks of interlaced branches, then a thick covering of young trees tied in place, butt ends up, branches pointing down. We wove them together to create an interlaced wall of vegetation.

Bundles of long-stemmed grass filled in the gaps; people in the future would use reeds in similar fashion and call it thatch. It was livable by the end of the day and we would improve it the day after. Our beds were skin pads; they would serve until we could build something better.

We left an opening in one end for a doorway. In time we would close it with laced skins, but that would have to wait until after the hunt.

I would also need to pack the end walls with mud and let it dry; it would resist washing away unless we got a heavy rain. Wattle-and-daub was still in common use downtime. I might also add more bundles of grass as my roof compacted. I would have used all grass thatch, but cutting the grasses with knives and short swords was an exhausting, time-consuming chore.

The improvements were not solely for comfort; we also needed to protect our supplies. After the visitors left, the lean-to would become our storeroom and pantry, freeing up living space inside the cabin.

The woodcutting was put on hold after we finished the lean-to; it was time to go hunting. Six of us went out, Lilia and I with bows. We killed a turkey and two of the big palmate-antlered stag-moose, good practice for later hunts. There was enough meat for our immediate use and we sent the excess to the mine. Lilia took Millie and Cindy back with our share of the meat, I went with Laz and René to the mine. The two dragged the travois while I served as route guard.

Robert thanked us, the mine guards glowered, and we headed out. We got home just after dark.

Chapter 22

Fitting a handle to the end of the saw converted it for two-man use, much more efficient than the one-man version. I recycled a pair of the copper rivets I'd kept from the short swords. Tapping the rivet ends straight, fitting them into place, then peening them over with my axe took most of the time, but finally it was done. The saw was ready for use in the morning.

"Laz, you and René use the small axe and the saw tomorrow. I'll cut trees using the felling axe, you trim off the tops and branches. After that, saw the trunks to a size that we can haul on the stone boat.

"We'll cut timber until after noon, then load the stone boat and haul what we've cut back to the cabin. We'll do the same the day after, get the logs back, buck them to length, and split the sections.

"We don't want to overload the stone boat. I'll help when I'm available, but when it's just the two of you it's easier and faster to drag smaller loads.

"I'll work on spears as soon as I can take the time away from woodcutting. Lilia's keeping watch, but you'll still need better weapons for yourselves. After I finish your spears, I'll make Cindy's bow. As soon as I'm finished, I'll help with the woodcutting. We're going on a long hunt, as soon as the weapons are ready and the firewood's split."

🌑

We started early. Sandra and Millie brought our lunch at midday and looked willing to hang around, but they had jobs back at the cabin. I put Laz and René back to work as soon as we'd finished eating. The women got the hint and left.

Lilia ate lunch with us, then went back to providing security around the work site. The wood piled up. Late afternoon found the three of us hauling the heavily-loaded sled to the cabin.

We offloaded the stone boat, stood it on end, and went in for supper. Lilia had bagged a couple of rabbits that she'd spotted prowling around our work site, and they got added to the pot.

Sandra, Millie, and Cindy had managed to fill a pair of the fired clay containers with more coarse-ground meal. Some of it would be added to our reserve. Drying preserved the grains the same way that smoking preserved meat.

We rested for half an hour after eating; cutting wood is hard work! But we had more work than we had time, so we were soon busy again.

The saw needed a touch-up with the file so I took care of that, then ran a stone along the axe's edge. As the final step, I used a leather scrap to rub beeswax on everything. When you have a limited supply of irreplaceable tools, you take good care of them.

We began working on weapons after the tools were put away. Lilia worked on making bowstrings and sinew backing, the others knocked chips from flint cores. I would flake the chips into arrow points later, which saved me a lot of time. I could concentrate on pressure-flaking the rough pieces into points. It's slow work, making arrowheads, but once you achieve a certain level of skill it's not difficult. The more you practice, the better you get. I already had a buckskin bag of arrowheads I'd made while learning, useable if not aesthetic.

Two spear blanks were finished and stacked near the fireplace, along with the blanks for making bows. Darkness and exhaustion put an end to our labors. We three would sleep in the lean-to, Lee stayed inside with the women.

All of us needed sleep, but one man still had to keep watch; we didn't yet have a door for the lean-to. Still, we each got almost eight hours of rest that night.

I was tired next morning but I could function. Even though we worked constantly, we still needed to get accustomed to the increased labor.

The spears were almost finished by mid-afternoon, blades lashed into place, needing only final sanding and waxing. But they were usable, so I handed them to Laz and René when they came in and went back to work on the bow I'd started.

They leaned their new spears against the cabin wall next morning while they cut and stacked wood. Lilia went along as guard when they took the stone boat out to bring in another load.

Drag a load back, offload, do it again. They weren't able to haul as much as the three of us had, but a respectable stack of wood was growing, ready for use during the winter.

Cindy had learned arrow-making from Lee and Lilia. She proved to be more meticulous than either. We developed a division of labor, a kind of assembly line; I was the master knapper, she was becoming the master arrow-smith. After attaching points that I'd made, she glued and wrapped turkey-feather flights to the shafts.

Rough-shaping chips from the stone cores continued after our evening meal. I finished the two spears by sanding the shafts with river sand on damp rawhide, then waxed everything to make the spears resistant to rain.

Final work on Cindy's bow continued until we were ready for sleep. She could try it tomorrow, and if it wasn't strong enough, I would glue on sinew backing that evening.

"We should be ready to hunt day after tomorrow. Lilia and I will be the primary hunters, but everyone will bring their weapons. We'll continue hunting after we bag something, Millie and Sandra will skin and quarter the meat for transport. Laz and René will help, then haul meat to the mine as soon as the hunt's finished. Millie and Sandra will bring our portion of the meat back here.

"Cindy will stay at the cabin with Lee; until she's had a chance to practice, I'd rather have Millie and Sandra with us. The plains are just too dangerous for someone who's not ready.

"A sled or two, something like our stone boat but lighter, will make transporting meat easier. I don't expect to get more than two hundred pounds of meat from an animal and a light sled will make hauling it easier. We can't use the sled in the grasslands, the clumps are too high and they grow too close together, but it should work fine after we're back under the trees. The grass is short and there aren't many bushes after you get back in the woods.

"We'll cut out the larger bones and leave them, the head and lower legs too. The less weight we haul, the better. Ideally, we'll only transport what's edible.

"Use the hides flesh-side-up to protect the meat. Laz and René can pull a sled and still be ready to drop the straps and use their spears, Lilia will go along for added security or I'll go myself, whichever seems best."

Laz asked about using the heavy spears.

"They're tip-heavy. They don't have the right balance for throwing, but they work fine for thrusting or hacking. I'm mostly right-handed, not quite as good left-handed, so my right hand goes near the butt of the spear to provide power. I've rounded off the ends to make it easier to push with your palms, but you probably won't need to do that.

"Put your left hand a foot or so behind the blade to guide it, then use that strong right hand and your body weight to provide power. Brace it against your hip for stability, but use your legs and get your body into the thrust. Don't hold back; it's not easy to punch that spear point all the way in.

"You can use the same grip to swing the blade. A chop works if you're in too close to thrust. That's one advantage of using the steel blades, it gives you an option that flint-tipped spears don't have. Even so, the best option is usually the thrust. The object is to get the steel into the vitals, the heart, lungs, or brain. Hacking kills by blood loss, so it's unlikely to finish the critter before it kills you.

We went through a few slow exercises until they had the hang of using the spears. They could have benefited from more practice, but summer would end soon. We needed meat for ourselves as well as for trading. Lee could teach Cindy to use her new bow while we were gone.

◉

We ate an early breakfast and departed. We had packed the night before, so we lost no time getting on the trail.

I led, Laz and Sandra followed, René and Millie trailed behind Sandra. Lilia was rear guard. Lee and Cindy seemed content to remain behind.

Did the pairings mean anything? Was an attraction building between the couples behind me, maybe also between Lee and Cindy? Social rearrangements seemed to be happening; I'd assigned people to the various jobs because they seemed to work best that way, and if relationships grew because of that it wouldn't necessarily be a bad thing.

Nothing had happened around the cabin, so far as I knew. I'd wondered if Lee and Sandra had established a relationship before Cindy arrived; they'd had the privacy. Lilia had taken Sandra with her on some of her foraging trips, leaving Lee and Millie alone. Lee was young, but grown-up enough; maybe something had happened there too. Time would tell.

We camped early and ate a cold supper. Conversation was low-voiced around the small fire, kept going to keep animals from getting curious, and the conversations soon lagged. I took first shift, the rest slept. Lilia relieved me at midnight and I got some sleep too.

There was a small stream to cross tomorrow morning, so we could take turns bathing before continuing on. Human scent might be the difference between success and failure; it was worth taking a few minutes to reduce our smell.

There was indeed something going on; Lilia and I stood watch while the others washed; they acted more like couples than casual bathers sharing the same water hole!

They stood guard for us, keeping their paired arrangement while Lilia and I bathed. If our baths went faster than the other four...well, they were younger and we had more responsibility. But there had clearly been shifts in the group's social arrangements.

Full sunrise found us watching over the grassland. Sandra and Laz shared a tree, Millie and René had their own tree. I climbed one a few yards off to the left, Lilia went off to the right, giving the four least-knowledgeable people the most protection. We settled in to watch.

I saw no animals nearby. There were huge, slow-moving masses far out on the grasslands, too big, too far away, and too dangerous. Killing something that size was only the beginning; we'd still have to butcher the animal and carry as much meat as possible back across that dangerous plain. Much meat would unavoidably be left behind. The predators would be waiting too, ready to exploit any opportunity.

Mammoths? Elephant-sized ground sloths? The animals were probably at least a mile away. Whatever they were, they appeared to be grazing in small groups.

There were bison in herds of perhaps a hundred or more, huge things compared to the 'buffalo' I'd seen downtime. Closer to the trees than those distant giants, some were almost near enough to where we waited. One herd was grazing in our direction. Maybe, if they kept on coming...

But not yet. I kept watching.

The animals had the wooly coat of American bison but wide, spreading horns instead of the short, curved horns found downtime.

The herd was extremely dangerous to hunters on foot, lone animals probably less so. We could try for one if it got close enough to the trees. My new bow was a powerful weapon and I had gained considerable skill in using it. Lilia also had skill, although her bow wasn't as powerful as mine.

Meantime, even if we never got a shot at the bison, there might be camels or stags. We might also see horses or pigs, much safer quarry for hunters on foot.

The pigs were around. They had torn up the ground as they searched for roots.

I would need about twenty people to hunt sloth or mammoth. We'd need them not only to kill the beast, but to butcher it and transport the meat. Otherwise, we'd have to leave meat behind.

I didn't like the thought. I was still modern enough to believe that killing was wrong unless we intended to use the meat, all of it if possible.

Darwin's World was my world now. There were dangers, sure, but I liked this world just as it was. It might kill me, but everyone dies. And I wouldn't go quietly!

Predators had to be there in the grass, even if I hadn't seen them. The grasses moved against the wind from time to time.

I was watching the bison herd when I heard a faint murmur. It sounded like Sandra's voice. Exasperating; this was no way to act while hunting! I descended and slipped toward their tree, the voices becoming louder as I got closer. I murmured myself, scolding them in the harshest voice I could muster. Conversation and hunting simply do not mix.

I continued past the tree where Millie and René waited, but heard nothing. I went on to Lilia's tree and called her.

She joined me on the ground. She had seen the bison and had also seen the large animals in the distance; she thought they were likely mammoths.

"I don't see any way we can get at that herd. Some of us would get killed. They're big and thick-skinned enough to take a lot of killing and we can't escape because of the thick grass. There are predators too; I think we have to wait and see if they keep coming this way."

"I can confirm the predators," Lilia said. "I spotted two lionesses and there may have been more, but two of them were together for a while before they split up. I glimpsed another one that might have been a male, bigger than the two females. They're following the bison."

"If that's the case, they're heading our way. I hope they can't climb trees! But you and I need to share a tree, Lilia. If there are lions, two people are better defensively than one." She nodded agreement.

I took a minute to let the other four know about the lions. A low call up their trees took care of that. They were well hidden in the foliage. They needed to be concealed, but it would help if they also watched!

Lilia and I selected a tree between the ones occupied by the others. Climbing it with our awkward weapons wasn't easy, but we managed.

It got easier as soon as we were about ten feet up. Limbs were closer together, smaller but still strong enough. We took up positions, separated, but close enough to easily hear each other.

Lilia murmured after a short time, "Look there. That's definitely a male. See the mane?"

I looked, but saw nothing at first. The lion was barely visible, but then he moved and finally I saw the mane. It was dark brown in color while the rest of the animal was a tawny shade. The lion was creeping slowly toward the bison.

"Lilia, if the lions attack, the herd will scatter. If any of them run this way, we might be able to take one. I'd prefer a yearling bull or cow, but only if the lions stay with the rest of the herd. It's too dangerous otherwise, stealing prey from hungry lions."

We waited, but nothing happened for the next half hour. I lost sight of the lion.

The big animals had drifted toward us as they grazed. They were now no more than a hundred yards away.

Chapter 23

The bison grazed, insects buzzed, we waited. And waited. I finally decided that the lions had gone in search of easier prey.

Wrong! There was a thunderous roar from out in the grass! The old bull lumbered in that direction, head down and tail up, finally stopping between the threat and his cows and yearlings. He snorted loudly, and clumps of grass and dirt flew up as he pawed the ground.

The herd also showed signs of anxiety. They shifted around, the yearlings moving to the center, the cows surrounding them, all looking in the direction where that coughing roar had come from.

Suddenly, two tawny streaks shot from the grass across the herd from us and landed on a cow. One had claws sunk into the animal's withers while the other paw hooked the animal's nose, pulling back in an effort to break her neck. Grip secured, the lioness bit the back of the cow's neck. The other lioness had the loose skin of the cow's throat in her jaws, attempting to strangle her. The doomed cow collapsed and the others scattered.

Even as they panicked, most instinctively kept their matriarchal pairings. Most had run farther into the grass, but not all; a cow and yearling had stampeded past us, finally slowing about a mile on. The pair were no more than a hundred yards from the nearest tree, perhaps less.

"We might be able to take one by using the trees for cover. If they're in range, we'll try for the yearling. The old cow might be harder to kill and I'd rather not wind up with one of her horns stuck in my guts.

"We'll stay together. Make sure you've got everything, we won't be coming back this way."

I led off, the others followed, Lilia was rear guard again.

If the cow happened to be closer, I would take her instead of the yearling; the farther away from the trees, the more hazard, so I would take the less-desirable animal if that reduced our danger.

I stole along, watching for threats while looking ahead to where the pair of bison had stopped. Well back in the covering woods, I still looked for trees we could easily climb. The lions probably had gone after the herd and some were feeding on the dead cow, but there was no certainty. Some of them might have come this way.

We slipped through the trees, estimating distances. Finally we'd come nearly a mile, so I slipped toward the forest's edge. The two bison were still there, out in the grassland. I signaled the others to stop and eased ahead.

Lilia came up beside me and whispered, "Are they too far?"

"Well, they're too far away to shoot from here. They're two hundred yards out, maybe two hundred fifty. The lions, I just don't know. They must have gone after the rest of the herd or stopped to feed, because these two aren't acting as alert as they would if a lion was around.

"I can't believe any other predators would be around lions that are actively hunting. Even dire wolves wouldn't attack that many, not in this thick grass. We'd be taking a chance ourselves, but we need the meat and the lions aren't around.

"We could try slipping upwind through the grass until we're close enough to shoot. Put a couple of arrows into the yearling, he's the one nearest to us anyway. When the cow runs off, we put ropes on the carcass and just drag him to the forest. We can field dress him after we're back in the woods, dump the parts we don't want. What do you think? Too much of a chance?"

"No, I think you're right, the lions will be feeding farther away. It's dangerous, but going hungry this winter is dangerous too. We need the meat and skin, the help we're getting from the mine has to be paid for. I think we have to try."

I explained our plan to the rest. "Lilia and I will try for a shot. But we're going to need help after we kill the yearling. We'll wrap a pair of ropes around the head, grab on, and drag him back here; that's where René and Laz come in.

"We'll field-dress the carcass and skin it after we're back in the trees, then break the carcass down into five or six parts to make it easy to transport. Nobody takes on a lion if there's any way out of it, just climb the nearest tree if you're threatened. Any questions?"

The others looked scared or determined, depending. Lilia had her bow, quite adequate for anything short of a mammoth, Millie had my old bow, and Sandra had the crossbow. Laz and René had their heavy spears. We were as ready as it was possible to be.

Our companions split into pairs at the edge of the treeline, each pair by a tree they could climb if threatened. I took a deep breath, glanced at Lilia, and bent forward. I crept out into the grass and she followed close behind me.

I wasn't liking the feeling at all, but as Lilia had said, we needed the meat.

The yearling was grazing but the cow was nervous, raising her head every few seconds to look around and sniff the breeze.

Feeling naked, I stole around the heavy clumps of grass. The trees had always been nearby since I arrived on Darwin's World, but every step I took now put me farther away from the woods. I had to do this, but I didn't have to like it, and I didn't!

Was Lilia as nervous as I was? Was she doing what I was, hiding fear while we concentrated on the task at hand?

I estimated we'd come about a hundred yards into the grass when I slowly straightened up to have a look.

The bison were closer. Either we'd moved faster or they had drifted toward us. Ten yards, maybe a bit more, and we would be in range. We crept on.

Finally I judged we were close enough. I glanced at Lilia, nodded, and slowly stood up while bringing my bow to full draw. I glimpsed Lilia doing the same.

She probably got her arrow off a fraction before I did; my heavier bow was a lot harder to pull.

Both arrows thumped into the yearling bull. He bolted ahead twenty yards and fell. I could hear him kicking the grass, but I couldn't worry about that.

The cow hadn't run away. The yearling had been about thirty yards away when we shot, the cow about fifty, but she'd seen me stand up. Tail up and head down, she charged. I dodged to the side, crouched behind a large clump of grass to hide, and she hesitated. Maybe she'd lost me, maybe she couldn't decide whether to go after Lilia or go back to the yearling, still kicking.

The others, back at the treeline, had seen what happened; now they ran toward us. Sandra was close enough; when the cow paused she shot the cow with the crossbow. The heavy bolt struck just forward of the withers and punched in with a thump. The cow dropped.

I wasn't certain she was dead; the bolt might have gone into the spine, or it might have only stunned her. I wavered for a moment, wondering whether to use another arrow or go in with my spear; Lilia moved up and her arrow went into the side of the cow's skull from a range of only a few yards, which answered that question.

In the space of seconds we had killed two of the huge animals. I had dropped my bow and grabbed my spear before Lilia shot, more from reaction than reasoned thinking. I was still holding it as Laz and René came up. Millie followed behind them.

The lioness chose that moment to charge. So much for my analysis of what the lions would be doing!

We had taken her intended prey, but she had no intention of losing it to insignificant humans! She would swat the presumptuous things aside, then enjoy the bison as her reward.

I heard no growl, just the warning swish as she came through the grass. She made two fast jumps toward us and I had almost no time to prepare.

"LAZ! RENÉ! Spears!"

I grounded the butt of my spear, point toward the lioness; by chance I was on the left. Laz was a step behind me and René was on the right, closest to the lioness. Her third or fourth leap put her into the air on a level with my head, mouth wide, fearsome fangs exposed as the claws reached for me.

She hit three spear points, two of them braced against the ground, shafts pointed up at a shallow angle and blades tracking her as she came. René didn't have enough time to brace his spear, but he was holding it firmly and stuck the point deep into her shoulder. My own point landed low, skidding off the breastbone before plunging deep into her belly. The entire blade had gone in and part of the shaft as well, driven in by her falling weight.

Laz had managed the best placement of all. His spear was now half-buried above the spot on the breastbone I'd struck. The blade had sliced into the neck between the shoulders and gone into the body. The heart, lungs, and major arteries are in that area.

She sank back on her haunches, then tried to rise. I still had a solid grip on my spear, so I yanked it sideways, pushing in deeper and causing the blade to slice organs and vessels in the abdomen. She glared hate at me even as she died.

I gave a couple more tugs on the shaft to widen the cut in the body, then pulled as hard as I could. The spear resisted, but finally pulled free with a sucking sound. I was bloody, but the blood hadn't come from me. I was unhurt. I glanced at Laz. He too was uninjured.

Then I looked at René.

The lion had gotten one of those huge paws onto his shoulder and raked her claws down. René's vest hung in tatters and blood oozed from four deep wounds. As I watched, the blood collected into a pair of heavy streams and slid greasily down his chest.

"Lilia!" I indicated René's injury. She said nothing, but moved quickly to his side. Laz and Sandra helped him to lie back on the grass while Lilia used water from her gourd to wash out the wound. I watched the grass around us; there might be another lion.

"It's bleeding but I think that might be good. Bleeding cleans the wounds, washing out whatever was on the claws of that beast." She spared a glance for the lioness, now looking much smaller, even a bit pitiful where she lay on the ground. "I'll let it bleed a little more, then bandage him. But we need to get him back to cover and let him lie down. He's going to be hurting pretty quick, if he's not already feeling it! Wounds like this sometimes take a few minutes before they start to hurt."

René said nothing. Was he was going into shock? Shock could kill; I knew that from my previous life.

"Let's get him to the woods and let him lie down if we can find a place. We need to get him comfortable and elevate his feet. Bandaging can wait."

We left Sandra with him in the trees, her crossbow re-cocked and loaded. She supported his head and gave him a drink from her gourd as we headed back across the grass to recover the bison.

We dragged the yearling back first, a heavy load for four. We left the carcass and went back for the other one.

Sandra would open the yearling's body cavity, letting it bleed out and cool, while we went back for the cow.

She had died with her legs bent and folded under; the carcass was almost upright. It took all four of us to turn her over, meaning she was too heavy for us to drag. Millie made the long cut to open the abdomen. then removed the entrails. The cow, considerably lighter with those gone, was easier to drag, so we soon got her back to where we'd left the yearling. Lilia and I moved out a few yards to provide security while the others began skinning and quartering the carcasses.

Laz and I would need to construct a lightweight sled to transport the meat to the mine. We were probably no more than six miles away from there, so the trip shouldn't take long. The others would set up a temporary camp half a mile to the north to get away from the spilled blood and entrails.

We finished the sled and loaded it before dark. The skin of the yearling protected the quarters; laid flesh-side-up, it had been folded over the meat and secured with ties.

We left early the next morning, intending to travel as fast as possible. The night had been cool and the temperature hadn't warmed up yet, so I didn't anticipate any spoilage if we kept moving. The meat had cooled out nicely and the skin, hair side out, helped insulate the load.

We nodded goodbye to the others and headed north toward the mine.

Chapter 24

I turned over the meat to the head cook and asked to speak to Robert.

He came in, yawning; we had interrupted his sleep. I didn't like waking him, but I thought he should know about René.

"Robert, we had an accident during the hunt. A lion got in close and clawed René. He's alive, but the wounds are serious. Lilia cleaned out the scratches, made sure that none of the leather from his vest was carried into the wounds when the lioness raked him. Lilia's knowledgeable about herbs and medical care and she's the best we've got for treating injured people. She did a good job treating Lee, and he's almost fully recovered now.

"Laz and I brought a load of meat in just now and dropped it off at the kitchen. We're about to head back, but since René is one of your people I wanted you to know what happened. We'll get him back to the cabin and do the best we can for him until he's recovered."

I paused for a moment, remembering.

"We didn't see the lioness. She got in close before we knew she was anywhere around. We'd killed two of the bison; Lilia and I shot a yearling bull, then the cow charged so we shot her too. Sandra got a bolt into her spine and we had just started field dressing her when the lioness jumped us. We were lucky she didn't maul more of us. That grass. . . it's perfect cover, and she got in close before we knew she was anywhere around."

"Yeah, they're dangerous. René is more than just a tribesman, he's a member of my extended family group. I need to go back with you, if you can wait long enough for me to let my supervisors know. I may also need to let my family know. I'll want to take him with me, if you can give me a hand and if he's well enough to travel. We've got someone in our camp, our Wise Woman. She's been dealing with wounds, done it since before she was transplanted. I'll decide when I see René, but if the wound looks bad I'll need to get him back to my camp. Laz didn't get hurt?"

"Laz is fine. He's here with me, helped me unload the meat. He can help you get René home, and Lilia can go along and help guard the three of you while you travel. She could also help care for René while you're on the trail."

We got food from the kitchen while waiting for Robert to return, enough for a quick meal and sandwiches for the trail. Robert got a sandwich too, and less than an hour later, we were on our way.

I had intended to abandon the sled...they're not difficult to make... but Robert thought it might help transport René. The skin from the bison remained on the sled, so we would use it as padding to make René comfortable on the trip. The sled barely slowed our pace back to where Lilia and the others waited.

We found them by spotting their smoke column.

They were drying meat on a rack built over a smoky fire. Sandra had remained close to René, Lilia took care of the drying meat, and Millie tended the fire.

Laz parked the sled and we went to examine René. The wounds were red and swollen and René looked feverish to me. He wasn't sweating, even though his skin felt hot.

Robert wasted no time. "We'll put him on the sled. Laz, you and I will pull, Lilia comes along for guard duty if she's willing, and we get René to the Wise Woman as soon as possible."

We put the second hide on the sled as an added cushion and wrapped it loosely around René. I hoped it might cause the fever to break; if we couldn't bring the fever down, René wouldn't survive. The wound wasn't severe enough to kill him outright, but infection and fever surely would if the Wise Woman couldn't get it under control.

I gave Robert the spear I'd made for René and they set off.

Two days later they were back.

René never made it home. He died on the trail about halfway to their destination.

He was likely not aware when it happened, first becoming delirious, then unconscious. Robert wrapped the skin around him and he and Laz pushed on, Lilia keeping watch. The next time they paused for a break, René's body had already begun to stiffen.

The skin that René had been wrapped in became his shroud. They left his body on the sled beside the trail. The three had gone on to Robert's group and told his family what had happened.

Robert's tribe had never practiced burial or cremation; bodies were simply removed from the settlement and abandoned to the elements. Whenever possible, this was on platforms to keep the remains out of reach of land-based scavengers. Birds would soon dispose of the remains, so predators weren't tempted to hang around the settlement and become a nuisance. Or get accustomed to eating human flesh.

Sandra and Millie were shocked, but we had little time to grieve. Winter was coming and we still had much to do.

We had come to like René during the short time he lived with us. His passing was a quick reminder that death could come to any of us at any time. This world would weed out the unfit, but it would also eliminate the unfortunate. We had tried to be as careful as we could, and still it had not been enough. There was no safety to be found anywhere on Darwin's World.

We finished smoking the bison meat and set off for the cabin. The preserved, dehydrated meat weighed less after smoking, and the replacement sled I made worked well for transporting it.

Robert helped to pull the sled on the way back to the cabin, understandably depressed by the death of René. Sandra and Millie regained their normally cheerful disposition after a day of mourning.

We took a break at the stream when we crossed and all of us washed off, but this time it was Lilia and Robert who provided security while Laz, Millie, Sandra, and I washed up. We watched over the other two when it was their turn.

Robert got the unenviable job of explaining René's death to Cindy and Lee after we arrived. I worked with the other women, unloading the meat and hanging it in the rear of the lean-to for storage.

Cindy was the most upset; she had known René all her life. But soon she came out to help us hang up the meat.

Lilia wanted to layer it with salt for a day to see if that would help preserve it longer. It didn't seem to hurt anything, but if there was any uptake of the salt by the smoked meat I saw no sign of it. It's better to coat the meat with salt before smoke-curing it, but we hadn't taken salt with us. It would have been an added burden, and anyway we hadn't intended to kill two bison.

Once they were down, however, we had no choice other than to abandon the cow's carcass, something I was unwilling to do. Some of the meat needed to be taken to the mine, the rest was for our own use. Winter was coming; we would need all we could get.

Robert offered to take Cindy back to the mine and send two other people to the cabin, but she shook her head. "No, Robert. We have to move on. He was not the first we've lost and there will be others. I have work to do here and more responsibility than I had when I worked at the mine. I will stay."

We didn't have time to dwell on René's passing. We who lived would have to concentrate on the never-pausing tasks of survival. Food, shelter, clothing, defense, we had more than enough to do. There was little time for grieving, for reflection. Danger was always present and death happened. Quick, brutal, commonplace; death was part of living in this survival-of-the-fittest dimension on the planet I'd named Darwin's World.

Robert headed back to the mine the following morning. I offered to go with him, but he was confident he could cope with the danger. I was equally confident in my own skills, because I had survived alone for months before I found others, so I accepted his judgment.

I was concerned for Robert, but even more so for the survival of my small group. I had accepted responsibilities and was no longer as free as I'd been. So Robert went off alone, and I settled in at the cabin.

Lee was nearly recovered. He took the remaining bandages off and vigorously scratched the newly-exposed skin. There were numerous scars, and his arm had turned pale in contrast to the rest of his tanned body, but he could use the arm. It would soon regain full strength.

Lilia spent a lot of time that first day fussing over him. Reaction to the death of René?

I cautioned Lee about doing too much too fast and he agreed that it would be at least a week before he was ready to begin cutting and hauling firewood. I planned another trip to the grassland in two weeks, but this time I'd be much more cautious. Lions might well be more numerous here in Pleistocene North America than they'd been in the Africa of my time, but we would have to face the danger; that was where the big game animals were, the ones we had to kill if we were to survive.

Still, thanks to Laz and René, we had a stock of food and firewood now, even though not as much as we would need, and we had a lean-to for a storeroom.

Lee moved into the lean-to with Laz and me; we spent our nights there, protected by the roof, the end wall, and a small fire we kept burning overnight. The fire was tended by whoever kept watch over the others.

Laz and I headed out the next day with the stone boat, now somewhat lighter because the wood had dried. The runners had also worn smooth while Laz and René used it for hauling firewood.

We also had the lightweight sled that we'd used to bring the smoked bison meat back. It would work better and could carry even more after snow covered the ground. But for now, we left it leaning against the cabin wall.

We worked as fast as we could; we wouldn't have much more time. Nights were already cool. Some of the skins we'd taken had been fashioned into parkas and gloves in anticipation of need, and the women worked now on making a kind of tall moccasin with the fur side turned in.

Lilia was still my preferred hunting companion, but Lee would soon resume that role.

Millie had resumed paying attention to Lee, but now she had to contend with Cindy's efforts. I didn't know what Lee thought about it and didn't really want to know. It was their business, so long as it didn't become a problem for the rest of us. Still, he was a teenager with two females attempting to attract his attention. I doubt it ever gets better than that on Darwin's World.

As for Sandra, she also had me. Whether Lilia would also become involved with us, time would tell. I thought it likely; the two of us were together whenever she wasn't busy working with the other women.

The weather continued to change. Leaves turned from green to reds and yellows, then began to fall. Nights grew colder and days were much cooler than they had been. We enjoyed the cool days and kept warm in our furs at night.

We managed two more hunts to the grasslands as fall progressed toward winter. Thankfully, the hunts went smoothly. Even so, I avoided going very far away from the trees. I wasn't ready for a deeper grassland foray just yet, but I noticed that the tall grass had begun to dry and some of it had blown over. Many of the stems had broken off. Visibility was better and travel through the grass was easier.

Robert had not managed to get us a replacement for René, but we continued to send meat to the mine. Sooner or later, we would need help from the people there.

We killed two more camels during the following weeks, plus something I decided was a llama. We also bagged another giant stag-moose, this one with even bigger antlers, and once again it took a lot of effort to kill it.

We would avoid those in future if possible; there was easier game to be had. Not even the bison had been that dangerous as individuals. Laz told me that people in Robert's camp had killed a bull moose and he had been almost as dangerous as our stag-moose. Considering the quality of the spears they'd had at the time, I could well believe it.

The weather was windy from time to time and we had occasional rain as summer changed to fall. Still, the weather never got bad enough to prevent us working around the cabin or in the lean-to. If there was nothing else to do, I could always sit near the small fire we kept burning at the lean-to's doorway. It was a good place to work at flaking arrowheads. My skills grew with practice; my points were as useful and aesthetic as those left behind by the Folsom and Clovis peoples of Earth-prime.

Lee was fully recovered now and took an equal part with Laz and me, cutting wood, hunting and trapping, and processing meat and skins for storage.

The rear of the lean-to now sported a heavy rack I'd built; we used it to hang quarters of meat, off the ground and out of the reach of rodents. The long, cold nights and shorter cool days kept the meat from spoiling. We used fresh meat when possible and saved our prepared meat for when we couldn't hunt. I hadn't trapped around the cabin for several weeks and I now saw rabbit droppings often, as well as sign left by large birds in the vicinity.

We made another trip to the bee tree and collected more honeycomb. During our hunting trips a second bee tree was found, then a third one. We raided those too. We now had all the honey and beeswax we could store. The jugs of honey were stacked on shelves pegged to the outside of the cabin wall, protected by the lean-to roof overhead.

A huge collection of dried firewood, cut, split, and stacked, stood against the other three cabin walls. More was stacked along the side and rear of the lean-to and even more was further away from the cabin. The stacks against the walls were ready fuel if snow made it difficult to reach the rest of the wood. For now, we carried in daily loads of firewood from the more distant stacks.

I had used my makeshift froe and a billet of wood to split a number of thick planks. Crude they were, but still usable as boards. I fashioned them into a large, square box using pegs, and we brought back enough salt to fill it during our frequent trips.

Lilia took the lead in gathering nuts, berries, and edible plant products. Sandra, Millie, and Cindy took turns accompanying her during the first two weeks. They learned enough that soon Sandra and Millie went out foraging on their own, while Cindy became Lilia's usual companion during her trips. One pair worked around the cabin while the other foraged, then the pairs would switch jobs the next day.

All became adept at supplementing our food supply with turkeys and another kind of large grouse, hunting or trapping them two or three hours travel away. We also had quail and small mammals from time to time, captured in my pyramidal traps. I usually set the traps, hunted for a few hours, then collected whatever had been caught on my way back.

It was usual for the foragers to leave early and not return until late afternoon. All of us now had spears, some with metal blades, others using my flaked obsidian or flint points. We had bows and plentiful supplies of arrows, and we had all gained considerable skill in their use.

We saved the furs we collected, now much thicker as the animals also prepared for winter.

One morning I took a gourd to the spring and there was a rime of ice around the edge.

Chapter 25

The weather remained cold for four days, then a warming trend set in. I didn't expect it to last.

The freezing temperatures were followed by winds. While it was never quite strong enough to strip limbs from the trees, the cold northwest blast was quite able to finish dropping the leaves from the deciduous trees. One day, the leaves had been green but turning to red or yellow, then they began falling like colorful snow. The colors soon faded to brown and the remnants of summer piled up wherever something slowed the wind.

Trees built up a layer of dead leaves underneath, nourishment to be recycled in the spring. The piles grew higher where the winds swirled around the trunks. A few pines and cedars retained their color, green islands in a world turned mostly brown.

"Ok, folks. It's here. We do as much as we can while we can. The winter got here earlier than I hoped and it will probably stay late. There are likely glaciers north of here. It took centuries before the main icecap melted and the last low-altitude glaciers disappeared. Our weather will almost certainly be affected by all that ice and cold up north.

"The usual weather pattern in my timeline ran northwest to southeast. Storms built up off the west coast of Alaska, then traveled south before turning eastward. Here, the weather pattern will likely avoid the glaciers, because the cold air above the ice-field will sink. That sinking air builds a kind of high-pressure area, a kind of polar high, but now displaced to somewhere around the 40th parallel. That's where I think we are, south of there, about where Oklahoma is located in the time I came from.

"High pressure circulates clockwise in the northern hemisphere and creates relatively stable weather, so whatever pattern comes in is likely to stay around a while. It's the low-pressure zones that create storms, especially when they run into a cold front. It's going to be cold here, probably rainy for a while, then snowy. Moisture will flow up from the Gulf and drop around here as rain or snow. Lilia, do you have any experience of weather near here?"

"Matt, I can't tell. Some years were really cold, and sometimes we got a lot of snow even when it wasn't as cold. A couple of times we got cold and snow both. We never got used to it. My husband always stocked as much food and firewood as possible and that lasted until spring, though sometimes we had to ration supplies in late winter."

"I understand his thinking. That's why I've been pushing so hard to stockpile things. If we aren't ready, maybe even if we are, it's going to be a miserable few months. Do we have enough? I just don't know.

"We've got more than enough stored to feed us and keep us warm if we were living in the timeline we came from. Here, we don't know what normal weather is. We may get pretty cold, hungry too, before spring gets here. We can at least gather more wood when the weather permits, the trees aren't going anywhere. It's food that will be critical. We depend on animals for meat, and they may hibernate where we can't find them or migrate south to where they can graze.

"At least, if the big animals move the predators will follow them. It's a silver lining to our dark cloud."

Hunting became more difficult. Animals sought warmer places to sleep and often these were on hilltops. The cold air from even slight elevations flowed downhill and pooled in the lowlands along the streams. Hunting rapidly became an exercise in climbing.

When we did manage to bag something, the coats were much thicker than we'd seen before. Long guard hairs covered heavy growths of insulating fur next to the skin. Animals lacking that thick undercoat had already migrated south.

Fires in the fireplace were larger now, for heating the cabin although we still relied on coals for cooking. We could let the fire die back slightly and rake the coals to where we wanted them, feeding in sticks of wood as necessary. Laz, Lee, and I brought in wood every time we went outside. Not all of it was seasoned enough yet, but I knew a way around that.

When I brought in firewood, I tried to mix seasoned wood with a few billets that needed more time to dry. The partially-dried wood was stacked near the fireplace, far enough away that there was no danger of catching fire, but close enough that heat would accelerate the drying process, substituting for the lack of drying time. After a day near the fire, the wood burned well.

We hunted when we could and took several large animals. Some of the meat went to the miners, the rest came back with the skins and furs to the cabin. We got metal from broken saw-blades and ground black pepper in exchange for the meat. The metal made excellent arrow points with a little work.

I guarded our dried meat supply zealously and rationed wood whenever I could. As a result, we were frequently a little hungry when meals were finished, and often the cabin was colder than ideal for comfort, but it might keep us from starving or freezing before spring arrived so no one complained.

Whenever the weather cooperated, we brought in new-cut wood and ate fresh meat and vegetables. Snow would put an end to this soon, but I had a plan ready for the first snowfall.

"Laz, I'd like you and Lee to take a close look at the sled, the one we've been using for transporting meat. If the runners are still good, check the lashings. Reinforce them if they need it and replace anything that looks like it might fail.

"The sled can carry a lot more weight after it snows, so brace the frame with crosspieces and replace any parts that won't stand up to heavy use.

"It's cold enough now for meat to keep without being smoked or salt-cured. From now on, we'll hang the quarters of any large animals from the big oak, the one that's closest to the door. They'll be safe from scavengers if they're high enough, and we won't have problems with insects now that it's cold.

"While you're working on the sled, I've got something else I need to do. I'll head down to the stream tomorrow. There's a large patch of willows there and I'll cut a supply of branches for a project I've got in mind."

They looked doubtful; we rarely used willow as construction material. It's too flexible, as well as not being very strong. But Lee acknowledged the task I'd given them, so the next day I headed for the stream.

There was a small herd of whitetail deer drinking from the stream. I carried my bow ready nowadays as a matter of habit; I came to the edge of the slope that led down to the stream, he was there, I drew and loosed without even thinking. I snatched another arrow from my quiver and managed to get a second shot off, this time at one of the does, but I had no idea whether I had scored a hit. The rest of the band scattered.

I quickly glanced at the buck, but I needed no follow-up shot. The heavy arrow had sunk to the fletching in his side, behind the shoulder, slightly more than halfway down from the withers. Somewhere inside, the arrow had broken. Otherwise, the point would now be sticking out from the side opposite the arrow nock. But the arrow had done its job; I would recover the steel point during butchering and use it again.

I had also scored a hit on the doe, but I needed to track her down and finish the job. There was a large patch of blood on the ground, not the bright scarlet of a heart or lung shot, but a darker red indicting a hit that sliced a large vein. Oxygen content gives the blood that bright red color, and depleted blood on its way back to the heart doesn't have the same appearance. Still, the amount of spilled blood meant she probably wouldn't go far.

I considered pursuing her immediately, but realized that tracking a wounded doe was a good way to lose a dead buck to scavengers. Regretfully, I abandoned the trail, field-dressed the buck, and went back for help.

"I've got a buck down, but there's a wounded doe I need to track. If a couple of you can skin and quarter the buck, someone else can come with me and we can bring back the doe after I catch up to her."

Millie and Cindy remained at the cabin and continued working while the rest of us hurried down to the stream. The buck was still there where I'd left him; there were fewer large game animals around now, so perhaps most of the predators had also moved on.

Laz remained to help the women process the buck. They would also carry it back to the cabin and hang the quarters outside in our natural refrigerator.

Lee and I easily found the blood trail. Two sets of eyes made tracking easier. One could look around for danger or watch for the downed doe, while the other kept the blood trail in sight.

The blood loss dwindled, and finally we had nothing but tracks to follow. The doe had stopped running and had even stopped to rest once. She pushed on after that, walking now, so we kept going too.

We found her a hundred yards or so ahead. It appeared that she'd just laid down and died. We made quick work of field dressing the carcass, removing entrails and then picking up the heart and liver to take with us as we dragged the carcass back. I also found my broken arrow end and put that in my pack.

I had become quite fond of deer liver roasted over coals! Our evening meal would feature the fresh livers and hearts, plus root vegetables and a few harvested nuts. Everything else would be hung from the oak tree, waiting to be used later. Both animals were fat; I knew we'd need that fat later in the winter.

Berries and fruits had been harvested during the summer as they ripened. Some were identifiable, some not, and even the identifiable ones were almost always smaller than the ones we'd eaten in our previous timeline. But they were far tastier, and they dried nicely when sliced thin. Lilia had even found wild grapes! She dried those on a rack placed near the outdoor oven, so we had raisins! Good tasting, even if they did have seeds. They were full of vitamins too, and we would need those before spring. Scurvy and other deficiency diseases could become problems if we didn't have enough vegetables in our diet.

Sealed jars now occupied more than half of the lean-to, some stacked on the ground, others on the shelving I'd built. The women had separated the different products by storing fruits against one wall, roots against another, and the back wall had jars of honey. Smoked and salted meats hung near the top where the lean-to's roof met the cabin wall.

I continued improving the lean-to as time permitted. The shovel made it easy to pile dirt around the lower edges for insulation. The walls barely sagged under the weight, not enough to be a concern. Snow would provide even more insulation later. Meanwhile, the stacked firewood served as a windbreak.

I went back to the stream that afternoon and harvested a load of willow branches and an armload of the thin trunks. They were twice the thickness of my thumb, as tall as I could get them, and still flexible, making them ideal for my purpose.

We stuffed ourselves that evening on fresh meat and the vegetables Millie and Cindy had brought in earlier. We were clearly eating much better now than when I'd first found the cabin!

I began working with the green willow stems after we finished eating. I wiped them with a damp piece of rawhide, then slowly warmed them in the heat from the fireplace. Already flexible, they were easily formed into elongated ovals, almost a foot wide and about three feet long. I took a temporary half hitch around the trailing ends, then slowly bent the rounded front of the oval upward at a slight angle.

I repeated the process three more times but only tied and completed forming one of the ovals produced by the bending.

Taking one of the others, I laced it to the first one I'd made. The oval middle of this one I laid atop the oval of the second, but with the thicker butt end of the willow aligned with the thinner end of the first one I'd formed.

Later on, I might be able to produce the snowshoe frames from a single thicker piece of wood. For now, bending and forming the wood using only muscle power required me to double-layer the willow, laminating it to make the frames stronger.

I laced small branches of willow across the layered frames, tying them carefully to make a springy platform. I then laced smoked leather strips, netlike, across the rest of the frame and stacked the two in the corner. A leather loop would still be needed, one that I could put the toe of my boot into to attach the snowshoe to my foot.

I would make snowshoes for each of us. Given time, I'd make a spare set or two. I had plenty of flexible willow to work with now, but I wouldn't have it later in the winter. The completed snowshoe sets went into the lean-to for storage, hung against the cabin wall. I might have to build another lean-to if we continued to accumulate things that needed to be stored under cover!

We went back to woodcutting the next day. We now had to haul the wood farther; I chose to do that rather than clear-cut the wood near the cabin. All the dry wood near the cabin had already been gathered.

We had fur garments ready for use when needed. For now, we simply worked. There's an old saying that burning wood heats you two or three times, and I certainly believed it! Cutting wood kept us warm, so warm that we frequently worked wearing only the sleeveless vests that we now wore under our coats.

I tried to stay clean, washing the sweat and dirt off in the stream when possible, but it was more of a chore now than in the summer. Get in, shiver and wet down in the cold water, wipe off, get out, and shiver some more while getting dressed.

Our furs were critical, so they remained in the cabin now rather than in the lean-to where we'd stored them before. The furs would be the difference between being cold or freezing to death. Conceivably, hungry critters might get in the lean-to and chew up the skins; the cabin offered better protection.

A cold breeze was blowing from the northwest when I went out next morning. I could see angry clouds building in the distance. We cut wood as long as we could, keeping apprehensive eyes on those threatening clouds, and made one last haul back to the cabin.

"We'll cut firewood until the storm hits. Laz and Lee, you work the saw, I'll split and stack. As soon as the weather socks in, we store the tools and stand the stone boat and sled against the front wall near the door. That way, we can find them even if they're covered with snow."

A chill rain began falling later, slow and misty at first, heavier as daylight faded. Lee, Laz, and I had been sleeping in the unheated lean-to; now it was time for us to move into the cabin.

I had waited for Laz or Cindy to suggest it was time for them to go back to the mine, perhaps even back to their tribe. But nothing was said, so I didn't bring the subject up. Finally, I simply decided that Cindy and Laz were part of our group and included them in our plans. Perhaps we had become a tribe. Lee and Cindy now spent as much time in each other's company as work allowed. Sandra and I stayed close as did Lilia, even though Lilia and I had not become physically intimate. Laz had Millie, and the two seemed content. It was never discussed, it simply was.

I thought this was probably the reason why Laz and Cindy never mentioned leaving, the pairing off with Millie and Lee. Perhaps they had found opportunities to be alone while I was away from the cabin working? If they were happy, I was happy.

I thought Robert might come by, but he never did. Had he gone back to his tribe and the replacement foreman forgotten about us? We hadn't delivered meat to the mine for more than a month now.

Rain changed to snow overnight. The rain froze into a sheet of ice atop the ground and the snow lay thick over that.

We had hide curtains now to keep rain or snow out of the lean-to. The hides overlapped across the opening, one tied to the left side of the entrance, the other to the right. Laces across the overlap secured the hides together. The lean-to was nearly full anyway, so all we really needed was the access provided by the cabin's back door.

The temperature was well below freezing now; Laz, Lee, and I moved our bedding furs to where we could share the heat from the fireplace.

We each had large fur pads now, with a bison skin we'd split down the middle as top cover for two of them. Those skins were huge! The curly hair and fur made them very warm. The third pad used doubled deerskins, cured with the hair still attached and stitched together with the hair between. That was the one that Lilia and Sandra now shared with me. Shared warmth could keep us alive, and of course it would make things a lot more interesting during those long winter nights!

I had been waiting for the first snow. It was time to hunt the grasslands again, but this time, we would have the advantage.

Chapter 26

We loaded the sled with tools and supplies in preparation for the hunt; two short swords, the shovel, axe, a small pottery lamp with extra fuel, furs for sleeping and heavy coats, these were our supplies. The lamp burned a mix of beeswax and animal fat. A spare pot held enough mix to refill the lamp twice more. If that wasn't enough, we would use animal fat if we killed something. Pure beeswax would have been better, but we used it for so many other things that only a little was available.

We also packed emergency food on the sled, but hoped not to use it.

We greased the outside of our heavy boots with animal fat to make them water-resistant. Even our supply of fat was limited; we needed to include fat in our diet, and that dictated how much we could trim off the meat for other uses. Small animals such as rabbits were a welcome supplement to our meat supply, but there was so little fat on them that we sometimes coated them with bison fat before roasting.

That was one of our problems, losing fat from roasting meat as it dripped while cooking. I had tried to capture the drippings, but so far nothing had worked. Our best solution for now was to not overcook the meat and collect the drippings in a clay pot while the meat cooled.

We were packed for the hunt, but there was a gray overcast when I glanced at the sky the next morning.

"We're not going anywhere today. See those clouds to the north? Looks like we'll get more snow before nightfall. We're safe enough outdoors as long as the weather is clear, but it's too easy to get lost in a snowstorm. We'll wait it out.

"The fur coats are warm. As long as we have food and shelter from the wind, even outdoors, we'll be OK. It might be more dangerous outside if the weather gets colder, but we can worry about that when it happens. The Inuit and Lapps work outside in Arctic conditions, weather that's even colder than it gets here. If we're careful, we can too.

"Hopefully, the wind will firm up the snow. Snowshoeing is easier when the snow is packed. If it gets really firm, we may not even need the snowshoes, but we'll keep them on the sled just in case. Anyway, we need to get meat while we can, so we'll go when the weather clears. Even so, if the animals have migrated I don't think we should follow them."

We manhandled the partially-packed sled into the lean-to and laced the skins back together across the front. Snow had fallen on the slanted roof, and some had accumulated near the top where the roof leaned against the cabin. Still, the roof's steep slope discouraged heavy accumulation. I had built the lean-to's roof sturdy as well; I didn't expect it to fail.

We'd cut a number of small hickory trees during the late summer, selected to be about half the thickness of my wrist and stored in the lean-to for seasoning. From these, I made a sled that would have done a downtime kid proud. Smaller than the two-man version we'd been using, it could be towed by a single person but could still haul a lot of weight over snow.

After finishing the first sled, I turned the task of making more over to Lee and Laz.

"Five of us will go on the hunt. The other two will stay behind to protect the cabin and our supplies. We can't afford to lose either, so the task for those staying behind is to keep the cabin and supplies secure.

"The small sleds will carry our gear on the way out and as much meat as possible on the way back. Whatever we take will come back with us; we just don't have enough spare gear to abandon anything.

"Bedding will take up a lot of room. We'll need most of the room on the two-man sled to haul meat, so our gear will be divided up and stacked on the small sleds atop the rest of the meat. Carry your weapons over your clothing; everything else gets packed on a sled.

"The big sled is for Laz, Lee, and me. We're stronger, so it only makes sense for us to haul most of the load. Comments or questions?"

I got only nods. It was the obvious way to divide up the work.

The storm brought wind and more snow in the afternoon. I could still hear the wind blowing outside the cabin when we bedded down that night.

More snow was falling the next morning when I looked outside.

We used the snowshoes whenever we left the cabin that day, going outside only to answer nature's call or to bring in wood and water. The lean-to got a daily inspection, not only by looking at snow on the roof but also by going through the cabin's back door to make sure no small animal had found a way inside.

I occasionally thought how nice a flush toilet would be. Bath tub or shower, too, for that matter. Heated water! I found myself thinking of that barely-remembered bathroom every time I had to go outside. We did what needed doing as fast as possible and hustled back in before anything important got frostbit!

The small sleds were soon finished and we went back to making arrows. We could never have too many arrows, so when the weather socked in, we worked on weapons. I had become quite skilled at forming sharp edges and points, but I still ended up with a lot of broken arrowheads. I pushed the material's limits to get the points as sharp as possible. Sometimes I pushed too far. I bagged up the broken shards; sooner or later, I'd find a use for them.

I flaked points, Lee and Laz made arrows. We'd collected shafts during the summer and stored them in the lean-to. Now, as I finished arrowheads, they attached them to the shafts. Some of the arrows would be for my use, some slightly lighter ones were for Lilia and Lee; the rest were intended for everyone else. Short, heavy shafts got points, but no feathers; those were bolts for the crossbow.

Laz had a better bow now, more suitable to his increasing strength. He'd already had archery skills, so needed only stronger muscles to draw the heavier bow. The four men had spears with blades salvaged from short swords. We carried those whenever we went outside the cabin, using straps lengthened to fit comfortably over the fur coats we wore outdoors.

The storm ended three days later.

The next morning dawned clear and cold. Millie and Cindy would stay at the cabin. They had shelter, food, water, firewood, and weapons, so I expected they'd have no problems while we were gone.

"We're as ready as we're going to get. Make sure you've got your heavy sleeping furs. You'll need them...sleeping cold is uncomfortable!" I got chuckles from that; all of us knew the truth of that statement!

Lee finished breakfast first. "I'll get the big sled out of the lean-to and we can finish packing. The small sleds too, so all we'll need to do is pack last-minute gear and get going. I'm anxious! I haven't been on a hunt to the grassland yet, but my arm has fully recovered. I want to use those snowshoes to see something besides cabin walls and a woodpile!"

We planned to collect dry firewood from standing trees every afternoon. Our primary source of food would come from what we killed. Still, hunting isn't killing; luck is involved. We had enough dried meat on the sled to last for a week if necessary.

With luck, the bison would still be there, but they might have migrated on if the snow there was as deep as it was here. There might be no game at all. Time would tell. But if not, we had jerky and our own version of trail mix, made from dried fruit and nuts. We wouldn't starve.

We had tried making pemmican by mixing dried fruits with animal fat, but none of us liked the taste. Perhaps it had to do with the kinds of animals we'd taken or the way we collected the fat. Or we might not yet have acquired the taste for pemmican. If we got bison, they were likely still fat; maybe it would taste better.

Lee got the initial job of breaking trail.

Walking on the packed snow wasn't difficult. Laz and I slung our bows, picked up the lines on the big sled, and followed behind Lee; we would switch places as soon as someone tired. Meantime, we weren't trying to set speed records. Heavy exertion causes sweating, and sweating is dangerous in cold weather. It can freeze when you stop working.

I'd hoped to make the open plains by evening of the first day, but that didn't happen. The snowshoes helped, and the sleds pulled easily, but travel over snow was slower.

The sun hung low in the sky. It had now passed the highest point that it would reach during the day, but even at noon it was well to the south. This confirmed my impression that we were in the area that had been north Texas or Oklahoma in my other timeline.

I thought we were south of downtime Kansas and Nebraska, but it didn't matter. That world was not the same as this one. The animals were different, there were no natives, even the geology might be different. There was nothing we could depend on to be the same here as it had been in that other time.

The sky remained clear but I decided to err on the side of caution.

"We'll stop here for the night and move to the plains tomorrow. I intend to build a snow house, a kind of igloo like the Inuit used in our time, but I've never built one, so I'll need time to get it right.

"We'll use it tonight and close it up before we leave tomorrow morning. There's no reason it shouldn't be just the way we left it when we come back through. If we get more meat than we can haul in one trip, we'll cache the extra in snow houses and seal the openings. It's possible that we could end up with a whole string of caches, ready to be used if we ever get caught out in a storm. The meat will last until spring if we don't get a warming trend."

Using one of the short swords, I made the first snow cuts in two parallel lines that would form the entrance. Undercutting between the lines allowed me to remove blocks, forming a trench that extended beneath the snow to the frozen ground. I then laid the blocks in a circle, the beginning of the snow house's wall. I laid a second course atop the first, using blocks cut from the snow inside the circle. I left a layer of snow atop the frozen ground.

Laz and Lee cut more blocks and stacked them ready for use. The trench I'd started would be the entrance. Below the level of the surrounding snow, it would extend inside the wall of the snow house. Adding blocks along the trench sides would cause the wall to rise; when it was finished, it would curve into an arch overhead.

A circular wall would enclose the hollowed-out area I'd made by removing snow blocks. It too would connect overhead, using a keystone block to make a final seal and stabilize the arch.

I left a central 'table' of snow beneath the snow arch, and a circular shelf around the walls. The shelf was where we'd spread our sleeping furs; heat rises, so we'd be more comfortable if we slept in the warmer area above the floor. Food and weapons would be kept inside, the sleds parked alongside the covered entrance tunnel.

I rapidly stacked the blocks as Laz and Lee cut, trimming and fitting as I went. The second, slightly smaller, course of blocks went directly above the first. Beginning with the third course, the blocks were offset toward the inside of the circle, resulting in an open-topped dome that was tall enough for me to stand upright inside it.

We smoothed it and patted snow into place wherever there were gaps. I learned about shaping the blocks as I went along; they don't work as well if they're perfectly square. The last few blocks, over the low entry trench, would keep wind from entering.

We then put a tapered, circular plug into the space at the top. I had two more things to do before the job was finished.

We passed supplies in and stored them wherever there was room, leaving the central table empty. The lamp went on the table and I used a piece of steel and a flint core to strike sparks into a bit of the tinder we all carried. The steel had come from the mine, a broken tool I thought, but adequate for our needs. The flint core was left from my chipping efforts. The tinder soon showed a thin trail of smoke, then flamed as I blew on it. This served to light the twisted grass that was the lamp's wick.

I watched where the smoke collected against the roof to judge the best location for a vent. Using one of the short swords and working from the inside, I poked a hole through the roof.

The tiny blaze stabilized and the smoke rose through the hole. We would all produce carbon dioxide as we slept and the small flame would produce carbon monoxide. Those gases had to escape if we were not to suffocate.

As a last step, I built up a snow shield atop the dome to keep wind out of the vent.

"It's not dark yet, but I think we should sleep. The moon will give us light enough to travel as soon as we wake up. We can be on the grasslands by morning.

"We field-dress the carcasses as soon as we make a kill, but I don't want to stop the hunt until we've got all the meat we need. The meat will keep if we open the body cavity and let it cool.

"I'll be happy if we can bag two or three bison. We should be able to drag that much meat, even if we have to make two trips. I don't expect predators, certainly not the big cats. Even if I'm wrong, we'll see them a long way off and they'll be slowed by the snow. Same with the big bears, if they aren't already denned up; they're heavy enough that the snow crust won't support them. I think we'll have the advantage now.

"Dire wolves are a concern. I don't know if they howl like the gray wolves, but I don't see any reason why they shouldn't. If they're here, they're hunting the same animals we are. They also won't sink into the snow like the big grazers will.

"If the predators have left downed carcasses, we'll trim off the areas they've been feeding on and salvage the rest. It won't have spoiled in this cold, and there's no reason to take chances if they'll do the killing for us.

Predators go for the organs first and leave the muscle tissue for later. Let them eat the guts and heart and liver; I'll be happy to scavenge the backstraps and hindquarters!"

I woke up soon after midnight, then woke the others.

It was surprisingly warm in the snow house. I had worn my leather undergarments and boot liners when I slipped under the thick fur cover. The deerskin had been warm enough, even after I'd pushed the covering fur aside during the night.

Dried meat, dried fruit, water from our gourds; this was breakfast. Lee finished first and crawled through the tunnel. I watched; he was careful, listening for noise outside before exiting.

We dragged our bedrolls, weapons, and food behind as we crawled out. We separated long enough to take care of personal necessities, then packed our gear on the sleds. Lee went back in and brought out his bedding, adding it atop the rest.

I had brought the lamp out with me. Some of the melted fuel still coated the bottom.

We were on the trail ten minutes later.

Chapter 27

The day dawned clear and cold. A faint breeze blew from the northeast. We looked out over the broad snowfield where the grasslands had been.

Dark objects stood out against the whiteness. They were a mile away, possibly more; it was difficult to judge across that field of white.

That triggered a thought; my eyes had been gummy when I woke up this morning. Could the snow-glare have caused it?

"OK, folks. It's time to make masks."

"Masks, Matt?" This came from Lee. Lilia only nodded; she understood right away.

"I should have thought of this before; the snow is too bright. It's a near-perfect reflector and it can hurt your eyes, give you snow blindness. A bad case of it can make your eyes swell closed and you won't be able to see anything until it goes away. Even if it's just temporary, you still don't want it to happen and certainly not now."

There were a couple of doubtful looks, Laz in particular. I wondered what else he'd done besides work in a mine.

"We'll use leather. Take a strip long enough to tie around your head, then cut two slits for your eyes. Measure, fold the leather where you want to cut it, then make two slices. Check the location again and if you're happy where the slits are, cut away the leather between the slices. You want the openings to be less than half an inch wide. Tie the mask on, not too tight. Make sure you can see, then adjust the cuts if you need to.

"Give yourself time to get used to wearing the mask. It should be just tight enough to keep it in place."

We rummaged through the stuff on the sleds and managed to find enough leather. It had originally been padding for a strap, but it worked fine for the masks. Half an hour later we were ready, looking like so many bandits from a downtime movie, but my eyes could tell the difference. That was more important than how we looked.

"I can't tell yet what those animals are. They're up to their bellies in the snow, and anyway they're a long way off. We'll head that way and watch out for surprises.

"If you look at the surface ahead of us, you can tell there's a slight dip in the ground. Be careful when we get near that point. We don't want to surprise something that might mistake us for dinner. If there's nothing dangerous in that hollow, we'll use it to conceal ourselves while we work into bow range of those animals. They can see us as easy as we can see them."

"You lead off, Matt," said Laz. "You've got a better eye for terrain and Lee and Lilia can go ahead with you. I'll pull the big sled by myself, Sandra can pull the two small sleds if she ties one behind the other. We don't have very far to go anyway."

"We can try it, Laz. If it doesn't work, we'll think of something else. I've got another idea; turn your coat inside out, everyone. Wear them with the fur outside.

"They'll still be warm, but with the fur side out we'll look like animals. We won't be as likely to alarm whatever those things are unless we try to get too close, and that wouldn't be very safe anyway. There's no hurry; the idea is to get into range without spooking the herd. They'll run soon enough when we begin shooting."

We slowly snow-shoed our way onto the snowfield, five bent hairy figures with sleds following behind. I kept an eye on those far-off shapes but most of my attention was on the dip ahead of us.

I hoped the animals were bison. They're quick to detect movement, but if you can move at the speed a grazing animal would use they won't realize you're a threat until it's too late.

We approached a small ridgeline ahead. The declivity I'd seen was just beyond the ridge. I paused for a moment; there were tracks of animals in the snow, but they were like nothing I'd seen before.

Snow collects in the hollows, blows away from higher ground; whatever had left the tracks had pawed through the thin snow on the ridgeline. Even a slight reduction in snow depth attracts hungry grazers, and that's what had happened here.

We'd probably find deeper snow between this ridge and the next, but it wouldn't bother us. The snowshoes would keep us from sinking in.

The foraging animals had left their dung on the ridge. The piled droppings were smaller than expected but still resembled that of bison. We might get lucky, not have to go all the way to where those other critters grazed. I held my hand out as a signal for the others to wait. If there were feeding animals on the other side of the ridge, one man would be less visible than five.

It's really not possible to be stealthy on snowshoes, but I tried. Slowly, put a foot ahead, bring up the other foot, ease it straight down, repeat. The snowshoes squeaked against the snow as I stole up to the crest.

The snowfield dropped away in front of me. The valley was not very deep and there were scrubby plants on the sides of the ridges. Animals had been browsing on them, or maybe they'd used them as shelter for bedding down.

There was a snort of alarm and suddenly a dozen animals bolted across the valley, charging up the low ridge across from me. It took a moment for me to shuffle the snowshoes around; you can't draw a heavy bow if you don't have good footing.

I still had time to put an arrow into the one on the right as the animals raced away. I hadn't yet identified them, but they appeared to be larger than deer. To my left, Lee and Lilia had charged up the ridge and launched arrows of their own.

The arrow had gone into the back of the one I'd shot. I missed the spine but the arrow had penetrated the ribcage. It was still lodged in the body somewhere.

The animal was camel-like in appearance, but with a head perched on an upright neck. It stumbled when my arrow hit but soon regained its footing. I put my second arrow into the body, this one a perfect shot that sank to the fletching just behind the shoulder.

That was enough; the llama collapsed.

Lilia and Lee had also bagged one; it had run no more than fifty yards before falling. Fresh blood blotched the snow.

I murmured to the others, "We'll dress out those two, then pack them onto the big sled. We can try to get closer to those other animals, they're probably bison, when that's done.

"Laz, you'll stay behind with Sandra after we field dress these two. Yell if you see anything dangerous. The rest of us will try to get close enough for a shot.

"They're still too far away now, but if we can work in closer we'll have a chance. It's taking them a long time to paw through the snow, so that will work in our favor. They don't seem very alert, either; most of them are just keeping their heads down and pushing ahead through the snow. Still, there's sure to be one watching. Look for him, and when he lifts his head to look around, freeze in position. We'll move in closer when he goes back to feeding.

"Don't shoot unless you can put the arrow into a killing spot. That way, I think we can get at least one without scaring them off. If they do run, I don't want them running over one of us! Let's also make sure we've got an escape route before anyone takes a shot."

Lee snow-shoed to the ridge and stood sentry while the rest of us field-dressed the two llamas. The snow should make it easy to see anything approaching, but even so, keeping someone on watch had become a habit. I didn't want us to get careless.

Sandra helped me dress out the llama I'd shot and Laz assisted Lilia with the second.

"You're pretty fast with that bow, Matt. I didn't even notice you draw back on the string, but suddenly this fellow was down. That's a heavy bow too. I'm sure I couldn't draw it!"

"I've been using it for a while, Sandra, and I've practiced a lot. You're also going to need a heavier bow. As soon as we get back, I'll make you one. You'll be able to handle it with a little practice.

"The rule is start light, work up to heavy. You've picked up a lot of skill and strength while using the bow you've got. All that's necessary now is for you to build more strength, then learn to control it before we go hunting. Having that extra killing power might just keep the rest of us alive. I'll adjust the draw weight to your strength, easy enough to do while I'm building the bow. You can keep using your current bow until you're comfortable with the new one.

"We'll make it strong enough so that you can barely draw it at first, so expect that your back muscles are going to hurt while you're getting used to the strain. I figure two weeks, a month at most to develop the muscles, but then you'll stop using the bow you've got now and stick with the new one. Keep the old one for a spare."

She nodded, but didn't seem convinced. Well, she would still have the lighter bow if I was wrong. It would still be useful; Laz could keep the new bow for a spare if it was too much for Sandra. He had strength, just not yet the archer's strength of arm and back that comes from frequent use. Medieval English and Welsh bowmen had been required by law to shoot at least weekly, and had later used those practiced skills and strong muscles to butcher a French army.

In time, Laz would be drawing a bow as heavy as the one I was using. By spring we'd all need heavier bows, myself included. The animals we would encounter crossing the plains were too dangerous to hunt with anything less than the heaviest weapons we could use.

Practice had made us into skilled butchers and skinners; an hour later, Lilia and I snowshoed up the ridge to join Lee. Laz and Sandra remained in the hollow, stacking the meat on the large sled to balance the load.

We passed an old carcass a hundred yards past the ridge. Judging by the long hair and short, curved horns, this had been a musk ox. The killers had torn up the snow around the carcass while feeding. They had also urinated and left dung atop the snow.

I glanced at Lilia and she nodded. Lee looked at me and I murmured, "Wolves. No way of telling which kind. The main difference between them is size. Dire wolves are bigger than the gray wolves we had where I grew up, but there might not be a lot of difference between them here; the grays might be larger.

"If they leave us alone, we leave them alone. It doesn't matter which species they are. They'll be after bigger game than humans anyway, things like bison and musk ox. I doubt they could kill a mammoth or mastodon. I don't know whether they hunt the ground sloths, but they would definitely go after llamas or elk. They could bring down a stag-moose too, especially if they catch one in deep snow."

Lee looked to where the bison had been foraging before.

"The herd has moved. They're going south, and they're moving faster than they were before."

"Think they might be migrating, Lilia?"

She thought about it. "Could be. We don't know much about them except that they like the grassy plains. They might be browsing on trees and brush now, since the grass has gotten hard for them to reach. But it's still early in the season. This bunch might be stragglers from the main herd that got separated from the others, but if the snow gets deeper they'll move south too."

I nodded and moved up to where Lee was watching the herd. They would reach a small copse of trees soon, if they kept moving.

"OK, now we need to move fast. Don't run, but walk fast. The snowshoes are slow and heavy, and if you hurry you'll fall. We can hide in those trees, and they'll protect us if the bison decide to charge. If we bag one, maybe more than one, we wait for the rest of the herd to move on before we leave the trees to butcher it.

"We can bring the sleds up, load everything we can haul, then build a snow house to store what's left. The wolves *might* find the meat, but there's a chance they'll follow the herd. Anyway, it's all we can do, and a cache of frozen meat might mean the difference between hungry and starving before winter's over."

We collected the rest of our party and followed the meandering shallow valley, pausing only to examine a trail when we crossed it.

"Bear, and a big one, Matt. Not like the one that broke my arm, though. Maybe this one was a grizzly."

I nodded. The trail didn't look fresh, and if the grizzly had been looking for a place to den up I hoped he'd found one. In a deep cave, preferably, someplace we weren't going to be.

We huffed our way into the clump of trees and moved up to watch the bison approach. "See that one on the right, a little back from the others? I think he's a young one, maybe from last year's calving. He looks fat and healthy. We'll take him if the herd keeps coming."

But they didn't. The yearling moved into the herd and an older cow ended up closest to us. We communicated by gestures and agreed that she was our target.

She was twenty-five or thirty yards away when we shot. We drew at the same time, and as soon as I released my string two other arrows streaked across the short space and thumped into her side.

She sank down as her forelegs folded and then rolled over. A rear leg kicked briefly, scattering snow, then she lay still.

She had rolled onto the side where our arrows had gone into the thick wooly skin. Last gesture of revenge on her part, or a little bad luck to make up for the good luck we were having?

Half an hour later the herd had passed on, taking no notice of the dead cow as they plodded ahead. Lilia followed as I moved up to the carcass and Lee went back to help Laz and Sandra bring up the sleds.

Within a short time we had the carcass skinned and quartered. Laz and Sandra removed some of the llama meat from the big sled, making room for the quartered bison, and packed it on the smaller sleds before packing bedding furs and equipment atop the load.

We would take only parts that contained the most meat. This included the neck, the four quarters, and the upper ribs. The hump was left attached to the backbone and ribs. The skin was tied hair-side-out over the load of meat on the large sled. As for what remained, the wolves could have it.

It took the combined efforts of three of us to pull the large sled. The two women towed a smaller sled each, manageable but still heavy for one person to pull. As soon as we crossed the shallow valley, we would have to leave the small sleds while all of us pulled and pushed the big one up the slope. Two of us could then recover the small sleds and join the others.

We left the snowfield and were soon among the trees. I estimated half a day's travel before we would reach the snow house where we had stayed overnight, and probably a full day after that before we reached the cabin. We would be ready to stop by the time we got to the snow house; it had been a long day and we were already tired.

A few high clouds had drifted in from the northwest and the breeze had gotten stronger. It was nothing to worry about yet, but we would also need to keep an eye on the weather.

We were more than halfway back to the snow house when I heard a wolf howl behind us.

Maybe the wolves had stopped to feed on the offal we'd left behind.

But maybe not.

Chapter 28

The breeze picked up and high clouds were stacking up to the northwest.

I heard more wolf howls behind us. They were getting closer. We pushed the pace as hard as we dared, considering the heavily laden sleds.

We were all puffing and beginning to sweat by the time we reached the snow house. Sweating in freezing temperatures is dangerous, but so is being caught by a pack of wolves.

"We'll offload half the meat and hides here and leave them in the snow house, cave in the entrance afterward and cover the vent with snow. The meat's frozen now and doesn't have much smell, and whatever scent there is won't have had time to escape through the snow.

"If the wolves do smell it, they might stop following us, at least for a while. While they're eating those frozen quarters, we might get enough of a head start to make it back to the cabin. We'll make better time pulling lighter loads anyway."

Lee asked, "Matt, wouldn't it be better to just take cover in the snow house and defend it if they try to get in?"

"I thought of that. But hiding while the wolf is literally sniffing at your door, and when that door is made of snow, well…."

"Point taken. Is there a plan, fearless leader?"

"Sure. If all else fails, we throw you to the wolves! I heard a story once that featured that solution, throw the baby out while everyone else escapes."

"I never heard that story and I don't think I'd like being the tossee. How about we throw Laz? I'm probably pretty bony and tough, you know."

"Serious plan, if all else fails, kick off the snowshoes and climb a tree. Put arrows into as many wolves as you can until they get frightened off or we kill them all. But we'll probably lose everything on the sleds, maybe even the sleds themselves. We used leather laces, so if the wolves are hungry enough they'll chew the leather.

"We worked hard for that meat, and we need those hides too. They're not worth getting killed over, but I'm not giving them up if there's any other way.

"Meantime, there are trees and we can climb one if we have to. Just be careful, the limbs are sure to be icy and you won't like what happens if you lose your grip!"

"How about we start planning which tree we might need to climb? Always keep one in sight, and if the wolves catch up, we put the women up the tree and see if we can keep the wolves at bay. Matt, you and I have faced cats and bears, killed them too. We've got bows and a good supply of arrows, and I see no reason why we can't kill wolves. If they get in close we've got the spears, but I'd rather arrow a wolf at forty paces than spear him while he's gnawing on my leg."

"I shoot better from the ground," Lilia said. "And Sandra can use a spear to stick anything that gets through the arrows. There likely won't be many wolves. They're big animals and they'll need meat, a lot of it. That small herd of bison was moving south, and the only other thing we saw on the open grassland was the llamas, so I don't think there's enough food to feed a large pack.

"I doubt there's more than maybe three or four of them, unless they're hunting mammoths, and I think those have probably gone south too. Same as the big bison herds, they need a lot of graze. They can't forage through heavy snow."

"It's a thought, Lilia. We'll just have to wait and see. But we know what we have to do, so we'll just keep going as long as we can. If they get close, we can decide what to do then.

"There's the snow house ahead. Lee watches, the rest of us unload the big sled. Top skin goes in, two hindquarters from the bison, two hindquarters from the llamas, get it done fast. As soon as you're out, collapse the entrance tunnel. Laz, you cover the vent hole. Try to make a tight seal but don't waste time."

We left the snow house a scant ten minutes later, pushing on through the trees. I regretted leaving the meat and skins; losing the meat endangered our long-term survival, but being caught by wolves was the immediate threat.

The next howls came from only a few hundred yards behind us.

There was no chance now to reach the cabin; we would have to fight.

"OK, those two trees, the ones close together. They'll protect our back. Put the small sleds between them to fill in the gap, put the big sled in front. Park it close to the trees.

"We don't have time to build a snow fort, but maybe we can still keep the wolves out. Laz, get the shovel and dig across our front. Pile the snow behind the trench as you dig. The wolves will have to jump the ditch and snow barrier before they can get to us, or maybe they'll drop into the ditch before they try to jump the wall. Either way, they'll slow down.

"The idea is that they'll have to jump the wall, so they'll have to come high rather than attacking from high and low at the same time. Slowing them down gives us more time to shoot, and the wolves will be easier to hit.

"Get out the axe too. Stick the handle into the snow where you can grab it if you need it. It's a good close-in weapon, just be careful not to hit one of us. Same with the spears, butt ends into the snow, angle the blades forward. They'll be handy if we need them and a wolf might even stick himself if he jumps the wall.

"If you have to climb a tree, hop up on a sled and go up from there. It will be faster. Let's get the snowshoes off. Oh, and get me a forequarter from the small sled. I'll use that, too. Lee would whine if we tossed him out, Laz too, so I'll give the wolves a forequarter instead. We'll save Lee for bait next time."

The banter helped us relax. The others weren't exactly whistling while they worked, but they weren't tense either.

I got the forequarter from Lee. We had a clear line of fire out to perhaps forty yards in the direction the wolves would be coming from. I hauled the quarter in that direction, feet barely sinking into the wind-packed snow, and dumped it about twenty yards past where Laz was digging the trench. I then tied a tow-rope from the big sled to the forequarter's shank and ran the other end to a small tree, tying it firmly. The rope would keep the wolves from dragging the forequarter away, possibly out of range for our bows. I barely got back inside our improvised 'fort' before the wolves came into view.

There were five of them, dark, heavily built brutes. A huge male led, a slightly-smaller female followed close behind; the other three trailed and were smaller than the female. They might be from this year's litter, not that it made much difference; even the smallest was larger than the gray wolves I'd seen down-time.

The big male was as large as a six-months-old calf and had a head the same width. But this head had a muzzle-full of sharp teeth and a pink tongue that lolled past the teeth.

I glanced around at my companions, but there was no need to say anything; we were as ready as we were going to get. There was no time to talk, and nothing to say anyway.

I pulled half a dozen arrows from my quiver and stuck them into the snow wall ahead of me. Lee was on my right, Lilia on my left, Sandra and Laz behind us. Lee saw what I was doing and also stuck arrows into the snow wall.

The lead wolf stopped to tear at the forequarter I'd tethered as bait. The other, probably the alpha female, moved in, despite a warning growl from the leader, and grabbed at the shank end of the forequarter. The other three paused, then decided we were a safer option than trying to steal meat from the adults. They came on, bounding toward us.

Adult wolves might have been more cautious; the three young wolves saw only food ahead. They had probably never seen humans before. Run straight at the prey, grab for the throat and the heels, and if there was a problem killing, maybe one of the adults would be there to help anyway.

The tactic would have worked against a llama.

But we weren't llamas, and we had arrows ready on our bowstrings.

The lead one fell to my arrow. He ended his life, kicking up snow less than five yards in front of the two leaders where they were now biting off mouthfuls from the forequarter. The big leader paid no attention to the dying yearling and attempted to drag the meat away, but succeeded only in pulling the line taut. He kept tugging at the remnants of the forequarter, but the female abandoned it and sniffed at the dead one.

Laz shot the leader of the two remaining youngsters as they kept coming. Lilia's bow thrummed too, but I didn't see where her arrow went. I grabbed one of my ready arrows, nocked it on the string and drew it back.

It seemed as if I had all the time in the world. I put this one into the big leader. The fletching, all that was visible after the arrow struck, stood out from just behind his foreleg. It might have hit a lung, but probably I had missed the heart. The big wolf went down anyway. The female finally realized that something was wrong. Four of her pack-mates were suddenly down, dead or dying.

Lilia had scored too. Her arrow had gone into the front of the other yearling, into the base of the throat. There was a small amount of arrow showing, but most of it was buried in the wolf's chest. Judging by where the feathers stood out from the throat, Lilia's arrow might have hit the beast's heart.

Blood spatters dotted the snow around the wolves. Not much of it came from where the arrows struck, because arrows tend to seal the wound closed, but all of the downed wolves had bled from the muzzle, indicating mortal wounds.

The female snarled as my third arrow punched into her open mouth and passed through the neck behind it. She was probably no more than fifteen yards from me when I shot. I nocked another and waited, but there was no need. Only the big male was alive, dying, but still snapping and snarling while scratching at the snow.

I swapped the bow for my spear, secured my snowshoes with the heel strap, then clumped out to where he pawed at the snow. Cold predator eyes glared as I drew back and drove the spear into his chest as hard as I could. I then went around to each of the other wolves and gave them the same treatment.

Tough animal; he'd taken my arrow in the ribs and most of it had gone all the way through, but he still kept trying to get up and attack.

We were all breathing hard. "Take a minute to catch your breath. This may be all of them, but maybe not. We can wait, we're not going to find a better defensive place than this."

"Matt, should we build up the snow fence, make it higher?"

"I doubt it's worth the effort, Sandra. If there were more of them they'd have been here by now. We're just making absolutely sure.

"We'll leave the carcasses for any others that might follow us. I want the skins though; they'll be good linings for the hoods of our coats. Wolf fur doesn't ice up, at least not as quick as other furs. If there's enough left after the hoods are finished we'll use it for hats. Russians downtime made warm fur hats and we can do the same."

I looked at the forequarter I'd used for bait, but it was too mangled to salvage.

The others had each begun skinning a wolf, so I skinned the big alpha male. I wanted as much of his fur as possible, so I started with cuts around each leg just above the paws. From there, I extended the cuts up the legs, peeling back the skin as I went. A final long cut from the lower jaw to the genitals connected the leg cuts.

The big knife worked, but it wasn't the best tool for the job. When time permitted, I'd make skinning knives for us all.

I wiped the knife down with snow, then dried it by wiping it on my deerskin trousers before putting it away. It would need a touch-up with a stone when there was time.

For making the fine cuts around the wolf's head, I used a sharp flake of obsidian. Nothing short of a dedicated skinning knife would have worked as well. No dummies, our ancestors; they had known just how effective flaked tools could be. I had only rediscovered some of their ancient knowledge.

The fresh skins were lashed on top of the sleds and we left the wolf carcasses on the snow after salvaging our arrows. Other wolves, maybe something else, would find the meat, and having it available might keep the scavengers from finding the cache in the snow house.

We made the rest of the trip without incident. The meat we hung from the nearest tree, high enough that not even one of the giant bears was going to get it. We thawed out in the cabin, then sliced up a forequarter for fresh meat that night.

Laz, Lee and I left the next morning to collect the cached meat and hides. We got there without seeing anything of note, loaded everything on the big sled, and headed straight for the mine. It took us the best part of a day to get there and deliver the frozen meat to the cooks.

I had met Colin, the head cook, when I first dropped off a load of meat. I spoke to him while his helpers unloaded some of the meat from the sled.

"Is Robert still here?"

"No. He left some time ago, six weeks or maybe two months. There's a different foreman now and I'm not sure whether he wants to continue the deal that Robert made with you. I told him about it, but he didn't seem interested. He wants to concentrate on producing ore, so I doubt he'll provide help for you to transport meat."

"It's just as well. We lost René a while back, a hunting injury that went septic. Hunting's gotten harder too. Most of the game has moved south. Is there any chance I can get a cooking pot in exchange for this load?"

"I don't see why not. Stuff breaks, and when it does we end up tossing it on a pile until someone can send it back. The mine supervisor doesn't care. For now, I've got two old pots and a fry-pan if you can use them. The pots are steel, dented but usable, and the fry-pan is cast iron. If that's what you're looking for."

"Perfect. Your share of the meat's unloaded, so if you've got them ready...."

"We used the fry-pan and one of the pots this morning. I don't think they've been washed yet."

"Not a problem. We'll take them and clean them later. I want to get started before we lose any more time."

We loaded the fry-pan and cooking pots, then moved off, traveling as fast as we could tow the now much-lightened sled. The sun went down before we got back, but the moon on the snow gave enough light so we pushed on.

We hung the remaining meat in the tree, then I scrubbed out the used pot and fry-pan with snow before taking them inside the cabin.

The women were happy to see the pots. The three of us were tired from the trip, so we went to sleep as soon as possible, taking time only to stand the sled on end and bring weapons and the skins from the cache inside. I was soon nodding off, too tired to eat.

I never heard the women when they banked the fire and joined us on our beds.

Chapter 29

I woke up the next morning pleasantly spooned into Lilia's back. She had to notice my interest, but didn't make any move to escape.

Well, well! Things were looking up.

I'm sure a part of my morning interest had to do with the need to visit the outdoors, so I pulled on my deerskins while shivering in the cold cabin. I took the time to poke the banked embers in the fireplace and add a stick of firewood, then put my parka on, grabbed my weapons and headed outside.

I took care of my morning needs and scraped snow over the evidence, then just enjoyed being outside. The inside of the cabin was close and not particularly fresh-smelling, what with seven people sleeping there. Not to mention assorted skins and other stored things.

The morning was cold and silent except for the slight breeze. Dark clouds dominated the northern sky. Sensible animals were probably denned up somewhere, keeping warm. I wanted to be a sensible animal, but I had things to do.

We needed guide ropes before more snow arrived, and I had just the thing. I stretched the first rope from the cabin door straight ahead to the nearest tree, the big oak that now held some of our frozen meat. A second rope ran between two trees so that it lay across the first rope. Some of my thinner string lashed the two tightly together, not an easy task wearing gloves, but I managed.

Now, if we had to go outside after dark or during a snowstorm, the guide ropes might keep us alive. Just follow the ropes when you go out, do what you have to do, then follow the ropes back to the door.

Simple, but necessary; if I'd had more rope, I would have stretched it in a circle around the cabin to keep anyone from wandering away during low visibility. But I had used all the available rope and finding more fibers wasn't an option now. I'd get some of the ropes back as we ate the meat we'd hung in the trees, but I'd need to be careful with my supply until I could make more.

I also carried several armloads of wood from the stacks, laying it in the cleared space by the door where it would be easy to reach.

Finished, I went back inside and replaced the locking bar. This was routine now; secure the bar, place my weapons by the door where I could find them even in the dark, hang the parka on a peg, then add another stick to the always-burning blaze in the fireplace.

It was time to sample Lilia's latest creation, 'eternal soup'. She began with water fresh from the spring, dipped through a hole chopped in the ice. That went into the largest of the pots I'd traded for, then she swung the grate over the fire and set the pot into position. As soon as the water began to boil, she added tubers gathered during the summer. Whatever vegetables we had that she thought might taste good in soup, those went in too. Toss in several chunks of meat, let the whole thing begin to simmer. Add salt.

We could pour in another gourd of water periodically and restock the pot with ingredients when the level got low. After supper, when the pot was nearly empty, we'd finish off what was left, clean the pot, and start the process over with different ingredients. The meat was usually the same, but changing the vegetables she put in gave us a little variety.

The soup was heating now, but the embers had kept it warm overnight. I dipped a gourd in and tasted the concoction, really more stew than soup, but it was just what I needed after working outside in the cold.

The fireplace had a built-in rack that could be swiveled in or out, and that's where the soup pot sat. There was a loaf of bread waiting beside the fireplace on a table I'd made.

The bread had been baked weeks before, then left in the lean-to to freeze. One of the women had brought the loaf inside the day before and it was now thawed; not fresh, but still good. Slicing a thick chunk took only a few moments and I laid my slice carefully by the soup pot for toasting.

There was honey in a pot with a honey-dripper. Millie had made the honey-pot and I'd carved the honey dripper myself; the honey came from the second bee tree we'd raided. I let a small amount drip onto my warmed bread and took a bite. Wonderful!

I enjoyed my breakfast while waiting for the others to stir. The Futurists had provided three chairs, but they weren't enough so we had made seats consisting of camel-leather slings and deerskin cushions, really only bags stuffed with grass. The slings consisted of leather suspended from a simple rectangular frame, just small branches tied together. Wrap the leather around the top of the frame, stitch it to hold it in place, allow the rest of the leather to hang naturally in a curve that ended several feet or so in front. Place the cushion on the loose end of the leather, then sit down. Weight held the leather in place, and the sling gave a comfortable back support to lean against.

This was half of a downtime sling chair; in time, I'd add the other half for greater comfort.

Sitting in the comfortable 'chair' I'd made and eating food I'd acquired was very satisfying. Such pleasures had been rare downtime. Except for the cabin and the outdoor oven, we'd made most of the other things we used in our home.

The leather for the sling-chair had been tanned using brains from small animals. Smoking the tanned leather finished the job. It had been a smelly and labor-intensive task, but the end product would last for years.

I had cut the branches and lashed the frame together, while Lilia had added the back-support. The sling-chair had also been her idea, but I was happy to take advantage of it. I leaned back against the leather and enjoyed the last of my honey bread before licking my fingers clean.

I lazily thought about how I could combine another frame piece with this, stitch the loose end of the leather sling to it, then tie the two frames together in an 'X'. Downtime chairs used a metal pivot point where the two frames crossed, but we could use loops of rope instead. The chairs wouldn't need to fold up in the way that downtime chairs did.

Coffee or a cup of tea would have been a nice addition to my breakfast. Maybe my descendants would someday be able to taste those.

Someday.

Sandra had promised a treat today; I wondered what she had in mind.

A heavy gust of wind shook the shutters over the window and I was glad I'd packed grass around the shutters. The cabin wasn't airtight, but it kept the worst of the weather outside.

A small snowdrift frequently collected alongside the door but I'd decided we could live with that. Laz had cleared snow away from the door and had also shoveled a path to the woodpiles. I had stacked the firewood I'd brought up in one of the areas he'd cleared.

The spring was a short distance in front of the lean-to's door, and Lee had cleared a path between them. We chopped the ice away each morning. Water ran out from the spring in a small rivulet, but we preferred to dip directly from the small pool that formed where the spring water emerged.

It took work to keep the paths cleared, but we had little else to do. Keep the track cleared, bring in supplies from the lean-to or cut meat from the quarters hanging from the trees, carry in an armload of firewood. Then just enjoy the results of the work we'd done during the summer and fall.

Sandra's treat turned out to be a variation of the 'tea' she'd made before. She dipped boiling water from the second pot, then added a mixture of berries and grapes, collected and dried during the summer. Simple; let the whole thing brew for a moment, then mix in a bit of honey for additional sweetening. It was quick, nourishing, and hot to take the chill off.

Might I be able to ferment something like this? Not now, but perhaps next year if we could gather enough fruit? A little experimentation might provide something drinkable!

Alcohol would also be useful to clean wounds. René had fallen victim not to claws, but to the microbes that lived on those claws.

Laz and Cindy asked if the two of them could visit their families in Robert's tribe. I agreed, but had concerns about their safety. They were not quite the woods-wise experienced travelers that I was, or for that matter Lee and Lilia were.

Lee quickly volunteered to accompany them, so I gave permission. They packed and set off early the next morning.

The cabin seemed almost empty with three people gone. But there were things that still needed doing, so my days stayed busy.

As it happened, so did my nights. Lilia left me in no doubt as to what she wanted that first night, and I happily obliged her. Twice. But there would be no third time. Sometime during the night, Lilia got up and Sandra took her place. I don't know how they worked out the rotation, but as a mere male the ways of women are beyond my understanding.

Fun, though.

It was puzzling, but entertaining. Lilia might have visited 'my' sleeping pad more than Sandra or Millie, but in the dark I wasn't sure. It happened, I enjoyed the differences, and tried not to disappoint anyone.

I found myself eating more, but still I lost weight during the week the other three were gone! I wondered briefly what would happen to this new arrangement when they came back.

They returned a week later. They brought back a different kind of bread, baked by someone in Robert's tribe, and they also brought Robert himself.

"Welcome, Robert! I'm glad to see you're doing well. How are things going?"

"We're doing fine, Matt. We've made more spears like the one you gave me when René died. We also went ahead with the bow-making project. Your ideas spurred a lot of creativity.

"We made several hunting trips after I quit the mine and brought back a lot of meat. We've been eating well, and we still have a good supply to last the rest of the winter.

"Anyway, I got a lot of good ideas when I was talking to you and looking over your equipment. Our bows aren't as powerful as yours, but there are more of us so we've been very successful.

"But I didn't just come by for a visit. I have an idea I'd like to talk over with you."

"Sure. Make yourself comfortable, grab a gourd of soup, and I'll make you some of our berry tea. You'll like this!"

I got him one of the spoons I'd carved and a gourd of the soup; he was quite appreciative when he tasted it. I toasted a slab of bread and dripped honey on it while he ate. He finished the first bowl and asked if he could have a second, so I got him another bowlful, then added more meat and vegetables to the pot. I topped off the mix with water and let it cook.

Lilia was the master soup chef, but all of us helped. Soup was available whenever you wanted it, plus there would be a slice of meat, bread, and the berry tea. Honey we reserved for breakfast and sweetening the tea. We might have to cut back later, but for now we were eating well.

"So tell me what you've been thinking about, Robert."

"Are you still planning on moving?"

"I am. The cabin has given us shelter, but the problems haven't gone away. It's not defensible, and there's not really enough room for all of us. There's also no arrangement for sanitation.

"The lean-to helps, but it's not enough. And there are still the rogue guards and deserters to deal with.

"They don't like us and they're envious. We've got things they'd like to have, so at some point I expect they'll get up the nerve to raid us.

"Even if they don't care about the things we've made, they'll want the women. We can't defend ourselves effectively and also forage for food if we're expecting to be attacked. We're also too few to spare someone to watch for raiders while the rest of us work."

"I think you're right about the guards, Matt. They would have raided you already, but they lost enough men to make them cautious. Still, they'll forget the losses eventually and just start thinking about the women. The mine bosses won't be able to control them.

"I expect they'll be coming as soon as the weather improves, maybe not right away, but after the snow melts and travel is easier. They don't like to work and I expect it will be too muddy to travel for a while after snowmelt, so that gives you a little more time to prepare."

"I'm not sure if there's enough drainage to get rid of all this snow, Robert. I'm afraid of flooding when the weather warms. This area is pretty flat and that small stream is simply not big enough to carry all the meltwater away. The snow would have to melt very slowly for that stream to not overflow."

"Do you think much of the water will sink into the ground?" Robert asked.

"I doubt it. The ground is frozen, and the snow will melt before the ground thaws. There's no place for the water to go."

"Good point, Matt. But I didn't see any evidence of flooding when I worked at the mine. There's nothing to indicate there's been high water near our camp, either. We're down in a protected valley that keeps some of the wind and snow away, so it's not as deep over there. Did you see anything to make you think that floods are a problem here?"

"No, but this area may not usually get this much snow, or maybe it melts slower than I expect; I just don't know.

"But I'm worried. It's likely that the glaciers up north aren't gone yet. They might extend south for a season or two, retreat, and keep that cycle going for years. Lilia told me that some winters are hard where she lived, some are easier. We don't have enough experience to know if this is just an unusually heavy winter or if it's something to do with the glaciers.

"This snow may not all melt during the spring. For that matter, if this is an extension of the glacier ice instead of just a seasonal snowfall, the snow might not melt at all this year."

Robert nodded. "It's something to think about, Matt. We've decided to leave too. We've also got women in our tribe and we don't have enough people to take on the mine guards either. What would you say to joining together and traveling as one large group?"

"I would have to talk to the others first, Robert. Tell me more about your tribe while I think about this."

"We've got equal numbers of men and women, plus a couple of indigenous youngsters now. Your people are all from North America, but that's not the case with my tribe.

"I suspect we got transplanted by two separate groups of Futurists. Four men and six women came from central Europe somewhere, east of downtime Germany and maybe all the way into Russia. The rest of us came from France.

"We had language problems before we finally settled on English. That's the only language all of us understood. The eastern men still keep to themselves, but the women have friends in each group.

"My group still speaks French when we're among ourselves. The easterners speak Russian or Czech or something, but everyone can speak English."

"That's interesting. Lee was born here and I think Lilia might have come from Canada. She might understand French too. They had a different rhythm to their speech when they first got here, though that's mostly gone now."

"The Futurists picked people from everywhere, Matt. Some of the guards are Asian. I haven't seen Africans yet, but they're probably out there somewhere."

"Seems likely. At any rate, there are too few of us to let feelings from our previous time bother us. We've got a whole world to live in. There's room for all of us.

"I found Millie and Sandra, but Lee and Lilia found us. Their home was raided, maybe by the mine guards, maybe by someone else. Lilia's husband was killed and the two of them just managed to escape. They joined us and have been part of our group, our own little tribe, ever since. People here look to me for major decisions, but I try to bring everyone in and get opinions if there's time. What I'm saying is that my group may not be willing to just begin following your lead."

"I've got the same problem. My own French people might be willing to accept you as a leader, but I'm pretty sure the eastern Europeans won't, at least not the men.

"What I was thinking was that we could share the leadership duties. You lead the movement, I could keep the camp organized—actually, the women will organize most of it—but I could keep friction from developing."

"If those eastern Europeans can't get along, maybe it would be best if they just left, Robert. Or got left behind."

"I considered that. But the women have made friends among my French group and they wouldn't want to see their women friends booted, so I haven't decided to split the tribe yet."

"OK, you talk to your folks, Robert, I'll talk to mine. We'll need to get together later and work out the details if we decide to join together. You've met my people, so I think Lee and I may come visit if that's acceptable.

"In a couple of weeks, say, if the weather doesn't get too bad? I could meet the rest of your tribe and we could talk about what my group thinks."

"That should be time enough. I'll see you then. I need to get on the trail now if I'm going to get home before dark."

Robert departed and I was left to do a lot of thinking.

There were real advantages to having more people working together, more efficiency from dividing up the work and certainly more safety. But it would depend on what the rest of the cabin people wanted to do.

Chapter 30

I could see advantages and disadvantages to Robert's plan. The next morning I brought it up for discussion.

"Robert wants his tribe to join with ours when we move west. Think about it for a while and let me know. Robert thinks that some of his tribesmen may not like the idea.

"I won't make a decision without the rest of you agreeing, and I think it has to be unanimous. I won't drag anyone into a merger if they don't like the idea, and nobody will be left out if we merge."

"I'll bet it's Pavel's gang that Robert's talking about," Laz said. "I've never liked those people."

"Pavel wanted to be the tribe's leader and he's never understood that the rest of us didn't want him," Cindy added.

"It will probably be safer, being part of a bigger group," Lilia mentioned.

"Yes, but I've felt safe having Matt watching out for us. He's got our interests in mind and I don't want to change that. We've seen what he does; when those rapists got in, he didn't hesitate. The bear, too; he wanted us to stay back while he went out and faced the bear, taking most of the risk.

"I trust Matt, but I don't know those other people. I think they've got their own ideas. Can they be depended on if the rest of us need help?" Millie looked troubled by the idea.

"Robert suggested we share leadership of the joined group. He thinks he can work it out, but I don't know if it's possible. I was prepared to leave here, just the seven of us, until Lee got hurt. We would need to be careful, but the added risks could be dealt with.

"Now we'd end up moving around twenty-seven people. That would provide more safety, as Lilia said, but we'd also have more responsibility and the trip will likely take longer too. We'll have to cross barriers on the way, rivers and probably other things; being responsible for twenty-seven people is going to make it much harder on me, maybe the rest of you too, and Robert's tribe has children, so that increases the difficulty.

"Whether we go with them or alone, we may have to leave before the snow melts. The animals won't be back until the grass greens up. Robert said his tribe has food and I'm sure he would share that with us in return for the help we provide. We've got our own supplies, so we might not need much from them, but it would give us an option in case ours started to run low.

"The snow might not melt this year. Robert and I discussed the possibility that the glaciers might be pushing south. I had intended to leave after green-up and hunt on the way, but now I'm considering whether we shouldn't just pack everything on the sleds and be ready to leave sooner.

"If we do, I'll need to make another large sled or maybe two. Three sleds with mostly furs and food would be all we could haul. That would mean two people to pull each sled and it would leave one person available for security. We could rotate the jobs so that no one's doing more work than anyone else and everyone gets a break from pulling a sled.

"We'd be dependent on finding firewood along the way and putting up temporary shelters at night. The snow hut worked well, so as long as we have snow we'll have building material. Water, too.

"If we go soon, we'll be able to cross the rivers easier. They're probably frozen over and the ice should be thick enough to support us. Hauling the sleds will be easier too. We've built temporary shelters, we can do it again.

"The best course would be for all of us to get ready, Robert's people too. If there's no sign of melting in a couple of weeks, we leave whether they're ready or not. Every day we wait, we use up some of our stored supplies and we aren't finding replacements. Even if Robert's tribe does have more food, it won't last forever."

Lee commented, "We've been lucky so far, Matt. That bear would have been even more of a problem if he hadn't been favoring that injured paw. The cat, too; he jumped into the river and that slowed him down. We didn't have a serious problem with the wolves, but suppose there had been more of them? What if we hadn't been able to put out that foreleg for bait and build a barricade? That pack didn't reach the barricade but the next one might. We might have climbed the trees, but again we might not have had time. If they'd jumped us without warning, some of us wouldn't have survived."

"I understand, Lee. Animals are dangerous, but starvation is dangerous too and if we start without enough food, we might not make it.

"I see it this way: we've got more food now than we can pull on the sleds, but if we wait too long we'll have more sled capacity than we have food. There's a point in between where we have just enough, all we can pull on the sleds but no more than that. That's the point where we should leave. If we wait, we'll be using up supplies and not getting anywhere."

We left it at that. I would bring up the subject later, after everyone had more time to think. But I didn't see any choice, we would have to take our chances along the way. Lee's injury had kept us here, now the heavy snowfall was pushing us to leave, ready or not. Robert was no more anxious to move than I was, but he would have been talking over the options with his tribe. We could get together in a week and decide.

I looked over our food supplies and concluded that the break-even point for us would occur in about three weeks. Whether Robert had sufficient food to wait longer, time would tell. It would be something for us to discuss.

Meanwhile, something had been prowling around under the meat that we'd hung from the trees. The unknown animal had not been able to reach anything, but it had made several visits and I decided to do something before the critter figured out a way to get at our food.

I made a quick trip out to the lean-to and brought in an armful of branches. They were nicely dried now, some of them warped, but that wouldn't matter for what I had in mind. I cut them to lengths of about a yard, then chopped through the center at a sharp angle, leaving me with two sharp-ended stakes about eighteen inches long.

Lee and Laz came over to see what I was working on. "Sharpened sticks, Matt? What are you going to do with those?"

"Something's been after the meat. It's not a bear. The tracks are similar, but narrower. Still, the print's almost as long as a bear would leave. Anyway, I think it's time to do something before it figures out a way to get at our supply of meat.

"I don't see any way of rigging a deadfall with all this snow, and this critter can probably gnaw through a snare. So I'm going to build a pit trap.

"We'll dig a hole under one of the hanging quarters of meat. We can dig out small hollows in the bottom and set the stakes upright, then pour water around them. We'll hold them in place until the water freezes. The trap might not kill it; the critter might even be able to pull itself off the stakes, so I'm going to fix it so that the animal won't be able to get away. I'll use ice for glue to improve the killing ability of the stakes."

"Ice? I never thought of that," Lee said. "How are you going to do it?"

"I thought of carving barbs, but then I came up with a better idea. I'll harden the points in the fire first, then glue on small flakes of flint or obsidian that were left over from chipping arrowheads. I've got bags of those. I'll dip the end of the flake in water, then just hold it on the stake until the water freezes. I may drip a little more water on to make sure the flakes won't come off.

"Anyway, after that we plant the stakes upright in the pit and pour water around them. The ice will fix them in place so that the animal falls on the spikes when it jumps.

"I'll hang a piece of meat over the pit for bait, lower than the rest, maybe just a shank off of a quarter. Then just cover the pit with thin branches and a few grass stems, sprinkle a little snow over it, and wait.

"The animal sees the meat, jumps for it, and falls into the pit; the sharp blades on the stakes will cut organs and blood vessels, so he'll bleed out even if a vital organ isn't punctured. The blades will act like barbs too, so the critter won't be able to pull free without causing more injury. We just wait and go out every day to see what we've caught."

Lee and Laz wanted something to do, so they jumped in with enthusiasm. We shared the job of sharpening, then fire-hardened them afterward. Laz did most of the ice-gluing of blades to the stakes, while Lee and I dug the pit.

By the time we were satisfied, the pit extended down to ground level and we had chipped holes in the frozen soil to accept the stakes. As Laz finished a stake, we planted it upright. I held the stakes in place while Lee dripped water around the bases. The water froze within seconds. We lightly covered the pit as soon as we'd finished.

I cautioned the women about going out where the meat was hung. A pit trap doesn't care what it catches. But it caught nothing that first night.

We left it in place and spent the next day working around the cabin.

Lee was making a drum from a gourd. He stretched rawhide across the gourd, then laced it underneath to provide tension. He dampened the rawhide slightly and let it tighten more as it dried; his drum wouldn't win prizes for looks, but I was impressed. He amused himself by tapping with his fingers, trying to find different sound points around the drumhead.

Laz, not to be outdone, began working on a carved flute. He hadn't yet achieved a sound, but he kept trying. Perhaps he had seen one used in Robert's tribe.

I was carving too, but making utilitarian things. After making spoons, I looked for other things I could make.

My knife wasn't suitable for carving, but I'd gotten several small scraps of steel from Robert. I attached a haft to one, then shaped it by rubbing on a stone. It was more scraper than 'knife', but even so it removed thin slivers of wood.

The shavings went into a leather bag, kindling for starting fires. We had too little to waste anything.

I made a simple 'plate' by splitting a board from a billet of firewood; the flat board would give us a place to put food while we ate, and scraping a shallow channel around the edge would catch liquids before they could spill. My spoons would also allow us to eat with more refinement than simply slurping from a gourd or using our fingers.

Those fingers didn't get nearly the amount of washing they needed; it was too difficult to wash in freezing water and doing so carried the risk of frostbite. Washing in the cabin made a mess that would have to be cleaned with the poor substitutes we had for soap and towels. We did what we could, and hoped the improvements made by the Futurists would protect us from disease. There was a risk, but frostbitten fingers were risky too.

Our would-be meat robber came back two nights later. I heard a squall from outside, but decided the beast could wait until daylight. The noises died away so I went back to sleep.

The musky smell was the first thing I noticed next morning. I had never seen one before, but I finally decided we had killed a wolverine. The trap had worked, even if not as I'd intended. The wolverine had actually ripped two of the stakes from the icy pit we'd made, then dragged itself into the woods. We found it, frozen stiff, about fifty yards into the trees. Laz and I tied ropes around the carcass and dragged it back to the cabin. I wanted the fur, but there was no way we could skin the thing while it was frozen; we would have to find a way to thaw the carcass first.

Skinning the wolverine inside the cabin was not an option.

"That thing stinks! You're not bringing it in here!"

Millie was the one who spoke up, but she wasn't alone in having that opinion. Even Laz and Lee were on her side. I considered pointing out that the cabin already smelled, but decided that wouldn't help my cause. Finally, I hauled it around to the lean-to and left it until I could think of a solution.

We kept busy. The women cooked and kept the beds fairly sanitary by rotating the skins in the stacks. The top skin from the night before was pulled off and the rest of the skins then placed on top of the one that had been removed. In this way, we always slept on a skin that hadn't been in contact with our human skins for three or four days. If things got a bit smelly, well, our noses were accustomed to the stinks now.

Cindy had finally gotten around to visiting my bed. I had no idea what the others were doing, but no one seemed jealous, so I figured that Laz and Lee were being visited too. There was no way to tell in the dark cabin.

Was Lilia visiting Lee? Did ordinary taboos even hold here? Did the genetic tinkering done by the Futurists remove harmful recessive genes?

I decided I didn't want to think about it. I didn't own either of them, so what they did or didn't do was their business.

The next storm arrived with a vengeance. Wind howled outside and snow fell for two days. During the daylight hours we shoveled clear the steps and pathways around the cabin. At one point I estimated that six feet or more of snow surrounded the cabin.

I kept moving the safety lines higher as the snow got deeper. Fortunately, the weight of the new snow packed what had fallen earlier in the season, and the depth finally stabilized at four, perhaps four and a half feet of hard-packed snow.

The temperature dropped even more.

We now went out in pairs to handle sanitary chores; there would be some unusual deposits here and there come springtime! But none of us went far from the cabin door.

As the snow level rose, we raised our quarters of meat so they remained beyond the reach of scavengers. But we saw no animals; they were hibernating, had migrated south, or now lived in tunnels under the thick snow.

I worried about the lean-to, but the sturdy roof held. I decided the steep pitch transferred a considerable amount of weight to the ground.

Whatever the reason, the lean-to survived.

Millie had been keeping a makeshift 'calendar' by counting the days. We were never sure, but finally decided that winter was half over, maybe as late as February.

I looked at our supplies again and decided that we might need to conserve food; despite wanting to leave at that 'break-even' point, weather might force us to remain longer in the cabin. Even if we did find game later, the animals would be lean from winter.

I might have to dig that wolverine out from where the snow had covered it; hungry people will eat things that well-fed ones won't.

It would take time for all this snow to melt, even if a Chinook wind blew up from the south. And the water would still have to go somewhere. We had coped with the winter cold and snow, at least so far, but we might yet be flooded out of the cabin in the spring.

Starvation, attacks by predators, flood, maybe even find ourselves surrounded by icefields from advancing glaciers; on Darwin's World, the interesting times just kept coming.

Chapter 31

We continued the discussion about leaving the cabin, even did some preliminary planning of the "what if" and "then what" kind.

There was little we needed to do outside; food and firewood were close to the door and the weather was such that we went out only when driven by necessity. The deeper cold that had settled in after the last storm was dangerous; even taking care of sanitary necessities was a serious matter.

It felt strange, not having a chore that had to be done before I was finished for the day! People in the cabin opened up more about feelings and opinions and there was considerable discussion about Robert's tribe. We became positively chatty, so unlike what life had been during the summer. We'd had little opportunity for conversation, often working apart from the others, and anyway trying to hold a conversation outdoors was dangerous. By the time we returned in the evening, there was always work to be done before we were ready for bed and we were too tired to talk. Summer and fall had been our silent seasons.

Laz and Cindy now shared what they knew of Robert's tribe. Millie, Sandra and Lilia were looking forward to meeting the other women. As for me, I knew Robert, but that didn't mean a lot. I needed to know more about the other people in his tribe.

Finally, the weather warmed slightly. The temperature was still below freezing, but not the killing cold of the week before. The snow showed no signs of melting, even though we'd had sunshine for the past few days.

It was time to see Robert's tribe for myself. I took Laz along; he knew the people and could advise me while I formed my own opinions. It would also give him time to visit his extended family.

There was a crust of ice on the snow that made walking without snowshoes difficult, so we strapped them on for the trip. As a result, we no longer slipped as much, but the ice caused the leather cross-lacings to wear. We would need to rebuild the snowshoes when we got back to the cabin.

Still, walking was pleasant and it felt good to get outdoors. Cabin fever? Not yet, but we had all become restive while we'd been forced to stay inside. The increased conversation was a symptom, but I would begin to worry when people *stopped* talking to each other.

We reached Robert's camp late that afternoon, although it was more small village than camp. No two of the habitations were alike, even though they shared features.

The houses followed two general plans, a log house and a kind made with stacked sod walls; both had steep roofs of layered plant material. The roofs were similar to downtime thatch, but differed because of the local materials that builders had used.

According to Robert, the sod houses had been built by the people from southern France, while the log variety had been built by the eastern Europeans. This small village clearly represented a considerable investment in time and labor, but I could see why they'd decided to leave. If the melting snow flooded the surrounding area, the houses in this small valley would be underwater. Despite their greater numbers, Robert's people were as endangered as we were.

We gathered around a campfire that evening.

"Matt, why don't you tell us what you're thinking."

"All right. We have to move; the cabin is a trap waiting to be sprung. Any extended siege, by people or even by animals, will leave us with a choice of coming out and fighting or starving to death inside.

"We don't have enough storage room to stock food and water enough to last more than a few days. The lean-to helps, but it has limited room because of the steep slant of the roof. Space where the roof meets the ground is wasted. And even if we built another room on for storage, we would still need to enclose the spring.

"We'd also need a permanent solution for our sanitation needs and I don't like the idea of putting a privy close to the spring that provides our drinking water. It's bad enough taking care of our needs away from the cabin, but those are widespread instances and natural processes soon break down the small amount of waste. Using a privy, an outhouse, means that natural breakdown will be slowed and the wastes will be concentrated.

"It's not as if we were using local groundwater from a well; a spring is the outlet for water that flows underground until it reaches the surface. That spring's water originates in the mountains farther north, so it's pure, more than anything local. But it doesn't matter; I don't want to take chances with our water.

"There are other considerations, too. The mine employs guards that are essentially lawless. The operators can bribe them with metal weapons and food, but we can't. Sooner or later, they'll come for us again. They might catch us by surprise next time, and there will probably be more of them than we've faced so far.

"Even if they *don't* attack, we'll still have to guard against the possibility. That takes people away from work, and the work must get done.

"Meantime, we've used up a lot of local resources. There are fewer game animals and plants convenient to the cabin.

"Without agriculture, which we haven't been able to attempt, we have no choice but to keep moving. We're nomads by necessity until we find a place where we can farm and keep animals. That means ranching or herding, efficient only with domesticated livestock, so domestication also has to be developed if we're to settle in one place.

"Even after we begin doing those things, we'll have to continue hunting and gathering until the agriculture develops enough to supply our needs. Our ancestors did it, but it took them centuries. Even with our knowledge, it won't happen immediately.

"We'll have to selectively breed plants and animals both. We can make each succeeding generation better, but we can't hurry how much time a generation takes. It's also going to take manpower, and if people are experimenting they're not hunting or planting.

"All this snow bothers me, too. I don't know if it will melt this year. It's a little warmer now, but this might still be the start of a new period of glacier expansion.

"Even if it's not, when the snow melts the water has to go somewhere. The stream's not big enough, so we'll have flooding. We've got to leave before that happens.

"Downtime, the area west of here had mountains, caves and fertile river valleys. There was also a lot of game. The first humans to move in there lived on bison and mammoths until they'd established farms. We can too.

"Those early people were called Clovis and Folsom, after the towns where we found flaked points. Those places are both in New Mexico, a part of the USA. After scientists started looking, they found evidence in other locations too. There weren't many people there at the time, but it appears they lived well."

The first question came from a man named Philippe. "I know little of this land. What direction should we go?"

"There are huge rivers farther east, and if the glaciers are advancing again they won't leave us much room to the north. The ocean, an arm of it called the Gulf, was south of here, so that leaves west.

"I think we should go south or southwest until we're clear of the snow, then turn more to the west. We'll have to adjust our direction of travel occasionally, but that's the way my group will be going, southwest. That keeps us away from the mine and its guards as well as taking us to where the climate is warmer. Downtime, the area was dryer than here but not desert. The American southwest didn't become that dry until long after the ice age."

"How long do we have?" A man named Anton asked this one.

"Less than a month, probably about two weeks if the weather cooperates. I originally intended to go shortly after green-up. The snow will be gone, the grass will sprout, and the animals will come back. But we can't wait that long or we'll run out of food. We'll also be flooded out; the grass won't begin to grow until the snow is gone and the water has very little natural drainage.

"Something else to consider, there are big rivers west of here. We can cross a lot easier on the ice, before the spring thaw. By heading southwest, we'll soon be into the area where the bison are wintering, so we'll find game. Instead of waiting for grazing animals to come to us, we'll be going toward them. They can't go too far south, too many rivers and canyons, and then there's the Gulf.

"We for sure won't be able to cross the rivers after the snow melts. Flooded rivers are incredibly difficult and dangerous, so we'd be stuck, running out of food while waiting for the water to go down."

"How do you plan on transporting our stuff? And what about shelter? And predators?"

"We'll be using sleds at first. They can carry a lot of weight over snow. My group intends to pull three two-person sleds, enough for everything we have to take, and that will leave one of us free to scout ahead. Knowing what's in front can save a lot of work, and we won't need to backtrack as far if we find a swamp or a river ahead. I can show you how to build sleds of your own; they're not difficult.

"As for shelter, there are several things we can do. We lived in a snow house, and if you've got furs and a small lamp it's not bad at all. We've also built a large lean-to. There's no reason we can't put two of them together, facing each other, and have a shelter big enough for eight or ten people. I imagine you have ideas too.

"As for predators, they'll be where the game is. We need the game, so we'll just have to face them. I doubt they'll range ahead of the game herds, so until the herds come north, we should be safe enough. After that, we've got our bows and spears. I can't see them attacking a large group. One or two isolated people, yes; eight or ten, no."

"Who will lead this trek? Do you intend to be our captain?" This came from a stocky man near the back of the group. I glanced at Robert and he mouthed "Pavel".

I showed no sign that I'd ever heard of him.

"I took care of myself until I met the others. They now ask me what I think before we act, but I don't give orders. I expect to be responsible for my group of seven, but as to whether we join into one group, my people aren't ready to accept a different person in overall charge.

"Robert suggested he captain the camp, I take charge during movement. But whatever is decided, we can probably travel together, help each other.

"It may be that after we get to know each other better, we might become more unified. But not yet. Instead, I suggest that my group go first and the rest of you follow. We're experienced hunters and we've faced dangerous animals and survived. If we encounter game animals, we have a better chance of adding them to the food supply than you would.

"You are free to travel and hunt as you wish, of course, but these are the ideas that we've discussed among ourselves. It may be that you will decide to go your own way. If so, we will help as much as we can while you get ready to travel, but when the time seems right we'll head out on our own.

"If the majority of you want to do what I've outlined, I'll do my best to keep you alive as long as we're together. I have a considerable amount of experience, some of it from my original timeline, some that I acquired here. But you can select your own captain, let him or her be responsible for your group and we'll be responsible for ourselves."

I wasn't going to demand that Robert's group follow me. No indeed; I wasn't running for office. You can't lead unless people want to follow. On the trail...well, I would take care of my own people first and hope for the best.

"I came to talk to Robert and meet the rest of you. If you decide you want our help, send someone to our camp within a week. We'll be getting ready to move by then and we may leave any time after that.

"If I have time, I'll help you as much as possible. Lee will help too, he's a good hunter and he's familiar with weapons. I think he might teach you a few things about using your bows and spears. Some of you have them now, but we've had them longer."

Most of the people were thoughtful, very few of them looking at Pavel. If anything, they were avoiding his gaze. He didn't look happy, but then he hadn't looked happy before.

Pavel finally spoke up. "What do you know about living in the cold? Can you predict when the snow will fall? Do you know the best way to prevent the cold from killing? My people have been doing this for centuries. The cold has often been our friend and our defense!"

I looked at him for a moment. "We're alive. We've been eating bison and stag-moose that we killed. We've been attacked by big cats, a giant bear, a pack of dire wolves, and dangerous people. We've kept ourselves alive, warm, and well fed.

"We're alive. Hunting the animals I mentioned is dangerous, but we did it and now we're using their skins and furs to keep warm. We've survived cold, predators, and hunting out on the open plains. The men who attacked us are dead and we're using their sword blades for spear points.

"But the choice is yours. I've told you what we intend to do, so now you have to decide for yourselves."

He looked like he wanted to argue, but I'd said all I intended to say. He could stay or go, and if he wanted to lead that was fine with me. But my group wouldn't follow him.

Laz got a chance to visit briefly with his family and renew acquaintances, but I cut the visit short. The division in the tribe, in fact the whole Pavel situation, bothered me.

We left early the next morning. Robert could let me know what his tribe decided.

Getting back to the cabin was coming home. Dark and smelly as it was, it had become a familiar place, comfortable, even though we couldn't stay. We got in late and were soon asleep.

The next morning I explained what had happened.

"We might have problems with Pavel and his group. The rest of Robert's tribe may also decide to go their own way. I told them we didn't intend a full merge but would travel with them as our own group. If they wanted to work with us I would welcome that, but if they choose not to, so be it."

"I think that's best, Matt," Lilia said. "Let's see how we do after we've been on the trail for a few days. I won't trust them like I do the rest of you until I've seen how they stand up to danger. Lee and I are glad we joined the three of you, and Laz and Cindy are now part of us too. Whatever we are, family or tribe, we've provided for ourselves. We still can."

She was quite emphatic as she spoke. Lee was nodding. In moments, I saw that the others were also nodding, and smiling.

So we had an agreement among ourselves. It was up to Robert now.

Chapter 32

Philippe and Marc, two men from Robert's tribe, showed up five days later. It was already late, so we got them warmed and fed before preparing places in the cabin for them to sleep. The rest of us moved our beds closer together to make room.

"You're trek captain, Matt. Robert wanted us to ask how soon you could begin working with our people to get us ready to leave?"

"We can start tomorrow, Marc. Laz, I'd like you and Lee to go back with Marc and Philippe. I'll follow as soon as I've taken care of a few things here.

"Philippe, how many of the tribe have weapons? Have they used them much? What about small children? How many are there, and how small are they? We'll have to take their needs into account. Are there any pregnant women who might deliver within two or three months?"

They gave me the information I wanted. What Philippe didn't know, Marc did.

It would have been nice if everyone in the tribe already had good weapons, but no; weapons were hit-or-miss and some of the 'spears' still had wooden points. As for having used the weapons, few had ever done that. Most of the men at least *had* spears, although only a few of their weapons had steel blades. Some had bows and a few arrows, but they were barely trained and the bows were not nearly powerful enough.

Robert's assessment of his tribe's capabilities had been optimistic.

I had my heavy bow, Lee and Laz also had stronger ones than before, but that was it. I realized I couldn't depend on Robert's people. Lee or I would need to see what they could do and I'd have to spend time making weapons and teaching others to make their own. Laz could help, but he lacked our experience.

Heavier bows should be our first priority, and we would have to allow Robert's men as much time to practice as we could. Heavier bows need heavier arrows, so someone would have to make those too. There wouldn't be a lot of time to get them equipped and trained.

The men's lighter bows could at least be passed on to the women.

There were no women in late pregnancy, but there were three young children. The trip would be hard on them, no question. They would have to ride on the sleds during the day and someone would have to be responsible for them at night. Were they even eating solid food yet? Lilia could check on that.

No one mentioned what hoops Robert had jumped through before his tribe agreed to make me trek captain; neither Philippe nor Marc knew what the final vote had been. Pavel had likely not approved. He was going to be trouble, sooner or later. He had a small group of followers, which made the problem worse.

It meant that I would be leading a loose collection of three separate groups. Whether they would cooperate with each other remained to be seen. People would get used to working together after a couple of weeks, but no question, I was going to be a busy man for a while!

I decided that Pavel and as many of his followers as possible would be split up to work with the scout and security crew. If we kept them busy and separated from the others, they might be too tired to cause trouble at night. Maybe even give Pavel some responsibility and see how he handled it? Meantime, putting him out front might just solve the problem, particularly after we began to encounter large animals.

I gave Lee a private briefing before he left. "Watch out for Pavel. Put him to work if you can, but don't take any back talk. If you have problems, get Robert involved if you have time. But you're in charge of security, so you're third in command. I'll back whatever decisions you make.

"Have him make arrows or build sleds until we're ready to leave. I intend to put him to doing something every day to keep him out of mischief, and I'll try to keep him separated from his little gang whenever possible. Make the easterners mix with the others and work for the tribe."

Lee nodded, understanding.

The next morning Laz and Lee loaded a small sled, then joined Marc and Philippe when they left for Robert's village.

I salvaged as many of the remaining steel blades as I could, then attached them to the last of my spear blanks. Some were bent and dented, scheduled for return to wherever the mine operators had gotten them. Robert had included them in the scrap steel he'd given me.

I was able to straighten them and pound out the worst of the dents, and sharpening with the file and a stone did much to repair the remaining damage.

The rest of the steel went into a pack, along with spear blades I'd chipped from obsidian. Maybe Robert's group had someone who could make spears; there wouldn't be enough steel blades, but obsidian was much better than the wooden points Philippe and Marc had described.

Lilia and I took the trail the following morning. Sandra, Millie, and Cindy remained behind, preparing our own gear for travel.

Following the trail to Robert's village was routine now, and traveling gave me time to think. I kept mulling over what needed to be accomplished before we left. We would take essentials, but nothing else; we couldn't afford the extra weight.

Considering the lack of weapons skills among Robert's people, their camping abilities probably wouldn't be much better. Everyone would have to do routine tasks and be willing to pitch in to help others get them done. We would also have to share things.

Personal weapons, clothing, and emergency kits, those belonged to the individual. Cook-pots were a tribal asset, as was food. A sled could hold bedding for four adults, and there would doubtless be some switching among groups as people adjusted to the hardships of the trip. Even my own small group might undergo some rearranging.

We needed to teach the tribe, but what? They had some skills, even if those were adapted to village life, which would be a help. We could build on those.

So, then; how to defend themselves, and when, because escape might be the only acceptable option someday. How to set up a camp and get tired people fed and bedded down; how to break down the camp and pack everything on the sleds, and after we abandoned the sleds, divide the goods into pack and travois loads. What to look for in assessing whether a sled needed an immediate fix, or whether repairs could wait until evening; for that matter, how to do repairs without wasting scarce supplies.

Add to that, how to build a shelter out of snow. Shelters later on would be made from whatever we could find, but we could figure that out when we got there. How to put up a protective barrier or organize a defense while the rest escaped; these would be essential trail skills. We couldn't foresee every problem, but the more knowledge the tribespeople had, the better our chance of survival.

We were nomads. Living in the cabin and in Robert's village had masked that fact, but we'd have realized it soon even without the problem caused by raiding mine guards or a harsh winter.

We had no old or sick people to care for; if we had any advantage at all, that was it. As for the incompetent, lazy, or uncooperative, we might have to deal with that issue at some point.

Knowledge? We had a lot, much of it useless. It would help us build a civilization someday, after we quit moving, but in terms of practical knowledge the nomads of my own timeline knew much more than we did.

For now, Lee, Lilia, and I would teach. If Robert or his people had the skills we needed, they could help too. What the tribespeople didn't learn before we left, they'd learn on the trail. That would at the least be time consuming. So our first few days after departure would progress slowly.

In addition to better weapons, Robert's people needed emergency kits. Maybe they had some of the things we'd need.

Otzi the Ice Man, found frozen into a Swiss glacier before my time, had such a packet. Our versions contained a small flint knife, a length of cord, a piece of steel, and tinder. The knives had short blades and rawhide wrapping for the handle, with thicker flint exposed at the end. The rawhide could be unwrapped and used to make a snare, the steel could produce sparks by striking the exposed flint of the knife's hilt, the cord could be used for another snare or fishing line.

Every adult on the trek would need such a kit, all enclosed in a pouch that would be tied to their belt. Anyone might find themselves separated from the group; the emergency packets could help the lost one stay alive long enough to rejoin us. We probably wouldn't be able to search for lost trekkers, although a final decision would depend on circumstances at the time; the well-being of the many took priority over the few.

Deerskin pouches were easy to sew, but steel strikers and flint might not be available. Flint-and-steel was efficient, such that it had survived until the development of matches; this was the method we seven used for starting fires now. Flint and steel was a huge improvement over friction-starting!

There was so much to do before we were prepared to leave, so very much; for now, push on, think, plan, watch for danger.

We arrived at Robert's village late that afternoon and were soon fed and bedded down.

Next morning, I helped Lee select the first group of people for trail security and scouting. He would be in overall charge, so he made the final decision about assignments. In time, we would rotate security so that everyone shared the risks.

Pavel was making arrows, so that kept him out of trouble. Philippe and Marc, not part of his eastern group, worked with him.

His small group of allies would be among those assigned as scouts and security when we moved out. Lee was now training them for the task.

Robert had charge of spear making and deciding who would get the steel-bladed ones. The longer blades required considerable strength to use; we didn't have enough to give them to people who couldn't use them.

Metal blades killed quicker, because they caused massive blood loss inside the body cavity. Obsidian edges were sharper than metal, but making the edges *too* sharp also left them fragile. Spear points could be no more than three or four inches long before they became too fragile, so while the obsidian and flint spears were useful, they lacked the penetrating ability of the steel-bladed spears.

Arrowheads took more shock in use, so obsidian arrow points were shorter than spearheads. Still, the points were lethal, and they didn't require the strength that the heavy steel-bladed spears did.

Robert and I conferred every night after work. On the second night, I brought up the topic of tools.

"Robert, can you get more steel tools from the mine?"

"Matt, I don't know. The stuff I gave you before was all I could get my hands on, and then only because the mine operators didn't know I had taken it.

"I had friends among the cooks and miners, some of the guards too. They'll remember me, but I don't know whether they can get more than what I already took. I can't ask the supervisors; they weren't happy about the stuff they knew about, and they'd have been really mad if they'd learned about the other stuff. I only told them the first time and they went along in order to get the meat, but after that I figured it would be easier to get forgiveness than permission.

"Their policy was to not pass anything to people that might give us too much of an advantage. They were like the transplanters, they wanted people here to survive as best they could. They were willing to risk introducing limited numbers of steel swords to get whatever they're taking from the mine, but they didn't like it. As for giving us things like bows or spears, forget it."

"Are you willing to try? We need as many pots as we can get and anything at all that's made of steel. We can make our own metal things someday, but it's going to take a long time. Life will be much easier if we have metal to start with."

Robert finally agreed, and we decided he would wait for two weeks before making the attempt. The mine operators would have little time to react, and if they waited more than a day before trying to recover the items, we'd be on our way. The farther away we got, the less likely we were to have problems with them.

So Robert would lead a small party to the mine and be ready to bring back whatever he could get. If he found it necessary to steal, he would try to clean out the shelter where the tools were stored. If the guards proved more alert this time, Robert's group would deal with them.

None of us had any love for the guards; the expedition wasn't intended to be a raid, but if guards got killed, we wouldn't weep.

As for Robert, he needed to show that he could lead fighters. That meant he had to be a proven warrior himself. He had supervised miners, but could he and his people be competent killers? Was Robert a war leader as well as an organizer?

Sending him off in charge of the group left me uneasy, but the trip would test him as well as the others. It had to be done, and better now than later; Laz would go along and observe. I would judge Robert by how successful the trip was and what Laz said after they returned.

Laz, onetime member of Robert's tribe, was now thoroughly integrated into our group of seven. He had used the weapons I'd made, he'd stood with us at the little snow fort. I could depend on him.

As for Robert, I liked him, but that wasn't the same as relying on him. I had to be certain. Only then could I feel safe when he was in charge. If I couldn't depend on him, we would have to leave the group.

If Robert was questionable, Pavel was on the bubble. I would use him if possible, keep him out of trouble as long as I could, and if that failed, expel him or kill him. If it came to a choice between Pavel and the group, I wouldn't hesitate.

Hopefully, I would never have to make that choice about Robert.

I spent the next morning teaching how to make a fire atop the snow.

We cut two small trees to make a base, sawed them into sections about three feet long, then laid them on the snow. Adding a second layer at right angles across the first made the platform thicker; the fire would burn longer before the base burned through. The two layers together were about eight inches thick when finished, and we had left narrow gaps for air circulation.

The fire was then built in the usual way atop this platform. It would burn through eventually, but people would have plenty of time to get warm and cook the evening meal before that happened.

Breakfast and lunch would be eaten cold, the noon stop would be as brief as possible. Building the platform and laying a fire took time, so we would only do that when we stopped for the night.

Laz, Lee, and I took separate groups out and showed them how to build a snow house and a hasty snow fort. The groups practiced, leaving space between the shelters for the sleds. Lilia moved from group to group, showing the women how to set up the snow houses for sleeping. She and Robert would still have to check them nightly to make sure that vents had been left open and had windbreaks. Some of the couples spent the night in the snow houses, while others went back to the village.

The tribe's hunters had ranged out on overnight trips during the summer, but the rest had become too dependent on them. Some, the potters and the Wise Woman for example, worked only within the village. That would have to change now; everyone would need to be self-reliant on the trail because there might be a time when no help was available.

Philippe and Marc had been two of the tribe's hunters; now that the lack of game kept people from hunting, they attached themselves to Lee, or to me if Lee wasn't available. Two of the others who'd been hunters were members of Pavel's group. They might have the skills, but I couldn't trust them.

The women from the cabin had spent considerable time outside. Since few men were available, our women had hunted and fought just as we men had. Not so the tribe's women; they had to be taught, and even then it would take time for the lessons to become reflex.

The teaching went both ways, however. Pavel and one of his men described dwellings two stories high with an entrance on the second floor, used when the snow was deep.

I thought about it and realized that a two-story house with a second-floor entrance and a ladder for access made a lot of sense. Building one would be labor intensive, but we now had people to help, and pulling up the ladder at night made such houses secure.

Something like the Pueblos of the southwestern Americans? Adobe bricks are fireproof and could be made large for thick walls. Making and stacking the bricks made building the walls easy, and adding an overhang by extending the floor beams and adding floors would protect the lower walls from weather damage.

Use the bottom level for storage, perhaps? Maybe put in a door for bringing in supplies, but with a sturdy crossbar that could resist even a bear? If we built houses such as this around a courtyard and included a sanitary system, we would have a fort that could withstand a siege! Especially so, if there was a water source such as a small stream inside the courtyard.

After we stocked it with food, of course. Take up farming, raise animals for food and work?

Such simple forts had grown into imposing castles during the Middle Ages. They had been the ultimate refuge until gunpowder ended feudalism.

Daydreams could wait. We would need to get there, find someplace for a secure settlement, then begin the long process of building a civilization.

For all of us to survive the trek would require a miracle.

Chapter 33

Robert and his small crew left two weeks later. We'd talked about his plans the afternoon before.

"Matt, I want to get there fairly late. I'll approach whoever's working in the kitchen, see what I can talk them out of. I'll want steel pots and utensils if possible, but I'll take anything they'll give us.

"If there are any maintenance workers around, I'll talk to them too. I know most of them from when I supervised a crew, they may have tools they can let me have. It's only been a couple of months since I left the mine, so I'm sure they'll remember me.

"The supervisors stay in the main building, so I doubt they'll see me. If they wanted us, they sent a messenger and we went to their office. I'll try to avoid the messengers just in case, but it shouldn't be a problem. Late afternoon is just before shift change, there'll be people moving around, so we won't stand out.

"I'll be on the trail before daybreak. The moon on the snow is bright enough that we can travel at night, and since I'm taking six men, there will be enough of us to handle problems if they crop up. The food and bedding will be on two small sleds and we'll take turns pulling them. It'll be cold food, jerky, and bread, but with some of that trail mix your people use.

"As soon as I've gotten everything I can from the mine, we'll start back before they can change their minds. If we find ourselves out on the snow during daylight, I have snow-masks. If the guards *do* send a patrol after us, they won't be prepared for snow blindness.

"I'll take one man into the camp with me. The sleds will stay in the woods with the other four. If the foremen say they can't give me anything, then the two of us will leave. We'll join the others, catch a short nap until it gets dark. As soon as the moon's up, we'll go in and steal anything we can find. With luck, we'll have a head start before they realize what we've done.

"Let's hope that there are no guards posted. They mostly watch for predators, and there aren't any around right now. Plus the guards are lazy, it's why they're guards. They won't be awake, I hope. If they're not asleep... well, I didn't like them before, and I don't like them any better now."

"Sounds like you've got it figured, Robert. Even if the guards are awake, I doubt they'll follow you at night."

"You're right about that. We'll travel for a few hours, find a place to set up an ambush, maybe four of us waiting while the others take the sleds on. I know what I expect, but maybe one of the guards is smart enough to do something different. If it happens, we'll make them sorry. But there's no reason why they should show initiative. The only thing they do is guard the mine, so unless there's a supervisor awake to send the guards after us, all we have to do is get away."

The foraging party, not a raid unless it was forced on Robert, had left before I woke up next morning. I was nervous, but I'd felt that way before. It's part of being in charge.

I grabbed a light breakfast and got to work. The tribe had made tremendous progress during the past two weeks, but there was still more to be done.

Lilia had spent the last two days working with the women. I wanted to get her opinion, so we ate lunch together. I picked a spot a little apart from the tribe.

"Are they ready?"

"Matt, they couldn't have done it before, but now they can. They know how to fight, they're armed, they can build a hasty shelter or a fort, they have the means to start a fire and know how to build one. They know a lot of other stuff too."

"That confirms my impression, but I wanted to hear it from you. I've spent most of my time with the men, but the women are going to be just as important. What about our own women?"

"We're ready. I want to move our group here today; all we're doing at the cabin is eating food that should be saved for the trek."

"That soon, Lilia?"

"Sooner the better. I think we should be ready and leave as soon as Robert's back, cross the grasslands while they're still under the snow, then just keep going southwest. We won't get a better chance.

"Working outside and traveling in cold weather, we've been doing it for several months. Unless there's a late blizzard, we shouldn't have any problems we can't cope with.

"Even if that happens, we'll just build snow houses and wait until the storm blows out. We've got food for at least six more weeks, but there's nothing left around here. Everything's under four feet of snow.

"If we wait another two weeks, we'll only have a month's supply of food left. We'd have to go on short rations before we got away from the snow."

I was surprised; I'd thought there was more food, but Lilia would know. She'd been working closely with a woman named Monika, the chief cook for Robert's tribe, and the two had a good handle on what perishable supplies we had left and how fast we were using them.

It had been three full days, and I was increasingly concerned.

I had expected Robert back by the end of the second day. Many things could have happened; the trip took most of a day each way, and Robert might have been forced to wait before he could slip into the camp. But there was no sign of them, and we found ourselves looking often to see if they were in sight.

I decided I would take a small patrol out if they hadn't returned by the fifth day. I let Lilia know what I had in mind and she just nodded; she was worried too.

I had converted a small shelter into a shop, and Lilia found me working there late on the fourth day after Robert had gone.

"Matt, you need to see this."

"Is it Robert? Is anyone hurt?"

"It's Robert, but come look."

I put down the bow I'd been working on—I was wrapping leather for a handgrip—and took time for a drink of water. After that, I had no excuse to stall any longer, so dreading what I might see, I went outside.

It was Robert, sure enough. But where he'd led out a party of seven,

I counted thirteen returning! They pulled loaded sleds, and most carried packs as well.

I looked on, bemused. Who were these people? One man looked vaguely familiar, but I couldn't remember from where. Had he been one of the kitchen workers? If so, he looked a lot different now.

"Robert, I didn't expect you to be gone long enough to have babies!"

He chuckled. "Matt, I didn't plan on this. But I had to decide, and this was the only solution I could come up with."

"OK, why don't you get your people fed and find someplace for them to sleep. Get some food yourself and after that you can let me know the highlights, if you're not too tired."

"I'm not tired. I got four hours sleep last night, and we've got decisions to make.

"Three of those, the big man and the two women with him, were part of the mine's kitchen staff. Half of the kitchen people and most of the miners have left the mine, the other three were part of the maintenance crew.

"Colin, he's the kitchen guy, told me that the guards have been making alcohol. They got drunk three days ago and the guard sergeant—they use military ranks now—and two of his men caught Colin's wife and raped her. They chased his daughter too, but by then Colin had heard the yelling and came out with a cleaver. One of those guards won't be guarding anything until he grows a new arm. The others finally went back to their barracks, and Colin's family has been barricaded in the kitchen ever since.

"The guards have gone hungry unless they cooked for themselves. Colin had control of the kitchen and most of the food supplies, but the guards broke into a storeroom and took what they wanted. No one's seen the mine supervisors since this happened, so they may be dead.

"Anyway, Sal—he's the maintenance foreman—brought his family into the kitchen with Colin's. They forted up there and they're in good shape, but they only had enough food for a couple of weeks more. They told me I could have anything I wanted, but only if I brought them out with me.

"So that's what I did. We took everything we could haul or carry and made tracks out of there. I set up an ambush the next day, but no one was following us. Some of us got a little sleep while we were waiting, the rest remained on watch. We hit the trail after that and traveled as fast as we could.

"We made tracks while the moon was up, slept when we got tired.

The mine people weren't accustomed to pulling the small sleds and we didn't have spare snowshoes, so I doubt we made ten miles that first day. We probably didn't make a whole lot more the next day. We were moving faster by the time we got here, though; the new people got used to the snow and pulling the sleds.

"We brought more food with us, so that will help. We got some large bags of salt and some spices too.

"I don't think the guards will come after us, but sooner or later someone will check on the mine. I don't know what they'll do. The guards will probably hang around until the food runs out, but there's no telling what will happen after that. They may decide we're their best source of food and women and come after us. We'll just have to keep watch."

"Robert, I don't see what else you could have done. You said Colin's wife was raped; is she able to travel now?"

"She's kept up with the rest of us since that first day. We hauled her on a sled until she'd recovered enough to walk. All three of them apparently took her and they were trying for seconds when Colin got there. Two of them hauled the third one away, less that arm that Colin chopped off. He looked after his wife as soon as they took off.

"She blames the guards and also the people running the mine for what happened. I think she's pretty much recovered physically, but it's got to have been traumatic."

"Lilia and I have been talking, Robert. She thinks we should go now. She says we're only using up supplies if we wait any longer. At least, on the trail we'd be making distance and the people are ready. They've learned a lot since we got here.

"We need to get off the snow as soon as possible. It might take us weeks to get to where the grass is greening up. Two or three weeks from now, maybe less depending on what supplies you brought back, we'll have to reduce the ration allowance.

"The animals won't come back north until there's something to eat. They'll follow the new growth, and that won't happen until the ground warms. The roots will be sending out new leaves and seeds will also sprout about then. It could take two months before the animals return, maybe even longer. And we don't have enough food to last that long.

"We have to push the pace as much as possible while we've still got enough for a full ration. It won't be fun if we have to reduce what we're feeding people. Working hard on short rations—well, it's a good way to make people sick. Even if transplanted people *are* resistant to local diseases, the ones born on this timeline may not be, and anyway no one's immune to starvation rations. Plus there are the kids, they'll suffer more than the adults; even if they survive on short rations, they may not develop normally. Later on, after we get to where there are animals, we can slow down.

"There's another problem to consider. According to what Lilia's told me, we'll still have meat when the rest of our food is gone. We're already short of vegetables and dried fruit. Lilia had some dried berries, but she's only got one more jar of those left. When the vegetables and berries are gone, we'll need to watch out for vitamin deficiencies. Scurvy can cripple people, cause them to lose their teeth, and lack of iodine causes brain development problems in kids. So I'm going to start restricting the dried fruits and berries immediately. The adults can have vegetables, not many but some, but only the kids will get dried fruit.

"If you agree, we pack the sleds tonight. Tomorrow morning we put our sleeping gear on top, tie it down, and get on the way. We've done enough practicing, it's time to go. If the mine people decide they want whatever you took, we can at least make them chase us."

"Let's do it, Matt. I'll tell my people, the ones who were on the trip. You pass the word to Lilia and she can tell the rest. I'll talk to Colin and Sal too, they're good men. I'll let them get a night's sleep, and I'll talk to Monika about sleeping arrangements and food."

Robert and I met with Monika before the two of them went off to begin organizing the tribe, I talked to Lilia and left her to organize our group. I packed my few tools before deciding to bed down early myself.

Lilia and Monika would be working tomorrow, but they wouldn't have to make decisions. Robert and I would be responsible for that, and neither of us could afford to be tired. Making decisions when you're short on sleep is a good way to forget something important or make a mistake. Mistakes on Darwin's World get people killed.

I stowed my tools and supplies on one of the three large sleds we'd be using, then went to bed. Lee was out with some of his crew, watching Robert's back trail. The women were doing the last-minute packing. I could hear one of the young ones, a little boy, fussing at the change in routine. Well, he'd soon get used to it.

Sometime during the night Lilia and Cindy joined me in bed, but I didn't wake up.

Chapter 34

We needed increased security on the trip, so I put Lee in charge of that.

I had no idea what the guards from the mine might do and the same held true for the mine operators, despite what Robert had said. His analysis had been based on what was normal when he worked at the mine, and things had changed in ways he might not know about. So we had to assume we were facing increased danger and would be until we'd traveled a considerable distance away from the mine.

The guards would know something had happened when they found Colin, Sal, and the women gone. As for the mine operators, I had few clues to their thinking. They were certainly Futurists, but whether they were from the same time as the ones who'd 'harvested' me, I didn't know. From what I'd been told, the Futurists who'd taken me had no need for mining. Their technology produced everything they needed. So who were the mine operators?

There couldn't be many of them available or they'd not have needed Robert's people to do the mining. If they used the same technology as the harvesters to cross timelines, perhaps there were limitations on their version. They'd not have needed me to provide supplemental food if timeline-jumping had been easy and cheap. There was another possibility, that the food the Futurists were accustomed to downtime wasn't what the local people here wanted to eat. If the food downtime was too different, that would give the supervisors a motive for trading with me to supply meat for their local hires.

Were the mine operators perhaps from earlier in the harvesters' timeline? Perhaps from shortly after the device was invented? They might need the mine's product to build the timeline jumper.

That explanation appeared to fit what I knew. Maybe the mine produced some sort of rare-earth element; something that was, by definition, rare. Something that was scarce enough for them to seek it on another timeline, something that had almost been used up downtime. And this timeline, uptime on Darwin's World, still had untouched mineral deposits and people to mine them. There'd be no need for extensive training before the transplanted people could begin work. And the transplants were desperate enough for metal that they could be hired cheap.

Were the operators, the bosses and supervisors Robert had mentioned, always the same people or did they work in shifts? Perhaps spend a week or a month here before being replaced? Had the guards killed the Futurists when they'd taken over the mine? If so, what would the other Futurists do? The kitchen crew hadn't seen any of the supervisors since the guards, fueled by alcohol, had taken over.

If I had guessed right, the Futurists needed the mine's output. They wouldn't give it up without a fight. And people who could build a timeline-jumper would also have advanced weapons. They might limit the spread of those weapons to the transplanted people, but that didn't mean they wouldn't bring in well-armed commandos to wipe out the guards...and maybe come for us. They might even bring vehicles or time hoppers.

It might be simple, timeline crossing, or it might require enormous expenditures of money and energy. The implication, based on the one member of that Futurist transplant corps that I had met, was that timeline crossing for them was routine. And yet, the mine operators wanted us to supply local foods rather than simply bring food for the miners from downtime.

I mulled this over and thought of something else. I'd assumed that the people from that abandoned dwelling were dead. But suppose they had been examples of what the transport corps had tried to achieve? Had they been harvested, to become educated in the same way that I'd gotten some of my memories, then sent out to rejuvenate that suicide-ridden future civilization?

Lee was back in camp. I told him of my fear that the guards or the operators might be looking for us.

He nodded and said, "I'll grab food and water and go back out. I'll move out a reasonable distance, keep one man with me, and watch Robert's trail. I'll leave a third man halfway between where we'll be and the camp.

We watch for a raiding party, he watches us. I'd like to put someone with him but we don't have people to spare. If something happens to the two of us, he can still warn you. I think that's necessary. I hope we can spot any raiders before they spot us. They won't have had much time to react, so I doubt they will be here this soon. And we'll be concealed while they'll be following Robert's trail across the snow, so I expect we'll see them before they can see us. What will you do, Matt?"

"If they get here before we leave, I just don't know. We'll do whatever we can, fight if it looks like we've got a chance, scatter into the woods if there are too many of them. If it's the mine operators and they bring a force with modern tech, infrared maybe, we can burrow into a snowbank. That might disperse our heat enough so that they miss us. Some of us, anyway."

He gave me a blank look when I mentioned 'infrared'. Well, he understood the part about fighting or digging into the snow. That would have to be enough.

Lee went off to finish setting up his early-warning system and I began chivvying people to finish packing.

I had hoped to be on the road early, but it was not to be. The scene was mass confusion, despite all Robert and I could do. Lilia and Monica helped, but for the moment it seemed that all the teaching we'd done had been wasted.

Well, the tribespeople would remember as soon as we got on the trail, or they'd relearn it the hard way.

I finally recalled Lee and he organized the rest of his small crew for security while we were traveling. One would scout the trail ahead, two others would be off to the left and right sides for flank security. My group would lead, Robert's would follow.

Lee wanted Pavel on the left flank, but got an argument. He finally sent him forward to scout. The Pavel question was clearly not resolved.

But with Pavel out front. . . where was a saber-tooth when you really wanted one to show up? Or a pride of lions, maybe a pack of dire wolves, a short-faced bear, anything?

I doubt we managed to get ten miles away from the village by mid-afternoon. I had hoped for more, but if everyone was as exhausted as I was, they weren't going any further.

We set up our first temporary camp and managed to get people fed and bedded down under thick furs. The sky was clear, so we decided not to build shelters. Our fire was out and guards were on duty before dusk, with reliefs notified which shift they'd be taking during the night. Robert and I walked through the camp, making sure people were as well taken care of as we could manage.

Colin, the former cook-supervisor, had proved to be a gem. He and his family, assisted by some of the tribe's women, had the kitchen set up and food heating in much less time than I would have expected. People had been able to stop, take care of necessary personal business, lay out sleeping furs, then eat a hot meal. That part of our planning had worked well, so far.

We'd build snow shelters when the weather threatened, but tonight we slept out under starry skies. Two sentries circled the camp during the night, the first ones relieved by a second pair and those relieved in turn by a third. They would wake Robert and me, we would wake everyone else.

Pavel took his turn without complaint and Lee paired him with Lilia. Colin's efforts had freed her from any need to supervise the kitchen activities, so she now worked with whichever of us needed assistance. Tonight, she watched the camp and also made sure that Pavel did his share.

Robert had been busy getting people bedded down. Neither of us planned to take a turn on sentry duty, but the rest of the men and most of the women would do so during the trek. We intended to pair two women together and only pair men with men, except for Lilia.

Lilia was up before her turn, and when she checked on the pair that she and Pavel would relieve, they were alert and watchful.

No problems were reported that night and we got on the trail early next morning. The moon gave us enough light to pack and go. Morning starts would have to wait for daybreak when the moon was down, but by then packing up every morning and setting up camp in the late afternoon would be routine.

We settled into a routine as the days passed. Robert and I got up early, woke Lee and Colin, and then let them get their own people working. Lee's three-person security team would eat something while they moved out to their positions. The rest of the people would get up and take care of morning chores. Children would be seen to and bedding packed. A quick meal, usually cold meat and bread; then finish packing and move out.

Sandra, Millie, and Cindy led off, because they woke up when I did and got a head start on packing. Lilia looked around the empty campsite to make sure nothing had been left behind, then took up position behind the last sled.

We'd pause for lunch at midday, the kitchen crew would pass out jerky and bread and sometimes a few dried vegetables from our dwindling stores, and half an hour later we'd be on the trail again.

Pavel became more of a problem two weeks later.

He loudly complained that Robert and I weren't pulling night duty. I attempted to make him understand that we were never really off-duty, but often got called to solve minor emergencies that always seemed to crop up during the night. That explanation wasn't good enough; he saw himself as a kind of deputy-leader because he still had influence with his group of easterners. Finally, Robert and I simply laid out his options.

"Pavel, you have a choice. You cooperate with us, and that means doing what you're assigned to do and working for the good of all the tribe, or you pick any other direction and go your own way. If your people decide to go with you, so be it. But we're not giving up any of the tools or equipment that we got from the mine. You can take your furs and personal possessions and the sled they're loaded on. Nothing else.

"As for the rest of us, we're packing. When we're ready, we will move out. If your group isn't packed, you'll get left behind. You have a few minutes to convince your group to follow you, but after that the decision will have been made."

Robert and I kept an eye on them. They argued loudly and then the discussion got quieter. Finally, they hurriedly packed their equipment and joined the rest, now about fifty yards behind us. We didn't slow down but they caught up and I took a moment to question Lilia, still following as rear security.

"Any idea of what happened back there?"

"I couldn't hear much, Matt. When they spotted me they got quiet. I don't think we've heard the last of them."

"Well, maybe they'll settle down. We need them to stay with us, but if they get to be a serious problem we'll cut them loose. I'll talk to Robert about it."

He reluctantly agreed with me. We would wait and watch, but in the meantime, we still needed to make as many miles as we could.

The weather had begun to warm but nights were still below freezing. The sun often warmed enough during the day now that we could pack our parkas on the sleds.

The snow pack grew thinner and became patchy in places. No plants were greening up but the trees showed buds; it wouldn't be much longer before spring arrived.

We crossed a large river without problems; it was still frozen, and other than slight difficulty pulling the sleds up the bank on the far side, the crossing was routine.

Two weeks later Lee came back with news. He'd been scouting ahead and he looked for Robert and me when he came back to camp.

"Matt, there's a river ahead. It's not very deep and the ice is thinner than what we've been crossing. People can walk on it, but I'm not sure it will support a sled. There are even places on the opposite side that are snow-free. It's muddy, but you can see the ground. Suppose we off-load the sleds and pack everything across? We might abandon the sleds anyway if there's no snow, especially if they start sticking in the mud.

"It'll be more work, but travois will do the same job the sleds did, Lee. Each travois will carry the possessions of the person dragging it and a little more. We may eventually switch to backpacks, but for now a travois can carry more with less effort.

"The furs are heavy...if the weather continues to warm, we might just abandon some of them. We could reduce the loads by dumping half the skins; the weather's warmer now, but we could still get hit with a late cold snap so we should keep some furs just in case. It's something to think about.

"But we already have less food to carry, so distributing what we've got won't add much weight to anyone's load. Hauling food and other supplies will end up weighing about what the sleeping furs weighed, and people can easily haul that much on a travois."

We decided to have a camp-wide discussion, share our thoughts with the others.

Robert, Lilia, Lee and I formed a kind of leadership council, but we were in no position to make decisions for everyone. We had come up with a number of options to consider.

Robert opened the discussion. "Here's the problem. We need to cross the river and Lee doesn't believe the ice will support the weight of a loaded sled.

"One option is to set up camp here and send out hunting parties. The weather is warming every day, so the snow will soon be gone. There might be game animals just south of here. The hunters can spread out in groups of two or three and look for something we can eat.

"We can find rushes or cattails along the river, so we'll want people to begin gathering food. The roots and seed heads can be added to our supply.

"Meantime, one of the hunting parties will look for a better crossing downriver and another party will look upriver. We might even catch fish in the river, maybe with lines and hooks or by setting up a weir to trap fish.

"The hunters stay out no more than three days. If they haven't found anything, we backpack everything across the river. We've got enough ropes for a safety line and hopefully the ice will still be there, but we will have to take some chances. Getting across is likely to take most of a day, what with packing everything and carrying the kids. We'll set up a temporary camp on the far side, then begin moving west the next day."

The decision was finalized after a short discussion. Camp would be established here and the various parties would set out. Michel and Philippe would go upstream and look for a better place to cross. Gregor and Vlad volunteered to cross the thin ice directly ahead and hunt there.

Pavel and I would go downstream and look for a better crossing while keeping our eyes peeled for game. Not good choices, but we had no time to wait for better ones.

Robert was working in camp the third day when Pavel and Gregor came in. He looked up as they hurried over.

"Robert, we lost Matt."

"What do you mean, you lost him? If you left him out there..."

"I mean he's dead, he's got to be. We had crossed on the ice and were looking for tracks along the edge of the river. The ice had melted near the bank, but it was still thick out toward the center. Anyway, the bank was muddy and Matt slipped. I tried to hold him but I could only get a grip on his parka."

Gregor spoke up, "I tried to help too. I grabbed him by the belt, this one," and he held up the belt holding Matt's trusted axe and knife, "But it came loose."

"I was holding onto his parka, but Matt had opened it because it was warm, and when the belt came loose he just slipped out of the parka.

"We tried to find him, but after he went into the river we couldn't see anything. Vlad stayed behind to see if he could find his body, but I thought we should come in and tell you what happened."

Robert was shocked. Lilia had come up during the last of the conversation and Lee was only a step behind her. Pavel had finished his report to Robert while glancing aside at Lilia. Now he looked down to admire Matt's parka that he was holding.

"It's too bad about Matt, but it could have happened to anyone. Still, now that he's gone, this is a nicer parka than the one I've been wearing. That wolf fur hood looks warm."

Lee answered, "You wouldn't like it, Pavel. The arrow holes wouldn't suit you."

"What arrow holes? I don't see any holes!"

"That's because I haven't put them there yet. But as soon as you put Matt's parka on, I'll put a couple of holes in it."

Lilia spoke up. "That goes for Matt's weapons, too. We'll take those. I won't believe he's dead until I've seen the body."

Pavel glowered, but he handed over the parka and weapons belt.

Robert slowly spoke. "Lilia, I understand how you feel. But we've got a tribe to get across that river, and no time left. We're going to have to pack everything across while we still can.

"We'll break up the sled loads and just carry everything. I'd like to look for Matt's body too, but we can't spare the time and everyone's going to have to help carry stuff. No, we cross now; if Matt was sucked under the ice, he's dead. The rest of us have to go on."

Lilia nodded. "I understand, Robert. When do you want to cross?"

"As soon as possible, and we'll make the crossing here. No one found a better place, and if the rest of that ice breaks up, we'll be stuck here using supplies we can't spare. We'll break the sled loads down, make up packs that people can carry. Roll up the furs we intend to keep, then carry them over a shoulder. When we get half the furs we want to keep across, we'll take the food. After that, we come back for the rest of the furs and whatever else is still here. I'll look at the ground over there and decide whether it's worthwhile to come back for the sleds. We move on ahead for a few days, then send the hunting parties out again. Maybe they'll find something.

Robert paused, and swallowed. "If Matt. . . survived, that'll give him time to maybe catch up to us. But if he slipped under the ice like they said, he's drowned. Still, it's hard to accept that Matt's gone."

Lilia nodded in understanding and spared only a moment to look at Pavel and Gregor as they headed toward the rest of their group. She noticed that Vlad had come in and had joined his friends.

It was a puzzle.

How had the three of them gotten together? Pavel had been with Matt downstream, while the other two were supposed to have crossed directly ahead. It was all very strange.

And how could Matt's belt have come loose? There had been no damage to the belt.

She spared a moment to look downstream. Poor Matt. To have done so much and then to have died in an accident while looking for a place to cross a river!

Well, he would have been proud. He had died working to help the tribe. She turned and headed for the sleds.

There was work to do; they could mourn Matt later.

Epilogue

Pavel was standing near the front of the column when Lee approached.

"Pavel, get food from the kitchen and head out; I want you guarding the left flank, so move off to where you can watch as we leave. Stay off to the left, watch for danger, and if you see tracks let me know. If there are tracks, then the animals are moving back and we really need fresh food. We'll send out hunting parties as soon as it's worthwhile."

"Do it yourself, kid. I'm busy with my group this morning, then I plan on looking in on your group this afternoon. I won't have time to wander around in the woods."

Robert had come up while this was going on. He watched, waiting to see how Lee would handle himself.

"Pavel, you were told before; do what you're told, work for the whole group, or take your personal stuff and hit the trail. You can go anywhere except where we are. That's still the only offer you've got; you're flank guard or you're out. We'll leave without you."

"Suppose we just keep up with the rest of you. We've been doing that and we can keep on doing it."

"Not you, Pavel. I'll lay it out in a way that even you can't misunderstand. We'll go on, you won't. If that means we leave you dead by the trail, so be it."

While speaking, Lee had unslung the spear that always hung across his back now. The long, sharp blade pointed between Pavel's eyes from less than a foot away. Pavel turned pale and took a step back.

"You would kill me because I won't pull your guard duty?"

"No. I'll kill you because you're eating our food and not doing your share."

Robert spoke up. "Pavel, are you leaving the tribe?"

"No, Robert. I'll do the guard shift if that's what you want. But this kid has no right to be giving orders! I've been part of the tribe a lot longer than he has, so why is he in charge?"

"He in charge because I trust his judgment. Matt and I delegated that authority to him. It's his until I decide it should go to someone better qualified. And I don't know anyone who's better qualified." When he said this, Robert looked squarely at Pavel.

Pavel stomped away and took up his post. Robert organized the train into family groups and soon had them moving.

Travel now would be slower by necessity; everything moved now by travois or backpack. But at least they were far enough from the mine that any danger from there had passed.

Robert missed Matt. It was not easily explained, but the man had exuded confidence. You simply knew that whatever came up, Matt would deal with it. It was hard to believe he was dead.

Briefly, Robert wondered how Gregor and Vlad had found Matt and Pavel. Coincidence? Well, perhaps they had all used the same location to cross the river.

Pavel came into camp late and decided to look in on the women of Matt's group. They now cooked for themselves, rather than sharing the communal kitchen; perhaps they had treats hidden away?

"Pavel, you should be over at the kitchen. They'll be shutting down shortly and if you don't eat now, you won't get anything before morning," Lilia said.

"I came over to get to know you ladies better. We need to work together now, right? So I thought I'd have my dinner with you. What are you making?"

"Whatever we're making, there's only enough for us. We're taking our meals with family members only."

"Still, there are four of you women; you'll need men around, especially if there's danger."

Pavel felt a sudden cold feeling alongside his ear. He reached up absently to brush it away...a bit of snow, fallen from the tree perhaps...but froze when he felt the sharp tip.

"I wouldn't turn my head just now if I were you, Pavel. Sandra's pretty good with that spear. And if she doesn't stick you, Millie's waiting for her chance."

Millie was holding her own spear, relaxed, the shaft held across her body but ready for instant use.

"I'll go, I'll go! There's no need for threats! I was just trying to be helpful, like."

"We don't want your help. You might remember that, because next time the lesson will be more painful. The kitchen is right over there," Lilia said and pointed.

Her expression might have been amused; Pavel didn't find it funny at all.

After they finished the meal, Lilia spoke to Lee.

"I'm not satisfied with Pavel's story. Matt somehow lost his parka and weapons while he was slipping on the muddy bank?

"And what happened to his bow? He had a backpack too, and there was a quiver of arrows. What happened to those? How could Matt lose his parka when he was wearing a belt and quiver strap over it? If he had taken them off, there's no reason why Pavel and Gregor shouldn't have brought them back too. And why were Gregor and Vlad even there? They should have been a mile or two upstream from Matt and Pavel.

"Their story is too pat; I think they surprised Matt and killed him. I can follow their tracks, there were three of them and they have about as much regard for hiding a trail as a mammoth! I'll look around for a while, but if I can't find Matt's body, I'll turn back. I don't like the thought of him just lying alongside the river someplace, no one to even look for his body.

"I can move faster than the group, so catching up won't be a problem. You explain it to Robert tomorrow; I'm leaving after dark, and I'll be back in a week or so."

The cold woke him. He was lying on a sandbar, where he'd washed up and been left as the water receded. He was shivering, wet, and his right eye was glued shut.

He pawed at the eye, trying to open the eyelid. Finally he washed his face, and in the process found a large bump over his eye. He had no idea where that had come from.

Washing removed the crusted blood and he got the eye open, but now he saw two images of the small tree that leaned over the bank. Blearily, he closed the eye again and that felt a little better.

He had a severe headache and the lump was sore, but at least it was no longer bleeding.

Muddy, shivering, he crawled away from the sandbar and found a pile of grass. Blown flat during the winter, left ashore when the river's spring flood receded, it now lay, slowly decaying, on the river's bank. He crawled into the drift and pulled the grass around him.

He needed fire, he knew that much, but the grasses would help him stay warm for now. He pulled handfuls and stuffed them in his shirt. They prickled, but he added more. Presently the shivering stopped.

He found the small pouch of materials at his waist and opened it; there was a roll of string, a small flint knife, a scrap of steel. The tinder was wet, useless, but he could find more.

He pulled more of the grass around him, making a pile of it. Judging finally that he had enough, he pulled off his wet clothes and wrung them out as best he could. Naked, he crawled into the pile and burrowed in until he began to feel warmer.

He was hungry, cold, and exhausted, but no longer shivering. It took only moments for him to fall asleep.

He had a strange dream; a man stood before him and said, "Your name is Matt."

Continued in Darwin's World II: The Trek

The Trek, an Excerpt:

Chapter 1

Lilia walked slowly through the camp.

It had been laid out with sleeping sites in two parallel rows on each side of the row of sleds. The kitchen, now deserted, was in the middle between the rows. Families with children occupied the sites immediately before and after the kitchen. Others had taken sites close to friends.

There had been little socializing this evening. Pavel's news had spread quickly and the tribe had discussed it briefly among themselves. After that, conversation lagged and everyone bedded down early. There was a lot of work to be done tomorrow and they would need to be rested. Friends died, the rest had to move on with their lives.

Lilia waited at the edge of camp for the sentries to pass. They circled the small camp every half hour or so, and she didn't want to attract attention. Lee and the others from her camp already knew she was going and the rest would find out soon enough; she intended to be well on her way before that happened.

Most of the snow had melted. The ground was slippery where the sleds had passed, so she moved away from the tracks, remaining close to the trail but not walking on the disturbed ground.

Even so, the ground beside the tracks was also muddy and she slipped a number of times. Finally, she gave up and picked a tree to climb. She would spend the night in the tree and go on in the morning. It was unlikely that anyone would miss her immediately. Robert might ask, but since she routinely made the rounds from camp to guards to kitchen to help as needed, it would probably take some time before he noticed.

In any case, the rest of the tribe would be occupied packing and moving on. There would be travois to build and no one would have time to look for her.

She unstrung her bow and slung it across her back with the quiver as she climbed the tree. A large branch projected from the trunk some twenty feet up, and there were limbs extending from the branch that would provide a place for her to lie back in relative comfort.

A safety rope attached her loosely to the main branch and she settled down to sleep. She was wrapped in her parka against the chill and had pulled up the hood to cover her head. Her bow and quiver lay beside her across two of the limbs and the small pack she'd been carrying cushioned her head. If the tree wasn't as comfortable as her sleeping furs back at camp, well...she'd slept in more uncomfortable places. She ate a piece of jerky on a slice of bread and drank from her water gourd before falling asleep.

She woke up once during the night. Something moved through the forest below; the animals were moving back north. She thought it was a deer, but it might have been something else. She had nothing to fear from it, whatever it was, and she was soon asleep again.

Matt woke up thirsty and sore. He crawled out of the pile of drifted grasses that he'd slept in and continued the few yards down to the river. The water level had gone down considerably. The bank remained muddy and he slipped near the water's edge. He saved himself from a dunking only with difficulty.

Had he walked instead of crawling, he would almost certainly have fallen into the water. He drank, waited a moment, and drank again. The water was muddy, but he washed his face and immediately felt better.

Matt crawled slowly away from the water after drinking. He was shaky but able to stand by holding onto a tree. Waiting until he felt secure, he took a few experimental steps before examining his surroundings.

Both eyes were clear and fortunately, he was no longer seeing double. Reflexively, he rubbed at the barely swollen lump on his forehead. It was still sore, but that would pass.

He brushed off the sticky grasses that clung to his body. Shaking out his deerskins, he pulled them on. They were clammy and cold, but not as dripping-wet as they'd been when he took them off. The skins stretched and soon felt warmer as he moved around.

He needed food. Nearly equal in importance was the need for weapons. He hadn't seen animals before winding up in the river...he still had no idea how that had happened...but there might be something else to eat. Plants had just barely begun to green up, so there would be no fruit or even leaves from sprouting plants just yet. There might be roots from cattails growing in the river, but he wouldn't be able to get to those until the water level went down.

But there were always insects or larvae. There might be fish in the river too. He'd caught them before, using hooks and weirs for fish-traps. He could do so again.

The sky was clear and the sun was well up. He had no idea how long he'd slept, but the sleep had helped him recover from the injury and near-drowning.

Bits of grass still stuck to his deerskins and some of the grass rubbed and prickled at his skin. For the moment, he could tolerate the itching. He had no urge to expose himself to the cold by removing his clothing again. Perhaps it would warm enough later for him to strip and vigorously brush away the grasses that he'd missed earlier. He could shake the deerskins and get rid of most of the grass stuck to them, then brush off the rest. Even dare a quick dunk in the river to get the mud and the last of the grass off?

That could wait. It was time to forage for something to eat. Matt wasn't fussy. Grubs would serve for now and he could use the cord in his emergency pack for a fishing line. When he spotted the first signs of small animal activity, he could unwrap the rawhide from the handle of his small flint knife and put out snares.

He found a dead log, downed a year or more ago. There was evidence that insects had been burrowing under the bark, so he used a stick to lever a section of the bark free. Under the bark he found a number of white grubs. They might have been round-headed larvae of woodboring insects, the things that woodpeckers seek when they hammer at the bark of dead trees. Regardless, there were many of them. He pinched off the black head sections and ate the bodies.

Hunger was a problem, but eating too many insects that his gut couldn't tolerate would be worse. He ate a half-dozen of the grubs and waited to see if they'd stay down.

While waiting, he began fashioning a gorge hook, using the flint knife. He could eat more of the grubs later if they didn't cause nausea, but one would serve as bait for a fishing line while he waited.

A short length of his precious cord was cut off to make a sinker-line. He tied this around a rock that lay beside the riverbank. The other end of the line he knotted to the longer fishing-line he made from the cord in his emergency kit.

One end of the longer line was tied around a circular groove he carved around the middle of the gorge hook. The other end of the line he tied to a small tree on the bank.

The two ends of the gorge hook were sharpened, designed to catch in the stomach and turn sideways after a fish swallowed the bait. The sharpened ends would then catch in the stomach's walls and prevent the hook from coming out while he pulled the fish ashore.

He threaded a large grub onto the gorge hook, then tossed the rock sinker into the river. This pulled the fishing line taut and the bait sank beneath the surface.

While the grub enticed fish, it was time for Matt to see what weapons he could contrive.

There was a large rock on the riverbank that had washed down in some past flood. He soon found a solid stick, apparently a branch from a tree that had broken away from wind or perhaps the weight of ice. It would do.

His strings and rope had been made from plaited fibers he'd extracted from leaves and grass stems. Neither source was available this early in the season, but there were roots. Flexible roots would do until he could begin making more cord.

He found several thin ones where the soil of the riverbank had been washed away in the flood. Being as careful of his flint knife as possible, he cut the roots.

Matt used the flexible rootlets as crude cord to bind the rock to the tree branch. He felt better immediately; even if he should be forced to climb a tree to escape a predator, at least he had a real weapon now. If a cat tried to climb after him, it would get a face-full of rock!

He checked his fishing line but felt nothing tugging back. Perhaps the bait had wriggled free? He pulled in the line and the grub he'd used for bait was still there. Still, a fresh one might be better. He loosened a section of bark from the dead tree and selected another large grub. The newly-baited gorge hook went back into the river to wait for a fish to bite.

The club was good, but a spear would be better. Two methods of getting a spear occurred to Matt. He could bend a small tree over, then use the club to batter the trunk until it broke. That in turn could be trimmed into shape, sharpened, then hardened in a fire. He could also use fire or coals to cut the tree, as well as fashion a point and harden it.

He went back to the tree he'd been extracting the grubs from. Should he eat more of them?

He decided to wait. The physical activity had lessened his hunger. No longer a sharp gnawing, it was now only a dull ache. He could tolerate that.

Using the stone-headed club, Matt crushed a section of bark on the dead tree. He carefully peeled this free and beneath the bark was the powdered cambium layer. There was also a sawdust-like material left behind by the borers. The powder beneath the bark would serve as tinder while the splintered bark could be added as soon as flames appeared.

He took the steel scrap from the pouch on his belt. Holding it in his right hand and the flint knife in his left, he began striking the heel of the flint with the steel. Glancing strokes released a few sparks and he waited for one to ignite the tinder.

A number of glancing strikes shed sparks into the tinder before Matt saw the first wisp of smoke. He carefully blew on the tiny coal and it grew brighter before finally becoming flame. Matt added the bits of bark he'd saved and waited for them to catch fire.

The small flame grew, and Matt gathered more fallen wood from the surrounding forest. He piled this near the fire, adding it to the small amount he'd gathered from the downed tree. Small branches were fed into the little fire and soon it had grown to respectable size.

Matt went to check his fishing line as the fire grew. A tentative pull on the line was answered by a strong tug back so Matt carefully pulled his catch ashore. A large, thrashing catfish lay gasping on the muddy bank.

A quick tap from the stone club ended the gasping. Quick cuts of the flint knife removed the spikes from the dorsal and pectoral fins. Matt knew by experience how painful a wound those fin spikes could inflict! He gutted the fish and removed the head. It was quite an easy task using the sharp flint knife. Those ancient ancestors had clearly known a thing or two.

A pointed stick held the fish over the coals of his fire. Matt moved some of the burning sticks to the base of a small tree that would make a suitable spear. He soon had more sticks arranged around the tree and watched as his small fire grew larger.

Watching the fire burn and the live tree char at the base, Matt removed his fish from the coals. The fish barely had time to cool before Matt began stripping flesh from the bones.

Gathering up the head and the bones, he threw these into the river. The guts he kept; they'd be good bait for his gorge hook. The rebaited hook, removed from the fish when he opened the body cavity, went back into the river.

Matt tended the small fire he'd built around the tree. He experimented by bending and attempting to twist the trunk free, but decided it was too soon. Adding more wood, he settled down to wait.

He soon felt sleepy; the full belly from the fish probably contributed much to that drowsiness. He fought off the feeling while waiting for the tree to burn through.

A large pile of fallen wood waited beside the fire. The spear was a defensive weapon primarily, at least the wooden-tipped one would be, but fire was an excellent defense too. Tonight Matt would sleep in relative warmth with a fire in front and another behind.

A last check of the fishing line brought in another catfish, somewhat larger than the first. He gutted this one and left it hanging from a branch near his fire.

The tree finally burned through and Matt laid it near the fire. Safe and warm between his fires, breakfast assured, and with a tree that he could make into a weapon tomorrow, Matt slept.

Robert woke up early and went about getting the camp up and working. Lee was also up and munched on a piece of bread and chunk of dried meat as he went to check on the camp's guards.

Breaking down the sled loads into packs and arranging straps to carry them took longer than expected. Robert fretted. He had hoped to get a few miles farther before night, but he soon revised that estimate.

Shortly before noon the sleds were abandoned and the tribe straggled on their way. Well, they'd soon settle into the new form of travel.

Lee took charge of the group as soon as they moved away. He sent a scout ahead and had two others flanking the group, watching for danger and any animal that might add to their food supply.

Laz and Millie worked together, each pulling one branch of a heavily-laden travois. This contained their sleeping furs and a share of the tribe's food. Sandra and Cindy followed behind, carrying backpacks with the rations they'd eat during the day.

Robert noticed this late in the afternoon and wondered where Lilia was, but he was too busy at the time to do more than wonder. Later, he found Lee when the tribe stopped for the night.

"I didn't see your mother today. Is she all right?"

"I'm sure she is. She decided she didn't believe what Pavel and his two friends said, so she took off to backtrack them. She thinks Pavel and his cronies ambushed Matt and killed him.

"She'll find out and try to find Matt's body. If his death wasn't accidental...well, just keep out of my way. I'll settle Pavel once and for all, and if his little gang gets in the way, I'll do them too. That's assuming my mother doesn't beat me to it. She's no pushover. I watched her stick swords into a short-faced bear after it clawed me and broke my arm."

Lee thought for a moment before continuing.

"You don't want her angry at you. I've acknowledged your authority as leader, Robert, but in this matter I'm not willing to defer to you. I'll do whatever seems right at the time."

"You won't be alone, Lee. I'll be there with you and probably Marc and Philippe will too. Laz won't be hanging back, either. He liked Matt a lot. We all did. Pavel has few friends outside his gang of five.

"I don't favor hanging. We'll use the closest thing to a firing squad we've got. If we need to execute anyone, we'll do it by arrows or spears."

Lee nodded, not convinced, but willing to wait for now.

Robert wasn't the only one who noticed Lilia's absence. Vlad realized that two women, neither of whom was Lilia, now patrolled around the rear of the tribe. He remarked on this and Pavel took a walk past the camp Lee and the women had set up. No Lilia.

Pavel watched for some time, in case Lilia was off on one of her many errands. Finally, he decided she wasn't coming back. If she wasn't with her own small group, that meant she'd left the camp. Why would she leave, and where would she go?

He continued to muse on this and finally brought up the subject to the men of his group.

The women were away visiting other women in the camp. This made it easy for Pavel to tell the men what he'd found. The women might gossip; the men wouldn't.

"Lilia's gone," Pavel said. "She must have left last night. I saw her yesterday, but she wasn't around this morning and she's not in her camp now. Anyone see her today?"

He waited, but no one said anything.

"She's left the camp and I can't think of any good reason why she would do that. There's only one place she'd have gone. I think she's gone back to look for Matt.

"She won't find his body, that's miles downstream by now. But she might find his bow and quiver. Maybe his spear too. I knew too many questions would be raised if we brought those back with us and we probably should have thrown them in the river. Having his parka and his weapons belt was dangerous enough, but they were just too nice to leave. I thought it was worth it, taking the chance.

"After we dumped the body, I just wanted to get away from there so I didn't take time to pick up his gear and brush out the marks. I never expected anyone to go back and look for the site anyway!

"Robert and Lee don't have any witnesses. No one saw what happened but Gregor and Vlad, and they won't say anything. But there might still be signs where we dragged him to the river after I clubbed him. If she finds the bow and spear, she'll know she found the right place. If she's good at reading sign, she'll know too much.

"We've got to go after her. We have to kill her before she can tell the others."

The Trek is available in ebook, audiobook, and print versions from Amazon.

Made in the USA
Las Vegas, NV
20 August 2023

76348245R00159